THE FINAL TESTAMENT OF THE HOLY BIBLE

JAMES FREY

JOHN MURRAY

First published in Great Britain in 2011 by John Murray (Publishers)
An Hachette UK Company

First published in paperback in 2012

1

A CIP catalogue record for this title is available from the British Library

B format paperback ISBN 978 1 84854 319 5
A format paperback ISBN 978 1 84854 669 1

Printed and bound by Clays Ltd, St Ives plc

Designed by Graphic Thought Facility, London

John Murray policy is to use papers that are natural, renewable and recyclable products and made from wood grown in sustainable forests. The logging and manufacturing processes are expected to conform to the environmental regulations of the country of origin.

John Murray (Publishers)
338 Euston Road
London NW1 3BH

www.johnmurray.co.uk

He will come again
— The Apostles' Creed

This book was written with the cooperation of and after extensive interviews with the family, friends, and followers of Ben Zion Avrohom, also known as Ben Jones, also known as the Prophet, also known as the Son, also known as the Messiah, also known as the Lord God.

MARIAANGELES 11
CHARLES 25
ALEXIS 37
ESTHER 53
RUTH 67
JEREMIAH 85
ADAM 101
MATTHEW 129
JOHN 153
LUKE 169
II MARIAANGELES 213
MARK 241
JUDITH 271
II ESTHER 331
PETER 365
III MARIAANGELES 389

MARIAANGELES

He wasn't nothing special. Just a white boy. An ordinary white boy. Brown hair, brown eyes, medium height and medium weight. Just like ten or twenty or thirty million other white boys in America. Nothing special at all.

First time I saw him he was coming down the hallway. There was an apartment across the hall from where I lived that'd been empty for a year. Usually apartments in our project go quick. Government supports them so they're cheap, for people who ain't got shit in this world and, even though they always telling us different, know we ain't ever gonna have shit. There's lists for them. Long and getting longer. But nobody would live in that one. It had a reputation. The man who lived there before had gone crazy. He'd been normal. Sold souvenirs outside Yankee Stadium and had a wife and two little boys, real cute little boys. Then he started hearing voices and shit, started ranting about devils and demons and how he was the last man standing before us and the end. He lost his job and started wearing all white and trying to touch everybody on their head. He got his ass whooped a few times and his church told him to stop coming. He screamed at his family and played this organ music all night. Cursed the demons and pleaded to the Lord. Howled like some kind of dog. He didn't ever let his family leave. We stopped hearing the music and it started smelling and Momma called the cops and they found him hanging from the shower. Wearing a white robe like a monk. Tied up with an electrical cord. They found his wife and boys with electrical tape around their ankles and wrists and plastic bags over their heads. There was a note that said we have gone to a better place. Maybe the Devil got him or the demons got him or his Lord left him. Or maybe he just got tired. And maybe they did go to a better place. I don't know, and won't probably ever know, not believing what I believe. And it didn't matter anyway. Everybody heard about it and nobody would live there. Until Ben. He came down the hall with a backpack and an old suitcase and moved right in. He either didn't know or didn't care about what had happened before. Moved right the fuck in.

He was the only white boy in the building. Except for the Jews who owned the liquor stores and the clothing shops, he was the only white boy in the neighborhood. Rest of us was all Puerto Rican. A few Dominicans. A few regular old-school black motherfuckers. All poor. Angry. Wondering how to make it better and knowing there was no answer. It was what it was, is what it is. A fucked up ghetto in an American city. They're all the fucking same. Ben didn't seem to notice. Didn't care he was out of place. He came and went. Didn't talk to nobody. Wore some kind of uniform like a pretend cop during the week that made everybody laugh. Stayed in his apartment most of the time on weekends, except when he'd go out drinking. Then we'd see him passed out on the benches out front of the buildings, right near the playground. Or in the hallway with vomit on his shirt. One time he came stumbling home on a Sunday morning and his pants were all wet and he was trying to sing some twenty-year-old rap song at the top of his lungs. My brother and his friends started going along with him, making fun of him and shit, and he was too drunk to even know. We started thinking we knew why he was living among us. Why he didn't care he was out of place, didn't belong. We thought he must not be welcome where he came from anymore. They didn't want him around. And we was right, he'd been kicked the fuck out by his people, we just had the reasons why wrong.

First time I talked to him was in the hallway. It was probably six months after he moved in and me and my daughter came walking out of our apartment on our way to chill in front of the building. He was standing there in his boxer shorts and a t-shirt with his door open, holding his telephone. My daughter was like a year and a half old. Just learning some words. She said hola and he didn't say nothing back. She's like her momma. I say something to someone, I expect they say something back. Everybody wants that. Some basic level of respect. Acknowledgment as a human being. So she said it again and he just stood there. So I said hola motherfucker, don't you know how to be a decent motherfucking neighbor and say something back. And he looked nervous and sort of scared and said sorry. And then my girl said hola again, and he said it back to her and she smiled and hugged his leg and he laughed and I asked him what he was doing just standing there in the hallway with his drawers on and his door open and the phone in his hand. He said he was waiting for a new TV, that he had bought one on sale and it was being delivered. I told him he better have a good goddamn lock, that there's motherfuckers around here that'd kill a motherfucker for a good TV, no lie. He just smiled, still seeming all nervous and scared, and said yeah, I think the lock is good, I'll check and make sure. And that was that. We left him standing there. Waiting for a TV.

I know that damn TV came too, 'cause we started hearing it. Bang bang bang. Some explosions. Helicopters and airplanes flying around. Heard him whooping and hollering, saying yeah yeah yeah, gotcha you bastard, how you like me now, motherfucker, how you like me now. Could hear him pacing, walking around. Got a little scared 'cause he was sounding like the crazy man who killed his family and I started wondering if that place really was cursed. Made my brother, who dropped out of school the year before me and was still around then, go listen at the door. My brother got all serious and listened real close and turned to me and said this is bad, Mariaangeles, real bad, we got a honkey playing video games across the hall from us, I better round up some of my boys and take care of this shit. I laughed, and knew I shoulda knowed better. But that's the way it is in this life, you love your own, and you don't trust people who ain't like you.

If I'd a moved into a white neighborhood and one of my neighbors'd started hearing gunshots and hollering, there'd a been a fucking battalion of cops kicking my damn door in. That's just the way it is.

My brother liked video games. He started spending all his time in that apartment with Ben. They got a basketball game and a driving game where the more people they ran over with their car the more points they got. They started watching Knicks games and drinking beer together and sometimes smoking weed. I told my brother to be careful 'cause white people could be tricky, and you could never know what they might want. I thought everything in my life that had gone wrong had been because of white people, and most of 'em looked Jewish. My daddy got sent to prison by some when I was little. My momma had to work cleaning their houses most her life. My teachers, who all pretended to care so much but was really just scared of us and treated us like animals, was white people. They're the cops, the judges, the landlords, the mayors, the people who run everything and own everything. And they aren't letting go of any of it or sharing any of it. The rich take care of the rich and make sure they stay rich, and they talking about helping the poor, but if they really did, there wouldn't be so many of us. And it was one thing having a white boy live across the hall and saying hi to him now and then or watching him get drunk or wear some silly uniform, but it's another having my brother spending all his time with him. I didn't think nothing good would come of it.

My brother didn't ever listen to me. Never did. Wish he had, he might still be with us. This time, though, he was right and I was wrong. Even before he knew, before he became what he became, before it was revealed, Ben was okay. Nothing more, nothing less, just okay. I first found out when my brother took me over there. He had got tired of me telling him all the time that the white boy was no good, so one day he says you either come with me and see he's cool or you shut the fuck up about me spending time over there. I ain't one to shut the fuck up, only a few times in my whole life, so I went with him. We made sure Momma was okay and we went across the hall and we knocked on the door and he answered in his boxer shorts and t-shirt with tomato sauce all over it and my brother started talking.

What's up, Ben.

Ben wiped some grease off his face and talked back at him.

What's up, Alberto.

This is my sister Mariaangeles and her daughter Mercedes.

Yeah, I met them once.

Ben looked at me.

How you doing?

I gave him a dirty look.

You gonna invite us in?

I guess.

He opened the door. Stepped aside. And we went in and I started looking around. Big TV in the living room. A grubby old couch with cigarette burns that looked like it was made out of old carpet.

Video game disks and controllers. Kitchen was nasty. Pizza boxes. Empty cans of soup and pasta with spoons and forks still in 'em. Garbage bags filled on the floor. I opened the fridge 'cause I was thinking of having a soda or something and all it had in it was some ketchup and that was it. Whole place smelled like old food and stale beer. Went to the bedroom and there was a mattress and a pillow. Some clothes on the floor. Closet had his uniform hanging up in it, and it was the only thing that looked cared for. Bathroom, the bathroom where that man was hanging, was worse than the kitchen. Stains in the toilet and sink. Tissues overflowing out of a little garbage can. No toilet paper to be seen and I doubt he had ever cleaned it once. Even by the standards we was used to seeing, his place was bad. And more than bad, or nasty, or disgusting, it was just sad. Real sad. Like he didn't know any better. Like he thought it was normal for a grown man to be living like that. Made me think he didn't have nobody in his life that cared about him. Like he was all alone. Alone in a place where he didn't belong because he didn't have nowhere else to go, and no one else to go to. They'd have done something if they was around. But they weren't. He was all alone. I went back into the living room. Bang bang bang. Him and Alberto shooting Nazis, throwing grenades at 'em. Mercedes sitting on the floor chewing her blankie, watching people explode on the TV. Too much. There's enough ugliness in the world already without pretending to do more. Too much I said, and I smacked Alberto on the back of the head. He got all mad, said you knew what we was doing here, you didn't have to come. I said play another game, play some game where you don't gotta see blood squirting everywhere, and Ben said we'll play the NBA game and changed the disk. While he doing it I ask him where he from, and he says Brooklyn, and I ask if he got family there, and he says yes. I ask him do he see them, he says no. I ask him why and he says I just don't. I ask for how long and he says a long time. I ask him how old he is and he says thirty, I ask where he been living before this and he says he don't want to talk about it. Answers made me sad. I always thought white people had good lives. Even the worst of 'em had it better off than me and everybody I knew. Just what I believed. But this boy didn't have it better. Worse. Just him and his video games and his shitty apartment that no one else would live in. I had my girl and my family at least. He had it way worse.

Their game started back up and I didn't like being there 'cause it was sad and depressing so I got Mercedes and we left and went back to our place. And that was it. For a long time. Six or nine months or something. Alberto played video games with Ben. I'd see him around. In his uniform if it was day, drunk if it was night, sometimes in the hall in his underwear while he was waiting for a pizza. I turned eighteen. Went out with some of my girlfriends from around the project and some girlfriends from when I was in school. They was all around my age, almost all of 'em in a situation similar to mine:

no diploma, a kid or two and a couple had three, boyfriend still around but not really there, no way to get out or move up. Just ways to make it through the day or the week or the month. One of the girls was wearing nice clothes and a nice watch and smelled good like expensive perfume and she started saying she was working as a dancer and making plenty of money. Said you had to be eighteen, but could make three, four hundred, maybe five hundred bucks a night dancing in clubs. We started saying she was hooking but she said no, she danced naked on a stage and gave men lap dances in a private room and they gave her cash. That it was easy. Men from Manhattan would come up, tell their wives they had meetings or was working late, or they'd come over after baseball games at Yankee Stadium. They was stupid and it was easy to make 'em think they was getting some ass and the more you could make 'em think it the more they would pay you. She said it wasn't a churchgoing job, rubbing her ass and tits all over white men, but none of us was churchgoing girls, and a good shower at the end of the night and she was fine with it, especially 'cause she was making so much money. She said maybe she was gonna leave the neighborhood. Find her a place where her kids would be able to go to a good school. Because even though almost all of us was dropouts, we knew the only way out for real was an education. Just none of us could do it.

Next day I called the girl. She took me to the club. I met the manager. Fat white man from Westchester.

He made me strip down to my panties and bra and show him how I danced. Made me rub my ass on his crotch and rub my titties down his chest and whisper shit his wife wouldn't say to him in his ear. His hands started wandering and I asked him what he was doing and he said he test drove all the girls before he let 'em out on the track. Made me sick. But we needed the money. Momma wasn't working and who the fuck knew what Alberto did. Made me sick. But I let him. I let him do anything and everything. Took me for a test drive. Made me fucking sick.

Started working a few days later. It wasn't hard but I had to close up part of my heart, part of my soul. I had been with three men before. One when I was twelve. Mercedes' father, who I was with from when I was fourteen until he left when I was seventeen. The manager. Except for that manager, I'd waited. Tried to make sure they loved me. I know I loved them. Would have done anything for them. Killed for them or died for them. Hit the cross for them. I thought they felt the same, loved the same. But love is different for every person. For some it's hate, for some it's joy, for some it's fear, for some it's jealousy, for some it's torture, for some it's peace. For some it's everything. For me. Everything. And to let a man touch me like that, or to touch a man like that, I had always had to love. So I shut it down. Closed it. Buried it somewhere. And I danced and touched and whispered and got them hard and took them as far as I could and took them for

as much as I could. They didn't know but they took
more from me. A shower at the end of the night
wasn't enough. Not even close. Didn't clean nothing.

Three nights a week I worked, sometimes four.
Started saving up. Got Mercedes some clothes
that hadn't been worn before, some of her own
shoes, brand new. Got my momma a sweater, and
new magazines every week. Didn't put none of the
money in a bank 'cause I know what happens
with white people and their banks. I put it away.
Where Alberto wouldn't never look. Where nobody
would look. A couple months, a couple more.
Making money but hurting. And changing.
Keeping myself closed and hard all the time started
taking it out of me. One of the girls gave me some
shit to smoke and it helped. So I did more of it.
And it helped. More than a shower or anything else.
But when it wore away it started hurting more so
I was taking more. Sleeping and working and
getting high. Starting to do things I would have
never done before because I didn't care, because
I was hurting so much that more of the hurt
wasn't nothing. And it brought more money.
One night I was working and Ben came in and one
of the girls smiled and said look who's here.
And I asked her what about him and she said he was
an easy mark. Would come in with his paycheck
and get drunk and give the whole damn thing away.
I told her he was living in my building and that
he was mine. She got in my face about it for a minute
till I told her how far I'd go. I was dipping into my

money too much and I needed more. Momma was getting sick and Mercedes was getting sick and I needed them to get to a doctor and I didn't have no insurance. And I needed more.

I went over to him. He was already drunk. He smiled and said hi and I said hey baby, nice seeing you here. And I didn't even ask him. Took his hand. Led him to the room where we did the dances. And I went at him, giving him what all them men wanted and whispering in his ear about what we could do back at home now that I knew what kind of boy he was. I told him I wanted to suck his cock and I wanted him to fuck me, that I would ride his ass all day and all night, that I was getting all wet thinking about it. And I kept ordering drinks and feeding him. Just kept it going. And he took it. And was wanting more. And after an hour he was gone. His mind was gone and his money was gone. And I felt bad 'cause I knew what he was and I knew he wasn't bad. Just sad. And alone. Man without anything or anyone, alone in that apartment where no one else would live, with his TV and his games and his pizza boxes and soup cans and his garbage and his sad mattress and his dirty bathroom. That's all he was. He passed out. Right in the chair with my ass between his legs. The bouncers came and took him out. He didn't have no ID or driver's license or credit card. Nothing with his name or address or nothing. I told them he was my neighbor and I knew where he was living. They was gonna throw him on the street, in the gutter. Leave him there.

Let whatever was gonna happen, happen. He'd been there before, I know. And shit had happened to him, I know that for sure. I told them I could at least get him back to the building. I had just taken everything he had and I was figuring I could do that much. We got a cab and put him sleeping in the backseat. I sat next to him. He was snoring like a baby. And when we got to the projects the driver helped me get him out of the cab. And I got him into the building and into the elevator. Got him into the hallway front of his door. And I left him there. And I went back out and got high. Spent some of his money on what I needed. And when I came home later he was still there.

Next time I saw him was like two days later. He was coming home in his uniform and I was going to work. We didn't say nothing to each other. I don't even know if he remembered. Just looked sad and nervous like he always did. And the next time I saw him after that was a long time. And he wasn't the same no more. He had changed. Changed and become someone else. He had become something I couldn't even believe. And then I did. I believed. I believed.

CHARLES

I felt sorry for him when I met him. He had come in to apply for a security position at my job site. We ran two guys at a time, on twelve-hour shifts. There were weekday guys and weekend guys. Pay was minimum wage. No benefits. It was a shitty job. You walked the perimeter of the site, stood around for hours at a time. We didn't have a security shack. You bring one in and the guards end up never leaving. They buy little TVs and drink coffee all day. Take naps. This was a sensitive site. We were putting up forty stories in a neighborhood where the tallest building was twelve. There had been community opposition. A couple protests, and a big petition. I needed guys who were willing to work. To make sure that the site was secure. It's harder than you think finding them. Most people want something for nothing. They want everything to be easy. When a job is hard, they demand more money, more time off, they complain to their union reps and try to renegotiate terms. That's not the way it works. Life is hard, deal with it. Working sucks, deal with it. I'd love to sit home and collect a check every two weeks for watching baseball games and spending time with my kids. Doesn't happen that way. You gotta work for everything in this world. Scratch and claw and fight for every little thing. And it never gets easier. Never. And it doesn't end until you die. And then it doesn't matter.

Learn to deal with that. It's the way of the world. You fight and struggle and work your ass off and then you die. Deal with that.

He came in with a resume. It said his name was Ben Jones, that he was thirty years old. He was wearing a button-down with the logo of a security guard school on it. My first impression of him was that he was very eager, very excited, and very nervous. His hand was shaking when I shook it. His lips were quivering. Aside from his basic biographical information, and an eight-week course at the security school which made him officially qualified for the job, the resume was empty. I asked him where he was from and he said Brooklyn. I asked him if he went to college, he said no. I asked him when he left home and he said at fourteen. I told him that seemed young and he shrugged and I asked what he'd been doing for the past sixteen years and he changed, just a little, but he changed, and something in his eyes came out that was really sad and really lonely and extremely painful. It was only there for a second, and normally I wouldn't notice anything like that, or pay attention to it, or give a shit, but it was very striking, and he looked down at his feet for a moment and then looked up and said I've had hard times and I'm ready to work and I promise I'll be the best worker you have, I promise. And that was it. He didn't offer anything else and I didn't push it. I just thought to myself sixteen fucking years, what the fuck has this guy been doing. And I still think about it, all the time, what the fuck was he doing. And I imagined, and still do, because of the flash of deep sadness and loneliness and pain that I saw, that whatever it was, and wherever it was, it had been truly truly awful.

So I gave him the job. He was very excited. Like a little kid at Christmas. A big smile, a huge smile. He said thank you about fifty times. And he kept shaking my hand. It was funny, and very endearing. It wasn't like he'd won the fucking lotto. He got a minimum wage job walking around a construction site for twelve fucking hours a day.

I put him on the five-days-a-week day shift. Thought that would be best. That he'd be proud to have that position. And he was. It showed in how he did the job. He was always on time. His uniform was always clean. He never tried to extend his breaks or his lunch. He never complained. He seemed fascinated by the process of putting a building up: knocking in the pilings, setting the foundation, the construction of the skeleton frame. He'd ask different people questions about what they did, or why they did things a certain way. He'd listen very intently to their answers, like he was gonna be tested on it or something. He was generally the happiest guard I'd ever seen or had on a job, and he became sort of the site mascot. Everybody liked him and enjoyed having him around. He knew everyone's name and would greet everyone in the morning and say goodbye at the end of the day. There were only two things that ever seemed off, and I dismissed them both because he did such a good job and seemed so happy. First was right after he got his first paycheck. He came and switched the address in our files to an address in the Bronx. The previous one had been in Queens. I don't know why but I was curious, so I looked up the address in Queens. It was a state-run transitional home, a place where they send men coming out of either prison, rehab, a homeless shelter, or a mental institution. I thought about looking into it more, but I had other things to worry about and Ben seemed fine. Second thing happened one day during lunch. I had a doctor's appointment and had to leave the site. On my way to the subway, I saw Ben sitting on a bench a few blocks away. He was crying. It was the middle of the day, and he had seemed like his normal self when I had seen him earlier. I did a double take because I couldn't believe it was him. But it was. He was sitting on a bench with his face in his hands and he was sobbing.

The day of the accident was a beautiful spring day. It was sunny, no clouds, slight breeze, in the mid-70s. A perfect New York day, not one I thought would fucking blow up. I had never had a major accident on one of my sites before, and it was a point of great pride for me. I believed there wasn't a building on earth that was worth sacrificing a life for, and I still believe it. Safety matters more than speed. Safety matters more than anything. It was one of the reasons I had been hired. Because the job was a sensitive issue in the community, and so many people were against it, the developer couldn't afford to have anything go wrong. Accidents are the best weapon community activists have against developers. While it would be nice to think developers care about safety, they don't. Like almost everyone else in America, developers are fucking greedy. They care about money, and activists with weapons cost them money. My job was to stay on budget, stay on schedule, and keep that site safe.

The skeleton was done. Forty stories of steel frame rising. We were putting in the windows, which were ten foot by ten foot mirrored panels. We had finished the first thirty-three stories without any problems, and we were installing on thirty-four. We'd lift seven panels at a time. Bundle them, secure them, rig them to a wire, bring them up with a crane. I'd done it literally thousands of times at job sites, and I had never had any problems.

I don't know what the fuck went wrong. Still don't. We had investigators from the city, the state, and the insurance company all look at the rig, and nobody could figure it out. To this day, the cause in all of the paperwork is listed as unknown. I could call them and tell them that it didn't matter what we did that day, that no rig would have held that glass, that there were other forces at work far beyond any that the city, state, or insurance company could muster, but they'd think I was crazy. And sometimes I'm not sure that I'm not. But that's part of faith. Believing and knowing despite what other people say, and despite what the world might think of your beliefs.

I was on the ground. Standing near our trailer, which was on the edge of the sidewalk. I was holding a clipboard, going over some budget numbers with one of our construction accountants. They blow an air horn right before any large load goes up, and the air horn went off. I looked up and the panels were slowly rising. We stop traffic when we lift panels, and there were no cars coming down the street. Most of the workers were standing around talking, which is what they did when work was halted. Ben was standing at the edge of the site, looking towards the stopped traffic, ready to stop anyone who might try to get around our traffic controller. Normally I would have gone back to the clipboard. But I felt something, something inevitable. If you can somehow feel fate, or destiny, or the power of the future, I felt it, very literally. And it made me watch. It forced me to do something that I normally wouldn't do. I couldn't turn away. I couldn't not watch those panels.

The panels continued to go up, and they drifted a few feet, just like they always did, like anything that heavy being lifted that high would drift. The crane was working perfectly. The rig was set perfectly. The panels were in wooden crates sealed with iron nails. At that point we'd lifted and installed hundreds of them. It was no big deal. Just part of our routine. Nobody was watching, and I'm the only one who saw. I saw the nails slip out of the crate. I saw the back of the crate fall. I saw the angle of the crates change. I saw them drift. I saw the panel fall out. A ten foot by ten foot glass panel. Probably weighed a thousand pounds. I saw it fall.

It hit him on the back of the head and shattered. There was a huge noise, an explosion of glass. He got flattened. A total collapse. Everything stopped, everybody turned. There was a moment, a long hideous moment of silence, of never-ending fucking silence. Then the screaming started. I dropped the clipboard and started running towards him. Pulled my phone out of my pocket and called 911. There was no way he was alive. I told the operator a man had just died on my construction site and gave her the address. I could see the blood before I got there. It was everywhere. And there was glass everywhere. All I could hear was screaming. People were getting out of their cars, running, calling 911. And above me, for a brief instant, I saw the rest of the panels being pulled onto the thirty-fourth floor. There was no way that one should have fallen.

When I got to him, I was positive he was dead. The back of his head was crushed. There was blood and something else, I assumed it was brain fluid, leaking out of it. There were shards of glass imbedded into his entire body. He was literally shredded, blood pouring from his arms, legs, chest, stomach, face. There was fucking blood everywhere. I couldn't really even see him. I didn't know what to do, if I should touch him, move him, try taking the glass out of his body. There was no way to try to stop the bleeding with a tourniquet, or ten tourniquets, or fifty tourniquets. And I didn't believe in God so I couldn't pray. I just waited for someone to come who would tell me what do.

A crowd started gathering. The other workers tried to keep them back. Sirens in the distance. A group of women kneeling in a prayer circle. People still screaming. As they got closer and saw what I saw, they turned away, covered their eyes, a few vomited. And the blood kept flowing. I was kneeling next to him, and it was running around my legs, soaking my pants. I took hold of two of his fingers where there was no glass, and I started trying to talk to him. I had no idea if he could hear me. I thought it might help him if he could, it might comfort him, give him some kind of solace as he died. No one wants to die alone, even though that's how it happens for all of us, even though we pretend there's some other way. I thought my voice might make it easier. Calm him, make him less scared. I can't imagine how fucking shocked and terrified he must have been, if he was aware of anything. I told him that help was on its way and that he was going to be alright. I felt sick to my stomach while I said it. I could see his brains through his shattered skull. Literally see his brains. I just held those two fingers and talked to him and watched him bleed away.

An ambulance arrived. The crowd parted and two paramedics came rushing through with a gurney. I heard one of them say Jesus fucking Christ, the other said no way this guy's alive. They dropped their bags and went to work. They started checking him, but they didn't seem to know where to start. One of them asked me what happened and I said a plate of glass fell on him. They checked his pulse, talked about how to proceed, leave the glass in him, get him out of here, let the surgeons deal with it if he's even still alive. He had a pulse, and they both seemed shocked. They lowered the gurney, asked me to step away. One took his lower body and one took his upper body. They lifted him onto the clean, white surface. Blood streamed off his body, stained the gurney, dripped to the ground. They started back towards the ambulance and I followed them. They asked me his name, I told them. They asked where he was from and I said he lived in the Bronx. They got him into the ambulance. I asked to come, told them I was his boss, that it was my job site. They said get in and I did and they closed the doors.

I sat on the bench near the door. One of them drove. The other worked on Ben. He put on a heart monitor, wove the wires around the shards of glass protruding from Ben's body. When it was on and working, he tried to stop the bleeding from cuts without glass in them, but there were so many of them it was almost useless. The monitor stopped, and the paramedic gave Ben CPR, and his heart started again. I don't know how long we were in the ambulance. It felt like ten seconds and it felt like ten hours, and Ben's heart stopped four or five times. He died in that ambulance four or five times, and the paramedic kept bringing him back. Something kept bringing him back.

Once the monitor stopped and the paramedic didn't do anything. Just stared and shook his head. I didn't blame him. It seemed like a lost cause. Ten seconds passed, maybe twenty, it seemed like forever. I just stared at Ben, or what was left of him, and tried to figure out what the fuck went wrong, how this could have happened. I started to say I'm sorry, as if apologizing to a dead man would mean something, though it seems that's how it works most of the time; we say the things that matter to people when it's already too late. Before the words came out of my mouth, the monitor started registering a pulse again. Something kept bringing him back. Something was not going to let him go.

We pulled into the hospital and they rushed him away. I followed them into the emergency room. I gave the administrators all the information I could. I filled out all of the forms as best as I could. I called back to the site and asked for a change of clothes because the ones I was wearing were covered with blood. Men from the site started showing up. We were all in shock. Just sat and talked about how we couldn't believe it happened, how awful it was. Media started showing up and trying to interview people. Nobody said a word. We knew it wouldn't matter if we did, that the media was gonna write what they wanted to write regardless of their so-called ethics, and their supposed belief in truth. We just sat and waited to hear that Ben had died. We assumed it was so. Though I had seen what I had seen in the ambulance, at the time I didn't believe it was anything more than coincidence.

More men from the site arrived. The crane operator and window installers came in. They were deeply and visibly shaken. I sat with them, asked what happened. They didn't know. They claimed the crate was intact. That there was no way that glass should have come out, or could have come out. I told them I saw the nails fall, and saw the back of the crate fall. They claimed that was impossible. That the crate was intact. There was tape around it, tape that had been applied at the factory, and that it was unbroken. The crate was empty. They could tell that by its weight. But it had never been opened. I figured someone was trying to cover their ass. Someone had fucked up and didn't want to take responsibility for another man's death. Ultimately the responsibility would have fallen on me. But it turned out they were right. The crate was unopened and empty. City and state accident investigators all agreed. The crate was fucking unopened. How the glass fell has never been explained. And Ben didn't die. Somehow he survived. More than survived. So much more. Something kept bringing him back. Something wouldn't let him go. Something, or someone, or I don't know what, wouldn't let him die.

ALEXIS

I was on break when the call came in, watching a baseball game with some of the guys who work in the cafeteria and were also on break. It was a Yankee game, and I love the Yankees, and though my schedule tends to prevent me from seeing as many games as I would like, I try to see two or three a week during the season, and I always watch during my breaks. I love the systems and the order of baseball, and I very much appreciate the cause-and-effect nature of the game. As a surgeon, my entire life is based in the systems of the human body, the systems of the hospital and a surgical team, the order or orders under which those things operate, and the cause-and-effect nature of trauma, injury, and the surgical attempts to remedy them. Though it often seems chaotic and anarchic and spontaneous, all life is system, order, and cause and effect. Try as so many do, it is impossible to escape them. I gave up at a fairly young age and decided to dedicate my life to the service of them.

The call was white male, late twenties or early thirties, massive trauma, massive head wounds, massive blood loss, and then the unusual part, which was the first of so many unusual occurrences with Ben and his case, hundreds of shards of glass imbedded in his body. I'm a geek about my job, and after doing it for many years—I was forty-one when the case began—I still get excited when a case comes in that sounds different or challenging for some reason. At the time, I didn't even think about the human element of it, that someone had just undergone some horrific event and was experiencing feelings and emotions that are far beyond anything within the realm of my experience. I just thought about the potential medical and technical challenges involved and how I would solve them. Ben changed that for me. Now much of what I think lies within the human realm of the surgical experience, what the patient is feeling, what the people who love the patient are feeling, and how I can help with those issues as well. I understand that all of our lives revolve around what we are feeling at any given moment. There is nothing more human than emotion.

I got up and I said goodbye to my fellow Yankee fans and I quickly made my way to the trauma suite. Everyone was getting ready, the nurses, the assistants, the residents, and I was the last to arrive. At that point, and again this was before my experience with Ben changed me, because my position as the head surgeon is one of authority, I tended not to speak to any of the people I worked with unless I needed something from them or needed to discuss a specific aspect of the impending surgery with them, both of which were rare. While I scrubbed in and prepared myself for whatever it was that was arriving, I was silent.

The moments while a team waits for a patient can be very tense. You stand at the ready. While you have a general idea of condition, you do not often know what the specific medical issues are, and you have no idea if you will be there for ten minutes or ten hours, though there is rarely anything in between. Different surgeons handle it differently. I think of myself as a batter in a baseball game, actually in the seventh game of the World Series, with the bases loaded, a three-and-two count, down by three runs, in the bottom of the ninth inning. I have one swing to either succeed or fail and the result entirely depends on what I do and how I perform. Unlike in baseball, though, I cannot hit a single, a double, or a triple. I either hit a home run or I strike out, and the patient either lives or dies.

As I mentioned, I was intrigued and excited by the call, and had no idea what a patient who had shards of glass imbedded in his body would look like or what I would need to do to make that patient survive. When paramedics enter the hospital with a critical case, they are greeted by ER doctors and members of the surgical team, and there is a transfer of information related to the patient: the circumstances of the trauma, issues, if any, during transfer, a preliminary diagnosis, if one is possible. Once the transfer is made, the patient is brought into the trauma bay, where I, and the rest of the team, go to work. It is usually a fairly seamless process, and it is one that is repeated with great regularity.

Not so with Ben. The EMTs were covered with blood, as was the stretcher. They started to describe the scene, and one of them kept repeating something I myself said many times later, which was that there was no way the patient should be alive, and that he had no idea what was going on with him. The doctors and nurses, who were incredibly seasoned and experienced, and had seen all manner of horror and gore after years in a public New York City emergency room and trauma unit, were shocked almost into paralysis, and one of the nurses vomited. Each looked to the others for direction, which is not entirely surprising. In life we often look to others for simple, but difficult answers, despite the fact that we have those answers ourselves. They needed to get him into surgery, and they needed to do it as soon as possible.

One of them took the initiative and urged the others to act, and they started moving towards me and my team. We can always hear them as they bring the patient into the trauma bay, hear the wheels of the gurney, the various squeaking sounds it makes, hear the nurses talking to each other, sometimes the patients scream, cry out, or moan. As they get closer, I tend to become calmer, more focused, and more aware, and time slows down in a way that makes those few brief moments seem incredibly long and peaceful. I sometimes wish I could live forever in that state, and believe that those who find enlightenment, people like Ben, though he discovered so much more than that, live their entire lives that way.

The doors opened and he was brought into the trauma bay, and for the first time in my fifteen-year career I heard an audible gasp come from every single person in attendance. It was a surreal, unbelievable sight, like something out of a Hollywood horror movie, something that shouldn't have been possible and isn't possible, but was right in front of my eyes. There was blood everywhere. There were huge, deep lacerations everywhere. When I heard glass shards, I expected small pieces of glass, maybe an inch long at their longest. What he had in his body were not shards, but actual pieces, some as tall as ten inches, some as wide as twelve inches, and we were only seeing what was visible above the level of his skin. The back of his skull had been crushed, and there were pieces of it that appeared to be missing. We could not see his face at all because it was entirely covered in blood. Everything was entirely covered in blood.

The first stage of treatment in any trauma situation is the stabilization of the patient. Death from blood loss was the obvious first concern. If a patient has lost more than 40 percent of their body's blood volume, they are likely to be in decompensated hypovolemic shock, which usually results in multi-organ failure. While we checked his blood pressure, which was at 40 over 20, the lowest I'd ever recorded in a living patient, and checked his pulse, which was 30, again an absurdly low number, we gave him injections of epinephrine and atropine to jumpstart his heart and get his blood pressure and pulse up.

Simultaneously, we tried to get heart-rate monitors and BP monitors on him, but it was incredibly difficult because we were weaving the wires around glass shards that had very sharp edges. We inserted a central venous line and transfused him with type O negative uncrossmatched red blood cells. Though we wanted, at some point, to take the glass out of him, we needed him to be stable first, and we needed to figure out which pieces to remove first, and in what order the rest of them would come out.

He shut down three times in my care, went into full cardiac arrest. We defibrillated him, which was difficult because of the glass, and on one occasion I absolutely know the defibrillation worked, but on the other two his heart appeared to start functioning again on its own, which was both surprising and confusing. We kept putting blood into him and he kept bleeding and we kept putting it in. I don't know the actual amount, but it became something of a game, a game where a man's life appeared to be at stake, and in which I and the other people in the room were working with incredible urgency and resolve, making sure we were transfusing more blood in than he was losing, a game that we knew would result in death if we did not succeed. What we could see of his skin was white, and I don't mean the Caucasian white, I mean truly white, alabaster white, like he was carved from marble. And no matter how much blood we put in, his skin didn't change, and his body showed no indication that it was actually maintaining the blood.

While we were stabilizing him, I also needed to cover and protect his head. He had sustained a comminuted skull fracture, which means it had broken into a large number of small pieces, through which I could clearly see his brain. I assumed there was intracranial bleeding, most likely subdural, epidural, or intraparenchymal, and even if I could keep him alive, he would suffer from massive brain damage. We applied compression dressings using sterile surgical bandages, gauze, and surgical tape and moved his head as little as possible. We found pieces of his skull that were the size of nickels and bagged them in case we might be able to use them later.

Two extremely long and stressful hours after he arrived at the hospital, his heart rate and blood pressure were stable, or at least stable enough for us to attempt to start removing the pieces of glass from his body. I took a step back and took a deep breath and looked at what was ahead of me. There were three IV lines transfusing blood into his body. We were applying pressure everywhere we could, but blood was still coming out of him at a rather alarming rate. We had been able to clean him up and cut away his clothing, and his skin was still deathly white. There was glass protruding from his legs, his arms, his abdomen and chest, there were smaller pieces in his face, and there were a number of large pieces that had been deeply imbedded into his back when he hit the ground.

I tried to identify pieces of glass that had nicked, punctured, cut, or potentially severed major veins and arteries: the jugular veins, carotid arteries, and subclavian arteries and veins in the neck, and the femoral arteries and veins in the legs. I wondered what I couldn't see, possibly damage to the aorta, the inferior vena cava, or the pulmonary vasculature, which are deeper in the chest and torso and were beneath my field of vision. While the conventional wisdom of a non-medical professional might say it would be best to remove the pieces of glass from those veins and arteries, there was the very real possibility that they were tamponading further bleeding and had sealed areas that had been damaged or destroyed. Getting through this part of Ben's treatment would be part luck and part strategy and, if successful, part miracle.

I had a vascular surgeon and his fellow join me and offer their opinions. I felt they might have something to offer that would help me, and help Ben, in some way. None of us had any idea where to start, or what to do, or what path to take, or what we might have in store for us when we started to actually remove the pieces. So I just started. I had three residents with me, and I had two of the residents prepared with suture in case sutures were needed, and I had the other prepared with a bipolar bovie, which is an electrocauterization instrument. We had two surgical nurses with suction and another with an aspiration wand that delivered an anticoagulant. There were other nurses monitoring his vitals and continuing to transfuse him.

Once we started, we moved very quickly, because every movement, especially removing the largest pieces, resulted in blood loss, sometimes fairly significant blood loss. If we hadn't moved quickly, Ben would surely have died. There were a number of scares, and a number of times when his vitals dropped dramatically, and a number of times when we couldn't stop the bleeding in what I considered a timely manner. But Ben wouldn't die, and now, at this point, after everything, I believe that what we did that day probably didn't matter very much. Ben was not going to die.

Nine hours after we started, we tied the last suture. He had a total of 745 stitches, both internal and external, and an additional 115 external staples. We had used 40 units of blood, which is approximately double the amount any human has in their body at any given time. We also gave him multiple units of platelets and fresh frozen plasma. And for him, the day was far from over. There was a team of craniofacial surgeons and neurosurgeons standing by to deal with his skull and brain injuries. As I stepped back from the table, I saw one of his hands twitching, which I took to be a good sign, and I stepped over and took hold of it, hoping that somewhere, on some level, he might find it comforting. To my great shock, his grip was very strong, very firm, and I immediately felt something similar, but deeper and more profound, to what I feel in those moments just before surgery, an intense calm and sense of peace and contentment. It was unreal, and obviously unexpected, and it ultimately changed my life in so many ways. I didn't want to let go. I didn't want that moment to end and I didn't want that feeling to ever leave me. But all things leave us, all people, all feelings, no matter how we want them to stay, no matter how tight we hold on to them. We lose everything in life at some point. I lost that moment the instant I let go of his hand.

After he was hemodynamically stable, he needed a CT scan of his head to determine the extent of intracranial injury. Moving a patient as critical as he was can be very difficult, very complicated, and very slow, so I knew I had some time to take a break, and I needed one. I went to our break room and took a shower and tried to take a nap but couldn't fall asleep. I was extremely awake, felt electric. I imagine I felt the way people feel when they take cocaine or ecstasy, though I have never used either of those or any illegal drugs. I got dressed and found Ben back in the OR, where the surgeons were now working on his brain, and I gowned up so I could watch the procedures. They had basically completed what was already a craniotomy, and evacuated both epidural and subdural hematomas. I watched the surgeons do some skull reconstruction using titanium plating, though they appeared to leave much of his skull as it was in case of cerebral edema, swelling of the brain, which can lead to brain herniation downward and death. Four hours after they started, Ben was taken to the post-anesthesia care unit.

He was later moved to the surgical ICU, and even though he was stable, he remained on life support: supplementary ventilation, intravenous therapy with fluids, drugs, and nutrition, and urinary catheterization. He was kept sedated using propofol so that we could monitor brain swelling and function. The ICU took over his day-to-day care, though I would continue to treat him, as would the craniofacial surgeons and neurosurgeons. When I left the hospital, I felt very good, given the extreme nature of the situation and the trauma, about the care we had provided and Ben's prospects for some type of recovery. It was very early in a case like this, and normally it takes quite a while for us to really know how and if a patient is or is not going to recover. I assumed that I would come back the next day and everything would be more or less the same. I should have known better.

When I arrived, there were no urgent cases, so I went to the ICU to check on Ben and see if there were any new developments. I picked up his chart, and I noticed immediately that his name had been changed from Ben Jones to John Doe, and that his date of birth had been changed to unknown. I placed the chart back into the wall file and went towards the ICU offices, where I saw the ICU attending standing with two uniformed police officers and another man who appeared also to be a police officer but was wearing a suit. The attending introduced me to the men and told them that I had treated the John Doe when he had first arrived and had performed the first surgery on him. I asked them why he was being considered a John Doe, and they proceeded to tell me that his name was fake, his driver's license was fake, his fingerprints did not show up in any city, county, state, or federal databases, and that they could find no records of a man named Ben Jones born on the date listed on his driver's license in any of the city, state, federal, or law enforcement databases at their disposal. Needless to say, I was surprised. I told the officers that I didn't know anything beyond what was on his chart and what I'd experienced with him in surgery, and I had no idea who he was or where he was from. I also suggested they speak to the men who had been gathering in the waiting room, who had said that they worked with the patient on a construction site. They said they had spoken to those men, and that all of them knew him as Ben Jones, and they had examined all of the paperwork the site manager had on file, and that all of it contained the same information that appeared on the fabricated driver's license. Again, I told them I knew nothing. They asked if anybody else had asked about the patient, or if there had been any other inquiries about him. I said not that I knew of, but that I had been either performing or observing surgery with him for almost twenty-four hours and normally didn't have that type of contact with individuals looking for information on patients. They said thank you, and they left.

I went back to Ben's room with the ICU attending and we started talking about his case, his prognosis, and started exchanging ideas about treatment.

He had ordered an electroencephalogram to test brain function and was hoping to get a quantitative electroencephalogram to fully map Ben's brain and see what areas had been damaged and how badly. When he left, I had a moment alone with Ben and I reached for his hand, the same hand I had held before, but there was no reaction. It was limp and cold and felt like the hand of a corpse.

I continued to follow the case over the course of the next week. There was a fairly significant amount of press related to the accident—it was a controversial building being put up by a high-profile developer—and it gave the newspapers and blogs a few days of salacious headlines. We had hoped the coverage would help with an identification, but no one came forward. I got harassed by a couple of reporters who waited outside the entrance of my apartment building and stuck tape recorders in my face, hoping to get me to say something they could write about, but I knew to keep quiet, and that despite the tape recorders, the reporters would write whatever they wanted and the newspapers would print whatever they felt like printing. My truth is in the life and death I witness at the hospital every day. Ultimately, life and death are the only form of perfect truth that exists in the world. Everything else is subjective, and subject to an individual's perspective. I don't look for truth in the media.

Aside from the mystery of his identity, Ben became a medical mystery. His lacerations healed in a remarkable, unheard-of amount of time; after a week we were able to remove all of the sutures, all of the staples, and his wounds were closed and starting to scar. He was weaned down on the respirator, and we continued to feed him intravenously. The electroencephalogram results were erratic and unexplainable. At times he appeared to have suffered brain death, where there is absolutely no activity of any kind registering on the EEG monitors. At other times he appeared to be in a persistent vegetative state, where cycles of sleep and some base awareness, but not cognition, were recognizable. Once or twice a day he went into a state of extreme brain activity, centered in two regions of his brain, the medial orbitofrontal cortex, which is one of our emotional centers, and the right middle temporal cortex, which is often associated with auditory verbal hallucinations. The activity was extreme to the point that it was almost immeasurable, and the neurologists working on his case had never seen anything like it, especially with someone who had experienced such severe brain trauma. The initial worries related to brain swelling, bleeding, and intracranial pressure disappeared, as his brain seemed to heal itself as quickly, and miraculously, as his body did. He would also, at times, twitch, shake, convulse, and make guttural noises, which should not have been possible with the levels of medication being used to keep him sedated. At the end of his first week with us, he had a second major craniofacial procedure, in which titanium plates were used to seal and close the remaining open areas of his skull. The surgery went well, and he was returned to the ICU. Two weeks later we learned his real name, or rather, we learned the name he was given at birth. He was still in a coma, though no longer medically induced. It was some time after that, probably a year or so, that I learned who he was, and that his name, or any name any person could have given him, was meaningless. He was, and that is what is important. He was and he will always be.

ESTHER

My brother Jacob did not allow the mainstream media to, as he said, infect our home. There were no newspapers, there was no television, unless it was Christian TV. We could only listen to Christian radio stations, and our computers had filters on them that prevented anyone using them from accessing MSM websites. He believed, and still does, that the mainstream media is anti-Christian and anti-family, and promotes a liberal homosexual agenda in direct conflict with the teachings of the Lord and Savior Jesus Christ and God Almighty.

Jacob was head of our home. My father had passed away when I was six and Jacob was sixteen, and he had stepped into my father's role. A few months after my father's death, Jacob was born again into the Kingdom of the Christian God. Shortly thereafter, my mother was also born again, and when I was eight, I was as well. Life changed dramatically, and very very quickly. We had been Orthodox Jews. My father had always said we were part of an ancient family, that we were Davidic, which meant we were direct descendants of King David, that we were, in a way, Jewish royalty. Life with him was tense, and he didn't, for reasons I didn't know until later, have a good relationship with my mother. They fought all the time, or my father didn't speak to her. I never knew why or what she did, it was just the way it was. And when my father wasn't at work—he was a kosher butcher—he drank, read the Torah at the kitchen table, or sat in our living room with our rabbi, and later with Jacob. When the rabbi was over, all of the children were required to go to our rooms and stay there until the rabbi left. At the synagogue, the rabbi was always happy and friendly and very welcoming. When he was with our father, he was very serious and full of intent.

I saw Ben on the front page of a newspaper. I was walking to church for Bible study and was walking past a deli. The headline said Miracle Man and there was a picture of him lying on the ground with a man in a hard hat holding his hand. There was glass sticking out of his body and his head was bleeding. There was blood everywhere. It looked like someone had taken the picture with their cell phone. I stopped and looked at the paper to make sure I was seeing it correctly. I hadn't seen or spoken to or heard from Ben in sixteen years, since my brother had told him he had to leave. It was hard to tell exactly, so I went inside to buy the paper. I was uncomfortable. I didn't normally go into places like that, especially if they sold any media other than newspapers, especially magazines, which Jacob often said were the books of the Devil. The man behind the counter asked me if I had read the story and I said no. He said it was pretty incredible, that the man had gotten hit by a glass plate that fell from thirty stories and had lived. He was a Muslim man. I had been taught to hate

Muslims, that they were evil. I gave him fifty cents, making sure not to touch him, and left.

Outside I read the article, and it said the man's name was Ben Jones, and that he lived in the Bronx. I knew then it was Ben, our Ben, our missing Ben, our exiled Ben. It said he was in a hospital in Manhattan in the intensive care unit. It was only a few miles away. I couldn't believe that after all this time he was only a couple of miles away. Jacob had tried for years to find him. He never said why he sent him away or why he wanted him back, but he desperately wanted him back. He talked to our church elders, and they hired a private detective who spent a year looking for him. They didn't find anything, not a single trace of him anywhere, and they looked all over America, and all over Canada, and even some places in Europe. So Jacob prayed and watched for signs. He hoped and believed that someday Ben might return.

I didn't know what to do, if I should tell Jacob or go see Ben myself or just let him be. Part of me wanted to obey and honor my brother as head of our home and as a pastor at our church. Part of me thought if Ben wanted to come back he would come back, and if the Lord and Savior deemed it so, then so it would be. Part of me was just scared, really scared, and I didn't know why, and normally I would have thought it was the work of Satan—that is what Jacob would believe and what they would have taught me at church—but for some reason it didn't feel like that was the case this time. I put the paper in a trash can, and after

Bible study I stayed at church and prayed to Jesus for some direction. I stayed all day, and I prayed all day. Normally if I stayed away from home Jacob would get angry with me and tell me my place was at home helping Mother with the cooking and cleaning. The exception was if I was at church, and especially if I was praying. Jacob believed that all things could be achieved through prayer, and at the time I believed that as well. I prayed real hard that day. I kept asking Jesus to show me the way.

I didn't see any signs or experience any revelations, so I decided I would continue in a similar way. I bought a newspaper every day and read about what was happening with Ben and I went to church and prayed for most of the day. It was hard on Mother because she was used to having my help around the apartment. And Jacob was very curious why I was praying so hard. I told them I felt like I needed some guidance from the Lord as I moved into womanhood and was on my knees asking for it. They both approved of that and let me keep doing it. I saw it in the paper when they figured out Ben Jones was not Ben's real name. I read about how they were trying to find someone who knew him. I saw him when they showed his driver's license picture and I knew for sure. He looked just like he did when he left except that he was older, and I stared at the picture for a really really long time. Me and Ben had always been really close when I was little. My father and Jacob never liked Ben, and they were always mean to him. I didn't ever know or understand why, but they blamed him for everything that went wrong and yelled at him all the time. Sometimes my father hit him, and sometimes, when it was just the kids, Jacob would hit Ben. And as he got older, they hit him more, and they hit him harder. I would hear him in his room crying, and I would go in and give him hugs and tell him I loved him. He always said I was the only person in the family who loved him, and he would tell me I was the best little sister in the world. My father and Jacob mostly ignored me, and my mother was always worried about my father, and Ben paid the most attention to me, so I was closest to him and loved him most.

Each day there would be updates, and new stories. Ben was improving faster than the doctors had ever seen. He had another brain surgery. He was stable but still in a coma. There were protests at the construction site, and people were talking about lawsuits, and the developer was saying it wasn't his fault. I couldn't believe how much attention it was getting. I thought somebody who knew our family when we were Jewish, before we accepted Jesus Christ as our Lord and Savior, would recognize him and come forward, but no one did. The papers just kept calling him the Miracle Man. It was really the first time in my life that I had ever read newspapers, and I could see why people hated them. They didn't seem dangerous, though, just sort of silly.

I kept the same schedule and waited until the coverage slowed down. I was worried that if I went to see him before the reporters went away someone might figure out who he was and I would get into trouble with Jacob and the church. I was also waiting for some kind of sign from the Lord. I believed, at the time, that the Lord always provided those who lived by his word with signs that told them which way to go in life. One afternoon I heard one of the women in the church choir talking about how she had just gotten a letter from a brother that she didn't see any more because he drank and slept with women other than his wife. Her brother had found Christ and had been born again and had given up his evil ways and wanted to see her. She was standing beneath a cross as she was talking, and she was holding a Bible, and there was light streaming through a window across her face. I thought for sure it was a message from above. Now I understand there is no such thing, that there is no above and no one to send us supernatural messages. There is just coincidence or our individual interpretations of what we see around us, and if we do see something it's an accident, and it means nothing. That is truly the word of God.

At the time, though, I was convinced otherwise, and I decided to go and try to see Ben. I rarely went into Manhattan. If I did, I was with Jacob and my mother, and usually other members of our church. Our senior pastor preached that Manhattan was part of Satan's Empire. An island filled with sin and devoted to greed, where homosexuals and perverts were allowed to live freely and prosper, and where the word of the Lord was defamed and blasphemed. I was scared of it. I was worried that if I went alone I would be raped or forced into sin in some way. There were temptations everywhere, on every block and in every building, bars and restaurants and banks controlled by Masons, stores that sold impure clothing, entire neighborhoods devoted to homosexual sex. Satan's hold was strong. I know now that it's a ridiculous way to think, but I didn't know then. So I prayed for strength, I prayed long and hard, and when I felt strong enough I slipped out of the church and took the subway under the river. I followed the directions I had gotten from a church computer and got off the subway and went straight to the hospital. When I went in, I asked for intensive care and took an elevator to the right floor. I was very scared. I was shaking as I stepped out of the elevator and started walking down the hall. I was holding a copy of the Bible that had been printed in Israel and blessed by the head of our church. I was wearing a cross that Jacob had given me when I turned seventeen and that he said would always protect me. I stopped in the waiting room and I prayed. And when I felt the Holy Spirit strong inside me, I went into the intensive care and found Ben's room. I stood at the door and looked inside. There was a woman, a woman dressed like a doctor, sitting by his bed reading a clipboard with some paper on it. She reached out and held his hand for a moment, and I was scared, because I believed women who weren't either related to or married to a man should never touch him. I couldn't do anything to stop it, though. I just stood at the door and looked at him. He was lying in a bed and there were machines all around him and there were tubes coming out of his arms and there were wires attached to his chest and his head, which also had a bandage on it. I just stood there and said his name, the name he was given when he was born: Ben Zion Avrohom, Ben Zion Avrohom, Ben Zion Avrohom.

The woman looked up and saw me and started to stand. I didn't want to talk to her so I left as fast as I could and went straight back to Queens. I went to church and I prayed to the Lord Christ for the forgiveness of my sins because I had indeed lied to my brother Jacob, and I prayed to the Lord and gave thanks for his protection while I was in Manhattan, and I prayed to the Lord and asked him to help my other brother, Ben Zion, recover from his injuries.

Over the course of the next two weeks, I was able to see Ben Zion almost every day. Our church was going through its biannual fundraising drive, and members of the youth ministry were expected to go out and solicit funds. Our church had never been rich in money, though all of the pastors, including Jacob, said its coffers were overflowing with devotion, worship, the fervor of the Holy Spirit, and the love of the Savior Jesus Christ. Most of its parishioners were, and still are, working-class people and immigrants, mainly from Eastern Europe. While every member of the flock was expected to tithe ten percent of their income to the church, the fundraising drive was very important. It usually paid for the church's pamphlets and books, which were used to spread the word of the Lord, and paid for expansion efforts and church renovations. The senior pastor wanted to triple the size of the congregation and find a much larger building to consecrate and use as our place of worship. The youth ministry was expected to raise a large portion of the money. I would tell Jacob that I was going out to solicit, preach, and spread the word of the Lord, and I would go to the hospital. The first couple of days, I would just stand outside the door and stare at Ben with all of his wires and tubes and listen to the noises the machines would make. I gradually moved closer, to the chair near the door, to the chair near his bed, on my knees next to his bed. I prayed for him to recover and I prayed for him to come home and I prayed for the pain I imagined he was feeling. There were cuts all over his body, these deep gashes with pink scars, and there were bandages on some of them, and I could see the little marks on others where there had been stitches, or maybe staples. His head was wrapped in a big bandage, a huge bandage, that made the back of his head almost twice as big as it was. Sometimes he would twitch a little bit or shake a little bit or make some kind of noise, like growling or crying. I assumed he was grappling with the spirits of the Devil and prayed harder for him. At the time I believed in spirits and in the Devil and that any and all things could be achieved through prayer. Now I know better.

Near the end of the two weeks, I was kneeling next to Ben's bed. I had finished praying and I was telling him about our life since he left. Our conversion, how we moved out of Williamsburg, into a part of Queens where there were almost no Jews, Jacob's schooling and his job as a pastor, Mother's sickness, our devotion to the church. I told him a little bit about my own personal relationship with my Lord and Savior Jesus Christ and how he was the only person I trusted and could talk to about problems in my life, how Christ was the only person who was always there for me and would always listen to me. At one point I said I love him so much, Ben Zion, I love Jesus Christ so much, and I heard someone behind me say what did you just call him? I turned around, and a doctor, the same woman doctor who had seen me before, was standing a few feet away from me. I looked at her, stood up, and tried to leave. She stopped me and said what did you call him? in a very firm voice. I was very nervous and very scared and didn't want to tell her anything, so I said I called him Ben, the name in the newspaper. She said no, you called him something else, and I just shook my head and told her I learned his name in the paper. She seemed very angry, and I didn't want to get into trouble. If I had to call Jacob and explain everything to him, he'd be angry, and he might hit me or lock me in my room or force me to do some form of penance that I didn't want to do. I tried to step around the woman, but she wouldn't let me leave. She asked who I was, and I said I was a member of the First Church of Creation in Queens and that I came to the hospital to pray for sick and injured patients. She asked me if I had permission from the hospital to be there, and

I said the only authorities I answered to were God and his only Son, my Lord and Savior Jesus Christ. She asked who Ben was, and I said that I only knew what I had read in the newspaper, and that I believed he was a man who might benefit from prayer. I stepped around her, and she let me go. I rushed out of the hospital and spent the subway ride home crying and shaking and asking the Lord for his forgiveness. I had lied and deceived, and though I believed I had done it for righteous reasons, I still believed it was a horrible sin and that I needed to ask the Lord in Heaven for forgiveness.

I ended up staying on the subway for a long time. I couldn't stop crying and I couldn't stop shaking and I kept asking for God's forgiveness, which usually made me feel better, but it didn't this time. I wondered if somehow I'd committed a sin that was unforgivable, and I was scared that I'd be damned to burn in Hell eternal. Eventually I calmed down enough to go back to the church. We were required to check in at the end of every day and turn in all of the donations we'd received. It was dark and getting near dinner, which I was required to help prepare every night. I knew I'd be in trouble because I didn't have anything, and I hoped that Jacob wouldn't be there. I would have prayed, but I was worried that praying for the absence of a pastor was some type of sin.

When I walked into the church, Jacob was waiting for me. He asked me why I was late and I said I was out spreading the word of God to sinners and trying to lead them to salvation. He asked how much I had taken in in donations, and I told him I didn't get anything today. He stared at me for a long time and I got scared. He grabbed my arm and dragged me into the back of the church. I told him he was hurting me and he ignored me and kept pulling me. It hurt my arm and I was scared and I knew that he knew I was lying. He took me into his office and let go of my arm and pushed me into a chair and stared at me again and I was so scared and he looked so angry and he spoke to me.

Where were you?

I was out trying to get donations.

He slapped me.

Where were you?

I started crying.

I was out.

He yelled.

Where?

I was crying, and he yelled again.

Where?

In Manhattan.

Why?

I was so scared. I tried to wipe my face, and Jacob slapped me again.

WHY WERE YOU THERE?

And he slapped me again.

WHAT WERE YOU DOING?

And again. And again. And again.

And then he stopped and I was staring at the floor and I was crying and he grabbed my face and forced

me to look at him and he was shaking he was so mad
and he said it again.
Why were you there, and what were you doing?
And I didn't want to say anything, because I was
scared and I didn't know what he would do when
I told him, but I was more scared about what he would
do if I didn't.
I found Ben Zion.
I started crying again.
I found Ben Zion.

RUTH

My life has been like all the lives, long and hard
and full of sadness and confusion and horror,
a frightening, difficult dream punctuated by brief
moments of joy. And as is the case with all people's
lives, the moments of joy are never often enough
and never long enough. They keep me going,
the same way a glass of water, or an idea of a glass
of water, might keep me going in marching across
the desert, except that the desert never ends,
it's many million miles long, and it never will end.

I was born in Israel. My parents had both survived
in the Holocaust of the Nazis, being in camps in
Poland. My father was a Polish and went in Stutthof,
and ended in Treblinka, and my mother, who was
a Slovak, was first in Theresienstadt, and later in
Birkenau. They met in Tel Aviv in 1949 and married
almost immediately. At the time Jews of their
ages were being encouraged to be married and
starting families in order to further populate Israel.
They didn't love each other truly, but on some level
they understood each of the other, understood
in ways that other peoples couldn't. Both of their
families had been put to death by the Nazis during
the war. Their entire families, parents, grandparents,
siblings, aunts, uncles, and cousins, had all been
murdered in the death camps. That was the basis for

their marriage. Their feelings of the extermination of their families.

I lived in Israel until I was twelve years. We had moved to a small settlement near what today is being called Gush Katif, on the southern part of the Gaza Strip. It was attacked by the mujahedeen of Egypt and my parents were both killed. I was in the school when it was happening and found them on the floor of our kitchen with their throats gashed open. Their closest friends had left Israel for living in New York a year before and took me into their home. They were childless and happy to have me with them, and like my parents, they were both survivors. Also like my parents, their marriage was without love and strained, the main common element of them being they had both been in the camps. Also like my parents, they had survived but didn't live through what had happened to them. They breathed and ate and spoke and went about their lives, but they didn't live, didn't truly be alive, because they couldn't after what they had seen and experienced. Trauma is survivable, but often not much more. It kills you while allowing you to still live.

They did the best they could with me and I accepted them as being my parents. Like my birth parents, they were being very protective of me, did not trust non-Jews, and were fearful of all the world outside our neighborhood, which was entirely Jews. My adopted father worked as cook in a kosher restaurant, and my mother worked being a laundress. We went to synagogue every week, observed the

Sabbath, ate kosher, and had a Shabbat dinner every Friday in the evening. We were happy, or as happy as we could be given the course our lives had all been taken, and we did not wish for anything more than what we had. In that way we were gifted. For if one knows nothing about what may be possible in the world, one will not yearn for it or be missing it.

When I finished yeshiva, I went to work with my stepmother being a laundress. I had hoped to be going to college and maybe becoming a doctor or a teacher, but we did not have the money for me doing that. When I was twenty, I started thinking about marriage and hoping for love. I got one of those when I met Isaac, who was to become my husband. He was working being a kosher butcher, and his family was said to be Davidic and had been in America since the early 1900s and owned their own family butcher shop. We met because the restaurant where my stepfather worked bought their meats from them and Isaac often was delivering it. My stepfather invited him to our home for Shabbat dinner and he came with his parents and we were sitting at the table across from each other. He was very handsome and very shy, with nice green eyes and blond hair, which are rarer among us, and I was very shy too. That first meeting we were hardly speaking and spending most of our time glancing at each other and hoping the other wouldn't notice even though we did. That night when I went to bed I knew he would be my husband. For my stepfather it was a good marriage and would improve his standing at the restaurant, and for Isaac it would be prestigious to marry an Israeli-born daughter of survivors because there were very few of us then. I believed we would love each other.

Our wedding was a simple and beautiful one and our wedding night was more complicated for us. Neither had ever in our lives been alone with a member of the opposite sex before and we were both scared and being nervous. I was very excited and waited for Isaac but he wasn't being ready and later he cried. We were both knowing we wanted children and it was expected for us. For six months Isaac was trying and not being comfortable about it and he was being more and more upset. One night he had too much to drink and we became truly man and wife and he cried again because of being happy. That night we were both very happy.

We tried for two years for me to be pregnant. Most of the time Isaac would be drinking but sometimes he would not be. We prayed and lived strictly according to our Jewish laws. When I became pregnant we were overjoyed, and our families too. We were finished choosing names for a boy or for a girl when I started bleeding. A few days later we put the names written on a piece of paper and we burned them and we never spoke of them again. For the worst things of our lives, it is sometimes the best way, to never speak of them again.

It happened three more times in our next four years, with two of the babies going to the full terms.

We stopped trying to choose names or even being thinking of names, always feeling we should only give names to the living. In our seventh year of marriage I was pregnant again and it stayed and our son Jacob was born healthy and right. We thought he was a miracle baby, and he was looking just like his father, and we didn't think we were going to be having any more children. Our families were tremendously pleased and we had two years of happiness, watching Jacob grow and learn, every day becoming more like his father. We never hoped for more childrens and we stopped trying to do it. One night we go to a wedding and Isaac has too much to drink and I have a little as well. The next morning we don't remember everything of the night before but I know I am pregnant and I know it will be okay and I know the baby will be a boy and I know this with all of my heart without any doubts at all, the same as I know I am alive and I breathe and that God, in any of God's forms, is all-powerful and all-knowing. There are no doubts in my heart.

Isaac had many doubts and he was always very confusing about the pregnancy. After I tell him about it he is very upset and angry though he will not tell why he is feeling these things. He sees our rabbi many times and then he is happy and ready for another child. When Ben Zion was born, there are some complications with him, and some things not normal, and he did not look like Isaac, for Ben has dark hair and dark eyes like me and my parents, and Isaac left the hospital very angry. Rabbi Schiff

examines the baby Ben and then comes to my room
and tells me it is a great day, a monumental day,
that baby Ben is truly a gift from God, and he stayed
by my bedside and read to me from the Torah,
and together for the rest of the night we prayed.

When I got to home, Isaac had been drinking and
waiting for me, and Jacob is with Isaac's parents at
their home nearby us. Rabbi Schiff is helping me
bring Ben home and took Isaac away while I settled
Ben Zion into a bassinet we have for him. Isaac also
went to his parents' home to sleep and Rabbi Schiff
came back with two other rabbis and they stayed
beside Ben for the rest of the night and the next day
as well reading the Torah and praying.

When Isaac came home with Jacob, nothing was
ever the same again. He was always very angry
and drinking and he did not like Ben Zion and
when I try to talk to him about it he would not do
any talking to me. He drank much more and
almost every day he was drinking and he wanted
to have another baby soon. He did not care that my
body was not ready and that I wanted time for
me to bond with Ben Zion. He wanted more babies
right away, I think to prove to himself that Ben Zion
was not a fluke. We started trying and it much hurt
me but it was my responsibility as a wife for my
husband.

We try for one years and it didn't work, which
enraged Isaac. He accused me of being with another

man and I said to him I have only been with one man in my life and it has been you. He did not believe me and he said I was with someone else, that Ben Zion did not look like him and could never be his child. He yelled at me often and would sometimes start to push me, and hit me, and call me a whore, even in front of the children. I went to Rabbi Schiff and he consults me and Isaac many many times and he often came over to see Isaac and talk to him and check on Ben Zion, who he said was a special boy, a gift truly from God. And that was our life. We try to have another babies, and Isaac would drink and yell and hit me, and Rabbi Schiff would try to talk to him and calm him down. The boys started to grow up and went to yeshiva and Hebrew school and learn how to be Orthodox men someday. We observe the Sabbath and have Shabbat and go to synagogue. And I would pray to God to make changes for me to make my life better. I would pray to God every day.

And then eight years later after still trying I am pregnant again by a miracle of God and I have a girl we give the name of Esther. She is a beautiful little girl who looks much like Isaac, with light eyes and light hair. I hope and pray that this child will make Isaac happy and return to the Isaac I married, but it did not. He became even more convinced that Ben was not his and he would start telling people at synagogue or at Shabbat that I was a whore who had a child with another man. Once he do it in front of Rabbi Schiff, who immediately take him away. They were gone for one day and almost two and when they come back

Isaac is different than he was before. He seemed scared and upset and when I try to ask him what is the matter he pushes me away.

Our lives were separate in the same house from then to the end of our time with each other. He loved very much Jacob and Esther but did not love anymore me who was his wife or his second son Ben Zion, who he would push away when Ben tried to hug him or he would tell to shut up when Ben Zion would try to talk to him. I would try to tell him that he was my husband and I loved him and he would be polite and say he loved me but I knew he did not love me. I knew whatever he had been told by Rabbi Schiff had changed him to make him different. The rabbi still came by and took special care with Ben Zion and would ask him all about his studies and his love of God, and Ben Zion was such a good boy, a kind boy who loved everyone, who was always smiling and doing good things for people. It was Ben Zion who got me through all those hard years. I had no longer Isaac, and Jacob was his son and Esther was his daughter and he told them not good things about me that I think made them not love me the way children should love a mother. And Ben Zion seemed to notice and loved me more and made sure I knew he loved me with his entire heart.

When he was thirteen, Ben Zion became a man with his bar mitzvah. I never knew why but many rabbis from New York and other places attended, and they were not just Orthodox, but also Hasidic and

Conservative and Reform, and two came from Israel. He read the Torah in a way that made many of the members of the synagogue weep, which is not something I had ever seen before in my life. His voice was clear and pure and sounded so strong, almost like a thunder, but also his voice had care and love without trying. I had never heard this voice from my son Ben Zion, and I do not know where it came from inside of him. Sometimes I wonder, especially now, if it was even him speaking, or if it was the Lord God himself.

After the bar mitzvah things got worse again, with Isaac drinking and drinking and not going to work and beating me and Ben Zion every day. One morning after a year I go to our room to see why he is not awake and I discover that he would never wake again, that he had passed into the hands of God. The doctor said his heart gave way but no one in his family had that so I always wondered if it was so. Rabbi Schiff did the tearing of keriah and Jacob said the kaddish. We ate boiled eggs for dinner and there was much sadness in our family. For seven days we sat shivah. Even though the Isaac I loved was gone many years before, I grieved deeply for losing him.

At the end of shloshim, after we mourned Isaac for thirty days, Jacob was head of our home. On that very day he told Ben Zion he must leave and never come back again, that Isaac had died because of Ben Zion and that God would punish him. Ben Zion tried to speak to Jacob and tell him he loved him and loved his father, but Jacob beat him very badly and threw him out of the house and locked the door while he bled on the sidewalk. I could not watch and cried myself in my room, and I washed the blood away the next day. Rabbi Schiff was shocked and very stern with Jacob and said he had made a terrible, terrible mistake that he needed to right. But he did not make it right. And Ben Zion vanished. I thought he would come back or he would be at a home of someone that knew our family but he was not anywhere and nobody saw him or heard from him again. And every night I cried for him and it never became more easy for me. My beloved son Ben Zion was gone.

And then sixteen years later, sixteen years of terror, where I was forced to give up my God and pray before one I did not believe in, forced to leave my community for one I did not know, forced to live like a slave to my son who did not love me, Jacob came home with Esther from the church like every other day, but this day would change our life for all times. When they walked in, I could tell Jacob had been hitting Esther like he did sometimes to her and also to me, and I knew not to ask or defy him about it because then he hit more and harder. He was not, though, like he usually is when he is in one of those times hitting, he did not seem so mean and angry, and I asked him what was happening and he said Esther had found him, found Ben Zion, that he was alive, in a hospital in Manhattan, that she had seen him with her two own eyes and had prayed to her Lord and Savior Jesus Christ at his bedside.

Even though I always knew the day would come when Ben Zion would return, I could not believe it was today. I asked Esther who was crying if it was true and she said yes. I asked her what hospital and she told me and I asked her why he was there in a hospital and she said he had an accident with a glass falling on him and was in intensive cares and she started crying. I went to her and held her and told her she would be okay and Ben Zion would be okay and I keep holding her until Jacob told me to let go of her, that she will be fine. I told him she needs me and he yells at me No She Is Not A Baby and he pulled her away very hard and pushed her to the ground and told her to stop crying. Then he turn back to me and say Mother, we need to pray to the Lord for guidance and I say no, I need no guidance, I only need to go see my son who is in the hospital, my son who I haven't seen in sixteen years. He said the Lord will tell us when to go and I say the Lord has already told me and I went towards the door. He reached for me and I pushed his arm away and he grabbed me hard with both his arms and pushed me against the door and yelled at me We Will Pray Together Until The Lord Gives Us A Sign. I try to struggle away because I just wanted to go to the hospital so I can see Ben Zion and Jacob hit me three times very quickly with his open hand on the same side of my face and I know I must pray with him, even though it is not for me and will make no difference for me, I must pray. We kneeled before a crucifix with me on one side of Jacob and Esther on the other side and Jacob begin asking the Lord for guidance. He said Jesus Christ I am your humble servant please show me the way, please guide my actions, please give me a sign so that I may know your intentions for me and my family. And he go on like this for four hours, asking for a sign, for guidance from his Lord and Savior Jesus Christ, for strength from the Holy Spirit to be righteous in his actions. I did not need a sign, that Esther had seen Ben Zion is enough of a sign for me. I just wanted to leave.

After we pray Jacob says we should also fast and have no dinner and tells us we must go to our rooms and continue to pray on our own. I go and pack a small bag and get some money from a small amount I have earned for myself and wait until the house is quiet and I leave without anyone hearing me. I know Jacob will be very angry and he will punish me for leaving but I feel I must do this so I do it. I say to myself if you believe deeply in your heart you must defy, and if you are willing to pay for your defiance, you must always do it, even though the pain may be much. Too many times in our lives we do not do it, and we pay even more, so this time I do.

I did not know the hospital or where it was being located so I got a taxi and told the driver to take me there. The driver was a Muslim and had something in Arabic hanging from his car mirror. I was already nervous from leaving home knowing Jacob would be angry and the driver made me more nervous because I believe that if he knew I was Israeli he would hate me. I know it is not right for me to be thinking that way but it is also the real way of the world. And it is the real way of the world that I hate the Muslim for wanting me to die and for believing I am not a human. Maybe if he was not what he was and I am not what I am we would be friends in our lives. But we are what we are, and humans will always hate. It is the ruin of our world.

He drop me off and I give him money but do not touch him. I go into the hospital and ask where my son Ben Zion is and the lady tells me the visiting times are over for the day. I tell her my son who I have not seen in sixteen years is here and I must see him. I tell her his name is Ben Zion Avrohom and she looks in her computer and says there is no one here with that name. I tell her my daughter see him here and that he is hit by a glass and in the intensive cares. She looks at me for a moment and picks up the phone and makes call and tells me to sit down and wait for someone to talk to me about this situation. I became very upset and said I just want to see my son who has been missing for so long and the woman say she is calling someone to see.

I sat and wait for someone to come and a lady arrive in a doctor coat and introduce herself to me as a surgeon who work on a young man she believe might be my son. I say I don't believe anything, I know, I know with my heart fully, that my daughter was here and saw my son Ben Zion Avrohom, who has been missing from me for sixteen years. The woman ask me about Esther and I tell her what she looks like and the woman nod and say I met your daughter earlier today but she told me she was here to pray for the sick and injured as part of a church in Queens. I tell her my daughter is a Christian who lives in Queens and was praying to her Lord and Savior Jesus Christ for the welfare of her brother who she loves. The doctor asks me again what is Ben's name and I tell her and she asks me when I have seen him last and I told her it has been sixteen years that he has been missing and that every day I prayed to God for him to come back to me. She asks me why he has been missing and I start to cry and I cry for a long time and she sits next to me and holds my hand and it is the first time in many years I have felt any kindness from anyone other than my daughter, the first time in many, many years. I stop crying and wipe my face and try to make myself composed. The doctor tells me her name is Alexis and she tells me she did surgery on Ben when he came into the hospital and has been treating him for his injuries which are very much serious and threatening his life. She says it was a miracle that he was alive and that there was no explanation for it. I did not give her the explanation I know because she would not have believed if I did tell her it. She asked me if I want to see Ben Zion and I say yes and she leads me through the hospital. When we reach outside his room, we stop and I am feeling very nervous and scared and happy. She tells me to prepare myself and I say I believe Ben Zion will be okay no matter what has happened. She smiles at me and says please be prepared. There is, though, nothing that prepares us for the worst of things in our life. There is nothing you can do to stop the shock, or buffer the pain.

I walked into the room. Ben Zion was in bed on his back. There were intravenous tubes in his arms and a mask on his face and monitors on his head that had no hair and on his chest covered with scars. There were scars everywhere on his body where he had been cut by the glass. Long terrible jagged scars on his body everywhere. I was scared to go closer to him, scared of my own son asleep in his bed, my beautiful boy who I had loved his whole life, even when he was not with me. My son with all of his scars, with all of his pain.

I walked slowly to him and I started crying again. I cry because of what happened to him, and for all those lost years, and for why he was sent out of my home, and for all the times Isaac and Jacob beat him and are mean to him, and for the times I was with him when he was a boy and a baby and he smiled and laughed and for all the love I had for him. I walk to him and I say his name and I start crying very hard and it hurts my body and hurts me inside like I am destroyed and I kneel by his bed and I can't touch him or look at him, I just say to him over and over I am sorry, I am sorry. There are no other words, and even those words aren't enough for my feelings. There are never words for the strongest of our feelings. There is just the pain that we cannot share. Pain we must all feel alone.

I stay at his bed for the whole of the night and when the sun comes up I sit in a chair next to his bed and I hold his hand and I tell him about the years he has been gone and what has happened in our life. I hold his hand and it's cold and there are scars on his wrist and his hand and he does not move except for breathing which is faint, and sometimes labored, and sometimes he twitches or shakes a little amount. At one point many doctors come in and ask me who I am and I tell them and they say the chart still says John Doe and it makes me cry to think of how long my son has been lying here alone being called John Doe. One of the doctors calls someone on the telephone on the wall and more people come but they are not doctors. Some of them work for the hospital and some of them are police and I tell them his name and where he is from and I tell how long it has been since I have seen him. They ask for my ID and I tell them my son does not let me have ID or driver's license because he does not believe in any authority other than God. They take me to a room where they say I must stay until they confirm me as who I say I am.

It is a long time, many hours I sit alone. When the door opens, it is Jacob and he says to come with him. I ask him what happened and he say he talked to police and tell them everything and show them the driver's license he has for himself and they say I can go. We go to Ben Zion's room and Esther is waiting outside the door for us and we go in together and we kneel and spend the day praying together for the health of Ben Zion. And for many days that is what we do. We kneel by the bed and together we pray for the health of Ben Zion. Jacob and Esther go back to Queens sometimes because they both have many responsibilities at church but I do not ever leave the hospital. I stay with my son. And I wait for him. And I know in my heart, because I have known all my life, and I have known all of his life, what he will become when he returns. I wait for him.

JEREMIAH

Jacob was like a brother to me and a father to me and a spiritual guide to me and a true inspiration to me. He saved me and believed he cured me and I loved him and admired him, and in many ways I wished I was him. When the MSM descended after Ben's real identity was made public, he asked me to stay in the hospital with his mother and help protect them from the reporters and their tape recorders and their cameras and their lies. He also wanted me to take notes whenever the doctors were there so he could have them for lawsuits he planned to file on Ben's behalf against the city, the construction company, the real estate developers, and the hospital, which he hoped would provide him with financial security and help to expand the facilities and the teachings of the church. I was truly and greatly honored, and I promised him I would take the job very seriously and lay down my life if necessary. Jacob said he knew, and that was why he chose me. The hospital's policy was that only family was allowed to stay, so Jacob told them I was his brother, his real brother. And we believed that in the eyes of God, the Holy Spirit, and our Lord and Savior Jesus Christ, we were telling the truth, and that because our aims were righteous, the sin of lying was not actually a sin. We did what people do all the time, we told ourselves something we did was right and we found a way to justify it, even though we knew it was wrong. We told ourselves God would allow it, but not because of the Laws of God, but because we wanted to do it.

I met Jacob when he was protesting deviant lifestyles outside a club where I went to meet men. I had seen him a few times before standing with three or four other people, all holding signs that said God Hates Fags, or Fags Will Rot in Hell, or AIDS is God's Cure for Faggots, and he would yell verses from the Bible at people smoking outside the club and hand out pamphlets about his church. My story was the same as a million others in New York. I grew up in a small town, liked boys and dresses, got teased and beaten at home and at school, ran away to New York at seventeen to be a model or a singer or an actor or whatever I could be that was fun and easy and would make me famous. It didn't work, and I got addicted to drugs and sex and clubs and lived a sad empty life that I pretended was fun and exciting. I always felt I had a hole in my heart, this big black hole that made me feel lonely and empty and worthless. I tried to fill it, everybody tries in some way, and it just got bigger and bigger. The night Jacob approached me I was on a date with a man who gave me certain things and expected certain things in return. He lived in the Midwest and was in town for three or four days a month. It was my second night out with him and I was hurting really bad. The man wanted me to get some meth, and on my way out of the club Jacob said I can cure you as I walked past him. I stopped and asked him what he would cure me of, and he said the vile, soul-damning lifestyle of sodomy and homosexuality. I asked him how, and he said the Bible offers a message of love and hope, and the Lord and Savior Jesus Christ will save you and show you the way. I started crying. I was surprised. I hated religion because of its treatment of me, and its absoluteness, and I never would have believed I would believe in it, but something opened inside of me, the Holy Spirit opened inside of me, and it was lovely and fantastic and the most powerful thing I'd ever felt, a sense of joy and peace and love, and I believed at that moment that for whatever reason God was calling to me and telling me to follow this man. Two hours later I was baptized and born again. The next day I moved into a basement apartment in Queens in the house of one of the church elders. It felt right and true and good to me, and it was lovely and joyful and secure and strong. To have the Holy Spirit inside of me and to cultivate a personal relationship with the Lord and Savior Jesus Christ. To have friends who called me brother and wanted to take care of me instead of use me. It was all I ever wanted in my life, all anyone ever wants. To have someone love you. To have someone tell you that they know the way and want to share it with you.

I spent most of my time in a chair near the door of Ben's room. We kept the door closed, and if it started to open I would stand and ask whoever it was what business they had in the room. It annoyed the doctors and nurses because I made all of them show me their credentials, even if I had met them before or had seen their credentials before. Twice MSM reporters tried to sneak in as doctors. One of them even tried to show me bogus credentials. Everyone wanted to see the Miracle Man who had disappeared into thin air for sixteen years and survived what he never should have survived. Aside from the reporters, there were lawyers, photographers, psychics, healers, and women. I took the lawyers' business cards, but had everyone else removed as quickly as possible. And I couldn't believe how many women wanted to see him or touch him or marry him. He wasn't even awake and they didn't know what he would be like if he did wake up, if he'd even be able to speak or move or walk. I handed each of those women a pamphlet and said maybe the void they were feeling in their heart could be filled with the love of God and the love of his Son, the Lord and Savior Jesus Christ.

For the first ten days I was there, nothing happened. Mrs. Avrohom prayed by Ben's bed and I read the Bible. I went to the gift shop or cafeteria for food. We both slept in fold-down chairs, hers next to the bed, mine near the door. Jacob and Esther came by after breakfast and usually stayed until just before dinner. They spent most of their time kneeling by the side of the bed, praying, though Jacob often stepped into the hall to speak with the doctors, and on a couple of occasions with attorneys. Nobody seemed to know what kind of condition Ben was in. The machines they hooked up to his brain would give them all sorts of different results, and sometimes they were happy and said he seemed normal and sometimes they said he was going to be a vegetable and sometimes they said they were seeing things they had never seen before, extraordinary activity as one doctor called it, and most of the time they had no idea what was happening. When they took the breathing tube out of his throat, it was a big deal. They made everyone leave except for Jacob, who refused to leave, and they were really worried he wouldn't be able to breathe on his own. I waited outside the room with Mrs. Avrohom and Esther, and we were all praying to Jesus to give Ben the strength to live. We were praying really hard, and when we heard the doctors and nurses clap and Jacob yell Hallelujah, Lord, we knew our prayers had been answered.

For the next five or six days, nothing good happened. Ben was able to breathe, but he didn't move, and all the brain monitors indicated that there was absolutely no activity, and the doctors were saying that he was going to be a vegetable for the rest of his life. The timing was terrible because Jacob was finishing the church fundraising drive and was going to announce plans for the expansion of the church's facilities. He asked me to take notes on everything the doctors and nurses said and he'd come by at the end of the day and review them. He also asked me to pray extra hard, and I told him I'd pray my hardest, but I knew my connection to God wasn't nearly as strong as his was, and I was worried that I didn't have enough strength, and wasn't holy enough, to make a difference.

The doctors came and went. I heard terms like severe brain damage, without detectable awareness, Apallic syndrome, post-coma unresponsiveness, continuing vegetative state, permanent vegetative state. They tested his response to stimuli and there was no reaction. They tried to get him to track things with his eyes but he just stared at the ceiling, though I don't think he could really see anything at all. One of the doctors suggested something called bifocal extradural cortical stimulation, which sounded scary and evil, and I told Jacob that I believed that particular doctor, who looked like a Jew and had a hooked nose, might be in legion with the Devil.

On the seventh night, I sat reading my Bible. This particular evening I was reading Revelations 12. It is a powerful chapter, one of the most powerful in the New Testament, and one with a great amount of truth. It's about the woman clothed with the sun, with the moon under her feet, and the crown of twelve stars on her head, and the great red dragon with seven heads, ten horns, and seven crowns who draws the third part of the stars of Heaven with his tail, and how as the dragon prepares to devour the child of the woman, the child who is to rule all nations with a rod of iron, the woman is drawn into the wilderness of God for 1,260 days while the archangel Michael and his army of angels make war on the dragon. I had read the chapter many times, and I believed that the events of it were going to happen soon, as they had been foretold to occur in the End Times, and I knew the End Times were coming, and that I would bear witness to them, and that I would be one of the 144,000 of the Lord's anointed who would be saved and raised up into Heaven. Mrs. Avrohom was kneeling next to Ben, same as she did every night. This night, though, this seventh night, she started praying in Hebrew. Jacob told me she might do it, and he wanted to know if she did because he had forbidden Jewish teachings, law, words, and language in his home, and he would punish her accordingly for violating his rules. I didn't know what she was saying, but I thought I should put down my Bible and try to write down anything I heard. As she was praying, Ben's mouth started moving. She didn't see it, but I did. There wasn't any noise coming out, but he was mouthing the words, the exact same words she was saying in her prayers. And then his eyes opened, and not like when the doctors opened them for their tests, this time they opened and they were clear and focused and alive, and there was something about them, something pure and heavenly, as if they were the eyes of the Savior himself, and I was entranced by them. Mrs. Avrohom was still praying, and didn't know Ben was with her, and she was quietly saying the Hebrew verses, and Ben started saying them with her, softly, in a voice that sounded very old and strong, and he matched her word for word, like he knew what she was going to say before she said it, and it sent chills down my spine. I tried to write what I was seeing, and feeling, and what Mrs. Avrohom was saying, and what Ben was saying, but I was paralyzed, paralyzed with joy and freedom and a lightness of spirit that felt like the moment I was saved, when the Holy Ghost was so powerfully alive inside of me.

Mrs. Avrohom became aware of Ben when he reached out and put his hand on her forehead. I watched it happen like it was in slow motion. His fingers started moving slowly, slightly, each of them on its own, like they were dancing. And then his hand and arm lifted off the white sheet and his fingers stopped moving and looked like they were stretching, like the fingers of Adam reaching towards God. Mrs. Avrohom was still praying, and Ben with her, and the sound of their words in synchronization was simple and ancient and had a beautiful rhythm to it and as his arm moved towards her forehead he turned and looked at her and it seemed like it took a million years for him to reach her and it seemed like there was nothing else happening anywhere else in the world, there was just this one thing, this one moment, this lost, damaged son reaching for his mother as they prayed to the Lord Almighty.

When he did finally touch her, she gasped audibly. I don't know if it was because she was surprised or because of something she felt, but she looked like she had had a huge bolt of electricity pass through her. His hand was firmly on her forehead, and she looked up, her jaw dropped, her body went limp, her eyes were full of joy and peace and contentment. And they both continued praying, there was no lapse, no stopping, the words just kept coming. Ben smiled, turned and started to sit up, and as he did, the various monitors and IVs that were attached to his body started coming off, and those that didn't he pulled off with his free arm. The alarms started dinging, shrieking, but he and his mother didn't seem to notice. He sat all the way up and smiled, and it was a beautiful peaceful smile, similar to so many of the smiling images I've seen of the Lord and Savior Jesus Christ, and his mother was staring up at him, and he moved his legs off the bed, and they were both still praying, almost singing, and his hand was still on her forehead, and he stood up. He was wearing a white robe. His body was hideously and terribly scarred, you could see the scars running along his arms and legs and on his face. His skin was so white, and so pale. And there were alarms screaming. And it was beautiful. He was so beautiful. If only I could somehow communicate the feelings it inspired in me. But that is the way it is with all of the important feelings and emotions and moments we have in our lives, words fail and don't express even a fraction of what we actually feel. All I can say is it truly did feel like I was in the presence of divinity, in the presence of God himself. And I couldn't move or speak or write or do anything but stare at him and feel love, and awe, and humility. He was just so beautiful.

The door flew open and a team of nurses and doctors rushed into the room, though they stopped as soon as they saw what was happening. Ben didn't turn towards them or acknowledge them in any way. He stared down at his mother, who was staring up at him, and then he closed his eyes and lifted his hand away from her forehead and raised it to the level of his chest and held it there and stopped saying the Hebrew prayers and took a deep breath and smiled to himself as he exhaled. And as soon as he was finished with the exhale, he collapsed onto the floor and had a seizure.

I got pulled from the room, but what I saw of the seizure was hideous. Ben shook, his whole body violently shook, and fluids immediately started coming out of his mouth and nose, and he made these awful guttural noises. His mother stood up and started screaming. The doctors and nurses immediately tried to hold him down and grab his tongue, but he was strong, shockingly and unbelievably strong, especially given that he had been in a coma for the last several weeks, and it took two of them on each of his arms and legs to hold him down. As I stood in the hall, I could hear him struggling, he sounded like an animal, like he was possessed by Satan himself, and I could hear the nurses and orderlies yelling for more help, and I could hear Mrs. Avrohom, who was backed into a corner of the room when I left it, screaming at the top of her lungs.

I don't know how long it was or what it took, because it seemed like hours and hours and hours, but Ben's seizure ended and everything calmed down and I was allowed back in the room. Ben was on the bed, either asleep or sedated, and his arms and legs were in straps attached to the sides of the bed in case he had another seizure. Mrs. Avrohom was in the corner, quietly sobbing into her hands. I wasn't sure what to do, but decided that if Jacob considered me a family member, I should comfort his mother as if I truly were one, and that things that might normally matter for a Christian man, that I was a single man and she was a widowed woman, that she had been using Hebrew in prayer, that she had been raised a Jew, didn't matter, and that if God judged me, he would also forgive when I repented. I moved over towards Mrs. Avrohom and I put my hand on her shoulder and asked her if she was alright. She looked up at me and between her sobs asked me what had just happened, what had just happened with her son. I told her that I didn't know, that God always had a plan and that we should never question it, but that I didn't know.

Jacob showed up later. The doctors had called him because he was the family member listed as a contact. In between the call and his arrival, doctors came in and out of the room, checking Ben's blood pressure and heart rate. I was no longer touching his mother when he walked in, but he was upset that I was sitting close to her. I told him what had happened, with every detail I knew, and he didn't seem surprised or upset. He looked at his brother, and said let us pray, pray for the man who may be sitting before us. I didn't know what he meant, and didn't feel like I should ask.

Together we kneeled and we prayed, prayed silently until the sun rose and another of God's glorious days began for us.

In the morning, Jacob took his mother home. She didn't want to leave, but he felt she needed some time away, and she obeyed him because he was the head of their household. He asked me to stay and try to learn everything I could about Ben's condition. The doctors kept coming in and out of the room, but when they spoke they did so in hushed tones, so I couldn't hear what they were saying. Around lunch they stopped coming in. It was just Ben, who had not moved since his seizure, and me. I started reading my Bible, turning immediately to one of my favorite sections, Matthew 4:1–11, which is about the temptation of Christ by the Devil while Jesus was living in the desert, and about the food the angels of Heaven brought him after he resisted the Devil's offerings. I often imagined myself in the position of Christ, resisting the Devil's foul gifts, which I had spent so many sinful years indulging in, and someday having angels descend from Heaven, their wings shining with holy righteousness, to bring gifts for me. When I heard a voice, I thought my prayers had literally come true. I closed my eyes and I said thank you, God, thank you for rewarding my devotion to you. And then I heard the voice again and I stood up and I was scared to open my eyes, not knowing what to expect, and knowing that angels had extraordinary powers that humans could and never would understand. The voice again, and again. I opened my eyes,

and there were no angels, but Ben was looking at
me, which was almost like an angel was there.
He spoke.
Who are you?
My name is Jeremiah.
Where am I?
You are in a hospital in New York.
Why are you here?
I am here because your brother, Jacob, who is
my brother in the worship of God and his Son,
the Lord and Savior Jesus Christ, asked me to
be here.
Jacob?
Yes.
He looked away from me, laughed to himself,
looked back.
Is Jacob responsible for me being restrained?
No. The doctors did that because of your seizure.
My seizure?
Yes.
Take them off.
I can't.
Please, take them off.
He looked at me, looked right into my eyes, and there
was something about his eyes, which were black, jet
black, and so deep they looked limitless, that made
me feel weak and vulnerable, humbled me, and made
me want to do whatever he asked of me. I understood
why he was restrained, but also knew that there were
many doctors and nurses very close by if anything
happened. He said it again.
Please.

It wasn't desperate or pleading, just simple and direct.
Please.
I set down my Bible, stood up, and took off the restraints. He smiled and said thank you, and he didn't move, just closed his eyes and took deep breaths, one after another after another. I don't know how I expected him to act, or what I expected him to do, but not that, not just lie there as if he were still restrained. I just stared at him, waited. After a few minutes, he started slowly running his hands along his body, feeling the scars, running his fingers along the length of them. He put his hands on his face, moved his fingertips all over, moved them along his head and the back of his skull. When he was finished with the back of his head, he continued moving them over his body and his face and he spoke.
What happened to me?
You had an accident at a construction site. A plate of glass fell and hit you.
How long have I been here?
A couple months.
How did Jacob find me?
Your sister saw you on the front page of a newspaper and visited you and she told Jacob.
Why would Jacob care?
Jacob has been looking for you for many, many years.
Why?
I don't know. I only know he desperately wanted to find you.
You said he's a Christian?
Yes, Jacob was born again and baptized into the

ministry of the Lord and Savior Jesus Christ. He's a pastor now, a holy man.
When did this happen?
Many years ago.
And my mother and my sister?
They're also Christians.
He opened his eyes and sat up and he turned to me and put his feet on the floor. He looked at me and the Bible I was holding, and again I felt this profound sense of peace and joy and love and contentment and humility. He reached towards me and put his hand on my forearm, and as soon as he touched me, everything I had struggled with, and tried to leave behind, my every urge and temptation, my need to sin and behave in a deviant manner, came rushing forward through whatever walls I had built to contain it.
I wanted him. I wanted him more than I had wanted anything in my life, more than any man in my life. I wanted to take him, and him to take me, and I never wanted it to end. I closed my eyes and said please protect me, Lord, please protect me, Jesus, but nothing happened, nothing went away. His hand was on my forearm and I wanted him in my mouth and inside of me and on top of me and behind me. I knew it was going to happen if he didn't let go of me, I knew I would ask him to satisfy me. Then I felt him lift his hand, and I opened my eyes and he was looking at me as if he knew, he knew what I wanted, and he didn't judge me or hate me for it. He stared at me. He took a deep breath. He smiled. And something in him changed. His eyes were in the same place, but he wasn't looking at me anymore. He was looking

beyond me, at something I could never know or touch
or comprehend.
And then he exhaled.
And then the seizure hit.

ADAM

I was certainly surprised when Jacob came to see me in my office at the synagogue, very surprised indeed. It had been many years since I had seen him, though I had never stopped thinking about him, or rather, I should say, I had never stopped thinking about his brother, Ben Zion.

Ben Zion was extraordinary from the day he was born, or more accurately, from the moment he was conceived. The circumstances were unusual, or confusing, or mysterious. There are a number of words one might use to describe it, and all of them would be appropriate. His parents had been trying unsuccessfully to have a second child, Jacob being their first, for several years. The night of conception, or what is believed to be the night of conception, they had been to a wedding together and had both most likely, though Ben's mother claims not, had a few too many alcoholic beverages, which, as everyone knows, can affect behavior and memory, along with a host of other things. Ben's father claimed that he did not have marital relations with his wife that night, while Ben's mother claimed they did. It caused a terrible rift in the marriage, and in some ways ruined both of their lives. Ben's father believed his wife must have been with another man. She hadn't been. But she did, I believe — though

I cannot definitively say—lie about having been with Ben's father that night. He lived with a great resentment and anger, which was transferred to Ben Zion, and he never trusted his wife again, or loved his child as a father should, and she lived with a lie that she perpetuated for far too long. If both would have accepted and acknowledged the truth, regardless of how unbelievable it may have been, and it was, I believe, quite unbelievable, they would have had dramatically different, and most likely happier, and more content, lives. And I have always found that to be the case: if you can accept the truth and live with it, your heart will be at peace.

Jacob arrived in the middle of the day, when I am often working on my weekly sermon, which I deliver during services on Saturday mornings. This particular sermon was focused on readings from Exodus 13:17 to 15:21, which deals with Moses and the Red Sea and the series of events that led Moses to use divine powers to part the waters of the sea, thus allowing the Israelites passage out of Egypt on their way to Canaan. In today's world, I find this story, and the story of the life of Moses in general, to be particularly relevant, as so many people, people of all faiths, are seeking an exceptional, perhaps even divine, individual who might be able to lead us into a place of greater safety, greater prosperity, greater peace. I was asking myself, and ultimately also asking the members of the synagogue, whether this search is healthy and productive, whether politicians should be mentioned in the same breath

as the Messiah, whether it is possible, despite the ridiculous preening that so many engage in, and so many people believe in, for a politician to really make any significant changes, despite their claims, and their promises to do so. There was a knock. I looked up and said come in, and my assistant rabbi, Rabbi Stern, entered and said a man named Jacob Avrohom was here to see me. Rabbi Stern knew of the Avrohom family, as I had often spoken about them with him, and about Ben Zion in particular, and he knew that a visit from Jacob might be of some significance.
I asked him to show Jacob in, and I put away the sermon.

Though he looked like the person I once knew, aged of course, by well over a decade of life, if I had seen Jacob on the street I am not sure I would have recognized him. He had very short hair, was clean shaven, and wore tan slacks and a blue sport coat. He carried a Bible with him, one that had clearly been read with great regularity, and where one might normally wear a tie, he wore a large gold cross on a gold chain. I stood and smiled when he walked into the office, and greeted him with an open hand.
He did not smile in return and didn't take my hand.
He asked if he could sit and I said of course, and before I could ask if he wanted a beverage, water, tea, or perhaps a cup of coffee, he spoke.
We found my brother.
I was surprised, but not shocked, for I had always believed that Ben Zion would return. I believed that he had to return, that God would impel him to do so.

I was very excited to have received the news, thrilled actually, and extremely curious. Given, however, Jacob's demeanor, and the fact that throughout the entire time I knew him as a child he was a very angry person, I thought it best to remain reserved.
Where?
He had an accident and is in a hospital in Manhattan.
What type of accident?
He was working on a construction site and a plate of glass fell on him.
Oh my. Is he okay?
Yes, he is okay, or at least I believe he is.
How long has it been since you've seen him?
Sixteen years.
Your mother must be very happy.
Obviously. We are all very happy. We missed Ben terribly, and we were all worried that we would never see him again.
Is he still in the hospital?
Yes.
May I visit him?
He asked that I find you and ask if you would. Just so you know, I was against it.
There's no reason for you to be angry with me, Jacob. I tried...
He stood and interrupted me.
I'm not here to discuss anything with you other than visiting my brother. If you would like to see him, I can take you there. If not, I'm leaving.
I would very much like to see Ben Zion.
Come with me.
I stood and put my sermon aside, knowing that

this, the reemergence of Ben Zion, was more
important than anything I would ever write or speak,
and that if he was what some, including me, believed,
he would make all of my sermons irrelevant. Jacob
turned and walked out of the room. We walked to the
subway station, took the train into Manhattan, and
walked to the hospital. I did not, as I did not
feel it would be kindly received, initiate any sort
of conversation, and Jacob did not speak a word to
me, look at me, or acknowledge me in any way.
We entered the hospital, took an elevator up to
Ben Zion's floor, and walked down a series of long
white hallways, hallways of the type that, because
I visit any member of my synagogue who is in the
hospital, whether it's for a broken leg or terminal
cancer or anything else, normally depress me,
but in this particular instance greatly excited me.
Jacob was a step or two in front of me, and he stopped
in front of a door and motioned for me to enter,
and as I did I said a silent prayer of thanks to God
for who I believed I was about to have the honor and
privilege of seeing, speaking to, and being in the
presence of, if even for just a moment or two.

Ben Zion was lying on the bed, above the covers,
wearing a hospital robe and watching television.
A handsome young man was sitting in a chair near
the bed, reading the New Testament. Ben Zion looked
up at me, and I was hit with the full shock of how
he had changed, and the extent of the trauma he
had survived. His head was shaved and ringed with
deep, jagged scars. His skin was white, an unearthly,

almost inhuman white, and was covered with scars, some of which were thick, some of which were thin, some of which were long, and some of which were short, but which seemed to be everywhere. His eyes, which had been deep brown as a child, but definitely brown, were now black, a black so deep and thorough that it was almost something else, something without a name or word or label that would apply to it. He smiled and turned off the television and sat up and spoke to me.

Hello, Rabbi Schiff.

Hello, Ben Zion.

He stood.

Just Ben. No Zion anymore.

Hello, Ben.

And we shook hands. Jacob was now standing next to me. Ben looked at him and the young man, and he spoke.

Would you mind leaving us alone?

The young man stood and closed the Bible and left the room. Jacob spoke.

I would prefer to stay.

Please respect what I'm asking you, Jacob.

I don't trust him.

But I do.

You know what he did to our family?

I know what you believe, Jacob, and I respect your right to believe it, but I would like to speak to him alone.

Jacob stared and Ben met his gaze, but without hostility or anger, and Jacob turned and left, though it was clear he was not happy about it. Ben sat down

on the edge of his bed, and motioned for me to sit
in a chair across from him, which I did. He spoke.
Long time, Rabbi Schiff.
It certainly has been. I have often wondered
what became of you and if, or rather when, I would
see you again.
He smiled, didn't speak, so I did.
Where have you been?
Here.
For a short while, as I understand it, but what about
all of the preceding years?
Drifting.
Through greater New York, America, where? And
how did you live?
Doesn't matter.
Were you happy, or safe?
It doesn't matter. I'm here now.
And I'm very excited to see you, Ben Zion, or excuse
me, Ben, I was terribly shaken when you disappeared
and your brother did what he did with your family. As
you know, I have always thought you were extremely
special, and did everything I could to watch over you
as a child and...
He waved me off.
The past doesn't matter. People cling to it because
it allows them to ignore the present. I asked for
you because I need to talk to you about the present.
Something happened to me, or is happening to me,
and I don't understand it, and I don't want it,
and I'm scared of it.
You've had a terrible accident and...
I don't remember much about my childhood, but

I remember enough. You weren't visiting me
out of some sense of charity.
No, I wasn't, though I did care a great deal about
your family and its well-being, as I do about all of
the families who belong to the synagogue.
Tell me what's happening to me.
Only you can know, Ben, and at some point, if not
already, you either will or you won't, and you will
either be, or you will not be.
I'm not ten or twelve years old anymore, Rabbi Schiff.
Tell me what's happening to me.
You need to tell me what's happening to you, Ben,
and if I can inform you or help you in any way, I will
certainly do so.
He sat perfectly still, and stared at me in a way that
felt very soft, and very gentle, almost quiet, if it is
possible to stare quietly. I felt he was somehow looking
into me, to see or learn my intentions. He took a
deep breath, but only through his nose, which gave
me the last piece of information I believed I needed,
and then he exhaled, and then he spoke, spoke the
words I had been waiting for thirty years to hear from
him, he spoke.
I think God is speaking to me.
And even though I didn't want to do it, and tried to
resist doing so, I smiled, perhaps as wide and true a
smile as has ever appeared in my life.
I have always believed this day would come.
I feel like I'm crazy, and I need to know why this
is happening.
First, tell me what he is saying.
God is not a man.

A woman?
No. God is not man or woman. Something beyond that, beyond our humanity, our notions of male and female.
If not a man or a woman, what does God sound like?
It's not some silly voice from above, like it is in the books of the Bible or in the movies, or like it is when delusional religious fanatics talk about it. It's not even a voice at all. It's just this presence, this feeling, this state where I learn things, where I'm shown things, where I see things.
What?
When I was in the coma, I was conscious. Not conscious like I am now, but definitely aware, definitely awake in a way. It was this state where sometimes there was silence and blackness, this infinite blackness, but other times I would see and hear and understand things I shouldn't.
It was beyond individuality, or identity. I wasn't Ben, not Ben Zion Avrohom or Ben Jones, or a man or a human being in any way, I was just part of this greater thing, or place, or force, or energy. I don't know.
That's why I wanted to see you.
I'm hesitant to comment, because this doesn't sound like God as I know or understand God.
This sounds like something that might be organic to your injuries, which I don't know the specifics of, but were obviously rather traumatic and related to your brain.
He smiled at me, pointed to a copy of the New Testament sitting on a small table next to his bed.
Pick up that book.

I reached over and I picked it up.
Open it.
Where?
Wherever.
I opened the book.
Put your finger down, and tell me the chapter and verse.
I followed his instructions.
Luke 12:5.
But I will forewarn you whom ye shall fear: Fear him, which after he hath killed hath power to cast into Hell; yea, I say unto you, Fear him.
You've been studying it, with your brother, perhaps?
Never read it. Never even held a copy of it. I can do the same thing with the Old Testament, with the Mishnah and Gemara, and the commentaries in the Babylonian Talmud. I know, by date, every day of all twelve cycles of the Daf Yomi, from today backwards to the day it started.
And you knew all of this when you woke up?
Some of it. The rest has come with the seizures.
Every time I have one I know more.
You're going to have to excuse me, Ben, but this is my first time seeing you in many years, and I'm not familiar with everything about you anymore.
What type of seizures are you having?
The doctors think it's some type of epilepsy. They're giving me CT scans, MRIs, all sorts of tests. I don't know what I should tell them, if anything, but what happens is that I feel them coming, I know a few minutes before. It's this heavy calm that very gradually covers me. It feels like someone is pouring water

very slowly over my body. And when I'm covered, I have this moment, just a brief, brief moment, an instant, where I feel everything, see everything, know and understand everything, and where the world, or the universe, or whatever we are and are a part of, feels perfect, and I feel perfect within it. The only thing it's like is having an orgasm, but this is a thousand times more intense, and it's beyond just the physical. It's like a giant, unreal orgasm where all the knowledge and wisdom there ever was and ever will be is mine, but only for that instant. And then the seizure hits. And I feel everything in the seizure, and the pain of it is unreal, and as beautiful as the moment before is, the seizure is its horrific complement, its terrible companion. Somewhere near the end, everything goes black. And when I wake up, I know more, like I've kept some of what I saw or felt or knew.

I imagine you have capable physicians caring for you. What do they say about this phenomenon?

I haven't told them. Just you and Jacob.

Perhaps you should.

They'll tell me I'm crazy.

I could speak to them for you. My position as a rabbi might lend some credibility to what you're saying.

Words of God mean nothing in the face of science.

I would disagree with you on that point, Ben.

Can your words of God cure cancer? Or AIDS?

Can your words of God save a dying child?

Some people believe they can.

They're delusional fools.

And if that is so, what are you, who is hearing the
words of God?
I might be a delusional fool as well.
The door opened and a doctor came into the room,
followed by Jacob and his companion, the young
man with the Bible. I stood and decided it was best
for me to depart, with the hope that I would be able to
return sometime in the near future. I said goodbye to
Ben, and remarked that I would like to see him again.
Jacob objected, but Ben said he would like me to come
back, the next day if possible. Jacob said his fellow
pastors from the church were coming the next day,
and Ben said he would like me to be there with them.
Jacob said absolutely not, and Ben leaned back onto
the bed and closed his eyes and asked the doctor to
begin doing whatever it was he needed to do.

I left the hospital and started heading home,
taking the subway, as I usually did when I moved
about New York, and especially when I was outside
of the borough of Brooklyn. As I rode the train,
I thought about Ben, who, while clearly the same
person, hardly resembled, physically, emotionally,
spiritually, or otherwise, the child and young man
I had known and tutored for so many years.
He was, I believed, or had been since the moment
I heard of his conception, the type of individual that
came along, depending on one's theological position,
once in a generation, once in a lifetime, once in a
millennium, or just once, once over the course of all of
mankind's existence. The signs had led me to
this belief, and while some of them were open to

interpretation, some were absolutely not, and I had never questioned the signs, for I had no reason to question them. This Ben, though, this new man, this new incarnation of a person I had not seen for so many years, and who refused to discuss what he had done or where he had been for all of those years, brought up a number of questions for me, and certain things about him, including the extensive knowledge, gained, he said, during a coma, of a book not recognized as valid by my religious authority, conflicted with some of the signs I believed would confirm his identity. I had had tremendous expectations going into my meeting with him, some of which I should have certainly tempered. I knew his brother harbored great resentments towards me, which he had extended out to include all Jews, and Judaism as a religion, despite what I was told were his new beliefs regarding God, Jesus Christ and the Holy Spirit, the End Times, the Second Coming of Jesus Christ, and Israel's required existence for those events to come to pass. I wondered if this wasn't some elaborate trick that would result in Jacob exacting some form of sad, unnecessary, and ultimately misguided revenge upon me, and if Ben hadn't been convinced to play along in order to regain his brother's, and thus his mother's and his sister's, favor. On the other hand, something about him did seem otherworldly, divine. His scars and his skin and his eyes, which were remarkable, and the fact that he had survived such massive trauma, it all supported my initial reaction, and I had no real reason to doubt what he was telling me, as it was, and still is, my inclination to take someone's word as truth until I have reason not to. And that moment, just before he told me that he believed he might be speaking to God, when he took a deep breath, and the way in which he took that breath, was indicative of something astounding, and unless he had somehow gained knowledge that only I or another rabbi could have passed to him, he would not have known it would mean anything to me.

When I arrived home, I went directly to the dining table, where my wife and three children were waiting for me to have our nightly family meal. My wife could see I was preoccupied, which I rarely am, and tried to ask me why, but I didn't feel Ben Zion was an appropriate topic of conversation, and didn't want to discuss him or his family in front of the children. When dinner was over, I excused myself and went to my study, where I keep a small library of Jewish scriptures and sacred texts, which I use in my own continuing study, refer to when I work on one of my sermons at home, or share and use with my family, particularly during holidays and High Holy Days. I walked over to the Babylonian Talmud, which alone takes up several shelves. The copy I own is comprised of sixty-four tractates, totaling 2,711 pages, printed in twenty-four folio volumes. The cycle of Daf Yomi involves studying a single page of the Talmud every day, beginning on page one and continuing for 2,711 consecutive days. It was conceived by Rabbi Yehuda Meir Shapiro of Poland at the First World Congress of the World

Agudath Israel, held in Vienna in 1923, which was the year 5684 on the Hebrew calendar, and the first cycle began on the first day of Rosh Hashanah that year. Each day, approximately 150,000 Jews around the world study, contemplate, and discuss the page, and there is a celebration at the end of each cycle called the Siyum HaShas. The most recent Siyum HaShas took place on March 1, 2005, known to us as the year 5766. The idea that someone could know the entire book, or even a single volume of it, was inconceivable, and frankly, quite ridiculous. I chose a volume at random and opened it. Its pages consist of the Mishnah, or Jewish law, printed in the middle of the page, with the Gemara directly below it. The Gemara is a commentary on the law and how it relates to the Torah, written by the Amoraim, a group of ancient rabbinical sages. The Tosafot, a series of commentaries by medieval rabbis, are printed on the outside margins of the page. This incredibly dense text, written in Hebrew, governs Orthodox Judaism. One could devote one's entire life to the study of it, and many do, and not even begin to fully and completely comprehend and understand it, much less have it memorized, which, if even possible, would be a superhuman feat. I placed the volume back on the shelf and went and kissed each of my children good-night. I returned to my study and I prayed. When my wife came into my study and asked me what was wrong, I told her that Ben Zion had been found, and I had spent the afternoon with him. Having been with me for so many years, she knew what that meant to me, and possibly to all of Judaism, and also the world. Instead of spending time together, as we did most evenings, she left me in prayer, and I prayed for several hours before going to sleep.

The next day I went to the synagogue, where most of my thoughts revolved around Ben, and I found my daily tasks and responsibilities, which I usually so thoroughly enjoyed, to be a tremendous burden. I tried to finish them as soon as possible, and went immediately to the hospital. When I arrived at Ben's room, the young man who had been sitting near Ben's bed, and who was still clutching his Bible, was standing outside the door. When I tried to go into the room, he stepped in front of me and said that Jacob was inside with Ben's doctors and that he had been instructed not to allow anyone to enter. I told him that Ben had specifically asked me to return, and that I had been the family's rabbi before their conversion, and that as far as I knew, I was still Ben's rabbi because he had not converted to Christianity. The man told me he knew who I was, and that Jacob had told him not to allow me inside the room. I asked him his name and he told me it was Jeremiah. When I offered him my hand, he did not receive it.

We waited for a few minutes, and while Jeremiah was not physically imposing, something about him seemed off, as if he were very angry, very nervous, or very scared, or some combination of all of those emotions. He stood in front of the door, reading his Bible, and would occasionally either glare at me or nod to himself while saying Praise Jesus or

Hallelujah Lord. When the door finally opened and several doctors stepped out of the room, one of them, a tall thin man who appeared to have some authority, walked over to me and addressed me. Rabbi Schiff?
Yes?
Dr. Wulf. Neurology attending.
Nice to meet you.
Ben is sedated right now. He's had two severe seizures today. Last night, however, he both asked and authorized me to speak with you about his case.
Do you know more than you did yesterday?
We do. If you can come to my office, we can talk for a few minutes.
That would be great. Thank you.
We went to his office, which was crowded with papers, books, degrees on the walls, and a large number of family photos depicting him and a woman, I assumed his wife, and three young girls, I assumed his daughters, on vacations, at ball games, in front of a church. There was also a crucifix on the wall. He sat behind his desk and I sat across from him, and he spoke.
We've been working hard to diagnose Ben. It's obvious that he's been suffering from some form of seizure disorder, most likely as a result of his accident. Jacob came to me last night, and he told me about what Ben has been experiencing. That information made it very clear to us that he is suffering from temporal lobe epilepsy, and a rare and specific type, called ecstatic epilepsy. Ecstatic epilepsy is characterized by an aura, which is a feeling the patient has right before a seizure. The

auras of someone with ecstatic epilepsy tend to be
extreme, often involving sensory hallucinations,
sometimes erotic sensations, and, more rarely,
religious or spiritual experiences. It can be, and was
in our case, difficult to diagnose because the onset
of the seizure isn't localized in a specific set point
in the brain, which makes it difficult to track using
EEGs, and because the experiences involved with the
seizures are so profound, and pleasurable, that the
patients don't tell their doctors about them because
they don't want them treated and stopped. Both seem
to be the case with Ben. I don't know what he has
spoken to you about, but he told Jacob he believed he
was communicating with God. As I told Jacob, that's
actually normal given this diagnosis, but unfortunately, it is entirely a function, or rather a malfunction, of his brain. It is not real, as much as someone
like you or Jacob or I would like it to be, and allowing
it to continue should not be encouraged. We need to
get Ben on a drug regimen and begin treating him.
I understand.
Has he spoken to you about his communications?
I don't discuss conversations between me and
members of my synagogue.
Even if it may affect their health?
I understand your position and your concerns,
and if they come up with Ben, I will address them
with him.
Thank you.
I stood and left and went back to Ben's room, where
his brother and Jeremiah were praying at his bedside.
He was asleep, on his back, and looked as if he was

at peace. Jacob looked up at me and I knew I was not welcome. Wanting to avoid an unnecessary confrontation, I decided it was best to leave. I said a prayer outside the door and went home.

After dinner I went to my study and turned on my computer and started researching epilepsy, and more specifically ecstatic epilepsy, on the internet, which I find a wonderful, though sometimes confusing and contradictory source of information. The diagnosis was perplexing to me. While Ben had clearly suffered major trauma to his head and body, and the epilepsy might have been a direct result of said trauma, if there wasn't a spiritual element, a true spiritual element to what he was experiencing, there was no way he would know the religious books he claimed to know. He had also, since before he was born, depending on who you believed, shown signs of messianic potential, which had grown stronger and more absolute following his birth and his childhood. On the other hand, I did not know if he actually knew the books, and he himself had stated that the words of God meant nothing in the face of science, and that he might well be a delusional fool. I found myself, until I knew more and spent more time with him and had more time for reflection and prayer, in the same place I was with God, which is a place of faith. I either had faith in Ben or I didn't. I either believed him, and in him, or I didn't.

My research proved to be very enlightening, and epilepsy turned out to be far more fascinating than I'd imagined it could or would be. Over the course of recorded time, some of the world's most important historical figures either were or are thought to have been epileptic, including Pythagoras, Socrates, Plato, Hannibal, Alexander the Great, Julius Caesar, Petrarch, Dante Alighieri, Leonardo da Vinci, Michelangelo, Isaac Newton, Napoleon Bonaparte, Ludwig van Beethoven, Lord Byron, Edgar Allan Poe, Fyodor Dostoyevsky, Vincent van Gogh, Alfred Nobel, Thomas Edison, and Vladimir Lenin. Many scientists and researchers believe that the genius these people possessed was either directly caused by, or most certainly related to, their epilepsy. The number of religious figures I found who are thought to have had it was astonishing, among them the Priestly source of the Pentateuch, Ezekiel, Saint Paul, the Prophet Muhammad, Joan of Arc, Martin Luther, Saint Birgitta, Saint Catherine of Genoa, Saint Teresa of Ávila, Saint Catherine of Ricci, Saint Margaret Mary, Ellen G. White, and Saint Thérèse of Lisieux. Among those who either definitely had or are thought to have had ecstatic epilepsy are Saint Paul, the Prophet Muhammad, Joan of Arc, Beethoven, and Dostoyevsky. The effects those moments, those brief moments before their seizures hit, had on their lives, and on the world at large, are astonishing: on the road to Damascus, Saint Paul had his vision of the resurrected Jesus, which led to his conversion to Christianity; the Prophet Muhammad is thought, by some, almost always non-Muslims, to have spoken to the archangel Gabriel and to have received the

Qur'an from him during those moments; Joan of Arc is believed to have received the instructions from Saint Margaret, Saint Catherine, and Saint Michael that inspired her to lead the French Army into battle and resulted in its victories against the English in the Hundred Years' War; Beethoven is thought to have conceived of his symphonies in their entirety, which is perhaps how he was able to compose them even when he was deaf; and Dostoyevsky is believed to have conceived of his novels in their entirety. In thinking specifically of Saint Paul and the Prophet Muhammad, who, while I do not worship in the same way as them or the followers of the religions that one preached and one founded, are certainly the two most important religious figures who have appeared on earth since the death of Jesus Christ, I was heartened in my belief that Ben might be divine, that his visions might be of God, instead of a false apparition of God, and that his condition might be a requirement of his potential rather than an impediment to it.

I returned to the hospital the next day, stopping first at the synagogue to ask my assistant rabbi to handle those responsibilities that are normally mine. When I entered Ben's room, Jacob and Jeremiah were sitting across from Ben, who was cross-legged on his bed. They both had their Bibles open and were giving him book titles with chapter and verse numbers, and as soon as they finished saying them, Ben immediately recited the text, in what I assume was a word-for-word rendering, back to them.

Jacob looked up at me and started to speak, but Ben told him he wanted me to stay. There were no other seats, so I stood a few feet away from the foot of Ben's bed.

What I saw was absolutely amazing. Jacob was using an Old Testament, the first five books of which, Genesis, Exodus, Leviticus, Numbers, and Deuteronomy, also known as the Five Books of Moses, constitute the Torah, and Jeremiah was using the New Testament, the primary focus of which is the story of Jesus Christ. For over an hour they drilled him. They'd quickly flip through the pages, the book, chapter, and verse they landed on, and each time Ben would recite the corresponding text correctly. Near the end of it, while Jeremiah was visibly awed and excited, and I was silent and, in a way, very proud, Jacob seemed very anxious and nervous. He stopped Jeremiah, closed his Old Testament, and spoke.
How do I know you didn't memorize these while you were away?
Because I told you I didn't.
Why should I believe you?
It doesn't matter to me if you do or you don't.
Why won't you tell me what you did for all those years?
Because it doesn't matter.
Where were you?
I was drifting.
Where?
Doesn't matter.
It does to me.

Let's end our conversation. I'd like to spend some
time with the rabbi.
Tell me what you did and I'll end the conversation.
I lived and felt and learned and hurt and fell in love
once and most of the time I wasn't happy but some
of the time I was and I never stepped foot in a church,
a synagogue, a mosque, a temple, or any other kind
of religious establishment and I never picked up
a book of any kind, much less memorized one.
You didn't answer my question.
I just didn't give you the answer you wanted.
Jacob stood and said he'd be back in an hour,
and he and Jeremiah started to walk out of the room.
Ben spoke.
I love you, Jacob. And I appreciate how much care
and concern you've shown me.
Jacob stopped and looked back and he almost smiled,
which would have been the first time I had seen him
smile since he visited me in my office, and he said
thank you, and he and Jeremiah left.
Ben looked at me.
You spoke with my doctor.
Yes, I did. It was very interesting, and very
informative.
What do you think?
Words of science mean nothing in the face of God.
Ben smiled.
It could just be a malfunction of my brain.
What do you know about Messiah?
The Messiah?
Messiah. Not everyone believes it will be a person.
Many believe, as they do with large sections of the

Torah, that the story, and the prophecy, of Messiah is symbolic, and not about an actual person who may have lived, may currently be alive, or may at some point walk among us, but about a period of time, a Messianic age, when Jews, and the rest of the world, will live in peace.
Is that what you believe?
No.
You believe in a person, an actual Messiah?
Messiah, or Moshiach, means anointed, or the anointed one, in Hebrew. It is a word that has been used to refer to many things and many people in the Torah, including kings, prophets, priests, and warriors. Some believe we may have seen many Messiahs already, the most prominent being David, Solomon, Aaron, and Saul. In at least three points in our history, a great many Jews believed the Messiah was among us. In 132 CE, a Davidic soldier named Shimon Bar Kochba united the armies of the tribes of Israel and led a revolt against Roman rule, which freed Israel. He established a new government in Jerusalem, and he started rebuilding the Temple of Solomon. Rabbis made proclamations naming him Messiah and stating that the Messianic age had begun, which lasted for two years, at which point the Romans returned, crushed the Jewish armies, and killed a large portion of our population, including Bar Kochba. Fifteen hundred years later, in 1648, a Turkish rabbi named Sabbatai Zevi proclaimed himself Messiah, basing his claim on a prophecy set forth in the Kabbalah text of Zohar, which predicted the Messiah's arrival in that year. Though he was

not Davidic, and possessed none of the requirements of Messiahship, by 1665, when he proclaimed himself Messiah again, he was able to convince eighty percent of the world's Jewish population at the time that he was indeed Messiah. He ultimately converted to Islam before Sultan Mehmed IV of Constantinople, humiliating his followers and embarrassing Jews around the world. Against all reason, there are people today who call themselves Sabbatians and believe he was Messiah, and that in order to herald the Messianic age, they pray for his return. The most recent individual thought to be Messiah was Menachem Mendel Schneerson, the seventh Rebbe of Chabad Lubavitch in Brooklyn, who lived from 1902 until 1994. He was undoubtedly a great man, and spent his life spreading Orthodox Judaism and working to unite Jews, but his call for prayer to hasten Moshiach was not a proclamation of his own Messianism, despite the belief of many of his own followers, which he neither supported nor rejected. You ask what I believe, and as you know, as an Orthodox Jew, and as a rabbi, I am required as part of my belief to subscribe to the thirteen principles of faith set forth by Maimonides. The twelfth principle states: I believe with perfect faith in the coming of the Messiah. How long it takes, I will await his coming every day. I also recite the Shemoneh Esrei, the eighteen prayers, three times a day, at morning, afternoon, and evening services, and in that prayer, I pray for the conditions of the Messiah to be met: the return of Jewish exiles to Israel, a return to religious courts and God's system of justice, an end

to evil and the humbling of sinners and heretics, rewards to the righteous, the rebuilding of Jerusalem and the restoration of a king descended from David, and the building of the Third Temple of Solomon.
And when that happens, the Messiah arrives?
Or he arrives and then it happens, or some of it happens before and some after, no one knows, and the prophecies aren't specific about it. We only know, or believe, the Messiah will arrive, and that the arrival could be at any time, or it could have been and we missed it, or it could be now, or it could still be coming, and that's part of the beauty of Messiah, the fact that no one knows. There are, though, beliefs that specific events will herald the arrival of the Messiah: if every Jew on earth observes a single Shabbat, or if no Jew on earth observes a single Shabbat, if the world is good enough to be deserving of Messiah, or if the world is bad enough to need Messiah, if an entire generation of Jews is born innocent, or if an entire generation of Jews loses hope. None are likely, though, so instead of waiting for them, or trying to bring them into being, rabbis, or at least some of us, myself included, have looked for specific signs, which have been known for centuries, that Messiah, or the potential Messiah, will possess.
Such as?
The Messiah, or potential Messiah, will have been born on Tisha B'Av, the day of the destruction of both the First and Second Temples in Jerusalem. The Messiah, or potential Messiah, will have been born circumcised, as were Adam, Noah, Joseph, Moses, and David, and some believe Jesus, though

Jews do not believe that particular myth. The Messiah, or potential Messiah, will be able to judge people, whether they are good or bad, whether they are honest or deceitful, whether they are deserving of Heaven or undeserving, with his sense of smell. The Messiah, or potential Messiah, will also perform miracles; though the exact nature is not revealed, the most common miracles are related to health and medical issues, and having the ability to heal either themselves or others. I watched Ben to see if he would react to what I said, as he knew he had been born on Passover. I knew, though I did not know if he did or not, that he had been born circumcised, which is one of the reasons I had tried, for the entirety of his life, to be close to him and his family, and to watch, guide, and counsel him when I could, and I believed, based on what I had seen, that he had acquired the ability to judge people using his sense of smell. The fact that he was alive, given his traumas, was an obvious miracle, though I did not know, at the time, whether he was able to heal others, or perform any other type of miracle. I doubted, because I did not, and do not, believe the Christ story as it is written, that he would ever have walked on water or turned water to wine. He did not react, which surprised me, because surely he knew he possessed three of the traits, and must have, given the difficult situation within his family, which had revolved around the circumstances of his birth for his entire life, suspected that he possessed the fourth and that he had been born as he was.
He stood up and looked at me and spoke.
I need to do something.

Shall I wait here for you?
It would probably be better if you went home.
Is everything okay?
He smiled and nodded.
Yes.
He turned and walked out of the room. He was wearing his robe and a pair of hospital slippers and I could see glimpses of the scars on his back, and large scars on the back of his head. I think often of that moment, if perhaps I said something wrong, if I should have withheld some of the information I gave to him, if I was too forward, or if perhaps I should have sensed something when he told Jacob that he loved him. I think often of that moment, and I wonder if I should have known when he stood and smiled at me, that he was going to walk out of the room, and walk out of the hospital, and disappear again, and if I had known, would I have done anything to stop him.

MATTHEW

Some people just ain't made for the world. Can't fucking take it. Can't deal with Momma and Dadda and school teaching you nothing and a fucking job with some motherfucking boss going blah blah blah and bills and neighbors and some kind of bullshit church and having a good credit score and a mortgage and getting married with kids and some kind of mysterious motherfucking retirement plan that don't ever let you do nothing but put more in and get none back. Lotta people ain't made for it. They the people you see on the streets, in dirty clothes, talking to themselves, screaming on the corner like they demonized, mumbling and crying, they the ones in your family and your town you always scared of and feeling sorry for and making excuses about, the ones you don't even thinks is fucking human. They is, they just ain't made like the rest of you and they can't deal with it so they go to drinking and getting fucking high and being criminal and getting locked-the-fuck-up and just saying who gives a fuck to all of it. People be thinking they're crazy and be needing some kind of fucking help, but the help ain't nothing 'cause a motherfucking soup kitchen or some kind of shelter that can't hold enough or a nuthouse where we get beat or some charity that's really about motherfuckers' friends knowing how good they is and how much they care ain't nothing but bullshit. And don't

even bring up that made-up motherfucker people
be calling God, ’cause that motherfucker don’t even
exist, and don’t be bringing up all these so-called
houses of God, ’cause they more about killing
and hating than they is about helping and loving.
Sorry to break the motherfucking news if you ain’t
heard it, but that’s it motherfucker, that’s the
fucking news.

I been living underground for a long-ass motherfucking time. Living underneath New York
fucking City, where there’s tunnels, and there’s
tunnels underneath the tunnels, and there’s
some more fucking tunnels under those tunnels.
Some of ’em empty, some still got trains rolling
through ’em, some of ’em got the subways and
some of ’em gots peoples. And then there’s some
so dark, so goddamn dark, darker than the darkest
night, and blacker than what you see when your
eyes closed, that most peoples, even underground
peoples, won’t go into ’em. And those are the tunnels
where miracles happen, where people like Yahya
and Ben go and come back something different,
where motherfuckers who got the gift go and in
the blackness they see. I know it be sounding crazy,
but the ones with gifts got to go into blackness,
’cause that’s where they learn to see.

I was born in New Haven, Connecticut. My daddy
was a respectable motherfucker who had him a
college degree and worked his ass off as a bank teller.
My momma finished high school and spent her life

being his bitch. He wasn't never around when I was growing up, saying he was always working to get promoted and going out with clients and his boss. When he was around, he was drinking and yelling and ignoring me and my two sisters and telling my momma she wasn't pretty enough or skinny enough or dressing well enough or getting them invited to the right parties with the right peoples and every now and then if she talked back to him he'd hit her in the fucking face. He didn't think nothing about me 'cept that I was a piece of shit, which was fine with me 'cause I didn't think nothing about him 'cept he was a piece of shit too. They sent me to all sorts of different schools, thinking the better name or more of 'em would make a difference, but it didn't make nothing 'cept them real pissed. When I was seventeen, I left 'em for good. Just walked the fuck away. I was figuring I'd do fine on my own, and even if I didn't, I'd rather be doing real bad my own way than be an asshole doing what other peoples thought I should be doing. I convinced myself I was breaking out in the name of some kind of fucking freedom. I hadn't learned yet that everybody's locked up some way or another. That's how life is; we're all imprisoned by something.

I lived in a park for a while. Lived in a cardboard box. Lived under a highway. Got my ass beat and got robbed and got addicted and got locked up a few times and got raped more than once or twice. Learned what I already knew, that the world is an ugly motherfucking place where people'll spit on you and fuck you up before they'll be good to you. I found my way into the tunnels just wanting to get the fuck away, lived like a fucking rat, scrounging for food, eating fucking garbage, taking what other people didn't want and using it to survive. First time down was for three years. Just by myself. Living by the trains that went to Long Island. Had a sleeping bag and flashlight and a baseball bat. Then I got busted for being in a fight with a knife over some pizza in a dumpster and had some crack in my pocket and got sent upstate for three years. Got out and came back to my tunnel and found some other motherfucker in my sleeping bag and wasn't in no mood for fighting after fighting the whole time in prison and went further down and found me an old electrical closet on an abandoned IRT track and stayed there for three years. I got back on the rock and drinking again and spent my days begging and going through dumpsters trying to find some shit to sell. One day I came back from up top and I had me a couple nice rocks and a bottle of wine and I see two motherfuckers sitting on the ground outside my closet. They wasn't in uniforms and they definitely wasn't working with the MTA or Amtrak, so I figured it was some undercover pig motherfuckers coming to drag me back to prison 'cause I didn't never go see my parole officer, and I think about running away but figure they'd shoot me or some shit like they always do to poor supposedly crazy homeless motherfuckers.

So I just walked over to 'em and asked them what the fuck was up and when I was close I could see for sure they wasn't no fucking cops 'cause they had these scars that was identical and looked liked someone had put two long slices on each of their arms and they said some motherfucker named Yahya wanted to see me. I asked them what the fuck Yahya wanted and they said to see me. I asked them who the fuck Yahya was and where Yahya was at and they said they would show me. And that's what they did. They fucking took me down into the blackness and showed me.

I was there on that first day we saw Ben. We was just sitting having some dinner and most of us was there, sitting at the tables eating some macaroni and motherfucking cheese. At that point I'd been with Yahya for almost ten years, and it had taken a long fucking time, lots of hard-ass work and patience, but we had everything dialed up just fucking right: electricity hijacked from the city power lines, water hijacked from the city water pipes, a tunnel that hadn't been used since the eighteen fucking hundreds that was blocked at both ends, holes that we could close that was going up to other tunnels in four different places, and one passage that went straight into a alley on the Lower East Side that we could lock the fuck up to keep people out. We had built little shelters for everyone out of scraps of wood and siding that peoples up top threw away. We had pots and pans and sheets and towels and beds and old tape players for music and radios for when the bad news started coming and we had thousands and thousands of batteries. We had enough canned and boxed food to keep us going for a year, and that was if we didn't start eating any of the rats or the other fucking animals that was living in the tunnels, which could keep us going for just about forever. And we had us a stockpile of weapons. Everything from old medieval-like shit, fucking swords and spears and shields we made out of scrap metal, to new-school shit like nine millimeters and assault rifles and tasers and mace. There was other tunnels that had peoples living in 'em, and there was other groups that had organized into some kind of community or something, but none like us. We was a movement, a fucking army, with a philosophy and a motherfucking plan. We was ready for what's coming. For what is going to befall humanity. We was prepared to survive when everybody else is gonna fucking die.

Yahya'd been telling us for a couple weeks he'd been having dreams about someone coming to see us. Yahya was a prophet, an old school holy man, like fucking Moses or Muhammad or some other motherfucker from the old books, so when he was telling us he was having dreams or visions we took that shit seriously. Yahya had been in the tunnels for thirty-three years. Came down when he was fourteen years old, living in some foster care fucking nightmare, getting beat by the other kids and raped by the man who was supposed to be caring for him. He got fed-the-fuck-up one day and lit the house they was living in on fire. The other kids got out but the man burned to a fucking crisp, just like his ass deserved, and as soon as he'd dropped the fucking match, Yahya walked into the nearest subway and hopped the fucking turnstile and walked off the platform and into the tunnels. He figured out how to live without being above, eating discarded food from the garbage cans of subway stations, finding clothes that people be leaving behind on accident, getting water from bathrooms at the big stations. He kept going down further and further, finding his own motherfucking way, like all the prophets and the great peoples of the world find their own fucking way, and eventually he found our tunnel we living in now, pristine and unopened for almost a hundred fucking years, and he lived in it alone for ten years, till he started building our society. He only been coming out one day a year for the whole time, just the day of the anniversary of the fire. He come out and he read a newspaper and he walk around the city and look at the shit going down, which ain't never any good, and been getting worse and worse every goddamn year.

So he'd been telling us 'bout his dream, that some motherfucker was going to find us, a man who'd wandered the world, suffered shit none of us could ever imagine, knew shit that none of us could ever imagine, that his arriving was a sign that the end was coming, the final motherfucking sign. And there we were, eating our macaroni and listening to Yahya preach, and this motherfucker comes walking out the darkness, skinny as fuck, white as paper, scars all over the fucking place, scars that made the scars we had, the scars Yahya cut into our arms as a sign that our life above was dead and we was in the tunnels for life, this motherfucker had scars made those scars look like little bandaid booboos I used to get when

I was a four-year-old shithead. Yahya, who preached every night at dinner, just stopped, stared. If he hadn't been having his dreams he'd a pro'ly killed the motherfucker. But he knew, knew he was coming, and knew who he was, knew why he was walking the face of the fucking earth, and Ben just came strolling up, not saying a word, just looking unhuman, but not scary like a monster or shit, but unhuman 'cause it looked like he was glowing, like there was some kinda light coming out of him or something. He came to the table, asked if he could sit down, and Yahya nodded. We was all shocked and I personally was scared, scared of the motherfucker who could silence Yahya. So he sat down at the end of the table, looked at Yahya, and asked him, real polite and shit, if he would continue preaching. Yahya smiled, and he was not the kind of motherfucker who smiled very often, and said yes. And then he continued fucking preaching. And I remember that sermon 'cause of Ben joining us. Was about how the governments of the world leading everyone towards death, disaster, ruin, and apocalypse. And how God and Jesus and the rest of the motherfuckers and the dumbass prophecies in the Bible had nothing to do with it. It was the greed and folly of the men who running the world. Their belief in silly religions that preach murder and hate and division. Their need to control other peoples who's different from them and kill them if they don't bend to some motherfucker's will. That's what's gonna end it all, some dumbass war over religion and money, and that's who's gonna end it all, the motherfuckers who believe and hold the purse strings.

Ben settled right the fuck in. He took a job like everyone had a fucking job. Most of us went up top to either beg for money that we used for buying weapons and long-term supplies or look through the garbage for food and building materials and shit we could use down below. Some of us took care of our business in the tunnel, working on the electric or the water, managing supplies, doing maintenance, cleaning the place the fuck up. The worst job was cleaning the area around the toilets, two deep holes that went into a tunnel down below us. We had built little outhouses 'round the holes, and peoples tried being hygienic and shit, but it was still nasty, still a place where peoples pissed and took shits and smelled fucking bad. Ben became the toilet man, cleaning and stocking the paper and dumping a bucketful of water down the hole to make some of that foul shit go away. When he wasn't working there, he'd help whoever else was needing help, doing whatever they was needing doing. When we was eating, he'd always sit at the end of the table, and he didn't hardly eat nothing. Maybe two, three bites of rice or pasta, maybe an apple or an orange or half a banana, one glass of water, and that'd be it for the whole fucking day. And when we was sleeping, we all went into our shelters, some of 'em being pretty fucking nice, with mattresses and TVs and more than one room, and some of 'em being more the simple way, with maybe a sleeping bag or some blankets. Ben would sleep on the ground at one of the dark ends of the tunnel, all by hisself, nothing but his clothes, 'cept when it got real fucking cold, then he used this thin-ass blanket that wouldn't keep a fucking cockroach warm. And he didn't hardly ever talk. If you asked him a question, he'd either nod or shake his head or smile. If it was needing more words, or was a more complicated kinda thing, he would always say just what he needed as quick as possible and then shut up. And with the way he looked, he was making all of us think he wasn't a person, not a real person at least, he was something fucking else beyond, something that wasn't like the rest of us, not even like Yahya.

About a week after he was being with us, his seizures started happening. One lunchtime he just fell backwards from the table and his body went fucking haywire. He was shaking and rolling 'round and had shit coming out his mouth and was grunting like a goddamn dog. People got up to help him but Yahya said leave him be, the man is doing what the man needs to do. So peoples left his ass alone. And the first time it lasted something like two minutes. When it was over we just left him alone, and at a certain point he came back awake and sat back down at the table like nothing fucking happened. Twenty minutes later it happened again. He just fell back and freaked-the-fuck-out. One of us was a doctor before he became a crackhead and ended up in the tunnels, where Yahya found him and saved him, and he was saying we couldn't just leave Ben alone, but Yahya kept saying this is what the man needs to do. And it was one of Yahya's beliefs, one of the tenets of our fucking society: a man does what he needs to do, he lives his life how he wants to live it, other people ain't got no fucking right to impose. So even though we was all scared, and we be seeing that the seizures were fucking his ass up, we left him alone. He was doing what he needed to do.

In our world, in our society, our civilization, our culture, and I ain't talking 'bout yours, the one above the fucking ground, I'm talking about our nation, the one in the fucking tunnel, the underground empire, in that subterranean realm, there was rules. If you got brought down, if you got found by Yahya and chosen, you learned the fucking rules, and you lived by them, and if you became part of us, you was saved. Yahya believed the end of the motherfucking world was coming, and he was right, because it sure as fuck is, and it is coming soon. If he found you, you was one of the ones who couldn't live above, who wasn't cut the fuck out for it, and he believed you was capable of living below, and he believed you'd be capable of fighting. You'd get brought down, fucking blindfolded and shit so you wouldn't know where you was, most of us was addicted so we'd get taken the fuck off whatever the shit was, and we was indoctrinated. You had to work, fucking contribute. You had to submit your will to the good of the community. You could drink, use, fuck, gamble, read, play chess, cook, write, paint, build, do whatever the fuck you want, but there was no addiction, whatever you was doing had to be under control. You had to live and let live, but not like motherfuckers up top say that, you had to do it for reals. There was no stealing, no fighting, no judging, no hating. There was no God, no worship, no time wasting on made-up shit. You had to renunciate the fucking world, free yourself from the bullshit of it, accept that at some point there was gonna be nothing but what existed in the tunnel. And you had to be willing to die for that. And once you was fucking cool with all that, and was ready to make the commitment, you was fucking saved. And when you was saved, you was scarred. Yahya would cut you, two long gashes along each of your arms, symbolizing your death above and your birth below. And when the blood flowed, when you lifted your arms and it started running down your cheeks, your neck, when you could taste it, when you could feel it in your fucking shoes, you was free. Never going fucking back 'cept to get shit to live below. Never accepting their rules or expectations or so-called morals and so-called fucking standards ever fucking again. When the blood flowed, you was free.

When Ben came, there was thirty-two of us. It had been that way for two years. Even though Yahya had prophesized his coming, he had to follow the same rules as the rest of us, had to become one of us if he wanted to stay. His seizures made shit a little more complicated, 'cause he couldn't be doing most of the normal kind of shit the rest of us was doing. And who he was, why he was walking the motherfucking face of the earth, the gifts he was given or acquired or whatever you want to believe, though I know what I believe, that made shit more complicated too. Not every day a motherfucker like him comes strolling into the motherfucking lunch line. But he didn't seem to care. Yahya moved him to sweeping and garbage, which was sweeping the fucking grounds and taking the garbage out, which meant taking it to another tunnel that was also empty, 'cept for the fact we'd been dumping shit in it for years. When Ben would have a seizure, he'd just sit down and let it happen. Though Yahya noticed it the first time, the rest of us started seeing how Ben would go to another place right before those fucking things would blast him. His eyes would be real still, like he was looking at shit no else could see or had ever seen or would ever see. It would only be a second, maybe, or two or three, but somehow, those seconds seemed like forever. When someone asked Yahya what was happening, he said the man was speaking to God, seeing through to the eternal. Someone else asked how he was talking to God, if God don't exist? Yahya said God don't exist like people on this planet believe he exist, some big powerful all-knowing motherfucker sitting on a chair giving a shit about what's happening here on earth and planning our individual destinies, that's just stupid bullshit, but there was answers we didn't have, things we didn't know, things beyond the little minds of little men who was stupid enough to think that in the entire universe, infinite beyond human comprehension in size and energy and dimension, we was the only motherfuckers around, and that all the stupid little shit we did and fucking worried about mattered in some kinda way. Ben went to those places, those infinite places, and understood 'em, even though he couldn't or wouldn't talk about what the fuck it was he was seeing and feeling and experiencing.

The seizures got worse and fucking worse and fucking worse, and longer and fucking longer and fucking longer. They would last ten, fifteen, twenty minutes. Started lasting thirty minutes, lasting an hour, lasting three or four hours, shaking and convulsing and spitting up and grunting, you could see it hurting him while it was happening, and you could see him being in so much pain when it ended that he couldn't hardly move. The crackhead doctor said Ben was experiencing some shit called status epilepticus, a state of persistent seizure, and that he could be dying from it, that he would be dying from it if we didn't get him out to a proper hospital. But Yahya said leave him, that man is not going to die, at least not down here. Then he had him a seizure that lasted for a day, twenty-four fucking hours straight. It was scaring everyone and making us think Yahya was wrong, that Ben was gonna fucking die. On and on and on and on. Worse than we had ever seen. Don't know how anyone could live through it or be surviving something like that. And even if you could be living through it, how you wouldn't be fucking insane from the pain, just crazy outta your mind from the physical fucking pain. When it stopped, he just lie there, on his blanket, on the floor of the tunnel. Slept for like another two days. We was always going over to check him, make sure he was still breathing, and he always was, but it was real light, and you had to be looking real close to see it. When he waked up, we was all sitting around after dinner. Yahya had given us a fierce preaching, along the lines of his typical but real inspired, saying the world above us was dying, that greed corruption hate and intolerance was gonna lead to a war that would destroy it all, that the war was coming soon, that we got to renounce that world and prepare to survive, that we got to love each other and let each other live, and help each other live, and respect each other. Don't matter where we from or what we had before, don't matter our color or our religion, that nothing matter but living, and letting live, and loving. After he was done we got to listening to some old-timey jazz on the cassette deck, some of us having cocktails, some of us smoking some fine-ass weed, some of us dancing, mens together, mens and ladies together, just ladies, all of them cool down here, sharing their love and spreading their love however the fuck they want, nobody judging them. Ben joined all the people dancing, probably about twenty of us. Nobody saw him walk up, one second he wasn't there, the next second he was. And he was moving real slow, slow and in perfect rhythm, like he was part of the music, another instrument to it or some shit, tied directly into it. His eyes was closed, and he hadn't fucking eaten in so long, his skin was even whiter than normal, almost fucking translucent. His eyes was closed and he started moving to each person or couple, and he touched them, held them, moved with them, slowed them down so they was feeling the music same way he was, he was holding their hands, holding their faces in his hands, pulling them close so their bodies was real tight with his, and he was kissing them, men and women both, slowly and deeply kissing them, and you could see in their faces, in their bodies, that none of them had ever been feeling anything like it, nothing as pure, as sexual, as ecstatic, as fucking sweet and beautiful, and it was like he was fucking them, fucking them like they hadn't never been fucked before, even though he was just touching, kissing, moving, moving real slow, real real slow, he was fucking all of 'em. And those he wasn't with, who wasn't dancing, we was watching, and we was as turned on as the people he was touching, he was fucking. When I was a boy living in a world in my head to escape the world I was living in for real, I used to dream I'd be able to do anything I wanted to people and whatever I did they loved me, just loved and let me be free from all the shit in the world that I hated and that hated me. When I was older, I stopped dreaming that type of dreaming 'cause I realized that kind of shit just wasn't real or possible or ever going to be happening. But then I saw Ben, and I believed it was possible, that fucking anything was possible, because I saw it and felt and knew it and believed it and even though it didn't look real or feel real it was the realest thing I ever knew, that I ever saw on this fucking hellhole of an earth. That love was the realest motherfucking thing any of us ever saw. When he had been with everyone dancing, Ben stepped away and walked towards Yahya, who had been watching and feeling and believing too, sitting at the head of the table where he was always sitting, and Ben kneeled before him and offered his arms. Yahya always had his knife on him, or near him, and he picked it up and he took Ben's arms and he made the cuts. Normally takes longer, a year or so before you get them, and only when Yahya decides, but not with Ben. His blood flowed and he lifted his arms and the blood streamed down all over him. When he was covered and his clothes were soaked, and the ground beneath him, he stepped forward and he kissed Yahya. I hadn't never seen anyone kiss Yahya before, or even touch him, not outside of his room, which was the only place he did things with people, and only women. And Ben kissed him for a long time, and when he pulled away, Yahya's eyes was closed and he was breathing real slow and heavy, and he was looking like he couldn't move, like he was fucking paralyzed. And Ben just stepped away and turned and walked into the darkness.

It was a long time before anyone moved. And when we was moving again, we just went silently, not one fucking word outta anyone, back to our shelters, where most of us just laid there in our sleeping places and thought about Ben. Next morning we expected to see him, having breakfast or being in his sleeping area, but he wasn't nowhere around. Peoples started talking 'bout where he might be at, when Yahya tell us he gone, that he had him another vision last night, that Ben be gone into the tunnels, where he got some things that he need to do on his own, some fights he needs to be fighting on his own. Yahya say let him go, let him do what he needs to do, when he be finished with it, he'll be coming back.

A week went by and he didn't come back. Another week and still nothing. Peoples started getting worried a little bit. I started wandering the tunnels, looking for places I hadn't never been, places further down, places that got the true darkness, the black that don't ever see no light. I was thinking even though Yahya be having his vision, and even though Ben obviously got something special about him, he still a man, still flesh and fucking blood, still got him a heart that does its beating. And being a man, he vulnerable, and he wandering around somewhere with big-ass motherfucking gashes in his arms and some kind of medical condition that fucks him up worse than I ever seen. So I went looking for him, and looking for the places that are hidden, that ain't supposed to be found, the places where I say before that the magic happens, where in the darkness you learn to see.

After four or five days looking, walking through subway tunnels, trains blasting by me just a couple inches away, walking through Amtrak and LIRR tunnels, walking through PATH tunnels, walking through abandoned tunnels, the old IRT, tunnels that got started and never finished, just empty fucking holes, I come across a door in the lower tunnels beneath City Hall. Normally I don't bother with the fucking doors, 'cause they all be locked and breaking the locks just draw attention that don't nobody be needing, but something 'bout this door draw me in. I checked it and it was open, so I look inside and there's a hole with this ladder going straight down, though I can't fucking see where it's going or how far or where it ends. Ain't nothing wrong with looking in life, looking for new things and places and feelings and beliefs, ain't nothing wrong at all, so I start climbing down, looking to see what I find. I go down and it's black and fucking silent and even though I'd been living down there a long time at that point, I was real scared, my heart thudding all fast and shit, taking short breaths, wondering if something gonna come out and get me, some fucking monster or something, or if I'm gonna fucking fall and break my damn neck. I was being real scared.

My foot hit ground and I could feel it wet and slippery, which was telling me I must be somewhere in the fucking sewers, which all of us stayed the fuck out of because they was full of rats and disease and lots of other shit no man don't want to spend time in or around. I started climbing right back up but as my foot start rising I heard me something that was sounding like a scream. I stopped and stood listening for more screaming and I heard another fucking scream almost right away. I got down and started walking towards where I was hearing it, stepping real careful and moving real slow because I couldn't see nothing. Even though my eyes was real adjusted, I couldn't fucking see nothing.

Took me a long time to go a couple hundred yards down that tunnel, long-ass time. All the while I was hearing those screams, and the closer I was getting to 'em, I was knowing it was Ben, 'cause it was sounding like some of the noises I heard him making during his seizures. When I was real close I started hearing trickling water and started knowing that the screams is coming from below me, and that the water be running down somewheres. My eyes had adjusted and I saw a few steps ahead there was a huge hole, like some kind of fucking sinkhole or giant pothole that happens in New York once or twice a year, and Ben must be down in that hole, maybe hurt, and can't get himself out. I was about to call out to him, tell him I was here and gonna help him, when I hear him start talking, talking real slow and deliberate, like he having a conversation with someone. So I slide to the edge of the hole and look down, and he be right there, maybe fifteen, twenty feet down in some other fucking sewer tunnel, and he just sitting on the ground like he Buddha, and I swear on my fucking life his skin was glowing, and his arms was already healed, the scars just blending in with the rest of his scars, and he was talking to the empty air right in front of him, and if I didn't know him, and know how Yahya felt about him, I'd a done thought he was plumb fucking crazy out his mind.

I lied there and watched him. I was nervous he was gonna see me, so I only just peeked over the edge of that hole. I could hear him saying shit like yes or no, yes or no, over and over again, saying why, saying how, saying no, I will not, I will not. He talked for like an hour or two hours and then I see him get real still and I know what that means and he starts seizing, worse than I ever seen before, his body literally coming up off the ground, he convulsing so fucking hard. And the noises he was making scared me, sounded like something I can only imagine hearing down in Hell, if there is one. And something felt wrong, like there was something else in there with him. Something dark and evil and old as the fucking sky, something with power that was beyond power, that was fucking so deep and black it was beyond power, and it made me shake and made the hair all over my body stick up and made me piss myself, right there I fucking pissed all over myself. Whatever it was, if it was anything at all, it scared me so fucking much I turned and got the fuck outta there fast as I fucking could.

I started going back to see Ben whenever I could. Didn't tell no one I had found him or knew where he was at. Most of the time he'd be in seizures, and they always bad. When he wasn't, he'd be talking or sometimes screaming, screaming into the blackness, screaming into the motherfucking abyss. Sometimes I'd go down and I'd feel that thing, that mean-ass evil fucking presence, and I'd turn and get the fuck out right away. Other times it'd come while I was there. Only once or twice it didn't come at all, and those was times when Ben was screaming, like he was keeping it at bay or some shit, like the sound of his scream had some fucking righteous power.

He was down there two weeks, three weeks, four weeks, six weeks. Down in that fucking nasty hole by himself. Far as I could see he never ate nothing, never drank nothing, never slept, never fucking left. And while he shoulda got sick or fucking died from fucking starving, it didn't happen. If anything I was seeing the opposite. He was seeming stronger, still skinny as fuck, but stronger. And it was looking like he could somehow be controlling the seizures. Like he could make himself go in and out of 'em when he wanted to go in and out of 'em. I'd hear him ask a question or say something, some heavy-ass shit like what happened before the Big Bang, or who were they, why were they, answer the problem of quantum gravity, can we unify the four fundamental forces. After he asked, he'd close his eyes and take a breath and open his eyes and be in that place, that place like eternity, and then he'd seize. And for the entire last week I went to see him, the seventh week he was in that foul fucking hole, he was seizing. And the entire time, that presence was with him, stronger, seeming somehow active, like it would ebb and flow, attack and retreat, made me wet my fucking pants every goddamn time, scared me to fucking death. At the end of the week, I went down and he was gone. Made me real fucking worried, scared something had happened, that the fucking evil had somehow got him. I went right back to our tunnel, was gonna get Yahya and take him back and tell him what I'd seen and what I'd been doing with myself and Ben and tell him we needed to find him and help. I went back as fast as I fucking could, ran in the darkness, ran from the darkness. And when I got back, Ben was there, with Yahya, looking just fine, like he'd never left, actually looking better than I'd ever seen him, skinny and shit, but glowing like some kind of fluorescent fucking lightbulb, even though I knew he hadn't had nothing to eat or drink in seven motherfucking weeks. He was back. And just like Yahya had seen in his visions, the end was near. The end was fucking near.

JOHN

I had heard there were people living down there. They were called mole people. There had been a book, a couple of documentaries. It was one of those things people would talk about at parties. Frankly, I didn't care at all. It didn't mean anything to me. If people wanted to live underground, let them. It relieved the taxpayer of the burden of them, and it kept them out of institutions. As long as they didn't cross my path in some way, I didn't give a shit.

The main function of my job was the tracking of weapons that came into New York City, and the apprehension and incarceration of those individuals who chose to illegally possess them. It is forbidden by law to own or possess a gun within city limits unless you have a permit, and permits are very difficult to get. Whenever we recovered a weapon, our first priority was discovering how it had entered the city. A gun dealer in upstate New York led us to the individuals in the tunnel. We came across the dealer when a gang member in southeast Queens arrested for murder was found in possession of an illegal handgun. The suspect had not, as is standard procedure with gang members and murderers, removed the serial numbers from the weapon, which allowed us to trace it. When we arrested the gun dealer for selling weapons to individuals who did not have the required license, he made a deal with us to keep himself out of prison and started providing us with the identities of other individuals to whom he had sold weapons. At that point, he told us about the group in the tunnel, who had bought approximately sixty weapons from him, and thousands of rounds of ammunition.

It wasn't easy finding them. There are a large number of abandoned tunnels under the city, some of which haven't been entered in decades. We initially undertook a search of the tunnels, which was fruitless. The gun dealer had told us that the members of the group, who he described as apocalyptic wackos, made their money begging on the street, and that they all had long scars on their arms. We started looking for individuals who matched that description, and after eight months found two of them, one a male and one a female. We put them under surveillance and found the tunnel where they, along with approximately thirty other individuals, were living.

We knew very little about them when we executed search warrants on them. There was some worry we might be entering a situation similar to that of the Branch Davidians in Waco, Texas, where a group of heavily armed religious fanatics, followers of a messianic leader named David Koresh, engaged a federal task force, which held them under siege for fifty-one days, until the Davidians' compound caught on fire and eighty people, including seventeen children, died. Fortunately, that was not the case.

Approximately fifty law enforcement personnel entered the tunnel through four different access points. Almost all of the individuals residing in the tunnel were asleep, and the three that weren't were taken into custody without incident.

I met Ben when we were interrogating the suspects, who were being held at the MCC, the federal correctional center in lower Manhattan. We had found more than three hundred firearms and ten thousand rounds of ammunition in their compound, along with small amounts of cocaine and marijuana. They were also in possession of a large number of knives, swords, and spears. When we ran their prints, we were able to ascertain the identities of all of them except for two, and all of them had records, most for things like drug possession and theft, though a few also had assault convictions. Of the two we could not identify, one went by the name of Yahya and was recognized by all of them as their leader. The other identified himself as Ben Jones.

Yahya refused to speak. He literally did not answer a single question we posed to him, nor did he request a lawyer. He stared directly into the eyes of both myself and the other agent interrogating him, and never said a thing. We assumed it was a ploy to intimidate us, but having been in rooms with drug lords, serial killers, and terrorists, I didn't find him particularly frightening or off-putting. I did Ben on my own. As with Yahya, his prints and DNA came back clean, and there was no record of him in any law enforcement database. And though there had been extensive media coverage of the raid, we had yet to release pictures of any of the arrestees to any media outlets, and had yet to receive any public help in making a positive identification.

Before I entered the room where Ben was being held, shackled to the floor at his ankles and to the table at his wrists, I looked in on him through a one-way window. One of my colleagues was standing near the window, observing him. He sat absolutely still, his eyes closed. He was wearing a jumpsuit, so I could not see his arms or body, but his head and face were badly scarred. His hair was on the short side, black, dirty, and disheveled. He was incredibly thin, the veins in his neck and forehead and cheeks plainly visible. Usually people who are being interrogated for the first time are incredibly nervous and anxious; the only ones who are calm, as calm as he was, are usually extremely hardened criminals. I asked my colleague if he had observed anything unusual. He said the man looks like a fucking freak, and he hasn't moved at all in the last hour, and if I didn't know better, I'd say he wasn't breathing. I laughed and entered the room.

Ben did not move or acknowledge me in any way. I waited for a few moments, assuming he would, but he did not. He was absolutely still, eerily still, still the way large bodies of water can be still, the way they don't appear to be moving, don't appear to be alive, but you know they are. I spoke.

My name is Agent John Guilfoy. I'd like to ask you a few questions.
He slowly opened his eyes. I hadn't had any contact with him during the arrests and hadn't seen his eyes when observing him, and I had never seen anything like them. At least, not naturally. They were black, obsidian black, the black of silence, the black of death, the black of what I imagine it must be like before birth. They startled me, scared me. I waited for him to say something, and I waited until I was over the shock of his eyes, and I spoke again.
Do you understand why you're here?
Yes.
Have you been treated well?
Doesn't matter.
I'm going to tell you upfront that the more cooperative you are with us, the easier things will be for you.
He smiled, laughed to himself.
Is there something funny about that?
Go on with your questions.
We've been trying to identify you, and you haven't turned up in any of our computer databases. I'm wondering if you can help us in any way.
I gave you my name.
Is it your real name?
I consider it so.
Is there another one we should be checking?
There have been a few.
Such as?
None of them will be of any use to you.
Try me.
He smiled again, didn't say a word, waited for me.

I stared at him, tried to intimidate him. I might as well have been staring at a rock. He was silent and still and unmoving. I spoke again.
Do you understand the charges against you?
Yes.
You understand they are extremely serious?
If you say so.
You're looking at years, maybe decades in prison.
Yes.
That doesn't bother you?
No.
Why?
I can be free anywhere, just as someone can be imprisoned anywhere.
Is that something your leader taught you?
I don't have a leader.
No?
No.
Yahya was not your leader?
My friend.
A dangerous friend.
If you say so.
He and his followers, amongst whom we count you, were in possession of hundreds of weapons and thousands of rounds of ammunition.
I possess nothing.
Did you know of the weapons' existence?
Yes.
Then according to the laws of the government of the United States, you were in possession of them.
He smiled again.
If you say so.

Do you find this amusing?
Yes.
Why?
I think your laws are silly.
Why is that?
People should be allowed to live and act as they
choose.
Not if they endanger or impose on other people.
No one in that tunnel was imposing on or
endangering anyone.
I would disagree.
As is your right.
You were living illegally on public land and hoarding
weapons designed to kill people.
If the land is public, why can't we use it?
Because it was designated for other purposes.
And how can the most heavily armed, most
militarized government in the history of civilization
tell its own citizens they can't arm themselves in
preparation for the coming annihilation?
The coming annihilation?
Yes.
The apocalypse?
If you want to call it that.
You believe it's coming?
Yes.
The seals have been broken and the signs are
appearing?
No.
The Bible says so?
It does, but those words mean nothing to me.
Christ is coming back to do battle with the Devil?

Is that what you believe?
What I believe is irrelevant. I want to know what you believe.
I've told you.
This have something to do with Allah?
It has nothing to do with religion.
Then how do you know?
Look around you.
And what will I see?
That it's coming to an end.
And you can see it?
In a way.
And it's coming soon?
Yes.
I took a deep breath. I wasn't sure if he was a fanatic or mentally ill. In either case, interrogation is virtually useless. Fanatics don't break unless extreme techniques are used, and those sorts of techniques were forbidden in my branch of the government, and whatever the mentally ill say is considered unreliable, and is usually unusable in court. He closed his eyes and started taking deep breaths through his nose. I asked him if he was okay, and he slowly nodded. I asked him if he needed something to eat or drink, and he slowly shook his head. He just breathed, and I waited. After a minute or so, I thought I'd leave him alone, grab a cup of coffee, and come back and try again. When I stood up, he opened his eyes, and he spoke.
I can take it away.
Excuse me?
I can take it away from you.

What are you talking about?
I'm sorry. Terribly sorry.
What are you sorry for?
For your loss.
What the fuck are you talking about?
You lost a child.
I was stunned. I was shot in the line of duty during my first year as an agent, shot in the shoulder with a .38 caliber revolver. The bullet entered my shoulder and exited my back. Ben's statement shocked, hurt, confused, and scared me more than that shot, more than anything in my life, except the event to which he was referring. There was no way he should have known. He had never seen or heard of me before I entered the room. I had asked all of my colleagues not to talk to me about it. We had not released an obituary, so it had not appeared in any sort of media. At the time, I believed there was no way he could have known, though that belief certainly changed.

I sat back down. I looked at him. He hadn't moved. He just stared at me and waited for me to say something. I couldn't speak, and if I had tried, I would have broken down. I stared at the table and clenched my jaw and thought about my little boy, about the first time I saw him, immediately after he was born, about the first time I held him, two minutes later, about a picture, which I could not look at until after I met Ben, of me and him and his mother, who I am no longer with, taken just after we brought him home. I think about his room in our house, about his first step, about his first word, which was Dadda. I replay his life in my head, and I think about how happy we were for the two years we were together. And then he started twitching, and having trouble walking, and he went into the hospital and he never came out and my life fell apart, except for my life at work, which was the only thing I could cling to in order to stay sane. I lost everything else when I lost my little boy. I lost everything that mattered to me.

Ben waited until I looked up. I can only imagine what my face must have looked like, certainly not the cool calm federal agent trying to be an intelligent, convincing, and intimidating interrogator. He spoke.
Release one of my hands.
I can't do that.
Yes, you can.
I won't do it.
You'll be able to walk through your front door without crying. You'll be able to sleep at night. You'll be able to call her, and tell her you miss her, and you'll be able to love again, and live again.
Fuck you.
I know how much it hurts.
You don't know fucking shit.
Release my hand.
You don't know what the fuck you're talking about, you crazy fuck.
I wish I didn't, but I do.
You motherfucker.
I can take it away.
You're a fucking freak.
Call me whatever you need to call me.

I want to know how you knew.
By looking at you.
Tell me how the fuck you knew.
I did.
This is not some fucking joke here.
I'm just trying to help you.
You're gonna help me? You in shackles and a jumpsuit and twenty years hanging over your fucking head?
If you let me.
I stared at him. I didn't know what to say. I was confused and angry and in pain. He scared me. He scared me more than anyone I had ever been in a room with, anyone I'd ever met, anyone I'd ever seen. Most people, as dangerous or violent as they may be, are easy to figure out. They come from somewhere, and they have experiences that have shaped them, and they have soft spots, weaknesses, places inside where you can open them up.
Ben wasn't like anyone I'd ever met, watched, or interviewed, he wasn't like anyone I'd ever heard about. He was absolutely impregnable. At the same time, he wasn't putting up defenses, and didn't appear to have any. He made me think of something I read when I was in college about Buddha, something that described his physical presence and his state of being. It said he was soft as iron, hard as rain, quiet as thunder, and still as a hurricane. Our professor explained the paradox of the description, that iron is one of the hardest substances on earth but also malleable enough to be shaped into anything we want it to be, that water is fluid and yielding, but strong enough to carve canyons.

That while thunder shakes the ground we walk on, a thunderstorm is also a peaceful and serene event, and that while hurricanes are among the most destructive forces we know of, the eye of the hurricane is an incredibly calm place, an eerily and almost otherworldly calm place. Ben stared back at me. He didn't move, and if he blinked, I didn't see it. He just took me in with his eyes, those bottomless black eyes. And our session as agent and suspect ended, and our conversation as two men, two men trying to live and be alive and find their way, which is all any human being can really do in this life, began. He spoke.

Despite your earlier statements, you believe in God?

Yes, I do.

And you have sought God out in order to deal with your grief?

I have.

You have gotten down on your knees and cried, and pleaded, and begged for relief, and for answers?

Yes.

Has your God answered you?

No.

What version of God do you believe in?

I'm Christian. Episcopal.

Your priest has counseled you?

Yes.

And he is well-intentioned, but he has left you empty?

Yes.

Has he spoken to your God about you?

What do you mean?

Has he spoken to him, the way I speak to you,
the way you speak to other people?
No one speaks to God that way.
And yet you keep trying, because you believe at
some point your God will answer your prayers?
I hope.
Hope is an illusion, a carrot dangling.
Hope keeps me going.
Going towards what?
I don't know.
Your God offers you hope. Hope offers you nothing.
You should seek another way.
What would that be?
I've told you.
Let you go.
I don't care if you let me go. I don't care if I'm in
a cell for the rest of my life. I'm telling you, if you
release one of my arms, and believe in what I tell
you, and trust me for a brief moment, I can do
what your imaginary God, your fairytale God,
a God no one has ever seen or spoken to and who
has not relieved your pain or provided you with
the answers you seek, cannot do.
I could lose my job.
If that's more important to you.
He sat there and waited. I looked away, towards
the glass, and wondered if my colleague was
watching us or listening to us. We also record all
interrogations, so video was a concern. Agents are
given a certain leeway with suspects. If we think
giving a suspect space or room to move might help
them open up, we are allowed to do it. If we think

giving something to eat or drink will motivate them, we are allowed to do it. This, though, wasn't anything like that. This was entirely personal. And it involved physical contact, which was expressly forbidden. It was against regulations. But I had been in so much pain for so long. I had been haunted and terrorized and destroyed by images of my dying child, of the pain he felt as he went, of the fear he must have experienced as his body failed, of the horror of the moment when he stopped breathing, with my wife and me holding his hands. I knew I would never recover from my boy's death, and I doubted the pain would ever subside, but I decided that if Ben could relieve me of it for a minute or an hour or a day, it would be worth whatever penalty I would have to pay.

I reached into my pocket and took out a key. I leaned across the table and unlocked the shackle that kept his right arm bound to the table. He did not move as I did it, but once his arm was free, and I was still leaning over the table, his arm shot up and he grabbed me and pulled me towards him with a strength that no one who looked like him should have possessed. I felt my feet leave the ground. He held me with my head on his shoulder, and he started whispering in my ear. I don't know what language it was, though I believe it was either ancient Hebrew or Aramaic. I was terrified, and I didn't know if he had tricked me and was going to hurt me, or if he was actually doing what he said he could do. And in a way it didn't matter, because he was so strong that I couldn't have gotten away if I had wanted to.

He kept whispering, and my body went limp. It felt like someone had just emptied it of everything, like what I imagine people who die and come back say they feel while they're dead and drifting towards the light. My emotions, my soul, and my physical strength, my pain and sorrow and struggle, it was all gone. I felt completely empty. I felt like I had always wished I could feel: peaceful, and simple, and uncomplicated. I wanted to be that way forever, to stay with him forever, my head on his shoulder, his voice in my ear. I heard the door open behind me and I heard people come rushing into the room. Someone had been watching us and assumed he was hurting me and I knew it was going to end. Ben stopped speaking whatever language he had been using and just before I was pulled away he said I love you.

I was carried out of the room. The last image I have of him before the door slammed shut is of one of my colleagues spraying mace into his face. I was later told he was also shot with tasers and beaten with billy clubs, and when the beating was over, he was carried out of the room, bleeding and unconscious. I was taken to a hospital, where I checked out normal and went home a few hours later and slept easily for the first time since the day my son went into the hospital. I was transferred off the case and Ben was bailed out two days later. I never saw him again, though I did try to find him. I wanted to thank him for doing whatever he had done, and for giving me a new chance at life, for teaching me to love as he had loved me. I wasn't surprised when I heard what happened to him. We live in a cruel and unfortunate world. The longer I am in it, the more I believe he was right. Hope is an illusion, a dangling carrot, something to keep us going, but going towards what? It all is ending. His end, cruel, unnecessary, and cloaked in a veil of religion and righteousness, like so much of what's wrong with what we've built, will be but the beginning.

LUKE

I'm a white man, brothers and sisters. From the great state of Mississippi. Born a Christian white man and raised with a strong sense of my Southern heritage and the belief that I was part of a God-given few: the few who founded this country, who built this country, and who run this country, even when it appears someone else might be doing it. I was raised in Jackson, Mississippi. A beautiful town, brothers and sisters, a beautiful town. My family had been in the state for two hundred years, and most of us had never seen a reason to go anywhere else. We'd been settlers, soldiers, plantation owners, slave traders, slave owners. We'd fought for the South in the Civil War, and a good many of us had died for her. We'd been gamblers, farmers, Indian hunters, sheriffs, thieves, lawyers, bootleggers, congressmen, and senators. My daddy was an oilman. Spent his life searching for the black gold, that thick, dark, elusive money juice. He bought and drilled some land in Laurel, Mississippi, and he struck it, brothers and sisters, struck it deep and made himself a bundle. When I was a youngster, he lived in Laurel during the week, working and spending his nights sleeping with his black mistress. My momma and I lived in Jackson, and my momma spent her nights sleeping with the golf pro, the tennis pro, the local police, and just about anyone else who wanted to sleep with her. On weekends my momma and daddy got drunk and pretended they loved each other. They went to cocktail parties and horse races. They played golf and went to events at the club. Occasionally they threw things at each other, and occasionally my daddy hit her. I didn't think it was anything but normal. Even after my momma killed herself, my brothers and sisters, I didn't think it was anything but normal. I just thought maybe my momma had got got by the Devil, or that she had had a bout with some kind of female insanity. Lord knows how many believe those kinds of things happen. Lord knows.

Back to me. I must declare that I grew up like a little prince. I had fancy clothes and fancy food and went to the fanciest schools in Jackson. I did whatever I wanted and acted however I wanted and I got whatever I wanted. I had black women who cooked and cleaned and cared for me, and though my momma claimed to be raising me, it was really them. And that was the way it was with all the white kids I knew, and we just thought it was the way of the world. When I finished high school, I went to Oxford to attend the University of Mississippi, where I lived like a gentleman prince. I didn't hardly ever go to class, because I knew I had a job waiting for me. I was the president of my fraternity, where we drank beer and played cards every night and flew the Confederate flag right outside our front door. And when I wasn't drinking and gambling, me and all my friends did whatever we could to get coeds to sleep with us, including forcing them to do it. It was four years of what I thought was bliss, brothers and sisters, before I knew what bliss was. There was no responsibility to myself, my family, or any sort of higher authority. My loyalty and faith resided within my own ego, and within the bonds established at the fraternity house, where, by the way, we had black women working for us cleaning our clothes and cooking our meals. And yes, brothers and sisters, occasionally we'd try to sleep with them, and if by God they said no, we'd force them to do it.

At the end of college, I went to work for my daddy, supervising his wells. I married myself a nice young blonde girl, whose daddy was in the oil business in Louisiana and had known my daddy for twenty years. We had ourselves a big wedding at her parents' plantation house, where everyone got drunk and ate too much and generally acted like we were Southerners before we lost the war. We settled in Gulfport, 'cause it was closer to her family, and in six months' time she was pregnant. We had ourselves a little girl, and then another. They were cute little things, brothers and sisters, believe me, they were pretty as buttons the both of them. I settled into a pattern like my daddy's. I was working in Laurel and coming home on weekends. Though I said I wasn't going to do some of the things my daddy did, I did them anyway. I found myself a black ladyfriend and spent my evenings in bars with her and in bed with her. I played some cards and lost some money. I drove a big fast car and yelled at the people who worked for me, even if they didn't deserve it, and I fired 'em when I felt like it, even if there wasn't a good reason. I was living a bad, bad life, and I didn't know any better. Some would say, and I have said at times myself, that I was singing with Satan, running with the Devil, walking down the dark dirty path of the demon Beelzebub. But I thought that was the way life was supposed to be led by a man of my type, brothers and sisters, a rich white man from the South.

As it is in life, what rises must fall. The mighty become the meek. Giants are stricken and empires razed. And even though nobody ever thinks it's ever gonna happen to them, it sure as shit does, brothers and sisters, and I can attest to that. My fall was swift and pitiless, like a box of rocks falling off the back of a wagon. I started smoking crack, which was a newfangled thing, with one of my ladyfriends. I could not for the life of me stop smoking it. Simultaneous to that little bit of nastiness, my daddy's wells ran dry and he had a falling-out with my father-in-law. Simultaneous to that, my daddy's stockbroker disappeared to Brazil with a mistress and all of our money. I stayed in Mississippi under the auspices of helping my family navigate the turbulent and troubled waters of financial Armageddon, while actually spending all my time in a cheap motel with a pipe and a torch and a stream of hookers. Upon returning home, I was greeted by my father-in-law, who had hired himself a private investigator, with a shotgun and some divorce papers. He told me my wife and beautiful daughters were in Louisiana, and if I tried seeing them or contacting them again I'd be strung up and castrated. Brothers and sisters, if you had seen the look in his eyes, you'd have known that was no joke.

So I went back to Laurel and smoked away everything I had left. And then I smoked away a whole bunch of what I didn't have. And then I started stealing things that weren't mine and smoking those. Brothers and sisters, I descended into the depths of Hell, where I laughed with Lucifer and made love to his dastardly disciples. I stayed there for three years, smoking and doping, hooking and whoring, wheeling, dealing, and stealing. When I was near a point where I believed I was shutting down and about to leave my earthly body, I had a revelation, brothers and sisters, a tremendous revelation, and I was born again, born again into the heart, soul, and spirit of the man who became my best friend and mentor, the man I believed to be the power and the glory, the mighty Almighty himself, the Prophet and the Son, our Judge and Redeemer, the Lord and Savior Jesus Christ.

It happened in a rotten old basement of a rotten old abandoned shack that a bunch of crack smokers used to hide out in and get high. We were like a bunch of rats. Gray and stinky and dirty, greedy and hungry, willing to crawl through a world of shit just to feed ourselves. I had been having some pains in my chest from lack of proper diet and too much of the drug and had been in a fight with another man over rocks he claimed I owed him. He showed up angry and fixing for a fight. I didn't want to fight, so I tried to ignore the man, which made him angry as a cut snake. He picked up a brick and smashed it right against my head, knocking me literally and figuratively right into kingdom come. When I woke up, brothers and sisters, there was light streaming through a broken window and coming right across my face. I heard the words, in a deep, strong pure voice, you must be born again. I didn't know who it was so I said who's that and the voice said Jesus Christ and I said how do I know it's you and he said look into your heart, my son, and I said what do you want me to do, Lord, what do you want me to do and he said you must be born again. I said I am, Jesus, I am, what do you want me to do now and he said spread the word of God the Father, preach the truth of the Gospels of the Son, and fill the hearts of sinners with the spirit of the Holy Ghost. I said I will, Jesus, I promise I will.

The light went away and I stood up and brushed myself off and walked out of the hellhole and went straight to the nearest church and got down on my knees and prayed. I spent two days praying. No food, no water, and no sleep. When approached by the clergy of the church, I waved them off and said I'm conferring with the Lord, brother, I'll talk to you when I'm done. Sometimes it felt like the Lord was sitting right there next to me, chattering in my ear. Other times I wondered why the silences were so long. Near the end, I believed the Father himself, the omnipotent one, the creator of all that we know,

told me that I was to go to the one city on earth
that held the greatest number of sinners, and the
greatest amount of sin, and start a church and start
saving souls. So there I went, brothers and sisters,
to New York, New York.

I walked the entire way. Walked with the shoes
on my feet and the clothes on my back and a Bible
in my hand. I was depending on the kindness of
strangers to sustain me, and, brothers and sisters,
as cruel and ugly as this world can be, there is much
goodness still to be found in it. Within a day I had
a full belly. Within two I had new shoes and new
clothes. Within three I had a couple of dollars in my
pocket. On the fourth I got a haircut and a shave.
Everything was given to me by blessed strangers,
all of whom I considered angels in disguise, angels
from Heaven sent to aid me and guide me, sent,
brothers and sisters, to insure my mission was
successful. Every night I prayed for several hours,
slept for three or four, and walked the rest of the time.
And while I was walking, every few minutes, I said
in a manner I would call and consider loud and
proud, Lord, I love you, I'm a humble man and a
humble servant and I love you with my whole heart.
After twenty-two days on the road, I walked across
the George Washington Bridge.

It was worse than I expected. I thought it a sinners'
paradise, brothers and sisters, a giant whorehouse
being run by the Devil. I found myself a place at
a homeless shelter. I stood on street corners and

preached the gospel of the Lord. I went to Central Park, which at the time was a sinners' field, where drinking and drugging, robbing and stealing, all manner of sodomy and sexual perversity were practiced with impunity, and tried to convert people to the ways of the Lord. I preached in Union Square. On Wall Street. In Greenwich Village. I stood in the center of Times Square, brothers and sisters, and shouted the word of the Lord at the top of my lungs. I felt like there were so many souls to save, so many sinners, perverts, homosexuals, and Devil worshippers that needed turning or needed to be brought into the flock of Jesus. I preached all day, every day, and I have to say, brothers and sisters, because I believed what I was saying with all of my heart, it was quite wonderful.

I started wandering into the other boroughs of New York, looking far and wide for people ready to be born again. I got beaten in Staten Island by some men in a Cadillac and threatened with my life if I ever came back. Nobody in the Bronx spoke English, and if they did, they looked at me like they wanted to kill me. With all the Jews in Brooklyn, I didn't feel like there was a place for me. So I stayed in Queens, and saved a man, and then two, and then three. Brothers and sisters, within a few months I had my own flock. A fine flock. People who believed in the righteousness of my words, and believed that I was preaching the one true word. We started meeting in the back room of a dry cleaner owned by a man I had brought into the arms of Jesus. I started collecting money after every sermon to start a real church. People started telling other people about my relationship to God and his Son, the Lord and Savior Jesus Christ, about how I knew his words and his Gospels, about my personal connection to Heaven above us, and my flock grew until the dry cleaner couldn't hold us anymore. And it wasn't just the numbers, brothers and sisters; it couldn't hold the power of our worship and devotion to the Holy Spirit, and it couldn't hold our love for God and his Son, and it couldn't hold the prayers we were sending on high. Lord have mercy, those were righteous days.

So I moved the church. We got our own building, one that used to hold an auto supply store. It wasn't pretty, but worshipping the Lord isn't about beauty, it's about spirit and devotion, and that was not lacking, brothers and sisters, we had worship and devotion in abundance. Around that time is when I met Jacob and his family. Jacob was a seeker, a searcher, a man trying to find his way into the heart of the Savior. He just didn't know how or where to go or have anyone to show him. He had been raised Jewish, and being a Jew had left his heart empty and his soul in turmoil. We met when I was preaching on a street corner. He walked up and asked for a pamphlet and I gave him one on the Second Coming of Christ, which I told him I believed was nearly upon us. He asked me how I knew, and I said no one but the Father knew the day or the hour, not even the angels of Heaven or the Son himself, but that it was my duty as a Christian to keep watch, and that my heart told me I would see something soon. Jacob asked me if I wanted to meet the Messiah, because he knew him. It was like a lightning bolt struck me, brothers and sisters, like the hand of God reached into my heart and said yes, yes, yes, like the mission of my life and my church had suddenly been revealed to me, the way the missions of their lives had been revealed to so many of the Bible's holy men. I asked him who this Messiah was, and he told me his brother. I asked him how he knew, and he said since birth his brother had been identified by Orthodox rabbis as the Messiah, and that he met all the criteria and fulfilled all the signs. I told him the Jew Messiah and the Christ returned were different things, and his response was that Christ was the King of the Jews and that it would make sense that when he returned, he would return as the King of the Jews. The logic was simple and sound, and I knew he was right, in my heart, because God was telling me so. Christ would return as he lived and died and was resurrected by the Holy Father, as the King of the Jews. I asked him where this brother was, and he said he didn't know, that he had disappeared, but that he would come back someday. Most people in my position would have thought this kid was crazy. But I was a believer in the Father, and his messages, and his history of choosing prophets, and I believed he worked in mysterious and unknowable ways. So I believed, brothers and sisters, and I opened my heart to Jacob, and took him and his family into my church, where I taught them traditional Christian values, and helped them rid themselves of their

Jewish faith and their Jewish traditions. He became like a son to me, my closest advisor and my partner in the church, which continued to grow, and continued to save souls from the Hell of eternal damnation. And for years, we searched for Ben Zion Avrohom. We searched all over New York, all over America, and a few times we believed we had found his trail overseas, once in India, once in Africa, and once in China. We never lost hope, and I never believed the Father and his Son, Jesus Christ, were sending me on a journey that would not have an ending. I knew we would find Ben Zion, or that he would return to his family. And I believed he would lead us towards righteous glory.

And he did return. He returned, and Esther found him. And it was a glorious, glorious day. Only the church elders knew of our belief in and quest to find Ben. We had prayed daily for almost sixteen years, and yes, brothers and sisters, we believed our prayers had been answered by the mighty Father himself. The Messiah had arrived. Jesus Christ, our Lord and Savior, had returned. First time I saw Ben, I knew what he was and who he was. Oh my, he was a powerful thing to behold. It didn't matter that he was on life support, and had wires and tubes coming out of him everywhere. He was glowing, brothers and sisters, he had the glow of God upon him, the glow of angels, the glow of Heaven, the glow of the Holy Ghost, the glow of eternity. I fell to my knees and I prayed and I thanked the Lord God for including me in his plans and I asked him for the strength to carry out his wishes. And when he survived the accident the way he did, which only a divine being could have done, and when he started having his seizures and speaking to who we believed was the Holy Father himself, and when he started reciting Bible verses and knowing the most ancient of the holy languages, and not speaking in crazy tongues, like the Holy Ghost makes some people do, but speaking in the holy languages themselves, brothers and sisters, how could there be any doubt? When something is staring you in the face in your life, and you see it with your own two eyes and feel it within the beating of your heart, only a fool doesn't believe it to be true. And my momma might have raised a lot of things, but she didn't raise no fool.

We prayed for Ben to recover, though there was never any doubt that he would. We allowed the Jew rabbi to visit him, because Ben insisted on it. We believed Ben would leave the hospital and return to his family's home and would join the church, as we believed the Father had destined him to do. Both Jacob and I had had conversations with God about it, and believed God's word to be true. When Ben disappeared while meeting with the Jew rabbi, we believed that the rabbi had taken him somewhere. There was no reason for the Messiah, Christ returned, the Lord and Savior himself, to flee the arms of a loving family and a loving church, unless someone forced him to do it. Jews had been trying, and in many cases succeeding, to control the world for two thousand years. They killed our first

Messiah, had him nailed to the cross and killed him, though thankfully he did it to redeem us of our sins. I believed that in their hands the power of Christ would most likely be used for a diabolical end. At the same time, every good Christian worth his salt knows that Christians are dependent on the Jews to bring about the End of Days. They have to be living in Israel, and Israel has to exist, for the End of Days to happen. The Temple of Solomon must be rebuilt. The war of Armageddon will take place on their lands. The trumpets will sound, and the four horsemen will ride on across the desert plain, and the Rapture will occur. Jews are necessary for all of it. Evil, I believed, but necessary. So we watched the Jew rabbi. We had people follow him. We tried to tap his phone, but we couldn't make that happen. There was nothing out of the ordinary. He went about his business in a seemingly normal way. We prayed extra long, and extra hard, and we asked the Holy Father for a sign to help us find his Son, and we promised that if we got him back, we would not let him go again. We read MSM newspapers and watched MSM news shows, even though we knew they were full of lies and propaganda, even though we knew they were controlled by Jews and homosexuals, hoping for a clue.

I saw the newspaper article on the black man's apocalyptic tunnel cult. The idea of it made me sick to my stomach. I believed that human beings were the product of God's glory and created in his image, and I can tell you, brothers and sisters, God would not approve of men and women living like worms in the dirt, even if they were sinners. After it came out, though, the Jew rabbi started acting different. He went to a bank, had long meetings with a lawyer, and went to the federal correctional center. The private investigator we had tailing him did some research and found out there was a man being held with the crazy black man that fit Ben's description. We believed that it had to be the work of the Devil, who never sleeps, never rests, and is always working to foment sin and evil in the world. The black man was surely an agent of Lucifer, meant to capture the Son and hold him in an attempt to pervert him, and when that failed, because no one and nothing can pervert the Messiah, the Son of God, the Lord and Savior, to kill him.

We immediately went to a bail bondsman. We had been raising money for a new church, in part to celebrate the coming of the Lord, and knew it would be irrelevant if the Lord were in prison. We also believed that when the lawsuits Jacob was filing on behalf of Ben were settled or went to court, our coffers would be overflowing. So we pledged our money, and the building we owned that held the church at that time, as collateral for a bond. A couple of the elders were worried, but I told them, if money can't be used for the glory of God and his Son, what can it be used for? And we wanted and needed to beat the Jew rabbi, who we believed was doing the same thing, though his sources had identified the issue before we did. That's the way I believed it was with Jews. That they knew everything first. And that was one of the ways they sought to control the planet.

So we went to the federal correctional center downtown, which is a cesspool of sin and degradation. We went with a lawyer and asked for information about the prisoner they were calling John Doe #4. Can you imagine, brothers and sisters, calling the Messiah, the Son of God, Christ returned, John Doe #4? It was a disgrace. It was an abomination. And though we could not tell the authorities, who I believed were evil and in legion with the Jews and the Devil, who Ben was, I certainly let them hear some of my righteous fury. We first saw Ben in a visiting room. Jacob and I and our attorney, Caleb, a fine Christian who believed in the words of the Father and the Gospels of the Son. He was led in with his legs and arms shackled, like he was some slave. His face was bruised and swollen, one of his eyes was black, and his lip was cut. He looked like he hadn't had a meal in a month.

We tried talking to him. He was very polite, but very distant. I assumed he was on some type of mind-control drug, which the government is known to have and use against people they believe threaten them. And the Messiah would certainly be a threat. The Messiah is going to bring it all to an end, or at least herald the end. Jacob hugged him and said we were going to take care of him. Ben said he was fine to take care of himself. Jacob said we were going to get him out of there as fast as we could, and Ben said he was perfectly happy where he was. Jacob told him how worried we were and how we had been searching for him, and Ben just closed his eyes and smiled. When I asked him if he wanted to pray with us, he told me I was free to pray, but it wasn't something that he did. I asked him if I had heard him correctly, that he didn't pray, and he said yes, you heard me correctly. It was mystifying. We were expecting a glorious reception from a holy man anxious to get into the world to spread the word of God. A holy man in the tradition of the biblical holy men. A holy man like Moses, or Isaiah, or John the Baptist. I was expecting to see Jesus before me. That ain't what I got.

We bailed him out anyway. I went to court, and we pledged all of the church's funds, along with the deed to the church property. Some of the other church elders thought we were risking too much, but I believed that if you can't risk everything for the Lord, and I mean everything, brothers and sisters, your life and money and family, then you must not truly believe in the Lord. For if you truly believe in anything in this life, be it God, be it love, be it money or greed, be it anything, you will risk all for it. And I did, hallelujah I did, I believed and pledged it all. I did not hesitate, not for one second, and in doing so, I thanked the Lord Almighty for giving me the opportunity to serve him. The judge issued a decree stating that Ben would be released into my custody and the custody of his family. He required that an ankle bracelet be attached so that Ben could be tracked. I objected, because I believed the tracker would be used by the Jew and his allies to track and capture him, that surely the device must be part of the Jews' plan, and by association, Lucifer's plan. Caleb told me to keep quiet, that the judge was also a Jew. I knew then that keeping Ben safe was going to be a battle. Jews, blacks, sinners, and perverts, we were going to have to fight all of them.

When we actually took possession of Ben, in a small room at the correctional center, I was with Caleb. Caleb was also a good Evangelical man, a member of our church, a man of Christ who believed in traditional American family values. He had been an Episcopalian, but had left what I believed to be a perverted faith, a faith that allowed women and homosexuals a say where they did not deserve one, a faith that was not in line with the real values of the Lord and his Son, and found the true Christ. He had become an alcoholic, despite attending his perverted church's services every week, which to us was a testament to the weak and blasphemous nature of his church's faith, and started hitting his wife and children without cause. He was born again after he had a car accident. He was driving and turned around to discipline one of his children. As he was reaching for the child, he lost control of the car and slammed into a tree. He woke up in the hospital and thankfully, brothers and sisters, his wife and children were fine. He was better than fine. He said the Lord had spoken to him in the second before he hit that tree. And the Lord Almighty, in all of his grace, wisdom, and mercy, had told him he would spare him if he devoted his life to his one and only Son, the Lord and Savior Jesus Christ. Devote he did, brothers and sisters. He left the firm he was working for in Manhattan, what we called the Devil's Island, and opened a practice devoted to Christian causes. He fought for the unborn children murdered in abortion clinics, he fought against laws granting queers and faggots the rights normal, healthy people deserve, he fought for prayer in school and for creationism to be taught in science, he fought for the right of Christian men to bear whatever arms they choose in order to protect their families. He was a nightmare for the ACLU, which we believed did nothing but promote sin and perversity and sought to control and subvert Christians for the good of the Jews.

Ben walked in, shackled. Both Caleb and I fell to our knees and bowed. We bowed before the Messiah, as one always should, brothers and sisters. We had met Ben before and had not bowed before him. We weren't sure, before our first meeting, what he would be like. No one, not even the holiest of the holy, not even the most righteous and pure of the Lord's flock, had met the Son of God before. He was not what we expected, and when we talked about it later, we realized that we should not have expected anything. God is God. Omnipotent and almighty. The creator of Heaven and Earth. The Judger and the Redeemer. We did not know God's ways and intentions. We did not know God's plan. Only he could know. And he revealed what he wanted to reveal. And we believed, and I still believe, that Ben was his beloved Son. And we also looked back, brothers and sisters. We looked back to Jesus Christ, the Lord and Savior, the man who sacrificed himself on the cross for the sins of humanity. We looked back to the man we believed had been reborn in the holy vessel of Ben Zion Avrohom. Christ was beloved by twelve men, twelve believers, twelve disciples, twelve apostles. He wandered the Holy Land, preaching the word of God. His message was unlike anything the world had heard before. His message was pure and beautiful and true, and straight from the Holy Father himself. His message was the future, and the world isn't always ready for the future. The world isn't always ready for the truth. He was a radical, brothers and sisters. A radical unlike any the world has seen, a radical sired for man by the ultimate authority on man. Christ was thought of as crazy by many. He was mocked and scorned. The rabbis of Israel laughed at him and dismissed him. His message was misunderstood and misinterpreted. There were only twelve who knew him in their hearts while he graced the earth. It took thousands of years for his true followers to find him, brothers and sisters, thousands of years. For people like me and my flock to be born again into the bosom of his love. Thousands of years and untold numbers of false churches with deviant messages. Thousands of years of popes and preachers and ministers and reverends and pastors spewing aberrant, heretical sermons and issuing meaningless edicts. They may have meant well, and their intentions may have been pure, but that does not relieve them of their roles as apostates. We determined, after much counsel and many days of prayer, and after untold numbers of conversations with God and with Christ, and after any number of intimate experiences with the Holy Spirit, that Ben was indeed the Messiah. We needed to accept him as such, and treat him as such, and protect him as such, and covet him as such, and worship him as such.

So he entered and we kneeled and bowed. I have never been so humbled, brothers and sisters, not even at the moment I gave my heart and soul to the Lord and was born again. As the guards took his shackles off, both of us prayed, and thanked the Father for his Son, and thanked him for the opportunity to serve him. The guards left but told Ben to stay and wait for the ankle bracelet. He stood above us, both of us still on our knees, still bowed. He spoke.
You posted my bail?
I spoke.
Yes, my Lord.
Thank you.
We are humbled and honored, my Lord.
Why are you kneeling?
We kneel before you, the Prophet, the Son, the Messiah, our Lord and Savior. We kneel before you, Christ reborn.
Please stand up.
We both looked up and stood. And there he was, brothers and sisters, the Prophet, the Son, the Messiah, our Lord and Savior. There he was, Christ

reborn. I could use words to describe him, but there aren't any that would mean anything. For the most profound experiences in our lives, and in the world, words are worth nothing. Can you describe love? Or death? Can you describe what it really feels like the first time you see your child? Or the first time your heart gets broken? You can try, brothers and sisters, but it won't come close to describing what it really was, or what it really felt like. And it was like that with Ben. He stood in front of us, scarred and beaten, sick and starved, the Lamb of God, the Light of the World, Ruler of the New Covenant, King of Kings, and we were awed. I spoke.
We are here to serve you, Mighty God.
I am a man.
As was Christ.
Yes.
Are you born of God?
We all are born the same.
Are you not the Prophet, the Son, the Messiah? Are you not our Lord and Savior?
Do you believe I am?
I do, my Lord. I do.
He stared at me, a slight smile on his beautiful face, his eyes black and motionless. It was a peaceful smile, still and calm, like the smile I had seen on so many images of Christ. Before I could say anything else, two men came in with an ankle bracelet and asked Ben to sit. They fitted the bracelet and explained how it worked, told him that the court would approve areas where he was allowed to be, and that the bracelet would track his movements. If he strayed from the

approved areas, he would be arrested and his bail would be revoked. I was sick to my stomach. Outraged and offended. The idea that the government and the Jews could restrict the movement of the Messiah, the man the world had waited two thousand years to see, could track his movements like he was some dog? It made me want to kill someone, brothers and sisters, and it made me look forward to the reckoning of the Rapture. They would all burn. Burn in Hell, where they belonged. Burn while I sat at the right hand of the Lord Almighty. Burn while I enjoyed the spoils of Heaven as the pastor who saved the Messiah from death in prison at the hands of God's enemies. I believed they would all burn.

The men left and we were alone with Ben. He was wearing rags. Loose black pants and a black t-shirt and black plastic sandals. Rags I wouldn't want to see on the worst sinner, regardless of whether they deserved it or not. We had brought him a fine white suit. One we had purchased with church funds from the best suit maker in Queens. He refused to wear it, said he would wear the clothes that he had. I told him his family was waiting for him. He smiled and said nothing. I told him we were at his disposal, and that we wanted to help him spread the word of God on earth. He stood and asked if we were ready to leave. We opened the door and motioned for him to lead us. He stepped forward, and we walked down a hallway and took an elevator to the ground floor. Ben said nothing. As we walked out of the correctional center, three men stood outside the door.

One was in a shirt and tie. He wore a gun, so he must have been some type of federal agent. The other two wore the uniforms that all of the correctional officers wore. They were clearly waiting for Ben. I immediately thought they must be assassins. I was ready to defend and die for the Messiah. Ready to demonstrate my love for him and for his Father. Ben smiled at them, and walked towards them. He stopped in front of each of them and hugged them. They held him tight. Like you hold someone going to war, or going into prison and not coming out again. Like you hold someone you love and you know you are never going to see again. He spoke softly to each them. Softly, so only they could hear what he was saying. And I swear, brothers and sisters, I swear on my life, I saw them change. They physically changed. Like they went from being weighed down to floating on air. Like they had been sick and were suddenly well. And when Ben pulled away from the last of them, he left them, and he did not look back.

We had a car waiting. We had gone first-class. A long black stretch limousine, with a driver in a uniform and a hat. Just like my daddy used to ride in sometimes. We had three Bibles inside and hoped to read with Ben as we drove back. We had chilled water and juices. It was first-class all the way, but Ben did not want to get in the car. He wanted to walk back to Queens. He wanted to walk across the Devil's Island and breathe its polluted air and mix with its deviant citizens. We tried to talk him out of it, but he just walked away. There was no choice but to walk with him.

It was a mighty powerful thing, brothers and sisters. Walking the streets of the Devil's playground with one of the two men ever created powerful and pure enough to do combat with him. He walked slowly. He didn't say a word. We walked on either side of him. He moved his eyes slowly as he walked, looking back and forth. He was clearly seeing everything, hearing everything, knowing everything. Every now and then he would close his eyes and take a deep breath through his nose. Every now and then he would take a step in the direction of someone, usually someone who was poor and dirty, more than one of them a homeless drunk or drug addict. He would lift his hand very slightly towards them. I saw him do it towards a crying woman. A man in a suit on a cell phone. A cop in the middle of the street. A woman in a nurse's outfit running down the sidewalk. An Arab hot dog vendor and some Africans selling fake handbags. He would do it to children. He did it to all of the children he saw.

It felt like hours and hours we were walking. Brothers and sisters, my feet and legs were hurting. We went up the east side of the island. We went through Chinatown, the Lower East Side, the East Village. There were freaks and sinners everywhere. Drug addicts and homosexual perverts. Caleb and I each held our Bible in our right hand. We wore crosses around our necks. We stayed close to Ben.

He did not speak, so we did not speak to him.
We walked through Union Square, up Park Avenue, through Grand Central Station, where hordes of sinners got off trains to indulge in their foulest fantasies. He kept lifting his hand, just a little bit. Always towards people who made me sick, who were clearly in legion with Lucifer. People I would have avoided; people I believed the Lord would have condemned. I was happy when we came out of the station, which felt like the bowels of Hell. I was overjoyed when I felt God's light on my face again and could breathe God's air.

We turned east and started walking towards the Queensborough Bridge. There was a big wind coming off the East River, as if it was keeping the fumes of evil away from Queens and Brooklyn. We entered the walkway to the bridge on Second Avenue and started crossing. It runs along the south side, facing all of lower Manhattan, the towers rising with all of Satan's menace. The walk is a simple sidewalk. There's a stone wall three or four feet tall, with a chain link fence built into the top that is about ten feet tall.
The wind was blowing fierce, brothers and sisters, whistling. Caleb said he believed it was the echo of the Lord's trumpeters announcing the return of his Son to the one true church, our church. And that was what it felt like. We were crossing the river.
The Messiah, the Son of God, who we had just saved from the clutches of the government and the Jews, and who had walked through the city, a newer version of the valley of the shadow of death, spreading

blessings and grace, was leading us. Of course the Heavenly Father, the Lord Almighty, the Ruler of all there was and ever will be, was heralding our return. It was a righteous moment, a truly righteous moment. One of the most powerful any man, woman, or child on this earth has experienced. I can't imagine anything greater. Praise be to the glory. Praise be, brothers and sisters.

As we got close to the middle of the bridge, and the stench of Manhattan was fading, and the Lord's trumpets were blowing, Ben stepped towards the wall. Before we could say a word, he had climbed to the top of the chain link fence. I swear I saw him jump onto the wall and climb the fence, but later, after everything else, Caleb said he floated up, like a gust from Heaven lifted him and placed him there. And there he stood. On a wire a quarter of an inch thick running through the top of the fence. He was a couple hundred feet above the river. His hands were at his side. He closed his eyes and he just stood there.

We didn't know what to do. I was terrified he would fall, though I also believed that if he did he would not die. Caleb got down on his knees and started to pray, saying Father God, I kneel humbly before you in Jesus' name, thank you for allowing me to serve you, Father God, and please show me a sign, Father God, so that I may serve you as you wish. He stared at Ben, said it again and again. The wind started gusting, and I joined him on my knees, and Ben just stood there. He shouldn't have been able to stand on that fence. He shouldn't have been able to keep his balance. The wind should have taken him away. The sky was blue above him, clouds drifting slowly past. Cars were blowing by behind us on the bridge and we could hear them honking and people yelling from their windows. The quiet drift of the river was whispering beneath us. And the wind, still there, was heralding his presence. It was the most beautiful moment of my life.

I don't know how long he stayed there. It could have been two minutes or two hours. I joined Caleb in prayer and I lost myself in the power of the Holy Spirit, which we could feel around us the way you can feel joy at a wedding or pain at a funeral. When he came down, he didn't say anything; he just started walking again. We stood and followed, and neither of us said anything. Like I said, brothers and sisters, sometimes words just don't work.

His family was waiting for him at their apartment. Our brother in Christ Jeremiah was with them. The women, as was their duty, had prepared a meal. A simple meal. A meal just like what we thought the Big Man, JC himself, would have eaten: rice, fish, bread, water, and wine. Caleb and I were dead tired when we got there. Ben didn't seem any different; he was fresh as a daisy. I wished he was in nicer clothes, or cleaner ones, but the Savior makes his own choices. I did not believe I was one to question them. He reached for the door, which was always locked with three locks, and it opened. He stepped inside.

It was the first time he had been inside his family's home in sixteen years. His mother immediately started crying. He stepped forward and put his arms around her and said I love you, Mother. She started sobbing. She put her head on his chest. He put his hands on the sides of her face, and lifted her face and looked into her eyes. He said it again, I love you, Mother, and I am happy to be home. He stepped away and towards his sister. She was looking very, very nervous. Her hands were shaking and her lips quivering. He smiled and said hello, Esther, I love you. He kissed her on the forehead and gave her a long hug. He stepped away and looked to Jacob. Jacob was very somber, and very serious. He looked very much, brothers and sisters, like the young man of God that he was. He was wearing a suit and a tie. He knew he was greeting his brother, his flesh and blood, but he also knew he was greeting the most important person to walk the earth in two thousand years. He was greeting the Son of God. Ben stepped forward and hugged him and said hello, Jacob, I love you. Jacob put his arms around him and hugged him back. Hugged him strong and tight, like a man should hug the Lord. It was the first time, in all the years we'd prayed and worshipped and studied the Bible together, in all the years, brothers and sisters, that Jacob and I had been preaching the gospel together, that I ever saw him show affection for anyone other than Jesus Christ. Ben pulled away and asked if he could take a bath. His mother said of course and went to show him the bathroom. Jacob led us into the living room, where me and him, Caleb, and Jeremiah sat down. We related the events of the day to Jacob, and then we got down on our knees, arranged ourselves in a circle, and we prayed.

Ben came down a little while later. He was wearing the same clothes. I know Jacob had had his mother and sister buy some new ones for him. We rose when we saw him. Jacob asked him if everything was okay. He smiled, and said yes, it is, thank you. He walked to the dinner table and sat down.

Everyone followed him. Mrs. Avrohom and Esther started placing the food on the table. Jacob insisted he sit at the head of the table. Ben said it wasn't necessary, that he was fine where he was, at the end on one of the sides. When everyone was seated, I stood and spoke.
Seven thousand years ago, the Almighty God created Heaven and Earth. He made man in his own image and placed Adam in the Garden of Eden. He made Eve from the rib of Adam, and the first woman arrived in Paradise. Satan tempted them, and man fell. For five thousand years, the world was filled with misery and sin. Two thousand years ago, the Almighty Father sent his firstborn Son, the Lord and Savior Jesus Christ, to earth, where he died on the cross to redeem us of our sins. He was resurrected, and took his place at the right hand of his Father. For two thousand years, we have waited for Christ to return to us, and to do battle with the Antichrist for the salvation of humanity, and to bring about

the Rapture, where 144,000 of God's true followers will be lifted into Heaven. It has been a long wait. And there have been many, the Jews, the corrupt, lying Catholics and their Pope, the Lutherans, the Presbyterians, and the Baptists, there have been so many who believed and still believe they are part of the holy family. They are not, never have been, and never will be, and they will all be sent to Hell for their blasphemy, which is where they belong, for all eternity. For true Christians, for those of us who truly live by the word of God in the Holy Bible, for those of us who live by the example of the life of the Lord and Savior Jesus Christ, for those of us who have the Holy Spirit inside of us, the wait is over. Christ has been reborn, and the Messiah has arrived. And the Heavenly Father has been generous enough to have given this woman, a proud member of our church, the privilege of carrying his Son, and this young man, a pastor at our church, and young woman, another member of our church, the glorious gift of living with him as a child. And to us, brothers, he has given the responsibility of protecting and guiding his Son as he spreads the message of the Gospels, and the true word of God, as found in the books of the Bible. Let us rejoice. Let us praise the Lord. Let us pray. Everyone bowed their heads and prayed. Ben did not. I was surprised, but then thought it was logical that the Son of God would not pray to himself. After a few minutes of silent prayer, I raised my head and spoke.
Ben, would you like to say a prayer before we eat?
He spoke.
Would you like me to say a prayer?

Yes, we would all be honored.
Everyone was looking at him. He reached up and took the hands of his sister and mother, who were sitting on either side of him. The rest of us followed his lead and took each other's hands, and we were an unbroken circle of faith and love and belief in the Holy Father. Ben smiled, and he spoke.
Thank you all for being here to share this meal with me. Thank you, Mother, and thank you, Esther, for preparing it for us. I love you both, and I always have, and I always will. Let us enjoy.
There was a long silence while we waited for him. I was, and everyone else was, expecting something more. He didn't thank the Lord, didn't thank the Holy Spirit, didn't thank anyone but his mother and sister. It was shocking, brothers and sisters. We were all shocked. He smiled and pulled his hands away. I opened my eyes. I looked at Jacob, Caleb, and Jeremiah. We all seemed to be waiting for something. Ben stood and reached for the plate of fish and asked if he could serve us. I laughed, said the Lord certainly does work in mysterious ways. It was all I could say, brothers and sisters. Now I know it's just life. Life happens in mysterious ways. Ben served each of us. He acted like he was some kind of waiter. He asked us how much we would like and put the fish on our plates. He did the same with the rice and the bread. He hardly put anything on his own plate. Not enough for a small child. Two bites of fish, one or two of rice, no bread. It was like he didn't need food. He was beyond food. What he did eat, he ate out of a sense of manners. So that his mother and sister weren't

offended. Everyone watched him. He did not appear to notice. When he looked up from his plate, he would slowly chew his food and smile. No one spoke. I know I had a million questions for him. This was the man who spoke to God, was of God, knew things no one on earth had known for two thousand years. I figured I'd start easy. Always good to start heavy things real nice and easy, brothers and sisters. Start with the small and work towards the big. I spoke.

How are you feeling, Ben?

Alive.

That's good. Better than dead, that's for sure. Bless the Lord for giving us this life.

He smiled.

Is there anything you want or need?

No.

We're very excited to have you see our church tomorrow.

He smiled again. Nothing more.

Do you mind that I'm asking a few questions?

Ask whatever you'd like.

What does it feel like?

What?

Being the Son of God.

I'm a man, like you.

But divine.

If you say so.

You can speak to him?

Him?

God.

In a way, yes, I speak to God.

What's it like? What is his voice like?

He smiled.
It's not what you would expect. It is not what
is written in the antiquated books you read.
The books of the Bible?
Yes.
Antiquated?
Yes.
The Bible is eternal, brother. As relevant today as
the day it was written.
The Bible was written two thousand years ago.
The world is a different place now. Stories that
had meaning then are meaningless now. Beliefs that
might have been valid then are invalid now. Those
books should be looked at in the same way we
look at anything of that age, with interest, with an
acknowledgment of the historical importance, but
they should not be thought of as anything that has
any value.
Brother, do you hear what you're saying?
Yes.
It's crazy.
What's crazy is living your life according to some
book written by someone who couldn't imagine what
your life would be like.
I respectfully disagree. I feel the world is very much
the same.
Do you live in a two-thousand-year-old mud hut
with no electricity, no heat, no running water, pissing
and shitting in a hole in the ground? Do you go to
an open-air market in a wooden carriage with stone
wheels, being pulled by an ox? Do you pay for your
food in trade with whatever you've grown in your

backyard? Do you cook your meals over an open fire made of wood you collected and started using a flint? Look around you. This world is not that world. That world is dead. Those books were written for that world. Those books are dead. They should be taken out of every church on earth and recycled, so at least they might do some good in this world. The oldest and most beautiful copies are historical curiosities and should be put in museums.

There was silence at the table. We were all shocked. Brothers and sisters, it was beyond shocking. It was blasphemy. Straight from the mouth of the Lord and Savior himself. Ben sat calmly, waited for one of us to say something. Nobody said a word. It felt like the moment after someone dies, and just before everyone in the room starts wailing. Heavy, brothers and sisters, extremely heavy. Finally, Jacob spoke.

And this is what God tells you?

God tells me other things. This is what common sense tells me.

Common sense is nothing when placed against the word of God.

And you think the word of God is found in the books of the Bible?

I know it is.

Did God write those books?

They are his word.

They are the word of writers. Men telling stories. No different than writers today who craft mystery stories, or adventure stories, or war stories, or stories of the apocalypse. Biblical stories were written decades, and sometimes centuries, after the events they supposedly depict, events for which there is absolutely no historical evidence. There is no such thing as God's word on earth. Or if there is, it is not to be found in books.

Then where is it to be found?

In love. In the laughter of children. In a gift given. In a life saved. In the quiet of morning. In the dead of night. In the sound of the ocean, or the sound of a car. It can be found in anything, anywhere. It is the fabric of our lives, our feelings, the people we live with, things we know to be real.

I have faith the books are true, and I believe I will be rewarded for that faith.

That is your choice.

I have faith that the stories in the books are true.

And that is also your choice, but it is the choice of fools.

Faith is something for fools?

Faith is the fool's excuse.

Faith is a gift from God.

Faith is what you use to oppress, to deny, to justify, to judge in the name of God. Faith is what has been used as a means to rationalize more evil in this world than anything in history. If there were a Devil, faith would be his greatest invention. Get people to believe in that which does not exist, and have them use that belief to destroy everything of value in the world. Get them to buy into an idea of something false, and use that idea to create conflict, violence, and death. If you opened your eyes, you would see that the end is coming, that our world is going to end. And it is coming, and it is going to end, because of faith.

It is coming because God has forewritten it.
Because man will cause it.
Because you have been sent to hasten it.
I will announce it, but not as the consequence of a false prophecy, or the wild imagination of a man, or many men, writing a book in a stone age society. I will announce it because I see it before me. Because all of the conditions for it exist. There is hate, aggression, pride, a lack of love and patience, a lack of understanding, and there are weapons, weapons that can end it all, weapons that can kill millions of people in a second, and there are men, leaders of nations, who are willing to use them. Apocalypse will happen because of man, not because of a nonexistent God.
So you are not the Messiah of the Bible? You are not Christ returned?
Do you believe I am?
I do not want to believe you are, but you have been given gifts. You claim to speak to God. You are Davidic. Born under circumstances which indicate divinity. Born circumcised. You survived the unsurvivable. You are able to speak the ancient languages. You know all of the words of the holy books without having read them. And I have heard that you perform miracles. Ben looked at him, same as he always was, simple and direct, calm. Jacob waited for a response and got none. He spoke.
Is it true?
Yes.
Then show me.
I don't think you'd like the miracle I would perform here.

Let me tell you one I'd like to see.
If that makes you happy.
He held up his glass.
Turn this water into wine.
And after, I'll walk on water, or make my face glow, or turn the food and drink on this table into my flesh and blood.
If you can.
Those are parlor tricks, not miracles.
Christ did them.
He did, or so your holy book says. And every casino magician in Las Vegas can also do them. A miracle is changing someone's life. Freeing them from whatever bonds tie them. Giving them the gift of being able to live the way they dream of living.
So show me.
Ben smiled. He looked around the table. He stayed on each of us, like he was trying to decide what he was going to do, and who he was going to do it to. We were all nervous. One of us was going to be changed forever. I believed one of us would be blessed by the Lord with a miracle from Heaven. Graced by the power of God Almighty, through his one and only Son. I wanted it to be me. I wanted to feel the beauty of the Heavenly Father inside of me. I wanted to be changed in whatever way God, and Ben, wanted to change me. I silently prayed for deliverance into God's hands. I had never wanted anything more in life.

He stood and pushed his chair out and walked around the table. We were all watching. We were all waiting. And we were, brothers and sisters, all hoping. He stopped in front of young brother Jeremiah, who was the last person I would have thought he would choose. Jeremiah was looking up at him. I could see his lips quivering and his hands shaking. He looked terrified. He was about to be given the greatest gift a man could ask for in this life. He was about to be given a miracle. Ben reached out and put his hands on Jeremiah's cheeks. Jeremiah smiled. Ben stood with his hands on his cheeks and stared into his eyes. He didn't move. He just stared at him. Stared right into his eyes. Did it for what must have been ten minutes. Not moving at all. Just staring. And we waited. And it should have been boring, but it was beautiful, and fascinating, and I swear on my life, brothers and sisters, as Ben stared at him, Jeremiah changed. His skin became flush. His posture improved. It was like he changed from a kid to an adult, from a boy to a man. We all knew something more was going to happen, though. We just didn't know what. Frankly, I wouldn't have been surprised if Ben and Jeremiah had risen from the floor and started flying. That's not what happened, brothers and sisters. Not even close. Ben stood there staring, and then he started leaning down. He leaned very slowly, staring into Jeremiah's eyes the entire time. There was no hesitation and no uncertainty. He went right in there and kissed Jeremiah. Kissed him right on the lips. And it wasn't the kind of kiss you give your grandmother. It was a real kiss. It started slow but got real heated, real fast. Within a couple of seconds, they were making out like drunk teenagers. Ben put his hands on Jeremiah's shoulders and pushed his chair back and sat down on his lap. And they were just going at it. We were all too shocked to do anything. At the time, I didn't understand what was happening or why. To me it was just a shocking and disgusting display of homosexual perversity and deviancy. One man in another man's lap, kissing like they were in love. Like the Holy Bible, the word of God, the truest of the true, the most divine of the divine, said was wrong.

I heard a fist slam down on the table. It was loud, brothers and sisters, sounded like a gun. Everybody turned except Ben and Jeremiah, who didn't seem to notice and didn't stop what they were doing. Jacob was standing up. He yelled stop at the top of his lungs, but they didn't stop. In fact Ben's hands were now running over Jeremiah's chest, and moving down to parts inappropriate for a dining room.
Jacob yelled stop again, and Ben pulled away.
He turned towards Jacob and spoke.
Your miracle, brother.
You're a pervert.
If you say so.
Jacob started coming 'round the table.
You're not divine. You're not a man of God. You're a foul pervert who is going to burn in Hell. Ben stood and turned towards him.
If you say so.
Jacob moved towards Jeremiah, who was still sitting.
And you. I pulled you out of a den of sin, out of the

depths of Hell, from the grips of queers and sinners.
I saved you. Brought you into the loving arms of the Lord and Savior Jesus Christ.
The closer he got the angrier he looked. His jaw was clenched and his veins in his neck were bulging.
How dare you faggots? Disgusting perverted freaks.
He rushed Jeremiah, hit him like a football player. He knocked him straight back over his chair and started choking him and slamming his head against the floor. Esther and Mrs. Avrohom started screaming. Caleb and I stayed where we were. We knew there was no stopping Jacob when he got something in his head. And for a second I thought Jeremiah was a dead man. That Jacob was going to kill him. Then Ben grabbed the back of Jacob's shirt and pulled him off. He dragged him a few feet back and pushed him down. Jeremiah was bleeding and had choke marks on his neck and stayed on the ground. Jacob got up and started after him. Ben pushed him back. Jacob screamed at him.
Do not touch me.
Ben looked at him, very calm.
Do not touch him.
I'll do whatever I want to him.
No.
Jacob went after him again, and Ben pushed him back.
You want to hurt someone, hurt me. He's walking out of here to live the life he was born to live.
Jacob pushed Ben. Jacob was breathing heavy, raging. He's going to die of AIDS and burn in Hell. You both will.

Love's going to kill us?
Jeremiah was up, crying, bleeding, breathing heavy. Esther and Mrs. Avrohom were tending to him. I looked to Caleb and back to Ben and Jacob, as if we should do something. Caleb shook his head. Jacob took a step towards Ben. God's gift to you and the rest of your kind will kill you. He pushed him. Ben just smiled.
You can't hurt me, Jacob. No matter what you do.
Jacob pushed him harder. Jeremiah was on his feet, still crying. Esther and Mrs. Avrohom were moving him away. Ben spoke again.
You've always hated me. This is your chance. Let Jeremiah walk out and I won't resist. Take out what you feel about him on me. Unleash your mighty God's wrath.
Jacob pushed him harder. Ben glanced back, saw Jeremiah being led from the room. He looked back at Jacob, smiled. Jacob pushed him again.
That's it?
He did it again, and harder.
That's not much from a powerful man of God.
And again, harder.
Seems more like a faggot's push. You sure you aren't ...
And Jacob attacked again. He threw Ben on the ground and climbed on top of him and started punching him in the face and on the head and on his body. Ben did not resist at all. From what I could see, he almost looked like he was smiling. Jacob was screaming faggot at the top of his lungs, and just kept hitting him. Caleb and I both stood, knowing

we'd have to stop Jacob at some point or Ben would die. We came around the table and Ben was clearly out. His body was limp and his face was covered in blood. It was also all over Jacob and all over the floor. And Jacob kept hitting him. Brothers and sisters, a man can only allow so much. A man can only watch so much. Whatever Jacob was doing wasn't about God anymore. I didn't understand or endorse gay behavior. Frankly, I found it sickening and wrong. But Jacob was killing his brother over a kiss. And kissing, and loving, whatever kind it may be, is not something the Holy Father would condemn someone to death for doing. At this point in my life, I believe—actually, brothers and sisters, I know—that God believes love, even between men and men, and women and women, is still love. And it is something beautiful, the most beautiful thing there is in this world. Let more of it exist. In every form. I say hallelujah. So we pulled Jacob off of him. His hands and face and shirt were dripping. He was still screaming, and we were struggling with him. He was yelling he deserves to die, I am God's soldier, he deserves to die. We took him out of the room and to his bedroom and convinced him that the best thing for us to do was pray to the Lord above for guidance and strength. I knew Ben was going to be needing a doctor. So I left the room to use the telephone. Caleb and Jacob were on their knees, holding hands, praying. The phone was in the kitchen, and I had to walk through the dining room to get there. I was going to check on Ben, make sure he was still breathing. When I came into the dining room, it was empty. There was a silhouette on the floor. And where the feet would have been, there was the ankle bracelet. I picked it up and it was still functioning. Wasn't broken and hadn't been cut. It was supposed to be impossible to remove it. But it was removed, brothers and sisters, it was lying there on the floor. I started to go back towards the other rooms to see if Ben had gone into one of them. As I did, I glanced at the table. And brothers and sisters, I am telling you, brothers and sisters, I am telling you because I saw it with my own two eyes, every glass on the table, glasses that had been filled with water a minute before, were filled with wine. They were filled to the top, and they were filled with deep red wine.

II MARIAANGELES

I was at home. Mercedes was watching TV. I'd just got back from the hospital, where my momma was dying. Alberto was in Rikers for killing some motherfucker. I heard a knock on the door. Figured it was the cops or some bitch from child services. Either way it'd be the same thing, some white person making threats on me and my baby, some white person saying they had the authority to tell me how to live my life and raise my girl. Like they could do better. With all their power and government money. Look what they done to the world. They couldn't do no better.

I opened the door. Ben was standing right there. Or some fucked-up version of Ben. I hadn't been seeing him for over a year. When he left we was wondering what happened. One day he was there being drunk and playing his video games, coming in to the club all fucked up, the next day he was gone. We didn't know where he went to. Figured he got tired of living with black folks and took off. It happens. People get tired of living with people that ain't like them and they go back to their own. And sometimes it's best. Sometimes I be thinking black folk and white folk ain't meant to be together. And you can give all the motherfucking speeches you want, it ain't gonna change.

He smiled at me. Said hello. Some of his teeth was broken and he had blood all over him. His face was all cut and swollen, his eyes turning purple all around them. And underneath the blood and swelling, I could see there was scars everywhere, like he'd been in a knife fight with twenty men. And his clothes was nasty, something I didn't even see 'round here with people who can't afford clothes. He reached up and put his hand on my cheek and said it's nice to see you, Mariaangeles. I had men's hands on me all the fucking time. Men grabbing my ass, my titties. Men trying to put their fingers everywhere inside of me. Never had a man put his hand on me like that. Just being gentle. Just being kind. Most men looking for some pussy and someone to take care of them, cook their meals and do their laundry. That's what they think love mean. Ben just touch my cheek and say it's nice to see you, Mariaangeles. Nicest thing any man had ever done for me.

I was wondering what he was doing. His apartment wasn't his apartment no more. After he left it stayed empty for a few months. My brother broke in and stole the TV and the video games and all the beer in the fridge. Said he'd give it back if Ben came 'round again and ended up selling it all to buy a gun. After a while white people with clipboards and phones on their belts came 'round and opened it up. Some old man moved in and died like two months later. Went to sleep and didn't never get back up. Then some family moved in. Woman and six kids and her husband, who didn't do nothing but yell and

beat the shit outta all of 'em and blame all his own shit on the Jews. He got arrested for something, don't even fucking matter what, 'cause he just another brother in the pen, and the woman and them kids went back to Puerto Rico, where they from. Now there was some girl like me. Eighteen and three kids with three different daddies, none of them giving a shit. Didn't think she'd want him coming in there, and she could have pro'ly whooped his ass, specially looking like he was looking. I was thinking what to do when he smiled and spoke.
I need somewhere to stay.
And you wanna stay here?
Yes.
Why you thinking I'm gonna let you stay here?
Because I love you, and I can help you.
What the fuck you talking about, Ben?
Trust me.
I looked at him. More than anything, I was feeling sorry for him. He was clearly fucked up. More fucked up than me, more fucked-up looking than anyone I'd ever knowed. He was all beat-the-fuck-up and skinny. I wasn't worried about him hurting me. And I was feeling a little guilty about taking all his money that time at the club. So I opened the door. He smiled and said thank you and stepped inside.

My place was bad. When I wasn't working, I was getting high. When I wasn't working or getting high, I was trying to be taking care of Mercedes. I didn't have no time for cooking and cleaning. I tried sometimes to straighten up, but it didn't happen.

There was dishes in the sink, trash in the kitchen. Didn't have nothing but milk and water and old macaroni and cheese from the deli in the fridge. I kept my drugs and my pipes in Momma's old room, and kept it locked so Mercedes couldn't get at it. Me and her was sleeping in the bedroom I used to be sharing with Alberto my whole life. I hadn't done no laundry in a long time so there was clothes everywhere. Mercedes was sitting on our couch, watching some TV show about crime, which she was doing all the time. Ben walked in and went to the couch and kissed her on the forehead. She didn't pay him no attention. He turned to me and asked if there was somewhere he could sleep. I told him he could sleep wherever he wanted.

He walked over towards Momma's room. I told him not to go in there. He asked where my mother was and I told him she was in the hospital. He asked why and I told him she had some cancer that was killing her. He said I'm sorry and he reached for the door and I told him it was a private place and he shouldn't be going in there. He opened the door and he stepped into the room.

I didn't know what to do. If I should be stopping him or if he was gonna be taking my shit or if he was just fucking crazy. I walked to the door. My shit was on my momma's dresser, where I always left it. Ben was in the bathroom, turning on the sink and starting to wash his face. I could see him doing it real soft because he was all beat to shit. When he put some water in his mouth and spit it out, everything was red. When he took off his shirt, he was so skinny I could see all his ribs and veins and his whole body was covered with bruises, all purple and black, like someone went at him with a baseball bat. He looked over at me standing near the dresser, where I had me a vial with one rock I was trying to save and a pipe and torch. He smiled and said it's fine, Mariaangeles, I will not judge you. After he was done with his cleaning, he come back into the room and took off his pants and layed down on the bed and closed his eyes. He didn't do no moving at all.

He slept for two or three days. I kept checking on him 'cause he was looking like he was dead. Only time I saw him moving was a few times I came in and his eyes was open a little and he was laying on his back twitching and shaking and doing some kind of grunting, but it was real soft like a baby. I started getting high in my room and just leaving him be. I knew he'd be waking up or dying at some time or another, and I thought either way it happened he'd be outta my apartment.

Thursdays sometimes I'd work a double shift. All the white boys from Manhattan would come up 'cause it was right before the weekend so they could get drunk but they could tell their wives and girlfriends that they was out for business dinners. They'd start rolling in right after lunch, looking for black girls, all of them thinking we was gonna fuck them. After the shift I'd stay and get real fucked up, smoking just to forget the day, and then I'd be coming home. I'd have my neighbor watch Mercedes and I'd pay her and then she'd put her to bed and lock the door. I told her about Ben being sleeping in Momma's room and told her to pay him no mind.

This shift was worse than most of 'em, and they was all bad. Had a man who knew the manager and was old friends, some rich white man wearing a suit and living in a big house in Connecticut or someplace. The manager gave him a private room for free without any champagne tip, and I had to go back there, wasn't no choice in it for me. Man was mean and cheap and I had to do everything he wanted. Sucked his dick, let him fuck me, putting his fingers where they didn't belong. Went on for four hours, and when he finally left there wasn't nothing to do but go out and hustle and try to make up for the money I didn't make while I was with him. I went into the back room three more times. Let them men do whatever they wanted and got fucking paid for it. When I was done, I left and found a quiet place behind a dumpster and spent the next six hours getting fucking high.

I came home knowing Mercedes was going to be crying, like she always was when she was hungry and alone too long. I wasn't in no mood for it either. Just wanted to drink me some water and go to sleep. When I put the key in the door, I could hear some laughing. I didn't know what the fuck was going on.

I opened the door and went inside, and it wasn't
even looking like my apartment. Whole place had
been cleaned. Like it was all shining. There was
some spaghetti cooking in the kitchen. And Ben
and Mercedes was both all cleaned up too, and they
was standing in the middle of the living room,
laughing and dancing together. Ben looked over
at me and smiled.
Welcome home, Mariaangeles.
What the fuck is going on here?
I'm teaching Mercedes to dance.
She know how to dance already. I taught her
how to dance.
Then I'm teaching her to laugh.
She know how to do that too.
No, she doesn't.
And what the fuck happened to my apartment?
Your life is going to change, Mariaangeles.
I don't want it to change.
Yes, you do.
No, I don't.
Yes, you do.
He walked over to me, holding Mercedes' hand.
I wasn't sure what to do. He was just smiling at me.
And my little girl was smiling at me, smiling real
wide. I hadn't seen her smile like that in a long time.
In a long long time. Broke my fucking heart.
And nothing in the world more beautiful than
a child's smile. And there was my little girl, smiling
all wide at a mother that didn't deserve nothing
like that. A mother that was feeling like she didn't
even deserve to be living this life that she had

been given. A life she know now can be something
she want, so full of moments like the smile of a beautiful child. Ben was right, even though I didn't want
him to be right. Life was going to change.

As they walked to me, Ben leaned over and whispered
something in Mercedes' ear. She smiled and went
running right up on me, and I bent over and took
her in my arms and gave her a big hug, a big hug like
I didn't ever give anybody, not even her. And as I was
holding her, she said I love you, Mommy. And I said
I love you, baby, and even though I didn't want to
be doing it, I started crying. And then Ben came over
and put his skinny-ass arms around both of us.
And he said I love you, Mariaangeles. And for the first
time in my life, when a man said I love you, I believed
it. I believed it with my whole heart. And he just stood
there, holding me, while I held my daughter and
I cried.

When we stopped hugging, Ben walked me to my
bedroom and told me to get cleaned up and get ready
for lunch. I took a shower and stayed in there a long
time, thinking 'bout my night, thinking about
what Mercedes made me feel. When I come out,
I'm wearing my best sweat suit and the table is set all
nice as it can be and there's spaghetti on plates and
my pipe and three vials of rock I had are sitting next
to my plate. Ben and Mercedes are sitting waiting for
me. I look at the pipe and the vials and look at Ben.
Why you putting that out like that?
Is there a reason you don't want it out?

I sat down and put everything in my pocket.
My daughter don't need to be seeing that.
Why?
You a fucking fool, man. Why you think?
You think she doesn't know.
She ain't old enough to know nothing.
If you say so.
I do.
You ashamed of it?
What do you think?
That you should stop.
You don't know shit, white boy.
He smiled and didn't say nothing. We started eating.
He was helping Mercedes using her fork. I just
watched her, and watching him with her made me
hate myself more, knowing what I had in my pocket.
I could feel it there. Heavy and bulging out. I was
always pretending Mercedes thought I was just
a regular momma. That our life was a regular life.
Or at least regular for where we was living, for where
we was from. I was just another girl with a kid trying
to do my best and struggling. And in a way it was that
way. But I was also knowing it was wrong. Knowing
I could do better. Even in the way that we was.

We finished our lunch and Ben told Mercedes it
was time for her to go napping and he took her into
Momma's room. I sat at the table and thought about
what was in my pocket 'cause it's all I wanted even
though it was hurting to think about it and I heard
Ben singing some kind of lullaby to Mercedes.
It made me remember when I used to sing to her,

before I was working at the club, before Alberto
got arrested, before Momma got sick. When he was
finished, he closed the door and came out. I was still
sitting and he sat down across and just stared at me.
His eyes was looking different from when I used
to know him. More black. Blackest things I ever saw.
And he had been healing when he was sleeping.
The bruising on his face was almost gone and his cuts
was healing good. It made the scars stick out more.
Made me be seeing them more. Made me really be
understanding how much he changed. He must have
been thirty or forty pounds skinnier. And he was
whiter. Most white people I don't notice. They all
be looking like they got the same skin. Just white.
Ben was white white. Paper white. And them scars
was even whiter. Like glossy paint over regular paint.
And he just stared at me. Them black eyes calming
me down so I could actually be feeling my heart
slowing down. And when I was real calm, and not
even wanting to smoke no more, I spoke.
What happened to you, Ben?
I changed.
No shit there. What happened?
It doesn't matter.
Does to me.
What matters is what I have become.
What's that?
Someone who loves you.
You don't know me well enough to love me.
One must know oneself to love, not know others.
You sound like a preacher.
I'm not.

You gonna try to save me?
You're going to save you.
How I'm going to do that?
Give me your pipe, your drugs.
What you gonna do with them?
Put them on the table.
They're mine.
Yes.
I need them.
No.
I do.
Why?
Because I fucking do.
Put them on the table. I'm going to show you something.
You try to use them and I'll fuck you up.
He smiled, stared at me, waited. If I saw him on the street, I'd think he was a crackhead for fucking real. But sitting with him and talking to him, I didn't think it. I didn't have no reason to trust him, 'cept how he was looking at me, but I did. Trusted him like I had never trusted no man or no white person ever. So I took my shit outta my pocket and put it on the table. Ben didn't even look at it. Just kept looking at me. And then he stood up and walked around the table and leaned over and started kissing me. Real slow at first, real light, just brushing his lips right against mine. And it felt good, felt right. So we started kissing more, using our lips like we was meaning it, using our tongues. Kissing like we meant it, like we was in love. And he lifted me outta that chair, like I weighed nothing. And he took off my clothes. And

he put me on the table. And he licked me, and sucked me, and fucked me till I couldn't see straight. Lying right next to my drugs. He showed me how to get high. He showed me what it felt like to feel good. He fucked me, and he loved me, and when he came inside me, it fulfilled more than any person, school, church, book, or God had in my life. He whispered I love you in my ear and he came inside me and it felt like I was right inside. It felt like what it was supposed to feel like to be believing in all those other things.

When we was finished that first time, he stayed inside me a long time. Just stayed inside and kissed me and held me. And then he picked me up, still inside me, and carried me to bed. And he put me down on that bed with his arms around me and we went to sleep. I didn't think about being poor. I didn't think about what I was doing for money. I didn't think about my brother rotting in a fucking cell. About my mother dying in a fucking hospital where nobody cared. About being black in a country where it means I ain't got no chance. About my daughter who wasn't gonna have no chance either. About a life stretching out in front of me where it never gets to be any better. The feeling of arms around me, of love in my heart, it was more powerful than any of the negativity I knew was existing in the world for me. That feeling of love killed it all.

When I woke up, he was gone. I went in to be looking in on Mercedes and she was still sleeping. I was supposed to be working so I started getting ready.

Taking me a shower and doing my makeup in the bathroom. When I went out to the kitchen, my shit was still there on the table. Made me fucking sick to see it there, made me sick to be thinking that's what I'd been doing for the last year. Made me sick to be thinking why I'd been doing it and why I was just getting ready. For money. For money that didn't make a difference. Didn't get me or my daughter out of anywhere or anything. Didn't change how I felt in my heart or how I was feeling when I looked in the mirror. Was just something I could hold in my hand. Money don't mean nothing when your heart is empty.

So I picked that shit up and threw it out the window. Figured some crackhead would find it and have a surprise, there was enough of 'em around. And I didn't go to work. Didn't even bother calling. They wasn't gonna miss me. They might not have even been noticing I was gone. Was gonna be easy to find another girl, 'cause they always too many out there willing to throw it around for the money. I ain't judging, 'cause I did it. It's the way of the world. You use what you got, and that's all that too many women got.

I waited for Ben. Mercedes woke up and I got her and gave her a big long hug. We went out and started playing in the living room, singing songs and tickling. I started getting a little sick, was starting to realize I might be needing the crack I throwed out. I went over to the window and looked down and it was still there. Was some kind of miracle it hadn't been picked up. I know in the Bible they be saying miracles is

withering some motherfucking fig tree or some shit, but in the world I live in, the real fucking world, a miracle is a vial of crack lying on the ground in an American housing project unclaimed for more than three fucking minutes. But there it was. Tempting me. Calling to me. Not even calling, it was screaming at me. I could hear Mercedes behind me. I started telling myself love stronger than drugs, stronger than anything, love stronger, but telling ain't always believing. You can tell yourself anything you want, but until you believe what you're telling yourself, you're wasting words. I was ready to go down there. Ready to go. So I turned and walked towards the door. When I opened it, Ben was sitting on the floor. He smiled. I started talking.
What you doing?
Sitting.
How long you been sitting there?
A while.
Doing what?
Just sitting.
I looked at him. Just sitting there on the floor.
He smiled at me, spoke.
You want to go back inside.
I smiled.
Yeah.
May I come in?
Yeah.
He stood up and followed me back inside. We played with Mercedes for a long time, singing and playing with her toys, and the whole time I was wanting to smoke. Dinner come around and Ben serve us more

spaghetti. We eat at the table. When we finished I'm feeling really sick, shaking, wanting to jump out the fucking window. Ben have me put Mercedes to sleep and when I'm done I come out and he waiting for me. He take me to my room and lay me down and spend the rest of the night licking and sucking and fucking. And every time I got to feeling sick he do it again, till I finally fall asleep.

And that's the way it stay for a few days, maybe a week. Ben go out in the morning while I sleep and find food somewhere. When I wake up he with Mercedes, and whenever she nap or sleep or whenever I feel sick he take me in the bedroom or on the floor or the table. And he was always telling me he love me. That I'm beautiful. That I can live however I want to live. That life can be beautiful. That Mercedes love me and I can be a good momma. And I stop hearing it. I start believing it.

And then one day I wake up and know. Know that I'm okay and going to be good, or as good as I can be where I'm at. And I tell Ben and he smile. And I stop thinking just about me and ask him more about why he here with me. He tell me about living in the tunnels and being arrested and he tell me how he leave his family. And how he skipped on his bail. He tell me about his being able to speak to God. He tell me that he know things about the world, and that he know the world going to end if we don't change it. That man is sick. That the leaders of the world killing us all. Making us think we progressing while killing us. And it ain't like there be some big grand plan, they just ignorant. And greedy. And thinking about themselves. And thinking about their Gods. Christians thinking they got God. Muslims thinking they got God. Jews thinking they got God. Everybody thinking God on their side. That God want them to kill and judge and dominate. And all of them wrong. All of them doing what they do in the name of something that don't exist like that. That fairy tales ruling the world. That God ain't part of the world that way. That God don't judge. God don't give power. That God something beyond the understanding of men or women on earth. That God ain't giving no gift of eternal life. The gift is the life we got, and when it's over, it's fucking over. No Heaven. No parties with relatives and people we love while the angels sing and play harps. No seventy-two virgins waiting for us to teach them how to fuck. No nothing. No God like we believe. Just the end. And all we got in the world is other people. And all we got with them is love. And not love like some dumbass pop song. Love is just taking care of each other, and fucking each other, and letting each other live how we want to be living. And protecting each other from all the shit that life throws us. That comes at us because that's fucking life, not because some fake silly God is trying to test us, or prepare us for the afterlife, or because he thinks we strong enough to deal with it. Bad shit just happens. Ain't no reason for it 'cept that it's life. It ain't no fucking God. And everything he say making sense to me. Making more sense than everything else I hear in the world. Making more sense than the bullshit politicians and preachers and popes spewing out every day. Making more sense than the bullshit in textbooks and newspapers and on TV news shows. Making more sense than the bullshit laws our government be trying to make us live by. The government that says One Nation Under God, but under what God? The old white man God with a beard who say blacks ain't got rights, Hispanics ain't got no rights, women ain't got rights, gays ain't got rights, and no one who ain't like him and believe like him ain't got no rights. Fuck that. And fuck that God. And fuck all the fools believing in that God. They can come kiss my black ass, 'cause that ain't no kind of Nation Under God, it's just fucking bullshit.

Life settled down for me and Mercedes and Ben. I started taking me some GED classes and got Mercedes in a daycare program in the project. It wasn't all daisies and bunnies and hugs, but it was better than sitting and watching TV. Ben would leave for the day. Said he would just wander around New York. Walk or get on the train and get off wherever he felt like it. Said he would just see people and talk to them and help them and love them. I know he was fucking some of them, 'cause I could smell it on him when he came back. Sometimes I'd ask him who and sometimes it was a woman, sometimes a man. I'd ask how he'd be helping people and he'd say however they needed it. I asked him how he loved them and he said however they needed it. I know he talked to some of them about how he could speak to God, about what God really is, about the way he

saw the world. About how it going to end. And people
believed him. They started showing up at my apartment. Sometimes they brought gifts, brought food or
clothes, sometimes they brought money. Sometimes
they'd be crying. Sometimes they'd be fucked up
on drugs or drunk. If he was home he'd let them in.
Some of them he'd take in his arms and whisper
in their ear. Some he'd sit with on the couch and take
their hands and stare at them. Sometimes he'd
stand by the window with them and talk real soft.
Some he'd take in the bedroom, men and women
both, and he'd close the door, and I know he'd be
fucking them, and loving them, and making them
better, same as he did to me. Some he put his hands
on their cheeks and he'd kiss them real light.
I don't know what he was ever saying or doing
to them people, but they'd leave better. They'd leave
different. They'd leave with that true belief in their
heart. And they'd be telling other people. So Ben
started having people saying things about him.
That he had powers. That he could perform miracles.
That he could save you or change you or make
your life better. That he was a prophet. That he was
a holy man. That Christ had come back. That he
was the Messiah. The Messiah the world been
waiting for and praying for and worshipping for,
that he was the man come to save us or let us all die.
He never said nothing about anything of that.
People would say things to him about it and he'd
smile and say nothing at all or say if you say so.
What he told me was important was him loving all
the people and making them so they was leaving

better than they was when they came. That was what God was. Making people still living their lives in this world feel better. All the rest was just made-up fantasy stories.

When it was just us, it was like we was married, but not hating each other like most married people being. Was like we was a couple. He didn't seem to be loving me any more or any different than anyone else, but we was together, and he always came back, even when he'd be gone for a night or two, and I was always knowing he'd come back, never doubting nothing. It didn't matter I was only nine-teen and he was thirty-one, and it didn't matter we was different colors and had been raised different or that our parents was from different countries, speaking different languages and believing in different Gods. We just loved each other. Didn't want each other to be no different. Didn't bitch about what we didn't like 'bout each other. Was accepting of each other as human fucking beings. Who felt the same shit. Knew the same kind of pain. And knew that love was the only weapon against that pain. Nothing else can end it or stop it. That's what Ben taught me more than anything. That we got this gift of life and we got it one time and we gonna get hurt in it and be hurt going through it and the only thing that'll make that hurt better or hurt less is love. And part of our love was fucking. Ben loved to fuck. He loved to kiss me and lick my body and suck on everything I got. When Mercedes was sleeping and no one was knocking on the door, we'd spend all our time fucking. Fucked for hours and hours. He never got tired of fucking. Said coming was the closest thing any human on earth would ever know about Heaven. That there wasn't no pearly gates, no trumpeters, no man waiting with some book 'bout all the good shit and bad shit we supposedly done in our lives, 'specially when most of what we do ain't good or bad, just boring. That there ain't no one gonna judge us and decide we can be in that all-time never-ending party or get sent to burn. That there ain't no party like that, just like there ain't no ball for Cinderella and her sisters, or prom for Barbie, or labyrinth with a bull that gonna eat your ass up. But there's the feeling you get when you cum. When everything disappears. When your body tells you it loves you and everything in the world is perfect and secure and safe. When you feel better than you ever feel any other time in your life. That feeling you wish wouldn't never end. He said people that try to say it's wrong is just stupid. That people who say fucking is wrong is just stupid. That say you got to fuck under certain conditions laid out by God are just fucking stupid. No one should tell other people how to fuck. Said people who take vows not to do it are denying themself one of the greatest gifts we got in the world. That men in silly robes singing songs in dead languages who ain't never fucked in their life certainly got no right. That maybe if they fucked, they'd understand God in a way no book and no cardinal and no pope could ever be telling them. He said if everyone who went to church or temple or mosque spent all that wasted time fucking instead of praying to made-up shit, the world wouldn't be ending soon. And he right. And you know he right. If you look in your heart, and if you've ever cum in your life, you know he absolutely right.

After my classes and before I'd get Mercedes and go home, I'd go see my momma. They had moved her to some place where people watched her and tried to make sure she was comfortable and she lied in a bed and her body was just wasting away. She was hurting real bad. Her body eating itself. Eating all its organs and eating all its bones. Cancer everywhere and no way to do a thing about it. There wasn't ever a thing to do about it. Most days I was strong and I'd hold her hand. Some days I'd just sit by her bed and cry. They'd just be giving her more and more drugs. Drugs that make her someone she wasn't, make her something not even a person. Just some flesh lying there breathing. You ever sat by the bed of someone dying you know what it's like. There ain't nothing you can do. You just sit there feeling pain like nothing else on earth. You sit there feeling helpless and empty. When they awake, every second you sit with them you know that they gonna die soon. Every word you say got this weight on it 'cause you know there ain't gonna be many more words. Everyone comes into the room do their best to be happy and seem cheery. To be talking about shit that ain't got nothing to do with death. But it's always there. The sickness. The death. The fact there ain't nothing to do about it. The fact that they won't be no more. That they gonna go in the ground and rot.

And that you gonna go on living. And you can say whatever you want and tell them you love them and do everything in the world to make their passing easier, but it don't change. They feel the pain. And the only way to stop the pain is load up on so many drugs that you a vegetable, or die. And in the meantime, everyone that loves you just feels the pain. The worst pain you can know.

Momma was getting worse and worse, but not dying. Just being in pain. The doctors wasn't even around anymore. Just nurses and people doing their best to have her be comfortable. She started telling me she wanted to die. Every day she tell me she don't want to go on, that it hurt too much, that she ready. I tell her she gonna be okay, that she got to keep fighting, but she tell me she don't want to fight no more. That her whole life been a fight. Growing up in a shack in a broke shitty country was a fight, coming to America thinking her life would be better was a fight, being in New York and realizing that nothing gonna be better, that the American Dream only for people with the right skin and the right accent was a fight. That raising two kids without no husband or man and without no money or family or help while she cleaned the houses of people who seemed to be getting everything real easy was a fight, that watching those kids drift and watching her dreams for them die was a fight. That getting cancer and not being able to afford to do anything about it was a fight. It was all a fight, from the moment she came screaming outta her momma 'til she ended up where she ended up, in some rundown place with cockroaches and rats and crack-heads outside and gunshots every night, what they call a peaceful place where they send poor people to die. She was done. She didn't want it no more. I cried, wailed, sobbed, begged her, told her I didn't want her to go. She smiled and said she loved me. And then they gave her more drugs and she passed out.

When I went home I was doing terrible. I couldn't stop crying. Mercedes come over to me, say it's okay, Momma, it's okay. And it make me cry harder 'cause I wish I could tell my beautiful little three-year-old girl that I love so much and that I want to have whatever she want in the world and that I would die for that it ain't okay, that the world is fucked up, that pain and suffering everywhere, that people hurt each other and hate each other and kill each other for no good reason, that we live and then we die and when we die that's it, we gone, just fucking gone. I wish I could tell her that she would be okay. That she gonna have a great life, but I know I'd be a liar. She gonna grow up, get hurt, and someone gonna break her heart and she ain't probably gonna have what she want in life and she gonna get treated like dirt and she gonna bust her ass alone and then she gonna die. There ain't no beauty in that, there ain't nothing but pain. So I cried harder. For Momma and me and her and everyone else in the world that ain't got and never gonna. I cried and I couldn't stop. It wasn't gonna be okay.

Ben came in and saw me and asked me what was wrong. I couldn't even be talking for a long time.

Just cried. And he put his arms around me. I wanted some of whatever he did to other people to make their pain go away. I waited for him to make me free.
He didn't whisper nothing in my ear. Didn't put my face in his hands and stare at me. Didn't talk. He just held me and had Mercedes come over and he put his arms around both of us. And he just hold the both of us. And I didn't stop crying for a long time. And then I did. And Ben ask me what's wrong and I tell him and I start crying again. Momma's in pain and she's dying and there ain't nothing to fucking do. She don't want to be living no more, say she ready to go, that she love life but she in too much pain. And I got to sit there with her knowing it, and feeling it, and hurting so much it make me want to die, and there ain't nothing to fucking do.

Ben waited for me to stop crying again. He looked into my eyes for a real long time, then spoke.
You would die for her?
Momma?
Yes.
Yeah.
You love her that much?
Yeah, her or for Mercedes. I would die for them.
And you know that without doubt or hesitation.
Yes.
He smiled. He took my hand and he standed up and he took Mercedes in her room and he put on her best dress and her best shoes and he make her hair pretty with some ribbons and barrettes. He tell me to get dressed in my best clothes so I go to our room

and I put on the nicest I got, a dress I bought when I was first starting working at the club and was thinking that maybe church every Sunday would make me feel better. It was before I learned that crack was stronger than God. At least that God they be praying to on the cross.

We left the project and went to the place where they had Momma. She was awake when we went into her room, lying there, and we could hear her moaning as we came down the hallway to her. Ben stood aside and let us into the room first. Momma had her blanket pulled down so we could see how thin she was, how there wasn't nothing left of her, just skin hanging off her bones. Mercedes went running over to the side of the bed, saying Abuela, Abuela. Momma lifted her hand just a little bit, put it right on her head, said hello. I went over to kiss Momma and she try to touch my head but she couldn't be lifting her hand enough. I ask her how she doing and she shake her head. Mercedes give her a kiss and she try to smile but she couldn't really even be doing it, so sick she couldn't even be smiling at her granddaughter. I told her Ben was there, the white boy used to be our neighbor. Ben step behind me so she can see him. She look at him long time, like she trying to recognize him, and I'm thinking it's probably being hard for her 'cause he looking so different. I see her looking real close, and he just staring at her, right into her eyes, just staring. She smiled and say real soft I know who that is, thank you for bringing him, Mariaangeles. I ask her what she talking about and she try to smile again, and do it a little better. Ben put his hand on my shoulder and ask me real soft if I'm ready and I look at him and ask for what and he say to say goodbye. I look at Momma and she still trying to be smiling at me all skin and bones just lying there in pain and dying. Dying too slow. Dying without no dignity or peace. Dying misery and shit in a bed that's held way too many other people who died in it. Every time I looked at that bed I was thinking about how many people died in it, and how my momma was just another one.

Ben told me to go around and take Momma's hand, so I did it. He had Mercedes take her other hand. He whispered in Mercedes' ear, and Mercedes kiss Momma and say I love you. He looks at me and smiles and I know what he wants me to be doing and I lean over and kiss her and tell her I love her and I thank her for doing the best she could be doing. I hold her hand real tight and I tell her how much I'll be missing her and how I'm going to do the best I can to be a good momma to Mercedes. I start crying again. I know what's going to be coming. And even though it's what Momma wants and is the right thing, I start crying.

Ben stepped around Mercedes and sat himself down on the edge of the bed. Momma smiled at him, first real smile of the day. He leaned over and kissed each of her cheeks and her forehead. He took her cheeks in his hands and started whispering to her, real quiet, and I couldn't hear what he was saying. She was occasionally answering yes, and after he finished he pull back and look her right in the eyes. He kiss her one more time, and he tell her he loves her, and she says I love you, too. He continue to stare at her, right into her eyes, and I see her eyes start to slowly close. I start crying harder. I know when them eyes close they ain't going to open again. Mercedes is saying Abuela over and over again, like she think her grandma is going to be able to say something back. And Ben just stared at her, and she stared back at him, and just before she went, before her eyes closed for good and she went into the blackness, I saw peace in 'em. I saw calm. I saw happiness. And I saw that little thing you see in someone's eyes when they got love in their heart.

More than anything else.

I saw love.

MARK

One of my parishioners came to my office and told me someone was having a seizure in the restroom. It was the third or fourth time that this exact situation had come up, someone telling me about a seizing man in the restroom, except whenever I went to check, the restroom was empty. Despite this, I immediately went to the restroom to check again, concerned for the individual's safety, if in fact there was an individual. We had had an elderly parishioner die of a heart attack in our lobby a year or so before, and he was there, alone and on the floor, for at least two hours before someone found him. Though I believed that a church would, in some ways, be an almost ideal place to pass on, I did not want another death on the premises. The first one had brought the diocese a fairly significant amount of unwanted negative publicity, and had generated a storm of paperwork. Given all of the controversies of the past years, and my love for the church and desire to protect it, I hurried to see if it could be avoided again, or if I could be of any aid to the man who was sick.

I entered the restroom, the men's restroom, and saw a man standing at the sink, washing his hands. I immediately thought he was Jesus Christ. I gasped and I was frozen and I could not speak. He had long-ish black hair, a short black beard, and alabaster white skin. He was extremely thin, wearing ragged clothes that hung off his body, and he was covered in scars. And he was glowing. Literally glowing. The restroom has no windows, as is proper for a restroom, and only one ceiling light, and I would swear on a Bible, or anything else I hold or held dear, that the walls were illuminated, and that he was glowing.

He looked at me in the mirror and smiled. He continued to wash his hands, very slowly and deliberately, very peacefully, if it is somehow even possible to wash your hands in a peaceful manner. I can only imagine what I must have looked like, standing before the Son of God, a man I had worshipped every day of my life, a man I had spent countless hours praying to meet. I couldn't move, and he just stared at me in the mirror. When he was done washing his hands, he turned and walked towards me. He put his arms around me, and I whispered My Lord into his ear. He held me for a moment and kissed me on the cheek and turned and walked out of the bathroom.

I stayed in the restroom for several minutes, standing exactly where I was when he left me. I was trying to reconcile what I had just experienced, which was, I believed, then and now, that I had been in the presence of Jesus Christ, the Son of God, the Messiah, the Savior, the earthly embodiment of the Lord God. He had smiled at me, and held me, and kissed me. He had placed himself within the sphere of my life, and my church, and my worship. I thought about how many people on earth could say that they had

had this profound experience, or could say that they had been literally touched by the Lord? Though billions and billions had prayed for it, and continued to pray for it every day, Christ had not appeared, or had not made his appearance known, for over two thousand years. It was a miracle. The greatest miracle. He had returned to save us and redeem us. He had come back to bring about the glory of the End Days. There are no words for what I felt at that moment, knowing what I knew, or what words there are, are inadequate. If forced to try to characterize it, I would describe a feeling of great peace, humility, and serenity, a deep sense of hope for both myself and for humanity. A feeling of enormous satisfaction in that all I believed in had been validated. And to be completely honest, there was something electric in it, something ecstatic, something I had felt only once or twice in my life, but never so strongly. It was something that scared me because it felt like I could lose control of it. And loss of control is always the source of fear. It is also, however, always the source of change.

After leaving the restroom, I went about the rest of my day. I met with one or two parishioners during my office hours, older women who attended mass most mornings and whose husbands had passed away. I went to a local hospital, where I pray for patients two days a week. I had a simple dinner in my quarters, which are in the rectory behind my church. I prayed to and thanked God for blessing me with his Son's presence. I read the Bible, focusing on the book of

Matthew, where the Second Coming is addressed in some detail. I prayed again and tried to sleep, but was unable to do so. So I stayed up, thinking about my life and how I had arrived at that moment, praying to a God I had met earlier in the day.

My childhood was, to say the least, troubled and difficult. My parents were Russian immigrants who had escaped from the Soviet Union in the '50s. Neither had believed in the Communist system, and both had dreamed of a life of freedom in America. In many ways, this is why they fell in love, or it was, in some way, one of the primary reasons they ended up together, for never in my life did I ever see any real love exchanged between them. Their fathers both fought in and died in World War II. My mother's father was taken prisoner near Raseiniai and died in a German POW camp, and my father's father froze to death outside of Leningrad. Their mothers both worked in factories near Daugavpils, and both were brutalized by German occupiers in the early stages of the war. My mother's mother had a child by a German as a result of a rape, and my father's mother was branded a sympathizer as a result of being forced to work as a prostitute servicing German soldiers. After the war, they were shunned by their neighbors and constantly harassed by the KGB. They were often taken in and held for indeterminate amounts of time at local prisons, and were denied the same rights as others who had suffered during the war. Also, because of this situation, neither of my parents was allowed to attend a decent school, or had a chance to become anything more than a basic service worker. They held jobs as cleaning people at a tank factory, where they met, and six months later they fled to Finland, initially leaving with four other workers from the factory. Though neither would ever discuss what happened during the actual escape, I know that all four of the other people they left with died during it. Once I heard mention that my father was somehow responsible for their deaths. I also know that they learned that as a result of their escape, their remaining family members were rounded up and sent to a gulag in Siberia.

Once in Finland, they went to the U.S. Embassy and asked for asylum. Because they had worked in a tank factory, the U.S. government believed that they might have valuable intelligence and flew them to a military base in Germany, where they were debriefed. Aside from knowing how to sweep and mop floors, neither of them knew anything. They were, however, given residency and sent to Detroit, and given jobs similar to the ones they had held in Russia, though this time in an auto-parts factory. They married, more because they knew no one else and had become dependent on each other, and I was born, though during my birth there were complications that prevented my mother from being able to have any other children, which she reminded me of almost daily for the rest of her life. They brought me home and continued on with their sad lives. They worked at the factory, and when they were home they drank and fought. My father beat my mother, and when I was relatively young, two or three, he started beating me. We both learned to leave him alone and not speak in his presence, though that made little difference. As I got older, the beatings got worse. At different times, both my mother and I had our noses broken, our arms broken, our ribs broken, and our teeth knocked out. The neighbors knew what was going on, but none called the authorities. It was a different time, and that was thought of as the correct way to handle such a situation. People at school knew I was from a troubled home and they spurned me. I had no friends, and no teachers who cared about me or believed I would ever do anything with my life. When I was sixteen, my father went over the edge. He saw my mother talking to a neighbor, a man, and believed she was having an affair. When she came home, he beat her with a wrench, and when I tried to stop him he beat me. When I woke up in a hospital room six days later, I learned he had beaten my mother to death, and had hung himself in his jail cell after being arrested for murder. To be completely honest, I wasn't upset at all. I felt bad that they had lived such miserable lives, but I felt relieved that their lives were finally over. My only concern was what I would do, or how I would take care of myself. I had no other family, and I was entirely alone. Soon, though, I learned I was not. A Catholic priest came to see me and told me he had spent several hours a day praying at my bedside. My parents were both atheists, and I knew nothing of God. I did, however, feel that this man was kind and pure and interested in helping me. He gave me a Bible and started talking to me about God, and about Jesus

Christ and the manner in which he gave his life
for the sins of man, and about the power of prayer.
I was in the hospital for several weeks, and over
the course of that time he indoctrinated me into
the ways and beliefs of the Roman Catholic Church,
and I became a Christian. He was the first person
to ever pay attention to me, and show me love, and
I came to love him in the manner I believe many sons
love their fathers. When I finished high school,
I entered the seminary and began training for my
life as a priest. When I finished, I took my vows and
entered the priesthood, believing I would devote my
life to the Father, and the Son, and the Holy Ghost,
and to what I believed was the one true church.
I believed I had found my true home, and that I had
found my true family, and that what I was doing was
the work of God, based on his word.

As I lay in my bed, reflecting on my life and praying,
I eventually fell asleep, though not for long. I woke
at five the next morning and prayed the Liturgy of
the Hours from my Breviary, as I do most mornings.
After praying, I would normally write the homily
for the morning mass, but I was feeling God so powerfully, and feeling so strong in my faith, that I decided
not to write anything and say whatever I was feeling
in the moment. I was very excited to celebrate mass,
which I do on most days, and which can be something
of a grind, especially on days when the church is
empty. On that particular day, I knew it wouldn't
matter if there were any worshippers or not. I didn't
believe I'd be celebrating with anyone but God

himself, who had blessed me so profoundly the day before, and I believed that none of the church's problems were relevant anymore, and that we were about to enter the greatest era in our long, distinguished history, an era when we would be proven righteous, and our glory would be confirmed by the Second Coming of Jesus Christ. The dwindling numbers of church members, and the aging of the remaining membership, would no longer matter. The controversies related to our policies towards women and homosexuals would cease to be. People would stop blaming us for the spread of AIDS in developing countries because of our stance on the use of condoms. And the never-ending scandals caused by the sexual abuse of children would end. We would be righteous.

I got dressed and left my quarters and walked to the church. I prepared the service with the deacon and the two altar servers and walked towards the altar to begin the introductory rites. I looked out into the church, and I saw four people, three elderly women and one elderly man, and the man appeared to be both homeless and asleep. Although this was typical of a morning mass, normally it would have disappointed me. This morning, though, it did not at all, for I knew at least three of these people were here to worship, and that at some point soon, along with the rest of God's true followers, we would all be in Heaven together. I began the service, and greeted them by saying In the name of the Father, and of the Son, and of the Holy Spirit, and my voice sounded pure and strong and true. When the people answered amen, I felt chills down my spine, and I thought yes, my Lord, amen, yes, my Lord Almighty, amen.

Normally, and according to tradition, during the Liturgy of the Word, I would read one passage from the Old Testament and one from the New Testament, but on that day I read two passages from the same book of the New Testament, Matthew 24:42–44, [42] Keep awake therefore, for you do not know on what day your Lord is coming. [43] But understand this: if the owner of the house had known in what part of the night the thief was coming, he would have stayed awake and would not have let his house be broken into. [44] Therefore you also must be ready, for the Son of Man is coming at an unexpected hour, and Matthew 25:31–34, [31] When the Son of Man comes in his glory, and all the angels with him, then he will sit on the throne of his glory. [32] All the nations will be gathered before him, and he will separate people one from another as a shepherd separates the sheep from the goats, [33] and he will put the sheep at his right hand and the goats at the left. [34] Then the king will say to those at his right hand, "Come, you that are blessed by my Father, inherit the kingdom prepared for you from the foundation of the world." Nobody noticed my indiscretion, not even the deacon, so I kept going, believing that God had endorsed my choices, and that he understood I was trying to alert people that his Son had arrived. The rest of the service was simple and beautiful, and as is the case sometimes with the things we do in life, whether they are part of our life's work, or simple tasks, or recreational events, everything felt right, and it was easy, and the time, which could sometimes pass slowly, seemed to speed up and move more quickly. After the mass, when I would normally go to my office and return mail and deal with administrative tasks, I decided to go for a walk through the neighborhood.

The church was in the Midtown area of Manhattan, on the west side of the island, in a neighborhood referred to as Hell's Kitchen. Directly to the east was Times Square, which, when I first started at the church, in the late '80s, after working first at a church in Newark, New Jersey, was a cesspool of sin, filled with pornography parlors, the streets teeming with prostitutes, drugs for sale on every corner. In the '90s, it was cleaned up by the mayor, a man I believed to be a fine, moral, righteous Catholic, a man who was holy without being part of the clergy, a man who was a warrior in the name of God and God's values. Hell's Kitchen, which had been an extension of Times Square, and a receptacle for the residual overflow of sin emanating from it, benefited greatly from the changes that the mayor imposed on the Square. Where it had once deserved its name, it became a neighborhood filled with actors, musicians, and young professionals who liked the idea of living near their offices in Midtown, and filled with restaurants and cafes and theaters that served them and provided them with venues. When I first started working there, I loved taking walks. While many of the neighborhood's residents were not Christians, or were lapsed Christians of some denomination, my clerical collar and position at the church commanded a certain respect. Shopkeepers were kind to me, and often went out of their way to help me. Policemen greeted me, and I often stopped and chatted with them. Mothers and their children would smile and wave to me. Even the prostitutes and drug dealers would greet me, saying things like hello, Father, how's the Big Man doing today? My walks made me feel good about myself, and about my choice to devote my life to God and service. I was proud to be a Catholic priest, and proud of my church.

Over the years, though, all of that had changed. My collar, for many, had become a symbol of shame and outrage. The press that resulted from the sexual abuse scandals had permanently altered the image of the church, and regardless of our individual positions on the issues, or our individual involvement in any of them, they had permanently altered how people viewed the men who served it. Inside the church, the most obvious effect was the number of parishioners who stopped attending our services. Outside the church, on my walks, I became something of a pariah. Shopkeepers were openly hostile towards me, and would sometimes ask me not to shop in their stores. Policemen looked at me in suspicious ways. Mothers and their children went out of their way to avoid me. I often heard people yell pervert or child molester after I had passed them. Once I was attacked and beaten. As I lay on the ground, being kicked and punched, I heard my attackers slurring me and slurring the church. I decided not to report them. And on more than one occasion, the doors of the church were spraypainted with epithets. I scrubbed them off myself.

All of this was heartbreaking for me. I had entered the priesthood in order to serve God, serve society, and do my part to make the world a better place. I had done everything in my power to live a life devoid of sin, and when I had sinned, I had confessed it and atoned for it. To know that, because of the actions of others, deplorable unforgivable actions, my life and work had been debased and tarnished was very difficult. It got to the point where I rarely left the church, and often when I did, I went out in civilian clothing so that I would not be identified as a Catholic priest. It was a nightmare. And not just for me, but for many of us in the church, or at least those of us who believed that some of the indiscretions had actually occurred. For those who didn't, and there were many, including Pope John Paul II and Pope Benedict XVI, there was no shame, just denial, confusion, defiance, and rage.

There was no nightmare, though, not on that day, that day after I had met the Messiah, the Son of God, Jesus Christ himself. There was only excitement and pride and tremendous optimism. I went out without an agenda, in my finest clothing, wearing my collar. The dirty looks I received did not bother me. The remarks I heard meant nothing. The way I saw parents hold their children's hands a little tighter when I passed was meaningless. I walked for three hours, and saw the glory of God everywhere, in everything. The city had never been so beautiful, despite the trash and squalor and desperation I saw, despite the fact that most of what went on in the city was done for the glory of money. I knew that soon everything would change. That soon, everything would be done for the glory of the Son, and of his Father, the Lord Almighty.

For the next several days, I followed the same routine. I would take care of my duties at the church, and celebrate mass, and in my spare time I would walk. During every service, regardless of the number of worshippers, I would scan the pews, hoping to see him again. With every step I took during my walks, I was filled with anticipation, and with every corner turned, I thought he might appear. I stared at the restroom door, and sometimes went into the restroom, hoping I would find him again. I knew it was only a matter of time. Jesus Christ would not appear in my life once and vanish. I knew in my heart that he would be back.

I saw him the next week during Sunday morning mass. The church was about half full. I was performing Communion, and the parishioners from the middle pews were at the rail. I glanced up and he was there, sitting alone, dressed in rags. It was a dreary New York day, cold and wet, and there was no sun coming through the church windows. There was, however, light coming from him, and light around him, in the same way you see light surrounding

Christ in classical depictions of him. I froze for a moment, and smiled, and was immediately flooded with a deep sense of love, and forgot that I was in the middle of mass, until the parishioner asked me if I was okay. I looked down and said yes and continued with the Communion, though I wanted to stop, stop everything, and tell everyone in attendance that God was literally in the room with us, that the Messiah had arrived, that all our prayers had been answered. As the service came to a close, I saw him stand and leave. Part of me was crushed, but a larger part of me told myself to trust God's plan, because I believed God would take care of me, take care of all of his people, and that all of what was happening was happening for a reason.

He was back again the next morning. And two mornings after that. And then he was gone for a week, and then reappeared again on a morning when there was no one else in attendance. Each time I saw him, I felt the same overwhelming sense of love. I felt the same ecstasy and electricity. The same peace. And each time I saw him, he stood and left just before the end of the service. And each time I believed he would be back, that it was part of God's plan, and that it would unfold before me as it was meant to be.

He came again during a Sunday mass. And this time, he didn't leave. As the rest of the parishioners left the church and I stood at the door and said goodbye to them, he stayed in the pew, unmoving, staring straight ahead, the light still emanating from him.

I was not the only person to notice him. A number of people approached him, all of them clearly feeling something similar to what I felt, as I saw them kneel before him, at which point he would motion for them to stand or sit next to him. As each of them left him, I saw him hug them in the same manner he hugged me the day we first met, and I saw them change, physically change, as if something had been taken from them, something sad or unpleasant, something tormenting, something that had prevented them from living or feeling or believing in the manner in which they wanted to. It was striking and beautiful, watching the touch of one man immediately change someone, watching whatever their burdens were lift and vanish. It was something that only God, or the Son of God, could possibly have the power to do.

When everyone had left, and the church was empty but for the two of us, I walked towards him. He was still sitting, silent and unmoving, and with every step I felt my heart beat faster and harder, and my hands started shaking. I stopped at the pew, and he turned and looked towards me. I spoke.
My Lord.
He smiled.
My name is Ben.
I kneeled before him.
Please get up.
The Bible says let us kneel before the Lord, our maker.
And I say no man should kneel before another.

I didn't move, couldn't move. I closed my eyes and held my hands in prayer in front of my chest. I heard him move and felt his presence come towards me. When I opened my eyes, he was kneeling in front of me, his face inches from my face. He spoke.
You like this?
He smiled at me.
You think it's required?
I spoke.
I am not God.
He spoke.
No man is God.
Are you not the Son?
Do you believe?
Yes.
He smiled again.
Sit with me.
He stood up. I couldn't move. He moved back to where he had been and sat down. I looked at him, but still couldn't move. He smiled.
Come, Father. Sit with me.
I stood slowly. My legs were shaking and my hands were shaking and I was both thrilled beyond description and absolutely terrified. I took three steps towards him and sat down. He smiled again and turned away, looking towards the altar of the church, above which was a statue of Christ hanging on a cross. I had a million questions for him, a million things I wanted to say, but I couldn't speak. I just stared at him, and he was beautiful, and he was God. I thought of Psalm 34:5, They looked unto him, and were lightened: and their faces were not

ashamed. I don't know how long we stayed that way, it might have been five minutes, and it might have been thirty, but once again, seeing him made me believe that my life's work had been worth it, that my commitment to God and the church had been worthwhile, and right, and just, and that God's light and glory would soon flood the world. He turned to me, and spoke.

You going to say anything?

I don't know where to begin, my Lord.

He laughed.

You look up there...

He motioned towards the altar, towards the crucifix hanging above it.

And you look at that piece of dead wood, beautifully carved, and beautifully painted, but still just a piece of dead wood, and you think it represents someone, and you think that someone is me.

Yes.

I'm not him.

You are.

I am not.

Is this a test?

No.

I know that God tests our faith every day, that being tested is part of faith.

God does no such thing.

And I believe this is exactly the type of test I would expect from him.

He laughed at me.

And I want to pass the test. I want to prove myself worthy of whatever God has in store for me.

God doesn't know you exist, and doesn't care about you.
I don't believe you.
So be it, but it is true.
How do you know?
Because God speaks to me.
Literally speaks to you?
Not with some silly voice, as it happens in the Bible.
Then how?
How doesn't matter. What does.
And what is that?
That this is all a fraud. This church, every church.
That the world's religions are bankrupt and meaningless. That the world itself is bankrupt. That it's all going to end.
As has been foretold.
I know every word of every holy book ever written.
None of them foretell what is coming.
Revelations does.
Revelations is a stone age science fiction story.
If that's so, who are you?
Who do you think I am?
Despite what you say, I believe you are Christ reborn.
I'm a final chance.
You're here to redeem us and forgive us.
There will be no redemption, and no forgiveness.
You're here to resurrect the dead, redeem the living.
I'm here to warn humanity that it is going to destroy itself in the name of greed and religion. That there is no God to save any of us. There is no Devil to take us to Hell. That man's only enemy is himself, and only chance is himself.

You're here to bring about the Kingdom of God
on earth, and to show that the Catholic Church
represents the one true faith.
Your perverted church has done more than any other
to bring this about.
If you feel that way, why are you here?
I've been going to churches, synagogues, and
mosques, trying to understand why people still
believe, despite the fact that what is said in these
places is ridiculous.
It's because God is real, and people know it.
It's because they're scared of death, and want
to disbelieve it.
The promise of eternal life is God's greatest gift.
The promise of eternal life makes people forsake
the life they're given.
Worship makes one's life better.
Love and laughter and fucking make one's life better.
Worship is just the passing of time.
I stared at him, and he smiled at me. And even though
I disagreed with everything he had said, or wanted
to disagree with it, his overwhelming physical presence, and the undeniable and unassailable feeling
that he was divine, and that, despite his denials, he
was the Son of God, made his words penetrate to
the core of my being, and the core of my faith.
He spoke again.
Stare at your cross.
I looked away and towards the crucifix hanging
above the altar. It was a realistic depiction of Christ.
Both the cross itself and Christ on top of it were
carved out of wood from an olive tree. The nails could

be seen through the hands and the ankles, and the look on Christ's face was one of peace, calm, and serenity. A crown of thorns could be seen on his head, and his eyes were open. Christ himself was painted in what I would call a realistic manner, giving one the sense that it was a close representation of what the real Christ must have looked like during the Crucifixion. I had seen it a countless number of times, and had stood beneath it while celebrating mass for many years. I had prayed to it, asked it for advice, begged it for help, and sought it out in times of strife and sorrow. And while it was, to me, a representation of the Holy Trinity and the Catholic Church, I would be less than honest if I said that it held my attention the way the man next to me did, or if its presence had the same power his presence had. After two or three minutes, during which the only sound I heard was the two of us breathing, he put his hand on my thigh. I felt an immediate, and extremely powerful, rush, unlike anything I'd felt in my life, something that was in my blood, my bones, my heart, and my soul, something that literally took my breath away. And as I turned towards him, he stood and leaned over to me and gently kissed me on the cheek, holding his lips on my cheek. I closed my eyes, and I felt myself become erect, a sensation I was not entirely comfortable with and had always resisted with the fear that it would lead towards sin, but that felt wonderful, absolutely and stunningly wonderful. He held his lips against my cheek for a moment, and then ran them slowly towards my ear, where he whispered.

Life, not death, is the great mystery you must
confront.
And he stood and he walked away.

Needless to say, I was stunned, and unable to move
or think, and I stayed in the pew, in a heightened
state, my heart pounding, my face burning,
my skin tingling, and my penis erect, for a long
time. When the physical sensations faded,
I started thinking about what had happened,
and felt a deep sense of conflict and confusion.
While I had never felt so good before in my
life, or felt love so powerfully, both physically and
emotionally, everything I knew, and had been
taught, and thought I believed, told me that what
had just happened was wrong, terribly wrong,
at best a sin and a transgression of my duties and
responsibilities as a priest, and at worst blasphemy,
heresy, and something that could result in my
spending eternity burning in the fires of Hell. In
my worship, I had never actually conceived, in a
real way, what it might be like to stand in Christ's
presence, to hear his voice, to speak with him,
and to have him touch me, to feel his love flowing
through and affecting every cell in my body and
every aspect of my soul. My thinking had always
been abstracted, about what it would mean to meet
Christ, but not what it would feel like to meet him.
And while I could not reconcile all of his words and
actions with those of the Savior, or what at the time
I believed might be the words and actions of the
Savior, the feelings I had felt when he spoke, and sat

with me, and touched me, and kissed me, and was left with after his departure, felt very pure to me, and very true to what I now believe Christ must have made his believers feel. It was, more than anything, an overwhelming and very profound sense of love, innocent, unconditional, deep, and true. And it was after feeling it that, for the first time in my life, I truly knew what it meant to be close to God. Not the Catholic God, or the Jewish God, or the Muslim God, or any other God, but the true God. The God that is life, and the God that is love.

When I could, which was at least an hour later, and probably longer, I stood and left the church. I asked the deacon to handle my remaining responsibilities, and I went to my quarters in the rectory, where I kneeled before a small crucifix on my wall and tried to pray. I wanted to say a prayer of examination and contrition, which is something I said most evenings before I went to sleep, in which I examined my thoughts and actions and asked the Lord to make me a better person, and a better priest. As I stared at the crucifix, I kept thinking about what Ben had said, about the cross being nothing but a piece of dead wood, and I kept thinking of the feeling of his hand, and his lips, and the difference between what Ben made me feel and what the crucifix made me feel. I recited the traditional prayer of contrition, O my God, I am heartily sorry for having offended you, and I detest all my sins, because I dread the loss of Heaven and the pains of Hell; but most of all because they offend you, my God, who are all good and deserving of all my love. I firmly resolve, with the help of your grace, to confess my sins, to do penance, and to amend my life, amen, but I did not feel any better, or any different. I kept trying, and tried to put more spirit into the prayer, but nothing changed, so I started praying, and speaking, directly to the Almighty Father, telling him about the conflicts I was having, telling him about the potential sins I had committed, and begging for his forgiveness. Nothing changed, and if anything, the fact that prayer was not helping me made me think more about Ben and what he had made me feel.

Whenever I was in crisis, or felt lost or confused, or needed earthly guidance, I reached out to the man who had brought me to Christ, and to the church, a man I considered my father here on earth, who had loved me more than my biological father, and who had brought me to the Holy Father. He had excelled in the priesthood because of his devotion and piety, and had become an archbishop of the diocese in Michigan where I grew up. I felt like I needed him that day, and though Sunday is obviously a busy day for a Catholic bishop, and normally I would never expect him to take time from that day, God's day, and a day when his diocese needed his leadership, I believed I truly required his counsel. It took two hours to get him on the phone, during which I only grew more confused and upset. When I heard his voice, and heard him tell me that he would always be there for me in my time of need, I felt better. I proceeded to tell him the entire story, from the moment I first saw Ben in the bathroom until the moment he left me sitting alone in the pew, and I included all my personal thoughts and emotions. When I finished, he told me that he was happy that I had reached out to him, and that my mortal soul was at great risk. The first issue he addressed was the church, and my feelings regarding some of its recent scandals. He said that while priests were human, and thus vulnerable to the same temptations as any human, the sexual abuse scandals were, in large part, a creation of the media, which was controlled by the Devil. He said that many of the allegations were invented as part of a smear campaign, and that the church protected the priests because they had done nothing except serve God, the church, and their parishes. He said that the campaign against the church was designed to destroy it, and was similar in conception to the Holocaust. And though the church did know of some transgressions, it had always handled them appropriately, and had done everything in its power to protect priests from unfounded accusations. He said he also believed that a large part of the campaign had to do with depleting the church's wealth through frivolous lawsuits, and he believed that if something truly bad had been happening, God would have stopped it. God, he said, always looked after the interests of the one true universal church. God, he said, would not have allowed anything so perverted to exist within it. He reminded me that he believed God chose each of the priests who became ordained within the Roman Catholic Church, and that God did not make mistakes.

We moved from there to my specific experiences with Ben. He said he wholeheartedly believed that Ben was an agent of Satan, most likely a demon in human form, sent specifically to tempt me and destroy me. He told me that God obviously must have something greater in store for me if Satan was sending someone so powerful, and that I should continue with a strict prayer regimen, which would give me the strength that I needed to fight. He also said that if the situation got further out of control, the Vatican had a staff of approximately ten exorcists who worked exclusively in the United States. They could be called upon to confront the demon directly, and had the power to send him directly back to Hell. He directed me to alert the other priests in my parish to the demon's presence, and said that all of us should keep holy water on our persons at all times, and that when the demon returned, we should splash him with it. I thanked him for his advice, and he told me he was proud of me, and that he was excited to see what the Holy Father had in store for me. I thanked him and said goodbye.

I spent the rest of the evening in prayer. I slept for a couple of hours and woke the next morning and resumed my duties and worked according to my normal schedule, celebrating mass, advising and comforting parishioners, and doing paperwork related to my church. Every free moment I had, I spent either reading the Bible or praying, hoping that God would respond to me in some way. I wanted, more than I had wanted anything in my life, to receive some sort of sign from the Holy Father, some sort of indication that all of the time I had spent on my knees and before the cross had not been wasted. Because of what I believed to be the gravity of the situation, I hoped to receive something quickly, and though I had been taught that God works in his own ways, ways that man does not and should not understand, I was upset when nothing came. A sense of loneliness, which in some way had always been with me, but through study, prayer, and activity I had always been able to ignore, deny, or control, began to overwhelm me. I had always felt that I was missing something, or had lost something, or misplaced something, and I assumed that that was a normal state of being, part of the pain of being human. Within a few days, however, the feeling became one of complete emptiness, hopelessness, and horror. I started weeping while I prayed, and weeping before I went to sleep. I wept when I woke up, and I wept whenever I was alone, and I had to force myself not to weep in the presence of other people. I didn't want to get out of bed and didn't want to see anyone. The job that had meant so much to me for most of my life had lost all meaning. It got to the point where I started thinking about killing myself.

I knew it was considered a mortal sin by the church, that it was believed I would damn myself to Hell for all eternity in committing it. I also didn't know what else I could do. I had no one to talk to about the situation. I knew that my fellow priests would tell me to continue to pray and that through prayer I would find my way. I had no other friends, and no family. I no longer felt close to the Holy Father or Jesus Christ. I was absolutely alone, doing something that no longer had any meaning for me, and I wanted to die.

I tried to identify why this was happening, and it was obviously tied to meeting Ben. This led me to a startlingly simple conclusion, which was that in my entire life, as a child, in the seminary, and in all my years in the priesthood, I had never felt real love. I hadn't received it from my parents, my teachers, or my fellow priests, and, despite what I wanted to believe, I had never got it from prayer, from the church, from Jesus Christ, or from my supposed relationship with the Holy Father. I realized that the most powerful form of love could only come from another human being. That the love that was spoken of in the Bible could only exist in a person walking the earth, and could not come from a representation of that person, regardless of how beautifully it was made. That love was something real if it was coming from a real person. I realized that I loved Ben, that even after my limited interaction with him, I loved him in a way that I had never loved anyone or anything. I also realized that, in some way, he loved me, that in his divinity, he expressed love for everything and everyone he came into contact with, and everything and everyone he touched. And for the first time in my life I understood Christ, and his importance, and I understood why I believed Ben was Christ reborn, and was the Messiah, as I still do. Like Christ, Ben loved unconditionally and without judgment; he loved men and women equally, and did not make distinctions between loving men and loving women; he made everyone who met him feel his love, and feel it in a way that was unlike anything they had ever previously felt; and he understood that religion as it was practiced had little to do with love. Love is something we must feel in our hearts, and in our bodies, and something we must express without fear of judgment or damnation. Love is something beyond rules and dogma. Love is beyond good and bad, or right and wrong. And love is beyond people who know little of it and have no experience with it deciding how it can be felt or expressed or who has the right to feel it or express it. I believed Ben would come back, and I decided to wait until I saw him again before I made any decisions about my future, though I already knew what I was going to do.

A week passed, and I continued to perform in my role as a priest, though it was entirely ceremonial for me. The words I spoke were empty, and I no longer viewed the blood and flesh of the Eucharist as anything other than what they were, and what they are, which is cheap wine and bad wafers. I spent most of my personal time sitting in the church, which was almost always empty, staring at the door, waiting for Ben to walk inside and sit down, but it never happened, and I thought constantly about what he had said to me the last time I had seen him, how he had whispered life, not death, is the great mystery you must confront in my ear. And he was right. I had spent my life worshipping death, fearing it, obsessing over it, and living my life according to what a book says will happen when it comes. I had functioned as a missionary of death for a dead church, praying to a dead man, and I came to understand that it's no way to live, and that living is all we have, and all we will ever have, and that it is not to be wasted. That love is life. That life isn't worth living without love. And that the Catholic Church, filled with celibate men who have no experience with it, has no right telling other people how to love or who to love or what kind of love is right or wrong.

I was faced with a choice, a very simple choice: I could continue to worship a God who promised me some kind of life after I died, or I could go live the life that I have been given. I could kneel before a statue, or I could find real people who might actually hear me. I could preach judgment and hate or experience love. It was an easy decision, and one morning, three weeks after my meeting with Ben, I took off my collar, and wrote a short note resigning my position, and thanked the men I worked with for their service, and walked out of the church. I walked into the street, a street where I knew he had walked, in a city where I knew he lived, and I started looking for him.

JUDITH

I'm a light sleeper. A very light sleeper. I always have been. As a little girl, my parents used to have to turn off the television and the phones after I went to sleep because if I heard them I'd wake up. And if I woke up, I always believed it was because something bad had happened, or was going to happen. I was very skittish. Everything scared me. At school and later, when I started working, even in my car, I was always scared. I didn't like being that way, but I couldn't help it. It's just how I am, I guess. Or it's how I was. How I was until Ben. After Ben, everything changed for me.

I've led a quiet life. Lots of people would say it was boring, and they're probably right. I was born in a small town in upstate New York. My dad was a farmer who grew potatoes and raised goats. My mom helped him and took care of me. I was an only child. My parents both wanted a large family, but there were complications when I was born and my mother couldn't have any more. My mother blamed my father for not getting her to the hospital early enough, and my father blamed my mother's body. I know neither of them really ever got over it because they used to tell me about it. The fact that I was such a disappointment didn't help.

I met Ben in New York. I love musicals and used to go into the city once a year to see a show. I would save all year and get a special outfit and a hotel room in Times Square and go by myself for a fancy dinner and a show. The next day I'd walk up and down Fifth Avenue and look at the windows of the fancy clothing stores. I knew I'd never be able to afford any of the clothes, and I knew they didn't make them for women my size, but I loved doing it anyway. I always dreamed of going into one of the stores and buying something, a bag or a dress or some shoes, but knew I'd never do it. Dreams are for people who can afford to make them come true. For someone like me, and for most normal people, dreams are just things that keep us going.

I was sleeping when I heard him. I usually stay in rooms on the first floor because they're cheaper. And because elevators scare me, and I don't like to use stairs. I had eaten a sandwich for dinner. It was roast beef and cheddar cheese, which I love. I had brought it with me from home, along with a bag of chips and some diet soda, and I had had some doughnuts for dessert, which are my true favorites. I had watched a couple of TV shows. One of my favorite shows is a dance competition show. The men are really handsome and always smiling, and the women are graceful and wear the most beautiful dresses. It's really like a fairy tale. And even though I loved the show, and never missed it, it hurt me every time I saw it. In some way, I know my parents loved me, even though they had trouble telling me, but no one else ever had. I'd never been on a date. I'd never danced with a man. I'd never really even had a man talk to me, at least not in a flirty way or anything. And it was what I wanted more than anything. Really, more than anything. To dance like one of the girls on the show.

After the show, I had gone to sleep. I had even put in earplugs because New York City is always so noisy. But I woke up right away. First I heard a rustling. Like an animal or something. It was a sound I knew from living on a farm. My dad had all his goats, and we had a couple of pigs, and there were lots of animals living in the woods near us. Animals aren't so scary, especially if they're not in your house. I thought I'd wait and it would go away, but it got louder. I thought whatever kind of animal it was, it was really loud. So I got out of bed and I walked to the window and peeked around the curtain.

At first I couldn't tell what I was seeing. There was a dumpster right outside. The lid was open, and there was tons of garbage in it. Something was moving around. Really moving around like crazy. I didn't want to open the window because I was scared whatever it was would come after me. And I didn't want to call the front desk because I could tell when I checked in that they didn't like me. I just stood and watched and hoped it would stop. I thought maybe even it would die. It was banging against the side of the dumpster, making really loud noises. I knew it must really hurt. And even though people try to pretend that pain doesn't do anything to them, none of us can really handle it. Everything bad we do in our life is because of pain of some kind. I couldn't imagine what it must have felt like. Twice I walked away from the window. I got into bed and put in my earplugs and put my pillow over my head. I closed my eyes real tight. I even balled up my fists. I just kept hearing it, though. A banging sound against the side of the dumpster.

Finally it stopped. It sure seemed like it took a long time. I went back to the window and peeked outside again. I saw a man lying in the dumpster. He was pale, and his clothes were really dirty and gross. He wasn't moving at all. He looked like he was dead for sure. But he didn't look scary dead, or mean or angry dead. He looked very peaceful. And normally I would have been very scared. I would have yelled or screamed. I might have hidden somewhere. I wasn't scared at all, though. I actually felt sort of wonderful. I just stared at the man lying in the dumpster. I forgot about everything. I even forgot I was me, which was something that had never happened. After a few minutes, the man started moving his hands and legs a little bit. I opened the window and talked to him.
Hello?
He looked up at me.
Hello.
You okay in there?
Yes, thank you.
You were banging around a lot.

He sat up and turned towards me.
Yes.
What were you doing?
I was looking for food.
In a dumpster?
Yes.
That's gross.
He laughed.
There's lots of good food in dumpsters.
No lie?
He laughed again.
No lie.
What do you find?
What other people don't want.
And you eat it?
Of course.
Is it good?
People throw away wonderful things.
Did you find anything wonderful tonight?
He smiled.
Maybe.
I smiled.
In there?
No, I got interrupted.
By me?
By God.
Excuse me?
I was speaking to God.
Like God, God?
Yes.
God from Heaven?
No, the real God.

Who's the real God?
If a bird dropped a pebble in the same spot once every thousand years, the time it would take for that pile of pebbles to grow to be the size of the largest mountain on earth would be equal to one second of infinity.
Yeah, so?
He laughed again.
God is infinite. And like infinity, too vast and too complicated for us to understand.
Then why do people worship him?
They've been tricked into believing something that is wrong but that they can understand. Humans cling to what they can understand, even if it's wrong.
If that's true, then how does God talk to you?
The sound you heard was me having a seizure, and my arms and legs and head hitting the sides of this dumpster. In the second before I have the seizures, I see things, and I hear things, I know things, and I am told things.
How do you know it's God?
Because of what I'm told, what I'm given.
Which is what?
I speak languages I've never studied, some of which are no longer spoken. I know the contents of the world's holy books, word for word, even though I have never read them. I understand general relativity, quantum mechanics, string theory, astrophysics, quantum gravity, physical cosmology, and black hole thermodynamics, even though I dropped out of school when I was fourteen.
What's all that got to do with God?
The first things allow me to understand

God as God has been written, and portrayed,
and worshipped. As people believe in God.
The others allow me to understand how close we
are to understanding the real God, the God that
doesn't need to be worshipped, that does not
exist as we do, that does not judge us, that does
not offer us anything more than what we have.
You sound crazy.
He smiled.
I haven't told you the crazy things.
Things crazier than going into dumpsters for food
and ending up having a conversation with God?
Yes.
I'm not sure I want to hear them.
He stood up, and in the dumpster he was almost
at the level of my window.
Give me your hand.
Why?
I'll show you.
Show me what?
He held out his hand. I stared at him. He was very
thin, skinny like he was starving. And for the first
time, I saw his eyes. They were jet black, and they
should have been scary, but they weren't. They were
beautiful. And when I saw them, for some reason
none of the crazy things he was saying sounded crazy.
They sounded right, and I saw everything he was
talking about in them.
Give me your hand.
Why?
To let you feel some of the things God tells me.
I reached out the window, through the bars that were

covering it. As I watched myself do it, I couldn't even believe it. I didn't like touching people. I knew they didn't like touching me. Not only that, I knew people didn't even like the idea of having to touch me. I always believed I was a good person, and I always felt I was kind and honest, but I knew what I looked like. I had to face myself in the mirror every day. I was, and I am, fat and ugly. It hurts to say it, but I know it's true. People have told me all my life what I am. They did it when I was a child, and all the way through school. They do it at work, even though I always smile and say hello. They do it as I walk down the street, like they think I can't hear them or something. And it always hurts. No matter how many times I hear it. It always hurts. So I couldn't believe this man was asking to take my hand. No man had ever done it. Part of me should have been scared. Once he had my hand, he could have done anything to me. But I guess I didn't care. His eyes told me he was something beautiful and eternal. And even if he had hurt me, I would not have regretted it. Just to have had it happen once. To have a man ask for my hand, and to have a man want my hand.

It was a little cold. There was a slight breeze coming into the alley. The dumpster smelled like bad meat. I could hear traffic out on the streets of New York. I could hear someone yelling the word tickets over and over. The alley was lit by two streetlights. They were yellow, and one of them kept flickering. The shadows were moving with the flickers. People walking the street were moving into the

shadows. I remember the moment very clearly.
More clearly than anything, ever, because it's the
moment my life changed. My hand went out between
the bars of the window. The bars were round and
painted black and some of the paint was flaking off
and my skin became cold, even though I was wearing
a long-sleeved nightie. He took my hand and held it
between both of his, and he smiled, and he spoke.
My name is Ben.
I had hoped to feel some kind of awesome romantic
electric charge, like from a TV drama or a romance
novel or even a Hollywood movie. What I actually felt
was even better. It was the best feeling I had ever had
in my life. My insecurity disappeared. My self-doubt
disappeared. My self-hatred disappeared. My sense
of disappointment in myself disappeared. The feeling
that I was bad and wrong and ugly and nothing, that
I was a fat, ugly failure, it just disappeared. That feel-
ing of being alone, always alone, truly and deeply and
horribly alone, disappeared. He held my hand and
smiled and looked at me. I smiled back and spoke.
God.
Yes.
I let go and smiled.
Thank you.
He smiled and stepped back.
I don't want you to go.
I need to find food.
I have food in here.
It's not just for me.
Who else?
My friends.

Who are they?
People who want to be loved.
What's that mean?
You know what it means. You felt what it means.
Can I get it for you?
No.
I have a little bit of money.
No, thank you.
I would like to give it to you.
I don't need money.
Why not?
Because I find what other people throw away.
And that's enough.
More.
He started to step out of the dumpster. I didn't want him to go. Ever. I knew that when he did, I would feel the way I always felt. The way I felt before him.
Don't go.
He stopped.
I don't want you to go.
He turned around.
Will you come inside, and sit with me?
Yes.
I'll meet you in the lobby?
Yes.
He turned and climbed out of the dumpster. I closed my window. I met him in the lobby a couple of minutes later. I was really nervous before he arrived. People were staring at me and laughing. I couldn't blame them, really. If I wasn't me, I would have been laughing too. When Ben walked in, everyone stopped. I was worried that they would stop him, or

call the police, but everyone just stopped talking and laughing and everything. They just stared at him.

He smiled at me and took me by the hand and we walked to my room. I opened the door and we stepped inside. He closed the door and told me to lie down on the bed. I was really excited. Really, really excited. Super excited. I had no idea what was going to happen. Whatever it was would be great. And as excited as I was, I was also calm in a weird way. Much calmer than I would have thought. I wasn't shaking or feeling like I was going to cry or scream at all.

He turned off the TV and lay down next to me. I couldn't believe it was happening. He started asking me questions. My name, where I was from, what my parents were like, and what they did. As we talked, and I answered his questions, he moved closer to me, and put one of his arms around me, and took one of my hands. He was so close to me that he started whispering. He asked me about my childhood. I told him it was unhappy. He asked me about school, and I told him it was always easy for me, but that I failed on purpose, because I didn't want to give kids another reason to hate me. He moved closer, and his hands started moving around my body. It was beautiful. Totally the best time I had ever had. And it wasn't dirty or perverted. His hands felt like they were part of my body. Everywhere he touched felt like it was absolutely the right spot, and the spot where I would have had him touch me if I could have asked him. We kept talking, and I started asking him questions. The same type of things he asked me. And he told me about his childhood, and growing up in Brooklyn. He told me his father hated him and beat him, and his brother hated him and beat him. He told me that his mother coddled him and that his sister worshipped him. He told me that he was Jewish. I had never met a Jewish person before, or at least not one that I knew was Jewish. He said his Jewish rabbis where his family went to pray had great expectations for him, and believed he would do great things, and maybe even change the world. I told him that must have been hard, that it was the opposite of my life, where nobody expected anything. He said it wasn't hard, because they were right about what they believed, but wrong in thinking about what he would do, and how he would do it. What was hard was waiting for it to happen. Spending all of his life alone, knowing it was going to happen, and just sitting around and waiting.

We fell into some kind of talking trance. He kept touching me and feeling me. He took off my nightie. And he took off my panties. And he whispered in my ear, and I felt him move inside of me. And it wasn't like some thunderbolt hit me, or like some passionate kiss in a rainstorm. It just felt full, and complete, and quiet. I felt like I could die at that moment and I would be okay with dying. I felt like however I had wasted my life, and whatever terrible things I'd seen and heard and felt, it didn't matter anymore. This man was inside of me and he was holding me and I was feeling love. True love. The kind of love that really could change the world.

We stayed that way for hours. For the whole night even. He stayed behind me and inside me. He was moving the entire time. Very slowly and gently. Sometimes so slowly I could hardly feel him moving. Sometimes a little faster. We talked the whole time. I told him everything about myself and my life. I told him how I lived alone on my parents' farm, which was overgrown and crazy. How I worked as a cashier at a superstore and tried to be nice but had people be mean to me all day. How I lived in a dead town filled with churches and bars and husbands beating their wives and children. How I spent all my nights alone in front of the TV, eating canned food and potato chips and ice cream. How I cried every night because I didn't believe anyone would ever care for me. I told him about all my best hopes and biggest dreams and my scariest fears. I told him all I wanted in my life was a friend who I could call sometimes and say hi. How I always dreamed about having someone tell me I was beautiful, or even pretty. How I was scared I'd die someday all by myself and no one would find me until a long time after I was gone. I told him that there hadn't been a time in my life that I hadn't been lonely and that I didn't want to feel it anymore.

He told me how he lived with a woman and her child in a small apartment. How he had been in jail and knew people were looking for him because he had jumped bail. How he spent his days touching people and helping people and teaching people about how to live in a world that is falling apart and dying. He talked about love. How love is the only thing in the world that is worth living for, the only good thing that we have left, and the only thing we haven't destroyed. That true love, God's love, isn't about beauty or perfection or man or woman. That love isn't about declarations made before false idols. That love isn't what a bunch of hateful old white men decide it is. That love isn't something that can be written into laws by corrupt governments. He said love is something shared by two people, any two people, man and woman, or man and man, or woman and woman, in whatever way makes them feel perfect and beautiful and peaceful in their hearts. He said love is what I was feeling as he held me and touched me and moved inside of me. He said that if I wanted to see God, see God as he did, and in God's true form, he could show me. He told me to close my eyes, so I did. He moved his hand onto me and moved his body a little more and he stopped talking to me and I could feel his breath on my neck and my cheek. It built inside of me. God built up inside of me. And the more he moved, the more it built. And his breath felt hot and smelled sweet. And he kept moving, real slow, and moving real deep inside, and it built until I saw it and felt it. It was love, and joy, and pleasure, and every part of my body sang some song I had never heard but was the prettiest, most beautiful song ever, and it was blinding and pure and my brain went the whitest white ever, and I saw infinity, forever and ever, I saw infinity, and even understood it, and understood everything else in the world, all the hate and rage and death and passion and jealousy and murder, and none of them even mattered. I felt one hundred percent secure. I felt nothing bad. I saw the past and the future. It was the greatest second of my life. Really the greatest, and I knew in that one second I was experiencing God. The real God. The true God. The eternal God. The God that can't be in a book or in a church or on a Sunday TV show or on a cross or a star. The God that can't be explained or described or written about or taught or preached. The God that can't be forced upon people or used to damn them. And I loved that God, that perfect amazing unbelievable true God. And I knew that none of the other Gods meant anything.

When that moment ended, Ben kept moving and breathing very slowly. I didn't know what to say and I guess I didn't want to say anything. Nothing I would have said would have meant anything or even mattered. So I just kept my eyes closed and listened to him breathe and felt him. And it just kept going, for the whole night, him inside of me. His hands moving all over me. The two of us loving each other. He kept speaking but I don't know what he was saying. All I know is what I felt. God, God, and more God. God all night. When the sun came up, he stopped moving but stayed inside of me and just held me. Finally I said something to him.
Ben.
Yes.
I don't ever want you to leave.

I'm going to leave in a little while.
Please.
Come with me if you want.
Where?
I have to find some food and go back to the Bronx.
What will I do?
Whatever you want.
What will your woman say?
She's her own woman.
What will she say?
She'll say hello, and welcome you.
He kissed me softly on the cheek and pulled away
from me. I felt him come right out of me. And not just
physically. I felt it right in my heart too. And I felt
like I had lost something. But not something silly,
like my keys or my gum. More like my arm or my foot
or something, something that really mattered.
Like something that I could live without, but would
make life much harder if it were missing. And life is
hard enough. Life is hard enough with everything
we're given. With what I used to think God gave us,
before I knew the truth. Before I realized that all that
Bible nonsense is just silly. That Bibles are just books,
like any book is just a book. Except maybe Bibles are
more boring and more ridiculous and harder to read.
And even though they say all sorts of things,
and make all sorts of promises, they're full of lies,
or lies if you're foolish enough to believe they contain
something real. I know that God doesn't give us
anything in life. So God can't take anything away.
But a real person can give, and can take away.
And when Ben was no longer inside of me, I felt

something was gone. Something that was more than anything I'd ever known. Something greater than a made-up God in an old dusty book.

He stood and I watched him get dressed. I felt sorry for him in his raggedy clothes. I wanted to get him some new clothes. Not that I could get him anything fancy, but I could get a discount on some clothes at the store where I worked. Simple clothes for a regular person. And I noticed his scars for the first time. Long thick scars over his whole body. They were really scary. Like someone had taken a white marker and drawn lines everywhere. Except I knew they weren't from a marker or anything. He had been really hurt. And I tried to imagine what it must have felt like to be hurt like that. And I could imagine it. That really truly awful terrible pain. The kind that can only be felt alone, and that no one can help you with. I really could imagine it.

As he was putting his shirt on, he smiled at me.
I knew if he left I would never see him again. I didn't want that. I couldn't even think of it. Of not having the feeling of being with him, or even near him again. So I spoke up. For the first time in my life. A life spent not talking and hiding and being scared and alone. He changed me away from it, and I spoke up.
I want to come with you.
He smiled.
Okay.
Really?
Yes.

No lie?
He smiled again.
No lie.
I stood up, and even though I look the way I do,
I wasn't even embarrassed. I started getting dressed
right away.
What should I bring?
You don't need anything.
Clothes?
He laughed.
What you're wearing.
Money?
Doesn't matter.
It will take me just a minute to get packed.
You don't need those things.
Will I be back?
If you choose.
You sure I don't need anything?
We don't need most of what we have.
I smiled, and pulled on my pants and put on my
jacket. He smiled at me while I got dressed, and
his eyes stayed on my body, and he made me feel
beautiful, which is something I had never felt,
not once, in my entire life. Once I was ready,
I grabbed my wallet and we left.

It was a crappy day. Cold and really rainy. It was the
kind of rain that hurts your skin when it hits it. It felt
like little needles. Ben didn't have a good coat. His
was an old brown sport coat like a librarian would
wear. It was really funny. And I don't think it kept
him warm or dry. He didn't seem to mind, though.

The rain hit him and he smiled. We walked along the street and he smiled. Everywhere we walked, he just smiled. He didn't talk at all. Sometimes he would take my hand. Like when there was a big crowd, or the cars were blocking the crosswalk. And sometimes I would get out of breath or have to slow down. He never seemed to even care. He would slow down and make sure I was okay. He was so nice and kind and gentle. It seemed like that was all that mattered to him. And it made all of the terrible things that had tortured me my whole entire life just go away. Kindness and love can make any pain go away. It's true. I know it.

After we walked a long time, Ben cut off the street and we went into the subway. I had never been in it before. I had always been scared to go under the ground. I thought I'd get mugged or bit by a rat or fall in front of a train. Or maybe I would just get lost and never find my way out. Or maybe people would point at me and make fun of me. I was just scared. Really scared. But Ben took my hand and we walked right down, and we waited for one of the exit doors to open and then we walked right through it. And we walked right to the platform and waited. I could feel people staring at us, but I realized they weren't staring at me. They were staring at Ben. Nobody was talking. And they weren't looking at their phones or little email machines or newspapers or the floor or even each other. They were looking at him. All of them, just silent and staring at him.

The subway train pulled up and we stepped on. There were empty seats and we sat down. I had no idea where we were going, and Ben and me hadn't said a word to each other since we'd left the hotel. There were a few other people in the car, and a few more got on with us. Everybody was sitting down. Ben closed his eyes and smiled and started breathing very deeply and slowly. It wasn't dramatic or anything, like some actress trying to calm down after being hysterical. It was just simple and pure. Just a man breathing. And people were staring at him again. Like they couldn't believe what they were seeing. Like their lives were all so busy that they had forgotten what a still silent man looked like. And as he breathed they all seemed to calm down. As if he were giving them what he had, or what he was feeling. Some of them closed their eyes and started breathing just like him. Some just smiled and stared at him. A few stood up and walked towards us to be closer to him. And at every stop more people got on the car. And whatever he was doing, he would do to every one of them. And even though it was roaring down the tracks at some crazy speed, that car was the most quiet and simple and beautiful and peaceful place in the world.

We stayed on the car for thirty or forty minutes. Nobody got off at a single stop. It got really crowded, but didn't feel that way. People were just breathing and smiling and being happy. I had never seen so many different kinds of people, black people and white people and brown people and all different kinds, smashed together in one place without looking suspiciously at each other or avoiding each other.

Without hating each other, or at least not liking each other at all. And it was just because of him, because of the way he sat and he breathed and smiled. Because he just looked like love, like peace, like he was content with things, even though he was dressed like a bum. As the car started to slow down before one of the stops, I felt Ben's hand on my leg. I looked at him and he smiled and motioned towards the door. When the car stopped, we stood and walked off. Everybody watched him go, and no one moved. They just stared at him and kept breathing. And as we were walking away, I looked back at the car. People were standing at the doors and the windows, staring. Watching Ben and me walk away. They were all smiling.

We came out of the subway into another part of the city. It was not very nice. I could hear sirens and cars honking and loud rap music and people yelling, mostly in Spanish. It smelled like meat was cooking. There were people everywhere on the streets, and none of them were white. The buildings were all big and rundown and looked the same. There was trash in the streets. Ben seemed the same as he was everywhere. Comfortable and calm. Like he wasn't scared at all. I was scared, though. Really scared. There were no black people in the town where I lived. Once or twice a week I might see a black person in the store where I worked. When people talked about them, it was mostly because they were on TV or on a sports team or something, or because they had seen them in the city being loud and were scared of them. I was scared of them, for sure. Me and Ben were the only white people I saw. It was like I was one of them where I'm from. It didn't feel nice.

We walked towards a group of big brown buildings. I guessed it was some kind of housing project. It looked dangerous to me. Nobody stared at us or even paid attention to us. Ben just walked along. And he didn't look so poor anymore. Lots of the people we saw were wearing old clothes that weren't so nice. Lots of the people looked poor. He just looked like one of them. Or like a white version of one of them. A beautiful scarred white version. But he was obviously still poor. And poor people are poor people, regardless of the color of their skin.

As we crossed the street and stepped onto the curb in front of the buildings, a large black man came walking up to Ben. I thought we were dead, for sure, and I wished I had a whistle or some mace or something. I thought about running, but knew I wouldn't get very far. Ben just kept walking and said hello to the man and the man said hello back. They hugged, and the man started whispering in Ben's ear. I was relieved, for sure, but something seemed wrong. Ben nodded as the man talked. The man looked real worried, and I could see his eyes looking around as he whispered. When he finished, Ben hugged him again and turned to me.
We need to go.
Why?
It's not safe here.

I know that.
Not for the reasons you think.
I could tell this was a dangerous place.
It's a poor place.
Yes.
Poor people are desperate, not dangerous.
Let's leave.
My friend is going to take us somewhere safe.
I'm scared of him.
You're scared of the color of his skin, not him.
That's not true.
Yes, it is.
He took my hand and nodded to the man and we started to walk away from the buildings. We were following the man and we were walking fast and I was still scared, but not as much. What Ben said hurt me, but mostly because it was true. I was extra scared because the man was black, and black people scared me. I knew it was wrong, but it was also just what I felt. I'm sure if he was walking around where I lived, he might be scared too.

We went around the corner, and the man opened the doors of a big SUV. We got inside and he started driving us away, but not too fast. As we came around another corner, I saw a group of policemen standing near their cars. All of their lights were flashing. Standing with them was another group of men in blue suits, and some had bulletproof vests. They all looked very serious, and they looked really mean. They were holding photocopies of a picture. I couldn't really see it very good, but I knew who it was. I knew that they were looking for Ben. He watched them as we drove past. He didn't look nervous or scared or anything. He just looked at them like he looked at everyone else, like he was best friends with them or something. I couldn't imagine looking like that at people with guns who were hunting me. But he did. He looked at them like he loved them with his whole heart, even though they wanted to get him.

We drove for a few blocks until we reached another set of big buildings. They looked exactly like the other ones. If I had been shown pictures of them, I would have thought they were all the same. The man parked the car, and we got out and started walking. We went into one of the buildings. It was dirty. There was trash in the entrance. A man was sleeping on the ground right outside the door. He was snoring and his pants were dirty. We waited for the elevator. I could hear it creaking on the wires. The big man who drove us was still standing with us. He and Ben weren't even talking. The elevator arrived and the door opened. We got inside and went up. It stopped at the seventh floor. The man got out first and Ben smiled at me and motioned for me to follow him and I did it. I stepped right out and followed him. And I should have been scared, but I wasn't. I was with a black man who looked like a killer and a homeless man who ate garbage. And I wasn't scared. I was just walking along with them like we were going to the mall to get some new pants or a computer game or something. What Ben had said before was right. I was scared of that man's color. What matters is what's in a man's heart.

We walked to the end of the hall and the man took out some keys and opened a door. He held the door for me and Ben and we went inside. It was a small apartment. It wasn't anything fancy, but it wasn't bad. There were five or six people sitting at a table, listening to a police scanner. They were all black. They were drinking water and eating fruit. They looked right at us. I didn't know what to say. A young girl, a really really pretty girl, with long curly hair
and beautiful caramel skin, stood up and laughed
and walked over to Ben. She started talking.
You know the trouble you cause?
He smiled and kissed her.
I'm happy to see you.
They kept kissing and talking.
They got an army out there trying to find you.
Michael got us first.
You lucky.
I know.
They catch you they taking you away.
I know.
I don't want that.
Neither do I.
We can't go back.
We'll find somewhere else.
We gotta leave everything behind.
That doesn't matter to me.
He put his arms around her and hugged her and kissed her neck and her cheek and her lips again.

And even though he seemed to love everyone, and make everyone feel loved, I could tell he loved her differently. Like he knew that no matter what he did or where he went he would always come back to her, and she knew the same thing. It was real sweet the way they held each other and kissed each other, really the sweetest thing I'd ever seen, including all the sappy stuff on TV and in the movies. There were no barriers between them. Like they accepted each other completely, and loved each other truly. I guess that's the way it's supposed to be between everyone. Love without conditions, love for the sake of love, love even though we're different. But it's never actually like that. Most of the time love is closer to something like hate. But with them it was beautiful.

They separated and the girl looked over at me. Ben introduced us and the girl, Mariaangeles, smiled and said hello. The people over at the table, an older woman who was fat like me, and a younger woman, and three men, including the one who had brought us here, were all still listening to the police scanner. One of the men looked over and smiled and said they're leaving, motherfuckers are leaving, and everyone started laughing. Ben smiled and walked over to the woman and kissed her on the cheek and said thank you. I asked Mariaangeles what had happened, and she said the woman monitored the scanner for some people in the projects and let them know when the police were coming. She had heard they were coming for a white man in his early thirties, with dark hair, who was heavily scarred. The only person who fit the description was Ben. She said Ben was known in the area because he was the only white person living there, and because he helped people, and gave them food and money. She said some people believed he could make sick children well and make drug addicts and alcoholics stop taking drugs and drinking. That people called him the Prophet, and believed he was a holy man, and they loved him and watched out for him. So the lookouts, who were normally there for other reasons, which I didn't ask about, had come to their apartment and brought her away, and watched for Ben to make sure he didn't get caught. I asked why the police and FBI were looking for Ben, and she said because he skipped bail after he got arrested for living in the subway tunnels. I asked if that was really something they would need all those guns for, and she said it was because Ben was living there with a black man who had a bunch of guns. I asked her where they would go now, and she said they'd figure something out, that there were people who would help take care of them, people who loved Ben, and they would give them somewhere to live.

I looked over at Ben, who was sitting with the people at the table. They were all speaking Spanish, which he seemed to speak just like them. The word policia kept being used and they were laughing a lot. Watching them, they looked like a family, a really really happy family. I was a little bit jealous, because they looked like the family I had always wished my family was, smiling and joking and being nice to each other. It didn't even matter that they all looked different from me. I wanted to be one of them. I had been living alone for a long time, and I had my parents' whole house and whole farm all to myself. It was not a happy place and never had been. It hadn't been awful or violent or scary, it was just empty. An empty house and empty fields. And I was empty. And I was tired of it. Tired of being sad and alone. I wanted to know what it was like to smile there and be happy there and to know love there. I wanted to hear someone laughing in my house. I couldn't remember ever having heard it, unless it was me laughing at a TV show that I was watching alone while I ate dinner or something. I wanted to come home from my job, which really stunk, just standing checking people out at a superstore all day, and feel like there was something or someone at home waiting for me. Who might even be happy or excited to see me.

Mariaangeles came out of a bedroom with a little girl. A beautiful little girl who looked just like her, though she sure seemed young to have a child. The girl ran over to Ben and gave him a hug and sat on his lap. Everyone was still talking in Spanish. I didn't know what they were saying at all, but I imagined they were talking about where they were going to go and what they were going to do. I sat down at the end of the table, in the only empty chair. I felt happy to sit down and be part of the table. And I had an idea. It was a great idea, I thought. A wonderful, really fun idea. I raised my hand, but nobody noticed, so I raised it a little higher, and waved it a little. Ben looked over at me.

You don't have to raise your hand.

I don't speak Spanish, so I wasn't sure about the rules.

There are no rules.

I didn't want to be rude.

You're not.

I have an idea.

About what?

About where to go.

We're okay here.

But those men, they're going to come back.

Yes.

And they'll keep coming back until they get you.

Probably.

I have a farm. It's upstate. There's a big house and land, and it's just me. I live there all by myself.

It's not just me.

Whoever you want could come. I'd like it a lot.

They might come for me there as well.

Oh man, if you think you have a good system here, we could really have one there. Our nearest neighbor is a mile away. We'd know for sure if someone was coming.

He smiled.

You're sure you want us.

I smiled.

Yes. I'd love it. It would be so fun.

And the yard would be awesome for the little girl.

We could get her a wagon or a bike or something.

Her name is Mercedes.

I smiled at her.

Hi, Mercedes.
She smiled at me. He tickled her.
You want to move somewhere with a yard?
She laughed.
Yes.
He looked at Mariaangeles, smiled.
She smiled at him.
She seems okay to me.
He breathed through his nose and nodded.
She is.
I ain't ever lived anywhere but here. Be nice to get out.
Yes.
She looked at me.
You sure?
I nodded.
Yes.
She smiled.
Let's go.
I smiled.
No way.
You asked for it, white girl, you got it. I hope you know what you in for.
I laughed and she laughed and I stood up and hugged her and she hugged me. The man who drove us asked when we wanted to leave and Ben smiled and said let's go now. The man stood and said cool with me and the old woman gave all of us hugs. One of the other women asked Mariaangeles when she'd be back and Mariaangeles said if she was lucky, never. We took the elevator back down from the seventh floor and we left.

I didn't even go back to the hotel and get my stuff. The man put my address into the computer in his car, and off we went. The drive was real easy. And it was fun too. We listened to the radio and sang along with some of the songs whenever we knew the words. Ben could sing beautifully if he wanted to, like an opera singer or something, but mostly he just sang for laughs. He'd make faces and do little disco dances and pretend to be crying during the love songs. He'd take Mercedes' hands and make her laugh and laugh over and over again. During a duet, he and Mariaangeles took the separate parts and sang to each other. We stopped a couple of times for food and bathroom breaks and stuff, but Ben didn't really eat anything. He would drink water and stand outside, staring up at the sky. I asked one time if he was looking at God or talking to God or something, and he just laughed and said no, he just liked looking at the stars and that he couldn't see them in the city. I looked up, and the stars were just coming out, and I have to say, they were pretty cool.

The drive took five hours. When we arrived, the house was dark and there were no lights. Mariaangeles said she'd never been out of the city before and Mercedes started crying. Ben held her and whispered in her ear and she stopped right away. The house was big and white and old. It had six bedrooms and four bathrooms and was sort of falling apart a little bit. There was a barn and the fields were overrun with weeds and little baby trees. When we pulled up right in front of the house, Ben got out and smiled and looked up at the sky again. I went right inside and turned on the lights. Mariaangeles brought Mercedes in and I told them to take whatever rooms they wanted, and the man who drove came in and I made him some food I had in the fridge. Ben stayed outside. I got a little worried and looked out the window and saw him walking into one of the fields. The moon was only out a little bit, and before I could go out to him he disappeared.

I waited up for him and watched TV. There are so many good shows on late at night. He never came back, though, and I fell asleep on the couch. When I woke up the next morning, I could hear Ben standing near the front door with the man, and I heard him say:
It could be tomorrow, or it could be in five years, but there's no stopping it. Protect the good around you. Love the good you know. Keep them safe.
How do I know who's good?
You know.
I can't tell the way you can.
We all know good and bad in our hearts. We can see and feel it. Trust yourself.
You sure you gonna be okay up here?
Yes.
What if they come for you?
Then they come.
They gonna lock your ass away if they get you.
They won't get me unless I let them.
You gonna?

Live your life. Love your children. Don't believe what you're told. Forget the lies of religion and government. And don't worry about me.
You need money?
No.
Anything?
No, thank you.
Get in touch if you do.
Go, my friend.
Ben hugged the man, and the man turned and got in his truck and pulled out. Ben came inside and smiled at me and kissed me. He asked how I was and I said great and he said thank you again for having us here, it's a beautiful place, a perfect place. I said sure and he hugged me and it felt great. When he let go of me, I missed him right away, even though he was right there. He asked what I was going to do for the day and I told him I had to go to work. He asked if I minded if he did some work around the house and I laughed and told him to do whatever he wanted. He smiled and said thank you, and walked away.
I got dressed and went to work. The store I worked in was the biggest store ever, the size of a whole bunch of football fields. It sold everything you could ever imagine, though the most popular things were steaks, beer, and guns. I just rang things up all day. I sat on a little stool when I could, but mostly I was standing up, which isn't easy for someone like me. On my breaks, I went to the break room and ate. I had a couple of people I talked to at work, but mostly I didn't talk to anyone. I sat by myself and watched TV. On the first day with Ben and Mariaangeles and Mercedes, I

could hardly sit at all. And I didn't mind being alone. I kept wondering what they were doing, or thinking about them walking around the house and the yard. I always tried to be cheerful with customers, but I was extra cheerful. And it didn't even bother me when they ignored me.

When I came home, I couldn't even believe it. The whole house was clean. Really really clean. Everything had been wiped down and the floors were all mopped. Even the kitchen was clean and the fridge was scrubbed. The yard, which I only had done three times a year, was totally cut. We had a push mower, so I knew it must have been hard work. I started looking around the house for everyone. I found Mercedes in her room, playing with a doll. I don't know where they'd found it, but it was one of mine from when I was a little girl. It was cheap but pretty cute, with a little pink dress and plastic hair, and I hadn't seen it in years and years. I went in and started playing with her. And she wanted to play with me. And it was awesome. Just playing with this little girl. Who didn't look at me and think bad things about me and wasn't scared of me. She was just happy. We played dance and nurse and singer. We played going to the grocery store and ice cream summer day. And the rest of the world disappeared. The rest of the world didn't even matter. I felt like I felt with Ben. Like what was important was right now, not sometime in the past or sometime in the future. It felt like life was what it is supposed to be.

We played for a long time, and near the end I heard some noise down the hall. I hadn't seen or heard Ben or Mariaangeles, but figured they must be around somewhere in the house. I stood up and told Mercedes I would be right back and went down the hall. The noises were closer. They were clearly hanky panky noises. They made me nervous and scared, but also pretty excited. The door was sort of open and I peeked around the edge. Mariaangeles was on top of him and she was really moving her hips. It looked like she was dancing or something. Ben was watching her, and smiling, and his hands were moving up and down on her body. I started to move away but Ben saw me. He smiled wider and motioned for me to come into the room, but I was too embarrassed and ran back down the hall and went back in with Mercedes. I kept hearing the noises for another half an hour or so. I had always thought of sex as dirty or bad. Something you weren't supposed to be open about with other people. Something that was against the rules of the church and God and that laws were made against. But they sounded happy. And when Ben was inside me, it was the best feeling I had ever had in my whole life. I had been in churches with my parents many times. And I had never felt anything in them. It was just boring. And it seemed old and silly. But when I felt that feeling with Ben, when I saw the light, and saw forever, and felt them, that was God.

When the noises stopped, Ben and Mariaangeles came into the room. Mercedes was really happy to see them, and we all went and had dinner together.

I wasn't sure how to act after what I had seen, but they just acted the way they always seemed to act, which was really happy. Dinner was great, my favorite, macaroni and cheese. After dinner, Mariaangeles took Mercedes upstairs to give her a bath and put her to bed. Ben smiled and walked over and kissed me. It was a long kiss. A real French kiss. I wasn't sure what to do so I just did it back. And it kept going. We kept going. Kissing like teenagers or something. And he pulled me out of my chair and started taking off my clothes. Thinking back, I can't even believe it, but at the time I couldn't think at all. I was just feeling so awesome. He took off my clothes right there in the dining room. And we went down on the floor. And he started going over my whole body. He was using his hands and his mouth and his tongue. Everywhere on me and in me. And I just closed my eyes and let him do whatever he wanted. It was wonderful. Like the best thing ever. He was whispering while he did it. And I tried to listen but it took me away from what he was doing to me. But what I could hear was about God. That this was God. That what I was feeling was God. That God in books could never make me feel like this. That I would never feel this way if it wasn't right, if it wasn't natural, if it wasn't part of God, the true God.

As he was doing all those things to me, I heard Mariaangeles come into the room and laugh. I opened my eyes and I was really embarrassed. Ben was the only person except for my parents who had ever seen me naked. I started to get up but she shook her head and smiled and kneeled next to me and put her hands on my shoulders and held me down and started kissing me. Something in me said it was wrong, but it wasn't. It felt as good as it did with Ben. And I did it back to her. Even though I had always been taught that being gay or doing gay sex things was against God's way, it didn't feel that way. God doesn't care if a man kisses a man, or a woman kisses a woman, or a woman and man kiss. God doesn't care at all. It's just love. Kissing or touching of any kind is just an expression of love, and it doesn't matter who is doing it. Anybody who says God believes something else doesn't know what they're talking about at all.

We were together for the rest of the night. On the floor in the dining room and then upstairs in my bedroom and then in the bathtub. What a night it was. My oh my, I saw God over and over, and I saw eternity, and I felt complete peace and understanding, and I felt loved, boy, did I feel loved, more loved than just about anybody on the whole earth that day, I think. When it was over, we all fell asleep together, right in the same bed. Ben was in the middle, and me and Mariaangeles were on either side of him. I slept really great and didn't even have any bad dreams. When I woke up in the morning, Ben was gone. Mariaangeles was still sleeping, but Ben was gone.

I got up and went to work, same as I did every day. When I came home, more projects had been done, like there was some wood stacked up and the barn was being cleaned out. Ben and Mariaangeles and me and Mercedes all had dinner together, and Mariaangeles put Mercedes to sleep. When she was done, we all went to my bedroom and did the same thing we had done the night before. We touched each other and we kissed each other and we licked each other. And we made each other feel wonderful. And we loved each other. That was what it was all about. What life is about. Loving each other. A man who was Jewish who could talk to God and a black Dominican girl from the Bronx and a fat white cashier from the middle of nowhere. We didn't care about color or religion or money or what kind of school we'd gone to or what kinds of jobs we had had or what our families were like or even what our bodies looked like. We didn't care that we weren't married. Or that we were sinners. Or that some people would even say we were damned to Hell. We just loved each other. For what we were. Which is how it's supposed to be. True love isn't about anything other than how it makes you feel. And if it makes you feel good, keep doing it, regardless of how other people may think of it or feel.

We fell into a routine. I would go to my job. Ben and Mariaangeles would work around the farm. We would have dinner together and go to bed. He was never there when I woke up. I asked one day where he went at night all alone. He said sometimes he went into the woods or the barn and had seizures, and sometimes he laid in the grass and stared at the stars, and he said sometimes he walked to town, which was three miles away, and went looking for things other people had thrown away, like food and clothes and stuff. I told him he was being silly and that he didn't need to do that anymore because I could buy everything we needed at the store with my employee discount. He said he didn't want bought things. That buying things just fed the system that was destroying the world. I asked him if he really thought the world was being destroyed and he smiled and said yes, it is, and it will be final soon. I asked him if he was mad that I worked at the store and he laughed and said of course not. He kissed me on the cheek and said that it wasn't his place or anyone else's to tell me how to live. I told him I wouldn't mind quitting my job and he said I should do what I wanted to do, that my life was my own, and when it was over, it was over, and that I should do and see and try and feel and experience everything I could and everything I wanted to. I told him I didn't know what I wanted, and he smiled again and said yes, you do, we all do, we just need to be honest with ourselves about it, and stop being scared of it. Fear, he said, ran all of our lives. Fear, he said, after religion, was the most destructive force in the world.

Other people also started coming to the house. At first it was just one or two a week. I don't know how they knew Ben or how they knew where he was. They would be there when I came home, or they would knock on the door. They all seemed crazy or sad or sick or on drugs. Ben would walk with them. He would go walking into the fields where my daddy used to farm. The fields were overgrown and scary.

Even though I knew better, and I was grown up, I was always sure there was something evil in them, like a monster or something. Ben would walk in there with people, and sometimes they would come back in five minutes and sometimes they would come back in five hours, but the people were always better. I didn't really know what to think about it. Something was going on out there, but it was hard to really think about it for real. Miracles were something people talked about, and I would read about in the newspaper, and people would pray really super hard for, but they never really seemed to happen, or if they did it was like one in a billion times. But people kept praying for them, millions of people did it, every single day they did it. Some of them were going to get lucky. And that was really all it was for them, and for their praying for miracles, just dumb luck. Something good is bound to happen like one in a billion times. Really most of the people who prayed for miracles were just wasting their time. It was silly. They begged and pleaded for some kind of help that never came. They should have spent the time having fun or something. Especially if it was for health reasons. They could at least have some kind of fun before they died instead of praying. And when these not really real miracles did happen, there wasn't really any reason for them. Like the people involved couldn't say what had happened or why it had happened. Not for real, at least. But with Ben it was different. Sick people would walk into the fields with him, and they would walk out healthy. Drug addicts would walk in with him and come out without wanting drugs anymore.

People on crutches would come out running. I saw a couple of people with sunglasses and white canes come out smiling and blinking. A man in a wheelchair skipped across the lawn. It was crazy. And beautiful. It was miracles for real. Not praying to some thing that wasn't even there and couldn't even listen. Not praying for some promise in a book that never made any of its promises come true. But having someone actually do something that changed someone. Knowing that because you met this one person, and he did something, that your life was totally different and totally better. That was a miracle. And Ben could make miracles happen. He could make prayers, which really are pretty useless considering how many there are and how little they actually do, he could make prayers actually come true. I don't know how he did it, except to say that he was the Messiah, and he had the same powers that that Jesus Christ man had, if that man was even real. He could make miracles. I've never heard of anyone else who could do it. But he could, for real. And it wasn't like it was easy or just some little thing. After he did it, he would always come out looking worse than when he went in. Like whatever he did took something from him. Like he was giving something of himself to the people so they could be better. Sometimes he didn't come back at all. The people would say he'd told them he was going to have a seizure and they should leave him. Or he'd walk out of the field and just have the seizure right in the yard. They were really terrible scary ones. He'd shake and grunt and spit and stuff would come out of his mouth. I'd get really worried and want to go help him, but I knew he wouldn't want that, so I'd usually just bite my nails on the porch. Once I asked why he did it, gave people the miracles. He said he did it because he loved them, and that miracles aren't done, miracles are given. And that anyone could do it. If people were willing to love enough, and to give enough, that anyone could change someone's life. And that that was the easy way to describe God on earth. People changing other people's lives. Not some heavenly being, or some made-up superhero, but people changing other people's lives.

After they were done with Ben in the fields, most of the people would leave. Some of them, though, would stay with us. It was pretty funny. They weren't like normal people. Or at least that's what I thought at first. They were men who dressed up like ladies, and ladies who looked like men, and they were people who were gay and people who liked men and women. They were homeless people who were on drugs, and they were black people and Hispanic people and Asian people and Arab people and people who were so mixed up I didn't know what they were. There were women who had definitely done some dirty things, and maybe even sold themselves for money. There were men who were the same way, even. There were criminals and drug dealers and beggars and people who had nowhere else to go. If I had seen these people on the street, I would have definitely been scared of them. If I had seen them in my town, I would have hoped the police were somewhere really close. All the God-fearing, church-going people I knew would have said they were damned to Hell for being sinners. They would have said these people were going to Hell for sure. But when they were in my house I loved them. And I loved them because I saw Ben loved them. I saw him hug them and kiss them. I saw them cry in his arms. I saw him spend hours listening to them and talking to them and laughing with them. I saw him heal them and change them. I saw him treat them like they were real people, which almost all of them said hadn't been done in a really long time. I saw Ben have sex with them, and all of them wanted to have sex with him, and he with all of them, and saw him marry them. Some of them came to the farm together and were in love or fell in love while they were with us. Men and men and women and women and men and women, every combination you could imagine, gay ones and straight ones. Ben told them that marriage wasn't about a man and a woman being together, it was about people in love being together. And he said that laws and restrictions against love and marriage, regardless of who was in the marriage and who they loved, weren't the way of God. God didn't care about those things. God was beyond those things. Marriage is a human issue, and all humans should be allowed to participate in it, regardless of how they love. And I followed his example. I talked and laughed and listened and hugged and kissed and had sex. I went to the weddings and cried and cheered, I was so happy for everyone, and I danced after, danced until my legs and feet hurt like crazy. I didn't think about anything except that I was loving people. That that was what mattered. That we were all human beings and we were loving other human beings. And that's God. Not some silly man with a beard wearing a robe, sitting in a gold chair in the clouds. Not some angry man who knows everything and says what is right and wrong. Not some old man in Italy talking nonsense, or some crazy man in the American South judging everyone. Not some man in Pakistan who thinks he has the right to kill, or some man in Israel who thinks he has the right to oppress. God is not a person or a man or even a being of any kind. God is loving other human beings. God is treating everyone you meet as if you love them. God is forgetting we're all different and loving each other as if we're all the same. God is what you feel when there's love in your heart. It's an awesome feeling. And it's the real God. The only real God.

People kept coming. And some who seemed to know Ben from before. A lady doctor from the city who said she had treated Ben in the hospital. A man who used to be his boss when he was working at a construction site. A sweet gay boy who was as pretty as any girl and who used to live with Ben's brother and who loved Ben and who Ben loved, and they kissed a lot and spent a lot of time in bed. An FBI agent who hugged Ben and cried and said thank you over and over again. Some people would stay for a day or two days, some would come and go, and some never left. Pretty soon people filled up all the bedrooms, and the attic, and the basement, and the living room, and the TV room. They were everywhere, really. And then they started sleeping outside. In the barn and in tents. Over the course of a couple of months, we went from the four of us to thirty or forty people, all living on my farm, and even more kept coming. I couldn't believe it. It was super fun. The house had never been cleaner. We started growing vegetables. And some of the people brought money and I'd buy things like food and blankets and fruit with my store discount. All day people would do jobs. Some would clean or make dinner or plant food in the garden. People would take care of Mercedes. People would go into town at night and go through dumpsters. And at night we would all sit around the front yard and Ben would talk to us. I wouldn't say it was preaching. Preachers are always trying to convince you they're right. Preachers are always trying to make you believe what they believe. Preachers are always trying to tell you if you don't listen to them you're going to pay some price. Ben didn't care if we believed. He said everybody should have the right to believe whatever they wanted. He didn't need to convince anybody. All anybody had to do to be convinced by Ben was look at him. When you saw him, you knew he was different from the rest of us. You knew he was special, or even something really beyond special. He was divine. He was what people prayed for and begged for and spent their whole lives worshipping. He was the real Prophet. He was the real Son of God. He was the real Jesus Christ born again. He was the real Messiah. He was everything all of the crazy religious people all over the world had been praying for and waiting for for all of these thousands of years. He was God. He was God.

And even though he told us all, every single one of us, that we didn't have to believe what he said, we did believe it, we believed everything he said, even when it was kooky. I remember the first night it happened. The sky was clear and there was no moon and it was warm. There were millions and billions of stars out, so many I couldn't even begin to count or guess how many there were. Ben had been in the house, having a seizure. Everyone knew to leave him alone when that was happening. Even if it had been happening in the kitchen or where we could see him, he told us all to leave him alone. He was having this seizure in the living room that night, right on our old carpet. He had been talking during it, talking in some weird language that sounded really old and scary and serious. Everyone had left the house and gone out to the lawn. We were just sitting on the grass, looking up and not saying anything because it was so beautiful we couldn't even believe it. It was when there were only eight or nine of us at the house. Me and Mariaangeles and Mercedes sleeping in her arms, and a gay man and two transvestites and a woman who had been a crack smoker when she came but wasn't anymore, and maybe someone else. Ben walked out and sat down with us. He took the crack lady's hand because she was having a really hard time being off her drugs. He kissed her on the head, and she smiled. One of the men asked him if he was okay, and he said yes. He asked if he knew he was talking when he was having his seizure, and Ben said yes. The man asked if he knew what he was saying, and Ben said yes, I was speaking to God. Everyone was quiet for a couple of seconds. Like they couldn't believe it, or maybe like they could believe it and did believe it but it was awesome and there was nothing to say. Me and Mariaangeles both knew already. The others looked at each other and one of the men smiled and said I told you, that's what I heard, that's why we're here. The other man asked Ben what God said to him, and Ben smiled and said God wanted to tell you hello, and to make sure you know you are welcome to stay here for as long as you like.

We all laughed. Ben laid down on the ground so he could stare up at the stars and brought the woman down with him and held her in his arms. It was really super sweet. She had been shaking before, her hands and her whole body and even her lips had been twitching and shaking. Ben just held her and ran his hand through her hair over and over and she got really calm and peaceful. We all laid down on the ground like him, like we wanted to see whatever it was he was looking at, and because he looked real comfortable. And Ben just looked up at the stars, and so did everyone else, and they went on forever and ever and ever. Nobody said anything for a long time. We just stared. And I saw stars that twinkled, and stars that looked like they moved, and really bright stars and stars that I could barely even see at all. I tried to count them, but there were too many, so I tried to count them in just one little square in the sky, but there were too many to do even that. Eventually I just got lost in them. I wasn't even thinking about anything. I was just staring at the wonder of the sky and stuff. And everyone else was the same way. We were lost, and when we had all forgotten he was going to, Ben spoke.

God isn't what you think, or imagine, or have been taught to believe. Much of what you have been taught to believe about everything in this world is wrong, but so much of it is tied to notions of God that it's easiest to start there first. We are animals. We were not created in the image of anyone or anything. We are a biological accident, and we are what we are now because of a long process of natural selection, and occasional spontaneous genetic abnormalities that made us stronger, and eventually became part of us. We started as single cells in swamp water, and rose from there, became fish, amphibians, reptiles, mammals, apes. It happened over the course of billions of years. The idea that this planet, this solar system, this galaxy, and this universe were created five thousand years ago is ridiculous. We know better. We might not have then, but we do now. And even then, when the stories were created, regardless of what culture they came from, they weren't created because the people creating them actually believed them, they were created in order to consolidate power, and to enslave people. They were created because a few men understood that if they claimed some direct relationship with God, some unique understanding of God, and that God was a God that created all life, and judged life, and knew everything everyone did at any given moment, and if that God was a God that controlled fate, and decided who would live and when we would die, and after death

granted eternal life in either Paradise or Hell, they
could use that power, that supposed relationship, that
supposed understanding, to make people live
as they told them to live, and make them do what
they wanted them to do. They could use that power
to make people slaves. Religion. It's remarkably
simple. A beautiful con. The longest running fraud
in human history. I know God. God created all,
knows all, and is all-powerful. Do what I say God
tells me you should, which also happens to make
you subservient to me, or you will burn forever.
The Christians are the masters of it. They have built
empires with their scam, murdered, tortured, and
terrorized literally billions of people. All in the name
of their bearded superhero, in the name of their crucified fiction. In today's world the Roman Catholics,
American evangelists, and fundamentalist Muslims
are particularly good, though all are guilty: the Jews,
the Christians, the Muslims, all the leaders of all
the various sects and denominations, anyone on
earth who thinks there is one God with the power
to know and judge all. They're all wrong. And they
are either slave masters, or they are slaves, worshipping things that don't exist. God is not a man. God
is not a reflection of man. God is not a being or
a spirit or a consciousness. God does not live in
some place with a staff who does God's work. God
is not a he or a she. God does not have an army
of angels or a mortal enemy who was cast out of
his kingdom. In terms that mean something to us,
God is nothing. God plays no part in our lives. God
doesn't care about earth or about humanity. God

doesn't care about the petty dramas that mean so much to us. God doesn't care what we say or who we fuck or what we do with our bodies or who we love or who we marry. God doesn't care if we rest on Sundays or if we go to some building to sing songs and say prayers and chant and listen to sermons. God doesn't care if we kill in God's name. God doesn't give a fuck. God does not give a fuck. Look up. There are twenty-five hundred stars visible in the night sky. Twenty-five hundred. Not that big a number. In our galaxy, our little galaxy, there are three hundred billion more that we can't see. Three hundred billion. We don't know how many galaxies there are because we don't have the technology to know, if it is even possible to know. There are estimates, guesses, darts thrown at a board. Some say a hundred billion, some say five hundred billion, some a trillion. Some say the universe is infinite, which is a concept we pretend to understand, but is beyond our minds. Humans worry about eating, finding shelter, fucking. We worry about jobs and money. We worry about class and status and what other people think of us. We worry about rules imposed on us by men who know nothing. We worry about death and when it is going to find us. We can't conceive of infinity. We can't grasp the idea of something that has no boundaries and no end. And that's where God is. That's what God is. Beyond our minds. Beyond our understanding. Beyond anything we can categorize or write about or preach about or place into one of our systems of rules. God is infinite. An infinite number of galaxies, an infinite number of stars, an infinite number of planets. Look up. Try to imagine infinity. Your mind shuts down and moves back to some number you can understand, some image you can grasp. Look up. Beyond what you see, beyond what lies behind what you see, beyond what lies behind what lies behind. What stretches out forever. That's God. All of it is God. An infinite God that we can't understand. That does not care about our little lives. That is beyond caring about anything, anywhere in this infinite universe. Look up and see God. Look up. Look up.

And we did. We looked up at all those pretty stars, and they were there shining and blinking and maybe moving around a little, but that was probably my eyes playing tricks on me. I tried to imagine all those numbers of billions and trillions and think about things just going on forever and ever and I couldn't do it, just like he said. My brain would come back to stars I could see and to the little sliver of moon glowing and the grass I was lying down on that was tickling my arms and the sounds of crickets playing and bugs winging real fast and a sweet little breeze moving through the trees and the other people around me breathing, just looking up and breathing.

After that we started doing it every night. It wasn't like it was required or anything, not like school or church, nobody was going to get in trouble, but almost everybody did it. We'd have dinner and go outside and lie on the grass and Ben would talk. He'd talk about life, about what he thought of it, and how he lived it, and about our world, about how we had allowed it to be destroyed, and about how it was going to end soon. He said life was simple, we were born and we were going to die. There was nothing for us before we were born, and there would be nothing for us after we died. While we were here we had choices. While we were alive we had choices. We could choose to be and do whatever we wanted. We could choose to become part of society, and follow its rules, which were mostly designed to control us and keep us in whatever place we were born into, or we could make our own rules and live our own lives. For him, he'd say, life was about love and fucking and helping other people. Life was about feeling everything he could and experiencing everything he could. Life wasn't about the accumulation of money and possessions, but the accumulation of friends. He'd talk about living simply. That the more complicated our lives became the more miserable we were. The more we had the more we wanted. The harder we worked the less we lived. He'd talk about patience, and say that there was nothing in life that was made better by being anxious or nervous or aggressive. He'd talk about compassion, how we should have it for ourselves and for other people and for the earth, and that if he could stop people from inflicting pain on everything around them, that the world might have a chance to survive, and that we might have a chance to survive. He said we needed to let go of the idea of death. That death was the end, very simply, and nothing more. That when death came it was blackness and silence and peace, but nothing we could experience. That our obsession with death was killing us. That our obsession with life after death, which did not exist, was destroying what we did have, which was consciousness and all of its gifts, the greatest of which was love. He said life, not death, was the great mystery we all must confront. He said it over and over again. Life, not death, was the great mystery we must confront.

When he talked about the world, it was usually about how we had destroyed it, or allowed religions and governments to destroy it, and how it was all going to end soon. He said religions and governments were never about what they claimed to be, which was helping people and making their lives worth living, but were simply instruments of greed and power and death. That none of them were worth a shit. That even the best of them were evil, and existed solely to control and exploit humanity, and control and exploit the earth's resources. That he couldn't, over the entire course of recorded history, find a single example of a government that didn't exist in the name of power, that didn't kill in its own quest for power, and that didn't use its citizens as servants of its greed. Though he said he didn't know how the world would end, it was obvious it would, that there were too many ways, and that one of them would happen, and it would happen soon. He said that too many people had too many weapons. That once the big weapons started flying, they wouldn't stop. That once one crazy man pushed a button, all of the buttons would be pushed. That too many people wanted to be right. That too many people wanted to control. That too many people wanted their God to be the only God, their system to be the only system. That Democrats and Republicans, and Capitalists and Communists, and Liberals and Conservatives, and Fascists and Anarchists, and Nationalists and National Socialists, whatever they called themselves, were all the same, and that they were no different than people who worshipped God. But that instead of pretending to believe in a supernatural God, they pretended to believe in Gods called social justice, and equality, and freedom, but that their real goals were no different than the religious people, that all they were truly interested in were money, and power, and control. That between them, they would destroy the world. That they would start a war that they wouldn't be able to stop, and that would have no winner. That the war to end everything would be coming. And that even if the war didn't come, everything would end anyway. There were too many people. There were no more resources. The earth itself couldn't support everything on it anymore. Soon all of its resources would be gone. And when we realized it, we would tear each other apart while we starved. And he said it was too late to try and stop it. That there was nothing anyone could do at this point. That no leader, no religious figure, no man, no woman, no nothing, could do anything about it. That we had jumped off the cliff, and that at some point soon we were going to land. And it was all going to end. And we were all going to die. And that it was best. It was the best thing that could happen. That destroying all of it, razing it, burning it to the ground, was our only chance. And that after it happened, he hoped, though he doubted it, that whoever was left would be smart enough to start again and forget all of it. And start something that revolved around the worship of love instead of the worship of God and money. God and money brought nothing but death and war. Love might bring something worth living for.

And he wasn't angry or mean when he talked. He didn't scream or shoot spit out of his mouth like lots of people did when they said stuff. He said it just like someone would say they were going to buy some milk or fill their car with gas. Just like it was something that was going to happen. He said we had choices about how we were going to live before it happened. We could either accept it and live as beautifully as we could before it happened, or we could not believe it and keep wasting our lives doing things and chasing things that didn't make us happy and make us feel good. He said his choice was to love as much as possible, and give as much as possible, and feel joy and happiness and ecstasy and pleasure as much as possible. Life was hard enough, he said, without denying ourselves the things that brought us into a state of bliss. Those who thought we should deny ourselves were fools. Our bodies were built for it. We should allow them to do what they were made to do.

After he finished speaking, he would always kiss someone. He did it with Mariaangeles the most, but sometimes it would be someone else, and sometimes it would be a man, and sometimes a woman, and sometimes a man that looked like a woman, or a woman who looked like a man. He would kiss them and touch them and love them. Most of us would follow his example and start kissing and touching and loving. Some of us would go into the house or into the barn or the fields, but most of us would stay on the lawn. It didn't matter who you were or what you looked like or what your background was or what color your skin was or if you had an accent or if you had money or no money or if you had gone to school or not gone to school or anything. Everyone loved everyone else. And everyone had sex with everyone else. And everyone came with everyone else. When we first started, it was just a few of us, but near the end there were lots of people staying all over the place and more would come or would be visiting for the day and people would be everywhere. And there was so much love. And we were all happy. And nothing else in the world mattered at all. Not one single bit.

Seven months after we all came to the farm together, after all of the space in the house and barn were taken up, and people were living in tents in the fields and the woods, and there were seventy-seven people living there, a girl came to see Ben. I was sitting on the porch when she came walking up, and I could tell something was wrong. She was young and sad and her face was bruised and her clothes were not in good shape. It was pretty normal for people like her to show up, but I could tell somehow that she was different. She asked if Ben was around, and I said he lives here but isn't around right this minute. She asked if she could have something to drink, and I said yes, of course, silly. She sat down on the porch stairs, and I got her some water and gave it to her. I tried to be chatty with her, but I could tell she didn't want to be chatty, and really she looked like she was going to cry in a sad way so I left her alone. An hour or two later Ben came walking out of the fields with a young couple who had been trying to have a baby but couldn't and they were smiling and I could tell the woman had been crying in a good way and Ben put his hand on her stomach and put her husband's hand on top of his hand and they both just looked so happy, like they knew everything was going to be fine for them. As they walked away towards their car, Ben turned towards us. The girl saw him and stood up and Ben smiled and she immediately started crying. He walked over and put his arms around her, and she just cried into his shoulder, really cried, like her whole body was shaking and sobbing. I could tell it was something really serious, so I left them alone there in front of the porch and went inside and read books to Mercedes.

Later everyone at the farm met outside for dinner. Ben seemed really happy and really sad at the same time and the girl was still there. She was sitting with Mariaangeles and they were holding hands. It wasn't unusual for women to be holding hands, but they were holding hands really tight. We had a really awesome dinner, and afterwards, instead of talking, Ben kissed every single person at the farm. He kissed everyone really nice, and everyone different, like he could tell what kind of kiss they liked and what kind of kiss they wanted and what kind of kiss they needed. When it was my turn, he kissed me real soft on the lips but not really sexy or anything. Just really nice and soft for like ten seconds or so, and then he pulled away and whispered I love you in my ear. After he kissed everyone, he took Mariaangeles by the hand and took Mercedes, who had dinner with us lots of the time, by the other hand, and they walked into the house with each other, and the girl walked with them, right alongside of them. It was really cute. Like he was Mercedes' dad and Mariaangeles' husband and the girl was part of their family somehow and it was really super cute. For a minute nobody was sure what to do, but then people started kissing each other just like we did every night when Ben was with us. And then we loved each other. And the sky was clear and it seemed more clear than ever and the stars were out and they seemed brighter than ever and it was a beautiful night, a perfect night, the most awesome I had ever seen and still have ever seen. And everybody loved each other. We all loved each other in some perfect way even stronger than before, like somehow the night made us better than ever and gave us more love. It gave us everything and it was beautiful. The most beautiful thing in the world. Love.

The next morning, when I woke up, Ben was gone. The girl was gone too, and Mariaangeles didn't come out of her room for the whole day. And when she did, she wouldn't say where Ben had gone or who the girl was or what had happened. All I knew was that Ben was gone.

II ESTHER

I think about my suffering. My sadness, loneliness, the fact that my family has been destroyed, that I've been beaten and tortured and forced to worship a God that is not mine, and live a life that is not mine. I think about the suffering of others in this world, this ugly, ugly world. I think about all of the violence and war, the poverty and hunger. I think about the addiction and abuse and oppression. I think about all of the sickness and disease and physical misery, and I think about all of the suffering of the soul, which is greater and more profound than any of the physical ailments that befoul us. I think about all of the pain that everyone feels every minute of every day. There is so little joy. So little freedom. So little security. So little that makes us feel as if this is all worth it. And what there is that makes us think it's worth it is love. Love is the only way to alleviate suffering. Love is the only way to find freedom. Love is the only place in all of humanity where there is security. And even love doesn't work for very long. Love always disappears or vanishes. Love is always killed or destroyed. Love always changes into something that isn't really love. Moments of true, pure, unconditional love are the rarest and most valuable things on earth. If we have two or three of them over the course of our entire lives, we're lucky. Most of us have none. Most of us live with the illusion of having love or seeking love or knowing love, but what we have or seek or know is desire and possession and control. What we know as love doesn't really make us happy. If anything, it makes us suffer more. It makes us more unhappy and more violent and more oppressive and more miserable. It increases our suffering. But if we could learn. If we could learn what Ben Zion learned. If we could live as Ben Zion lived. If we could feel as Ben Zion felt. If we could love as Ben Zion loved.

I always believed we would see him again. I hoped it would happen before our mother died. After he first left again, after his fight with Jacob, I prayed for his return. I prayed for hours a day. When I was supposed to be praying for other things, when I was supposed to be praying for things that Jacob wanted me to pray for, and told me to pray for, I prayed for Ben Zion. While I was praying, I thought about what it had been like seeing him again. I thought about who he was and what he had become, which my parents, and everyone in our family, and our rabbis always believed he would become. I thought about what he could do, how he could perform miracles, how he could make people feel, and how he could change lives with a word or a touch. I thought about all of the languages he could speak without having studied them and all of the books he knew without having read them. I thought about how he could speak with God. I thought about all of the signs of divinity that were recognized when he was born: his Davidic blood, his birthday on the day the Temple of Solomon was destroyed, his circumcision at birth. I thought about the burden he must have felt for most of his life. Being raised and educated as someone who might be the Messiah. What that must have been like for a little boy. A three-year-old who should have been playing with trucks. A five-year-old who should have enjoyed playing at a playground. A seven-year-old who should have enjoyed school like a normal child. A nine-year-old who should have been allowed to have friends. I thought about what it must have felt like for him to know what he was, or what he was believed to be, what made his father and brother jealous and scared and made them hate him. I thought about what it must have been like for him when he was thrown out of our home. He was still a child, barely a teenager. I wondered what he did for all of those years we searched for him and could not find him. I wondered where he was, who he met, and what he felt. I wondered if he was waiting to become what he became. If he believed it. If it was a burden. If he woke up every day in terror, wondering if today was the day he became Moshiach. If he ever spoke to anyone about it. If he had any friends or anyone who loved him. If he cared. If he knew how it would end, and I suspect that he did. I don't have answers, but I believe it must have been some kind of hell. To know that you were Moshiach, the Messiah, the Son of God, Christ reborn, the earthly incarnation of God on earth, even though his God was not the God propagandized on earth for thousands of years. It's a miracle he survived knowing. It's a miracle that he accepted it and waited for it, wherever he was, whatever he did, whatever he felt, however he suffered. It's a miracle. My brother was a miracle.

And while I thought about all of this, I let myself doubt it. Any faith, any true faith, involves doubt. If you say your faith is unshakeable, you have no faith. If you say you have no doubt, then you have no belief. The struggle of faith, the worthiness of faith, the value of faith, is holding true to that faith in the face of doubt. If you are to believe in God, you must allow yourself to doubt God. If you are to believe in anything, you have to doubt it. I believed in my brother. In his power and his divinity. In his righteousness. In his mission, which was to show us the folly of our beliefs, to show us the danger of our religions, to show us the stupidity we exhibit by placing our hopes and dreams in the hands of politicians, and to show us the value of living our lives believing in love, and living with love, not the false, judgmental love we have been taught, but a love where every human on earth is given equal value, and granted equal rights, and provided equal care. I believe that he was who he was born to be, and that he was the man that had been prayed for for thousands of years. I believe that in his death, in his sacrifice, he gave us a chance to redeem ourselves. He died willingly in order to redeem us of the sins of religion, the sins of our Gods, the sins of placing our lives in the hands of politicians who have defrauded us. He redeemed our humanity by showing how and why the humanity we have been sold is wrong. That the Gods we worship don't exist and don't care. That the systems we have been forced to exist in are destroying us. In the same way that Christ supposedly sacrificed himself for our sins, sins that are a natural part of our humanity, as natural as breathing and eating, sins such as love and sex and choice, Ben Zion sacrificed himself for our belief in the Christ story, and for all the stories like it, stories that enslave us, and oppress us, and destroy us. If we realize Ben Zion was right, and if we learn from what he taught us, we have a chance to save ourselves. I don't, however, believe we will take it. He was prophetic in that he knew the end was coming. He was Moshiach in how he showed us how to avoid it. He showed us we are all asleep. He screamed, and he kept screaming it until it led to his death. We have a chance if we remember that scream, if we listen to it. I don't, however, believe we will take the chance. It will all end.

And while I believe what I believe, there is doubt, there is always doubt, and there has to be doubt. Was Ben Zion just a man? Was he a child poisoned by religion and convinced to believe in ancient prophecies that will never come true? Did he become what he became because he was told he would? Was he mentally ill? Did his epilepsy destroy his sanity? Was he a criminal who deserved what he received? Was he an egomaniac serving his own self-need? Was he delusional and sick and dangerous? I allow myself to ask the questions, because when I think about the man I knew, and the life he lived, and the words he spoke, and the example he gave, and the miracles he performed, and the love he shared, and the sacrifice he made, the answer, to all of the questions I ask myself, is no. Or the answer is no to all the questions but one. He was dangerous. He was absolutely dangerous. Dangerous because if we listen to him we will wake up. If we listen to him, we will stop buying the bad goods that are sold to us, and we will stop falling for the cons of preachers, popes, and presidents, and the disease of religion will be cured, and the lies of politicians will no longer be believed, and everything that has been built, all of the sick, diseased institutions that rule us and control us, and deceive us, will crumble, and they will fall. He was absolutely dangerous. And they killed him.

After he left, after his kiss with Jeremiah and after Jacob beat him, and after he turned our water to wine, the priority became finding him again. When Jacob saw the wine, he immediately believed he had made a mistake, a major mistake, an irreparable mistake. He ran from our house into the street, but saw nothing. He got into his car and drove around the surrounding streets, but saw nothing. He went into local churches, believing that might be where Ben Zion would seek refuge, but saw nothing. He called the local precincts and hospitals, but nobody had seen anything. He searched for days, and when he wasn't searching, he was on his knees praying at the church, or talking with Pastor Luke, who, after meeting Ben Zion and hearing him speak and witnessing his miracle, was convinced that Ben Zion was Christ reborn. Jacob did not find him, or even any sign of him, and Ben Zion did not come back, or offer any clue as to his whereabouts, or contact us in any way. After Jacob realized Ben Zion was really gone, he started disbelieving what he had seen and claiming that Ben Zion had kissed Jeremiah only to upset, and had hid a bottle of wine somewhere in the house, knowing that he might get an opportunity to replace the water with it when he was alone in our dining room. He also started to become angry and say that Ben Zion had mocked him, and mocked God, and that what Ben Zion knew, the languages and the holy books, was something anyone could know if they studied long enough, which was what he must have done. When Ben Zion's court dates were coming up and he did not appear, thus jeopardizing both our home and the church, Jacob became enraged. He restarted his search for Ben Zion, and with greater vigor, and he also started screaming at, and eventually abusing, our mother, whom he believed knew where Ben Zion was living. Our mother knew nothing. As had always been the case, she became the focus of Jacob's rage. He screamed at her. He spit on her. He took all of her money and refused to give her any food. He would push her into our front closet and lock the door and spend time kicking it, and whispering through the door to her that she was the mother of the Devil, and telling her that our father had never loved her and regretted marrying her. Eventually he threw her out of the house. He let her leave with the clothes on her back and nothing more. She tried to go to other church members for aid, for they were the only people for years that she had interacted with, but they would not help her. She went back to Brooklyn, where we had lived as Jews, but the people we had known there would not forgive her for forsaking them. She lived in a shelter until her time there ran out. She went to another one. After a couple of months, she ended up on the streets, begging, hoping each day to get enough money for a meal. I tried to help her. I would bring her small amounts of money, blankets, clothes. Jacob caught me and beat me, breaking three of my ribs and three of my fingers, and quoted Ecclesiasticus 26:25, A shameless woman shall be counted as a dog; but she that is shamefaced will fear the Lord, after he was finished beating me. He told me if I did it again, he would beat me worse, and throw me out as well.

As the days went on, and Jacob became more desperate, and our mother became more desperate, I also became desperate. At the time I believed in the church, in Jesus Christ, and in the Heavenly Father as depicted in the Old and New Testaments of the Holy Bible. I knew nothing else. I had never been given the chance to learn anything or believe anything else. I did not want Jacob's church to fall apart, or to be taken by the government. Obviously I did not want to lose our home, as it was the only thing of value that my family owned. I started looking for Ben Zion on my own. I asked Jacob's permission before I started, and he initially said no. After Pastor Luke left, saying he could no longer reconcile his belief in Jesus Christ with what he had witnessed in Ben Zion, and he could no longer preach a gospel that he did not feel in his heart, Jacob granted me permission. Not only was he in danger of losing the physical building that held his church, but the congregation was losing members, as people felt the chaos, and saw the instability in the leadership, and started going to other churches.

I started by asking my mother, but she knew nothing. I went to the Bronx, where Ben had been living before his accident, before he came back to us, but no one would speak to me, and one large man recommended that I leave, that no one there would tell me anything, and some might hurt me if they thought I would hurt Ben Zion, who they knew only as Ben. I went to the construction site where he had worked, but the workers there had not seen Ben Zion, and the foreman of the site would not see me. I went to the jail and tried to speak to some of the people who had been in the tunnels with him. I saw three men and one woman. As soon as I told them who I was, they stood and walked away without speaking a word to me. I did what Jacob did, called police precincts and hospitals and homeless shelters. I went to the hospital where I had found Ben, but the doctor was not available. I went back to my mother, hoping maybe Ben Zion had contacted her, but I couldn't find her. I went everywhere she had been, or where I knew she had been, but she was nowhere to be found. I stayed home and at church for two days and prayed, and still nothing. On the third day, I decided not to go to church and not to pray. I was tired, and I did not like being around Jacob, who was becoming increasingly desperate and irritable and rageful. I stayed home. I listened to the radio. I put on a station that was not a Christian station, which would most likely have resulted in a beating had Jacob known or come home and discovered it. I listened to a pop station, like a normal girl my age might have done, like normal girls my age all over New York City were probably doing at exactly the same moment. I heard songs about falling in love, about being in love, about going to parties and dancing, and about losing love and mourning love. I heard songs about beautiful kisses and songs about sex. I heard songs about big dreams and people going after them and sometimes losing them and sometimes finding them. I had never known any of these things. I had never experienced anything like them. My life had been church and prayer and school at home and Bible study. What boys I knew were off-limits until marriage, and contact between us was strictly controlled and supervised. I had never walked out the door of our house knowing I was going to see a boy, a boy who might like me, who might kiss me, who I might fall in love with and laugh with and dance with, a boy who would make me happy. I loved the songs I heard, and they made me smile. And they made me hope. And they made me dream. I had dreams I had only dreamed of having. Maybe someday I would know something real about them. Maybe someday some of them would come true. After two hours of songs and dreams and smiles and some awkward dancing, the phone rang. Jacob answered the phone when he was home, and it was my job to answer it while he was out, though no one ever called for me. I immediately turned off the radio, assuming it was someone for Jacob, and knowing that if they heard the radio, I would pay for it later. I picked up and said hello, and a man asked me if I knew Ruth Avrohom. I told him she was my mother. He said he was a social worker from a hospital in Brooklyn, and that my mother was there, and that they needed someone to sign some forms related to her. I asked him what had happened, and he said he could not share details, but that he would discuss it if I came to the hospital. I asked him if she was okay, and he said she was in critical condition. I got the address and hung up.

Without thinking, or without thinking of the potential repercussions, I left immediately. I took the subway and found the hospital. It was in a poor section of Brooklyn, and I was the only white person there, at least among the patients and visitors. I asked a woman where to find my mother. She sent me to the critical care unit. When I got there, I had to speak to another woman, who gave me my mother's room number, but told me I had to wait for a doctor to speak to me. I sat down and I waited.

I waited for a long time. I was very scared. People looked at me like I didn't belong there, in that hospital, and I felt the same way. No one else was white. Lots of the people didn't speak English. I knew people who weren't white or didn't speak very much English at church, but there we were all united by our belief in God. At the hospital we weren't united by anything. I had no idea what they believed. I didn't trust them. I could tell by the way they were looking at me that they didn't trust me. One asked me if I was a police officer. Another asked me if I worked for the state and was there to take away someone's child. Most just stared at me for a minute or sat where they didn't have to be too close to me. Finally a doctor came to see me. He asked to see my ID and I showed it to him. He walked me to a room down the hall, where my mother was lying in a bed. Her face was hideously swollen and there were large bruises on it. There were tubes and wires going in and out of her arms and a tube going into her mouth and bandages all over her. Her eyes were closed.

I didn't know what to do, what to say. I was scared to step into the room. The doctor told me she had been attacked outside a homeless shelter. There were no real details as to what exactly had happened, but he had heard that there had been a dispute regarding food with a man at the shelter. The supervisor at the shelter had seen her leave, and she was found an hour later in an alley two blocks away. She had been raped and beaten. Her nose and cheekbones were broken and her skull fractured. She was stable, and would most likely live, but she was in poor condition. The police had taken a report, but there were no real suspects and they didn't expect to arrest anyone. He said that for the immediate future my mother could stay at the hospital, but that she would have to leave fairly soon. He asked if I could take her in. I started crying.

I stayed with her for a couple of hours. I sat at her bedside and tried to apologize to her. I knew she couldn't hear me but I did it anyway. When I got home, Jacob was waiting for me. I tried to tell him what had happened but he said he didn't care. Our mother was no longer our mother to him. I tried to talk to him about it and he hit me, and he kept hitting me. When he stopped, I went to my room and I stared at the ceiling until I heard Jacob go to sleep. I waited for an hour after that, and I got up and I got dressed and I left.

I went to Manhattan. The subway was empty. It was the middle of the night. My plan was to go back to all of the people I had seen and ask them again if they knew where I could find Ben Zion. I would explain the circumstances and why I needed to see him, believing if I could find him and bring him back, Jacob would allow our mother to come home, where I could care for her. I came out of the station into the city. The sidewalks were deserted. The shops were all closed. There were no cars on the street. It was quiet and still and beautiful. The long, straight blocks stretching out to the horizon line. The buildings in shadows, in black. The electric storefront signs were glowing red, yellow, blue. The streetlights were flickering. The blacktop was deserted. The closest location was the hospital, so I started walking towards it. For fifteen minutes I saw no one, though I did occasionally see shadows moving behind lit windows. As I got closer to the hospital, I started to see cars, and a few people. Hospitals are one of the few places in the world that never sleep, never stop, never have a chance to breathe, to be alone or quiet, to be deserted. The closer I got, the more people I saw, some in scrubs or white coats with badges on the front, some just sad or upset, some who looked sick and lost. I went to the emergency room, where the doctor worked. There were a few people in the waiting room. All of them looked scared, almost guilty. A young woman and a young man, both dressed like they had been somewhere fancy, looked like they'd seen a ghost. A little boy held his father's hand. An old woman sat by herself and stared at the floor. A couple was sitting together, the woman sobbing into the man's shoulder. As I walked to the reception desk, I saw the doctor standing in an office behind it. She was on the phone. She seemed very serious. The receptionist asked if she could help me and I told her I needed to see the doctor. She asked why and I told her it was about my brother. She asked if my brother was a patient at the hospital and I told her he was but not anymore. She asked why I needed to speak to the doctor and I told her it was very important, that it was about my brother. I asked her to give the doctor my name and tell her I needed to see her. She said she would and I sat down.

I waited for an hour. Every time a doctor or nurse would come in, everyone would look up, some mixture of great fear and great hope on their faces, knowing that at any minute they were going to be either saved or ruined. The fourth time, the woman doctor came in and looked at me and smiled and sat down next to me. She said hello and asked me what had happened. She could see fresh bruises on my arms and neck, and assumed I was there for some kind of care. I told her about what had happened with my mother and the situation at home, though when she asked if Jacob had beaten me, I said no, and I told her I needed to find Ben Zion, and that I had been searching for him for several weeks and couldn't find any trace of him, or anyone who would even talk to me about him. She asked me if I thought Ben Zion would be in any danger if I found him, and I said no, we're his family, we need him, we love him and we miss him and we need him. She smiled and said she'd be back, and she hugged me and walked away. She came back a little while later with a sticky note in her hand. She said he was living on a farm upstate and that she'd called the farm and spoken to him. He told her to give me the address and that I should come see him, and that he loved me. I took the sticky note and she hugged me and I left.

I walked to the bus station. I had enough money to buy a ticket most of the way there, but not all of the way. The station was disgusting. And frightening. It was dirty, and there were lots of homeless people and men who stood around waiting for something, or someone, and never seemed to leave. More people seemed to be coming to the city than were leaving it. As I watched them get off their buses, I wondered how many of them, if any at all, would end up happy, or would think they had made a good decision. I found my bus as fast as I could and got on and sat down in the seat directly behind the driver, so that if anything happened, I'd be near someone who could help me.

The ride was a few hours. The bus was mostly empty. An old couple sitting together holding hands. Three girls with shopping bags. A teenaged girl who looked tired and sad. A teenaged boy who looked like he was going to explode. I stared out the window at the green blur and the endless gray line stretching out in front of us. Three hours later I got off in a small town in upstate New York. It looked like it had been nice at some point in the past. The houses were clapboard Victorian, and many of them were very large, though most were now decrepit. There was a main street lined with shops, almost all of which were now closed and boarded. There were liquor stores and churches. Three gun shops. A discount clothing store and a thrift shop. A used car lot full of pick-up trucks, and crumbling factories at the edge of town. Most of the people I saw were sitting on their porch, or their lawn. Nobody seemed to be working. I stopped at a gas station and asked how to get to the town where Ben Zion was living. The man laughed at me when he asked me how I was getting there and I said I was walking, but he gave me directions anyway. He told me it was about seventy miles away. I started walking down the road. It was a two-lane country road with garbage and weeds along the sides. When I saw cars, I would step deeper into the weeds so that no one would see me, even though I knew they did. I was tired and my body still hurt from Jacob, and I was ashamed to be walking along the side of the road. I didn't have running shoes or walking shoes. Just my church shoes, cheap black leather flats with plastic soles. And I was wearing what I always wore, a long skirt and a long-sleeved blouse and long socks. I started sweating almost immediately, and I hadn't eaten or had anything to drink for a long time. I'd walk for a while, and then I'd sit down and rest. I was making some progress, but seventy miles seemed like a thousand. I could not imagine walking the entire way. And I knew that at some point I'd need to sleep, and find some food. I knew that at some point I'd need to find shelter of some kind.

I started praying as I walked. I was talking to Jesus and the Holy Father, and asking them for aid and guidance. I told them I was scared and needed help. I told them I was devoted to them and believed in them and would do whatever they asked of me if they helped me. I begged them for a sign, for something to let me know they could hear my prayers. I held my hands together, above my heart, as I walked, and I looked up towards where I believed Heaven was, and I asked for the angels to come down to me. I believed, because I believed in and lived by the word of God as expressed in the Bible and had a personal relationship with Christ, that help would come in some form. I prayed so hard. I kept walking, and I prayed so hard.

I don't know how far I got the first day, probably ten or fifteen miles. I slept in a park in a small town that looked exactly like the first one. All of them looked like the first one. I was woken by a police officer's boot. He was pushing me with it. Not in a violent or angry way, but enough to wake me. He asked me who I was and what I was doing. When I told him where I was going, he laughed at me and turned and walked away. I got up and got back on the road.

It was a long day. The longest day of my life. I drank water from gas station bathrooms. I ate food from garbage cans. I walked for hours and hours. My feet and my body hurt. I kept praying. I kept asking Jesus Christ and the Holy Father for help. Twice cars pulled over and I believed my prayers had been answered. Both times men offered me rides if I would do things with them, if I would defile myself for them. Both times I ran off the road into the woods to hide. When they pulled away I came out, and I just kept walking.

Three days after I got off the bus, I found the entrance to the farm. My feet were burning and my throat was burning and I felt like I was going to vomit. I thanked God for giving me the strength to make it. I literally got on my knees and looked to where Heaven is supposed to be and thanked Jesus Christ and God. I thanked them for guiding me and keeping me safe and showing me where to sleep and where to find water and where to find food. I thanked them for allowing me to recognize non-Christian predators and avoid them. I thanked them for allowing the doctor to tell me where to find Ben Zion. I thanked them for Ben Zion himself, and for the gift of having him as my brother. I stayed on my knees for an hour, praying and thanking Jesus and the Heavenly Father. I stayed on my knees until the urge to vomit disappeared and until I felt like they had given me my strength back.

The walk up the drive was easy. The road was long and straight and there were woods on both sides. It took about ten minutes. When I came to the end, there was a large white farmhouse and a barn, and huge overgrown fields behind them. There were people around. Some were working a garden, some just sitting around. They all looked happy. A large woman asked if I needed help. I told her I was looking for Ben. She said he was out and she wasn't sure when he'd be back. I asked for a glass of water and she got me one. She tried to talk to me but I asked her to leave me alone, and she did.

I watched the people around the farm. There were all types of people, all colors, different ages. Some of them were definitely strange, or what Jacob would call perverted or deviant. Men were holdings hands. Women were holding hands. I had been taught for my entire life that homosexuals were evil and damned to Hell. That they spread disease. That they were mentally ill. I was scared of them. I didn't want them coming near me, and although I had seen Ben kiss Jeremiah, I thought that was more just to anger Jacob than because he accepted them or their lifestyle, and I couldn't believe he was living with them.

I sat on the porch for an hour or so. Once I stopped moving, my fatigue caught up with me. I had trouble keeping my eyes open. It took a great effort to bring the glass to my lips, though the water was wonderful when I did. It felt like my chest was weighted down, and each breath was work, and with each I could feel my strength dissipating. The woman who had gotten me my water checked on me occasionally. The rest of the people, and they were coming in and out of the house, coming down the road with bags that appeared to be filled with food and clothes, people going out to the barn, seemed not to notice me, and when they did, they were very friendly, and seemingly normal. Finally Ben came walking out of the fields. He was with a couple, and they looked happy, and he hugged each of them. He turned towards me and saw me and smiled. He looked thin, and his hair was longer, and he was still pale, and his scars looked worse than I remembered them, or they seemed to jump out more. He walked towards me, and I started smiling. He sat down with me and took my hand and put his arms around me and said hello. I immediately started crying, sobbing, into his shoulder. I couldn't say anything, I just sobbed. And it felt wonderful to do it. I felt secure and strong. I wasn't scared anymore. I felt comfortable and calm. I felt like what I wanted to feel like when I was praying to Jesus and the Holy Father. I felt loved.

He took me by the hand and led me to a room. He told me I should lie down, and the bed was big and the sheets were clean and I was so tired. I tried to tell him about what had happened in New York and why I was there and how our mother needed him and how Jacob was going to lose the church and how Pastor Luke had left. He just smiled and said I should sleep. I told him he would only have to come back for a few days and he could leave again and come back here or go anywhere. He said once he left he'd never be back, and I asked why and he said because we both know what is going to happen when I get back to New York. I told him we'd get our mother home and he'd talk to Jacob and everything would be fine. He smiled and told me he loved me and would come get me later, after I'd slept, and he left the room.

I fell asleep almost immediately. I woke to Ben Zion sitting next to my bed, his hand on my arm. It was dark, and there was no light coming through the window. He smiled at me and said it was time to go. I got out of bed. He had a pair of shoes for me. Not new new, but someone else's shoes that were in better condition than mine, and were better for walking. I asked him why we were leaving in the middle of the night, and he said it was easier to walk because it was cooler, and there were more trucks on the road, which would increase our chances of getting a ride. He walked out the door and motioned for me to follow him.

We walked through the house. It was silent and dark. As we came down the stairs, I saw people in the living and dining rooms. There were five or six in each room. Most of them were nude, and they were

entwined with each other. I saw two of them kissing, and moving, and I immediately looked away.
I believed that whatever they were doing, it was wrong. Whatever they were doing, it was against the ways of God. Whatever they were doing was a sin. Ben didn't pay any attention to them.
We left the house.

The yard was the same. It was warm out and people were sleeping on blankets in the grass, and some of them were still awake. The moon was high and half full, so I could see them better, and they were doing the same sorts of things, and some of them were making noises. I saw two men kissing, their arms around each other, and I looked away again.
I must have tensed up, because Ben took my hand and spoke.
It's okay to look.
I spoke.
It's wrong.
Why?
It's a sin.
Why?
It goes against the word of God as expressed in the Holy Bible.
Two people making each other happy isn't wrong.
They're both men.
They're both human beings.
Leviticus 18:22 says you shall not lie with a male as one lies with a female; it is an abomination.
I can see that they're happy, and they love each other, and they're making each other feel good.

Their souls are damned.
You hate them for how they live?
Yes.
Your Bible also says, in 1 John 4:20, if anyone says, "I love God," yet hates his brother, he is a liar. For anyone who does not love his brother, whom he has seen, cannot love God, whom he has not seen.
In God's eyes, as I have been taught, because of what they are, they are not my brothers.
You've been taught wrong. We are all the same, regardless of who and how we love.
That's not what the Bible says.
The Bible is a book. Books are for telling stories. They're not for denying people the right to live as they choose. Live by what you feel, and what feels right to you, not by what some book of stories tells you.
I can't look at them.
You don't have to look, but it's no different than a man and woman in love, and you wouldn't look away from that.
If they were sinning I would.
There is no such thing as sin. Only control and guilt.
We walked away from the house, down the drive. He kept holding my hand. We turned off the drive and started walking down the road. I asked him where we were going and he said the highway.
We walked for thirty more minutes. We didn't speak, but it wasn't awkward. Ben Zion made me calm, made me feel safe, made my insecurities and anxieties disappear. He just held my hand and walked next to me. And as ridiculous as it may sound, sometimes

all any of us needs in life is for someone to hold our hand and walk next to us.

We made it to the highway and started along the side of it. There were lots of trucks, and very few cars. They would drive by us and the wind they created would move me a little, and I was scared because they were so close. Ben just walked and didn't appear to be scared at all. He told me that he had done this a number of times and that usually someone would stop and offer a ride, though it might be harder because there were two of us. And even though I had had some sleep, I was tired and couldn't imagine walking all the way back to New York.

After an hour or so, a truck pulled over. It was an eighteen wheeler with the logo of a grocery store on the side. The driver rolled down the window and asked where we were going and Ben said New York. He said he could take us to New Jersey, and we climbed into the truck. The cab of the truck had a small area behind the seats with a small cot mattress and a blanket. I went back and lay down. I tried to stay awake to hear what he and Ben Zion would talk about, because I was curious what the Messiah would say to someone he had just met, but almost as soon as we started moving, I fell asleep. When I woke up, we were in New Jersey. The truck was stuck in traffic, and we were barely moving. Ben and the driver were telling each other jokes. Silly one-liners and knock-knock jokes. They would tell a joke and laugh and laugh and laugh. I didn't really get the jokes, and when Ben heard me he turned around and said hello and put his hand on my head. Though I had been a bit sleepy still, I was immediately awake, and my heart was beating really fast, like I had just been running or something, or like what I imagined it must be like to be on drugs. All of the worries and fears and insecurities were gone. This weight I had felt my entire life, that I think every person feels, this weight that is our existence, or our soul, or the bad things that permeate our souls and infect us and make us do bad things, was gone. I didn't know what to say, so I said hi, and Ben Zion laughed and he told me we were almost home. I smiled and said good, and the trucker turned around and looked at me and said hello, and I smiled, but wasn't sure what to say. I rarely spoke to men outside of church. He told me my brother was a funny guy, and a good travel partner, and I smiled and said yeah. He asked me if I was shy, and Ben Zion said yes, she's shy, she's a good Christian girl, or she used to be before I came around, and they both laughed and I was a little confused by what Ben Zion meant and why the trucker would laugh. I did, though, feel different, felt better and lighter, felt the way I had felt before when I had been sick and woken up better, like my fever had broken or something, like I wasn't sick anymore. The trucker turned back around and Ben Zion told another joke and they laughed again and we kept moving slowly towards the city. That was it for the next ten or fifteen minutes. They told more jokes and the trucker called another trucker to ask about traffic and he called his destination and told them how far away he was. He pulled off an exit and to the side of the road and I could see the skyline of New York in the distance. The sun was coming up between the skyscrapers and streams of light were pouring through the spaces between them. And even though I had lived there for my entire life, I hated New York, and was scared of it, and thought of it as a cesspool of sin, a modern-day Gomorrah, a place where the Devil took the souls of innocents every day. This morning it was beautiful. The buildings were all shining. The Hudson was calm and there were ferries moving slowly across it, small wakes trailing behind them. I could see the George Washington Bridge, and cars streaming on both levels, full of people going to their jobs, or to see friends, or shop, or visit the sights, or do whatever they were going to do, and I felt happy for them, like the bright shiny beautiful place they were going was somehow going to help them, or make them better, or make them happy. And I didn't resent them for it. I guess growing up in an environment where I was told everyone was wrong and we were right and everyone was going to Hell and we weren't had me scared and hateful, and resentful, in a way, of people who didn't think like me or live like me. But for some reason this morning, all of it was gone, all of it was gone.

We got out of the truck and the trucker got out with us and he gave Ben Zion a big hug and said thank you over and over, and Ben Zion said no, thank you for the kindness of the ride, and the man started crying. I don't know why, but he did, he just stood there and cried and Ben Zion held him against his shoulder and let him do it. The sun was still rising behind them. And the light was still streaming. And the ferries and cars were still moving. And all of the people in the city and going to the city were alive and living their lives and I loved them all. And I don't know why, but I did. And I know Ben Zion did. And I know that trucker did. And I don't know why or what Ben Zion did to me or to that man while I was asleep and before they were telling silly jokes and laughing, but it's never left me, and while I may have wondered before, I didn't after. I didn't anymore.

The trucker watched us walk away. Ben Zion took my hand again and he smiled and we walked towards the bridge. It took an hour or so. Walking along empty sidewalks next to roads packed with cars. We crossed the bridge, and the closer we got to the city, the more beautiful it looked, the brighter it seemed. We were the only people walking on the bridge; everyone else was in cars or trucks, and almost all of them were alone. Tens of thousands of people, all of them going to the same place, all of them alone. We came down off the bridge and into the city. We were in upper Manhattan, where it's mostly long blocks of low-rent apartment buildings, and empty factory buildings, and warehouses, and where some of the subway trains run on elevated tracks. I asked Ben Zion where we were going and he told me the subway and I told him I didn't have any money and he told me we didn't need any. He led me into a tunnel where one of the trains came out of the ground, and it went from being bright and beautiful to being pitch black and terrifying. I told him I was scared and he said don't be, and I asked him if he knew where we were going, and he said yes, he had come across the bridge and into this tunnel many times.

We walked right down the middle of the tunnel, in the area between the two tracks. Occasionally there'd be an overhead light, but mostly it was black. I could hear dripping water and rats, and once or twice I heard some yelling. When the trains would come by, I'd put my hands over my ears, and the wind was really strong and the girders holding the tunnel up would shake a little bit. The trains were only a few feet away, and the people in them were a blur. Even though Ben was with me, I stayed scared. I felt like we were walking into Hell and the trains were full of souls of the damned, rushing towards eternal fire and pain. And though I would have once thought, having seen what I saw with Ben Zion, and having disobeyed Jacob, and having forsaken my mother, that I was going to join them, this time I didn't. If I was walking into Hell, I knew I'd walk out. Or if I felt like we were walking into Hell, I believed that there was no such thing. There is only life. This life that we live. If it is Hell, it is because we make it so.

I saw lights ahead of us, and we came to a platform and we climbed up and waited for the next train. There were a few other people on the platform, but they paid no attention to us and didn't seem to be bothered by the fact that we had come walking out of the tunnel. We got on a downtown train and switched to one going to Brooklyn. Nobody on the trains spoke or really even looked at each other. Ben held my hand and closed his eyes and leaned his head against the window and breathed through his nose, and though he looked like he was asleep, I don't think he was. Once a thin white man in a nice suit got on with a briefcase, and Ben immediately opened his eyes. The man was sitting across from us and further down, and Ben stared at him. He didn't give him a dirty look or a mean look, just stared at him. At the next station the man got off the train.

It took an hour or so. We got off and walked to the hospital. When we arrived, our mother was sleeping. The doctor said she was fine but not good. Ben Zion took me to the waiting room and left. I asked him where he was going and he said for a walk. I asked him where and he just smiled and walked away.

He came back three hours later. I had tried to pray while he was gone, but had had trouble doing it. It seemed strange to be talking to something that wasn't there, or that I didn't know was there, or that I believed was there but had no evidence was there. And I saw other people in the waiting room who were praying. I watched them carefully. Two of them were praying to a Christian God, and I know because one had a Bible with them and the other made the sign of the cross before prayer, and another was a

Muslim, and had a copy of the Qur'an. They were praying very hard, and they were very focused. I was used to praying with other people, sometimes many other people, especially at Bible conventions and Christian Youth meetings, so that wasn't it. I just couldn't do it at that moment, and wanted to see other people do it, and wanted to see what, if anything, happened. There were magazines in the room, magazines with movie stars on the front of them and silly headlines and bright pictures of pretty people in fancy clothes. I picked one up and looked at it. While I looked at it, I watched the people praying. If the outside of the magazines seemed silly, the insides were worse. The stories were about people who were very concerned with how they looked and dressed, and how much money they made, and the houses they lived in. And while I could understand worrying about those things on some level, they seemed incredibly insignificant in a hospital, a place where people were sick and diseased and dying, and where the people who loved them came to watch them suffer. At the same time, what the people praying were doing seemed equally insignificant. They were all begging for help, for aid, for some way to relieve their suffering, and to relieve the suffering of whomever they were praying for, begging to characters in books, characters that no one had ever met or seen or spoken to and was sure even existed. They were praying to whatever God or Savior they believed in to save them, and in the same way that some people worship the silly people in the magazines, who we at least know are real, they worshipped the people in their books, who we don't know anything about. I watched a doctor come in to see one of the Christians, and he had some type of bad news, because the person immediately started sobbing. A family member of the other Christian, or someone who I assumed was a family member because they looked exactly alike, came in to take the person away, and the family member had clearly been crying. The man with the Qur'an saw what I saw, that the prayer had clearly done nothing, but kept clutching his book and praying anyway. I wondered, and I still wonder, if I had replaced their books with the silly magazines I had been looking at, and if they had worshipped the silly people in those magazines, if they would have gotten the same result.

When Ben Zion came back, he smiled and told me to come with him. I stood and we left the waiting room and walked to our mother's room. When we went in, she was awake and she smiled at me. The tubes were out of her mouth, but there were others still in her arms, and she was still covered in bandages. I sat next to her and took her hand and told her I was so sorry and that I loved her and I started crying. She pulled me towards her, and though she was too weak to really do it, I understood what she wanted, and I stood and put my arms around her. I kept telling her I was sorry and that I loved her, and she put her hands on the back of my head and held me against her chest. Ben Zion stood a few feet away and watched us. After a minute or two, our mother let me go and I pulled away and sat back down, though I still held her hand. Ben Zion walked over and kissed me on the forehead, and leaned towards my mother and whispered something in her ear, though I did not hear what it was. She smiled and kissed his check, and he stepped away and sat with me. He stayed until she feel asleep, and when she did, he stood and kissed her forehead and turned and started to walk out of the room. I asked him where he was going, and he stopped and turned around and looked at me and spoke.

I'm leaving.

Where to?

I'm going to see Jacob.

Don't.

I'm going to make sure you never have to see him again.

Don't hurt him.

I wouldn't hurt anyone.

Then why go?

I want you to be free.

I'll be fine.

Fine is no way to live. Take care of Mom.

You call her Mom?

When I was little I called her Mommy, when I got older it was Mom. Only when we were alone. It was our little thing, away from the rules and formality of our home.

Is she going to be okay?

I don't know if she wants to live anymore. She's had a long, brutal life.

She didn't deserve it.

None of us deserve it.

He turned and walked to the door.
Don't let him hurt you, Ben Zion.
I love you, Esther.

PETER

I met Ben at his arraignment hearing. It was at the Queens County Criminal Courthouse. He had been arrested and charged with attempted murder and arson. I am an attorney and work for the criminal defense division of the Legal Aid Society. In simple, layman's terms, I am a public defender. I literally drew his file out of a basket. In doing so, I have been irrevocably changed. In almost every way for the better. Except for the rage I feel when I think about what was done to him.

I became what I am because of my father. He was a drug dealer. He was not a drug lord or anyone of importance in the drug trade. Rappers have not glorified him in their songs. Writers have not written books about him. Hollywood has not made his life into an award-winning drama. He was, like many black men, both now and in the '70s, when he was active, a street-level drug dealer. He literally stood on a corner and sold drugs. He did so because he believed there were no other options. He was not well-educated. There were no jobs available to him. He did not have parents who were able to support or nurture him. We lived, and still do, in Harlem. He and my mother were married, and still are, and they had three children, me and my twin sisters, who are a year younger than me. We lived in a fifth-floor walk-up. My mother worked as a checkout clerk at a grocery store but made very little money. My father looked for legitimate employment but was unable to find anything. He did what he had to do. He took the only job that was available to him.

As I said, he was a street-level dealer. He stood on a corner and sold heroin and cocaine. His customers were mainly whites from the suburbs and the more economically privileged areas of Manhattan, though there were plenty of local customers. In 1973, New York State passed a series of statutes known as the Rockefeller drug laws. The purpose of the laws was to stem the flow of drugs into the state by instituting harsh penalties for the sale and distribution of them. If an individual was caught with more than two ounces of either cocaine or heroin, and there was the intent to distribute, they faced a minimum sentence of fifteen years to life, and a maximum sentence of twenty-five years to life. When my father was arrested after selling cocaine to an undercover narcotics officer, he was in possession of a total of 2.5 ounces of cocaine. The cocaine had been processed into crack. It had been placed into small vials that held doses he sold for ten, twenty, fifty, or one hundred dollars. It was 1984. I was three years old, and my sisters were two. After a two-day trial, my father was convicted and sentenced to twenty-five years to life. While I don't condone what he did, the idea that he was given a harsher sentence than many murderers, than almost all child molesters, than the rich white-collar criminals who have bled this country and its people dry, than corrupt politicians destroying our cities, makes me absolutely sick to my stomach. My sisters and I were left without a father. My mother was left without a husband. My father was sent to a maximum security prison, where he still resides, and where he believes he will die. My sisters and I spent the rest of our childhood visiting him on his birthday, and on Christmas, and on the Fourth of July. It wasn't until I was older that I understood the irony of the July visit. Let us celebrate life in the Land of the Free and the Home of the Brave.

Having lost my father, my mother was determined to keep me from following in his footsteps. She took a second job, also working as a cashier, at a second grocery store. She enrolled us in a preschool at our church. She was able to dress us in secondhand clothes that looked firsthand, and she drilled into us that the system, the system of opportunity in America, and everywhere in the world, was rigged against us. We would have to work twice as hard to get half as much. We were poor and black and we lived in a ghetto. The schools we were supposed to attend were not going to educate us in a way that would prepare us for success. No doors would open for us because of the color of our skin or because of our last name. We would have to behave twice as well, work twice as hard, achieve twice as much. And if we could do those things, we had a chance. If we could not, we would end up like her, and almost all of the women in our neighborhood, working eighteen hours a day to support her family in a single-parent home, or like our father, and a large number of the fathers of children in our neighborhood, in prison for taking the only job available to him.

Though I do have happy memories, it was not a happy childhood. I studied most of the time. I was mocked and beaten by the other boys in my neighborhood, boys destined to follow my father's path. I started working part-time when I was fourteen in anticipation of college. The job was at one of the grocery stores where my mother worked. I took a weekend job picking up garbage in Central Park. I graduated third in my class in high school and got a partial academic scholarship to a large state school. I worked in the school cafeteria to cover what the scholarship didn't. I went straight into law school, which I did in New York, also on a partial academic scholarship. I worked in the school library at night and went back to my weekend job picking up garbage in the park. As soon as I finished law school, I became a public defender. And while I am not always successful in helping people like my father, or women who might have been my mother or my sisters, who both became doctors by working as I worked, I fight like a motherfucker to do what I can. I scream. I yell. I try every trick in the book, because I know the government is going to use everything they've got. I spend most of my free time studying areas of the law that I believe might apply to my work. I seek out experts in other fields who might have applicable knowledge to share with me. I don't bother speaking to young men to warn them of the evils of the drug trade, or of crime. They know the evils, and they know the potential consequences. They know the system has been rigged against them since the moment they were born. They know the world is rigged against them. If you aren't born with a silver spoon in your mouth, regardless of your race, religion, or sexual orientation, you might as well have been born in shackles. I'm not bitter about it. I accept it as it is. But I fight like a motherfucker against it.

As I said, I met Ben at the Queens County Criminal Courthouse, where I go to work every day. After an individual has been arrested, he or she goes to a precinct holding cell. From there, a prosecutor in the intake bureau of the DA's office looks at the case and files charges. The offender is booked and fingerprinted and sent to central booking. A criminal history, also known as a rap sheet, is brought up, and the Criminal Justice Agency looks at both the charges and the criminal history and makes a bail recommendation. All three are then put together in a case file. The case files are put in a basket when the individual is brought to court for their arraignment hearing. We, the public defenders, draw the files out of the basket, and the individual whose file I draw becomes my client. I meet them in an interview booth behind the courtroom. The interview booth is basically a Plexiglas box,where I communicate with my client through a partition. After briefly reviewing their file, I talk to them about their potential bail options. In the best-case scenario, there is a chance I will be able to get them out. In the worst, I can do nothing.

Looking at Ben's file, I knew he wasn't going anywhere. He had been charged with the attempted murder of his brother. The prosecutor claimed that he had also burned down a church and had charged him with arson. He had jumped bail on a long list of federal charges. I remembered reading about the federal case in the newspapers. Some kind of heavily armed apocalyptic cult in the subway tunnels. A large number of arrests. The leader of the cult had been killed in prison while awaiting trial, after supposedly attacking a guard. There were a number of questions surrounding the death, including whether he had actually attacked anyone, and even if he had, whether the force used in subduing him, which killed him, had been justified. Ben was facing life sentences in both the state and federal cases. He was considered violent, and an obvious flight risk. There was mention in the file of potential mental instability. He had been booked in Queens, but transferred for three days of treatment to a local hospital that had a secure wing. He had been taken into custody with severe facial swelling, multiple facial lacerations, nine broken ribs, a punctured lung, and a broken arm. Normally I would have assumed that the police had administered the beating. The file, however, said that he had been taken into custody in that condition, and that he had been injured by witnesses trying to subdue him after his alleged offenses. I saw him as I was walking to the interview. Needless to say, his appearance was startling. He was sitting in a hospital robe, chained to a chair. He was absolutely still, motionless. And he looked like he was in bad shape. Stitched gashes across one of his cheeks. Black eyes. A nose that had clearly been broken. One arm in a cast. And if he hadn't had his ass beaten recently, he would still have been startling. He had jet black hair and marble white skin. He was covered with the most severe scars I had ever seen, and I had seen plenty of them. He was extremely thin, though he did not look unhealthy. Actually, despite his wounds, quite the opposite. He looked like he was glowing in the way people sometimes describe pregnant women as glowing. He was staring straight ahead. Did not acknowledge anyone or anything around him. As I got closer, he started following me with his eyes, though he did not move in any other way. It was unnerving. Like I was being stared down by a statue. I sat down across from him. I set the open file down on my lap.

I spoke.

Hello.

He smiled.

Hello.

I've been assigned to be your public defender.

Thank you.

You've been charged with attempted murder, assault and battery, and five counts of arson. Do you understand these charges?

Yes.

Do you want to tell me what happened?

It doesn't matter.

If you want to try to stay out of prison it does.

What happens to me at this point is beyond anything you can do.

You're facing a life sentence. I'd like to try to help you avoid it.
Do you know why I'm really here?
I don't know anything except what's in this file, which is very basic information, and lays out some very serious charges.
Whatever's in that file is meaningless to me. And it doesn't actually have anything to do with me.
It has absolutely everything to do with why you're in court today.
I don't recognize that this court has any authority over me.
Unfortunately, you're going to have to.
No, I'm not.
I need you to work with me on this, Mr. Avrohom.
He didn't respond. He just sat there, staring straight ahead. It isn't unusual to have a client who won't speak. Or a client who has no respect for the legal system. There are times, quite often, that I too don't have any respect for the system, which is one of the reasons I do the job. Unlike other offenders I'd encountered who didn't speak, or seemed potentially belligerent, though, he didn't have a perp stare.
A perp stare is an offender's attempt to appear strong, intimidating, and fearless in the face of their charges, in the face of the system aligned against them, a system that often destroys them. There is always fear in a perp stare. That's actually all that it is. Fear. An attempt to control fear. His stare was quite the opposite. It was soft. Almost gentle. If I had seen him sitting somewhere other than where he was, I might have thought he had just received good news. He

seemed happy. And calm. Remarkably still.
He, and his expression, were absolutely devoid of any fear. I believed, in that moment, and still do, that if I had put a gun in his face, he would not have moved. If I had told him there was an electric chair in the room next to us and it was being prepped for him, he would not have moved. If I had told him he was going to be burned at the stake or crucified, he would not have moved. He was beyond it. He was the first and only person I've ever seen or met who was truly beyond fear. I literally did not know what to say.

We sat there for a minute. Maybe two. We did not have much time. We should have been talking.
I knew, though, that regardless of what I said, he was not going to cooperate with me. He smiled at me and lifted his hand. He placed it on the glass partition and held it there. He stared at me. Looked directly into my eyes and held his hand on the partition. Although I wasn't sure I wanted to do it, I raised my hand and placed it directly opposite his. And I don't know how it happened, but I knew absolutely and unequivocally that he was innocent. I knew it as much as I had ever known anything in my life.
You didn't do it.
Does it matter?
What happened?
I was brought here.
I don't think I'm going to be able to get you bail.
I don't need bail.
You'll probably be sent to Rikers.
I'll be safe there.

Nobody's safe there.
They don't want me in prison.
What are you talking about?
Do what you can to stop them.
He took his hand down. His name was called, and we went into the courtroom. It was a large venue. Very busy. People were, rightfully, concerned about themselves. They rarely, if ever, paid attention to anyone else. Ben silenced the room when he walked into it. Everyone turned and stared. The glow I had seen at the interview seemed brighter, more real. His skin was whiter. His scars more visible. And his presence. The presence beyond the physical. It was unlike anything I have ever seen. Before or since. Hardened lawyers, hardened criminals, bailiffs, and cops. They were all silenced. By his calm and stillness. By the glow.

When the judge entered, Ben refused to stand. He refused to acknowledge the court in any way. He just stared straight ahead and smiled. The judge threatened him with contempt. He just kept smiling. A pure, simple smile. Mouth closed and cheeks drawn. Staring straight at her. She asked him to stand again. He slowly and calmly shook his head. Normally she would have charged him immediately with contempt of court, but she didn't. She turned to me and asked if I was willing to waive the reading of the rights and charges, and I said yes. She turned to the prosecutor who gave grand jury notice, which meant that he would take the case to a grand jury for an indictment, which is required by law in New York.

The prosecutor then asked for denial of bail based on the seriousness of the crime and the defendant's background. I requested bail of ten thousand dollars. She looked again at Ben. He was still staring at her, and she was clearly unnerved. Most offenders are either deferential to the judge or belligerent towards her. He just stared and smiled. She asked him one more time to stand. He did not move. She denied bail. When the bailiff came towards him, Ben stood and allowed himself to be led away.

I had a full day, with a number of other cases. I took Ben's file with me when I left. I started reading it on the subway home. It seemed fairly simple. His brother was a pastor at a church in Queens. When Ben was incarcerated on the federal charges, his brother had put up both his home and his church as collateral for Ben's bail. Ben had disappeared shortly after being released, though how he had disabled his ankle bracelet was unknown. No one had heard from him for seven months. He had reappeared at his brother's home four nights earlier. He had a rabbi with him. They had dinner together, and the next morning went to services at the brother's church. The brother claimed they were going to the service so that Ben could repent before turning himself back over to federal authorities. There was some type of altercation at the church. Ben was beaten and taken to the office of the church. He was locked inside while they waited for the police. While in the office, he lit it on fire. When Jacob, his brother, came to the office after smelling smoke, Ben attacked him and said he was going to kill him. Once again Ben was beaten and subdued, and shortly thereafter, he was taken into custody.

There was nothing to indicate that anything was wrong with the case. It seemed airtight. Multiple witnesses. Physical evidence. The officers at the scene followed proper procedure. When I first get a case, I always look for holes in it. Look for spaces of doubt where I can move in and create openings. Look for small cracks that I can turn into fucking canyons. There were none in Ben's file. Nothing even close. Granted, sometimes it takes time to find them. Sometimes a witness will change their story. Or the evidence will prove to be something other than what it initially looks like. But Ben seemed to indicate, for whatever the reasons, that there weren't going to be any this time. And given how he made me feel, and what he made me feel, I believed him.

I thought about him at Rikers. Wondered what he was going through. A thin white man in his condition. He was out of medical and in general population. For the hardest men, the conditions are brutal. There's violence and rape. There are gangs, almost always divided by race, and if you're not affiliated with one, you're a target. People go in as petty criminals and come out as vicious predators. I doubted he would last long. Or if he did, he would be beaten and raped. Essentially enslaved. I stayed up with the file. Read it over and over again until my eyes hurt. Until I literally fell asleep with it in my arms.

I woke up. Got dressed. Went back to the courthouse, where I had a number of hearings scheduled. I kept thinking about Ben. About Rikers. About what I imagined was happening there. Midway through the morning, my phone rang. The prison's phone number showed on my caller ID. I took the call, expecting bad news. It was the warden of the prison. I was shocked. I had never spoken to him or had any contact with him. It was extraordinary to hear from him directly. He told me there was a problem. Asked if I could come to speak to him. I asked what the problem was, and he said he'd speak to me about it when I got there.

I took the subway to the bus and went over the Rikers bridge. I got through security and went to admin. The warden was waiting for me. I sat across from him. He spoke.
What do you know about your client?
Only what's in the file.
You ever hear of Yahya?
Heard of. Yes.
Know anything about him?
Very little.
He was a murderer. Killed his foster father when he was a kid. Disappeared for thirty years. Started some religious group in the subway tunnels. Preached about the evils of government and organized religion. Typical wacko shit. Scarred his followers, most of whom were drug addicts and petty criminals. Said the scars liberated them from society, freed them from its laws and obligations. They had their own

little world down there. Electricity, water. They did drugs and had orgies. Really fucked up. Near the end of their time, they built up a huge cache of weapons. Yahya said the apocalypse was coming. That the Messiah would arrive, heralding the end of the world. And when it came, he and his followers would be safe in the subways. I know all of this, more or less. They all got arrested. They were all held at the MCC. Yahya refused to acknowledge the authority of the court. Tried to reorganize his followers in prison. Got sent to solitary. Went on a hunger strike. Prosecutors got an order to feed him intravenously. When the guards opened his cell, he attacked them. As he was being subdued, he hit his head on the floor. His brain bled and he died. His followers went fucking crazy, and all of them ended up in solitary. Some got sent to other institutions, including this one. Everywhere they went, they preached the gospel of Yahya. And they preached the gospel of Yahya's Messiah, who had indeed arrived, and was the one member of his group who got bail and immediately disappeared.
My client.
Yes.
He's the Messiah.
He's a fucking lunatic that thinks he's the Messiah, and that some other lunatics think is the Messiah.
Anything happened since he arrived?
It took a day or so for people to figure out who he was when he got to our medical facility. As soon as they did, the inmates started talking. We had him isolated so there were no problems, though we tried to listen to the chatter. When he came back yesterday, he

entered general pop. I was watching when he went to the yard, where a group of inmates were waiting for him, which usually means someone's gonna get fucked up. As he walked out, they all stared at him. No one moved. The ones who weren't waiting for him stopped whatever they were doing and turned towards him. He went straight into the middle of the yard and sat down. First ones over to him were the ones who'd scarred themselves like Yahya. There are four or five of them. They have a few who follow them, who were all part of the initial group waiting for him. They followed. And then everyone in the yard, black, white, Hispanic, Blood, Crip, Latin King, DDP, Trinitario, fucking Hells Angels and mobsters, all walked over and sat down around him. I've never seen the yard so quiet, so still. Usually when it gets quiet it means there's gonna be a fucking war. It's the calm that descends before the killing starts. But not this time. Somehow he made men who literally spend most of their time trying to figure out how to murder each other sit around in a big circle. He started talking. We don't know what he said, and no one will tell us. We wanted to go in and break it up, but they weren't violating any of our regs, so we couldn't do a thing. He spoke for ten or fifteen minutes. At the end of it he stood up and walked around and put his hand on people's heads. Didn't say a word. Just put his hand on their foreheads and smiled. He walked back to where he had been and sat back down. Almost immediately, he had some kind of seizure. A fucking crazy, body-shaking, spitting, eyes-rolled-up-in-his-head seizure. Normally we would go in immediately and get the prisoner and take him back to medical. There was no fucking way this time. I knew absolutely, without any shred of doubt, if we had tried there would have been a riot. And men on both sides would have died, and this prison would have fucking exploded. So we left him there, left all of them there, and let him have his seizure. And waited for it to end. Ten minutes later it was still happening. Twenty minutes. Forty minutes. He just kept seizing. And the men stood up and started mixing with each other. All over the yard, men who a couple hours earlier were deadly enemies were talking, laughing, shaking hands. And Avrohom was still in the middle of the yard, having his seizure. And even though everyone had seemingly left him alone, it felt like they were all still watching him, watching everything he did, and waiting for it to end. The time passed when we would have normally brought everyone inside. We weren't sure what to do, so we left them out there. Two hours later the seizure stopped. Quickly as it started, it just stopped. He was still for a minute or two, looked dead. Then he stood up and walked towards the gate back inside. We opened it and he came in, and everyone else followed him. He went back to his cell, where he is right now.

The yard covered by cameras?

Of course.

Can I see the tapes?

You don't believe me?

I want to see it.

Fine.

We went to the control room where all of the surveil-

lance feeds come in and are monitored. He showed me the tapes, which showed more or less exactly what he had described. When they ended, when the last of the prisoners had reentered the prison, he spoke.
I can't have him here.
He hasn't done anything wrong.
If he can do that, he's a profound threat to the safety of this facility, and to the people who work here.
It looked more to me like he might be able to help you.
I don't know what the fuck he did out there, but sooner or later it will turn.
How do you know?
Because I've been working in prisons for most of my life and I've never seen anything remotely close to what I saw earlier today.
You can't punish him if he hasn't done anything wrong.
We're gonna recommend that the prosecutor have him declared incompetent and ship him to a maximum security mental institution.
That's fucked. I'm not going to let you.
Most attorneys would be happy to get their clients out of here.
I'm going to fight you.
Why?
He doesn't belong in a mental institution.
He thinks he's the Messiah.
He say that?
Enough other people have.
You can't hold things he hasn't done against him, and you can't hold statements he hasn't made against him.

He's fucking dangerous and I want him out of here. He stood and shook my hand. I asked him if I could see Ben, and he said no. I left and went back to my office. By the time I arrived, I had received notice that the assistant district attorney had filed an Article 730, which was a motion to declare Ben incompetent to stand trial and to have him examined for mental illness. Normally Article 730 was something used by defense attorneys. If they could have their client declared incompetent, they could avoid a trial, and their client would be sent to a mental institution for treatment instead of going to prison, which is obviously a better result for someone who's mentally ill. I had never heard of an ADA using it before. Normally they want the conviction, and the offender to be held in prison. Following its procedures, Ben would be examined by two psychiatrists. They would write reports. We had the right to have him examined by our own psychiatrists. They would write reports. All of the reports would be submitted and the judge would make a ruling. If he was deemed competent, he would stay in prison and face trial. If not, he would be sent to a mental institution.

I could not ignore or displace my other clients or cases, so I went back to the courthouse. As my day moved along, I was informed that Ben had moved into solitary. The next morning he had another seizure and was moved into the secure medical unit. Over the next several days, he seemed to move in and out of seizures. None of the drugs that were given to him were able to stop them. They would stop for a few minutes, start again. He had had no food and no sleep. Psychiatric examinations were scheduled and cancelled. I spent all of my free time trying to find a way to stop the 730, but there didn't appear to be one. I met and interviewed his mother. She was still in the hospital. She told me about the circumstances of his birth. About his immediate identification as the potential Messiah. About the pressure it had put on her, her husband, her family. About his childhood, where he had appeared normal but was expected to be anything but, and how those expectations had weighed on everyone in the family. I met and interviewed his sister. She told me about the relationship between him and his brother. His brother's hatred and fear of him. His resentment of him. His feelings of jealousy towards him. She told me about the farm and the life he appeared to be living there. I met his rabbi. He told me about the accident, how he had survived it, the condition he had acquired because of it, and the gift within that condition. He told me about the unreal amounts of knowledge Ben possessed, the languages he spoke, the books he knew word for word. He told me Ben could never have learned all of that through studying, or from school, that it would have taken five lifetimes, maybe ten. I met and interviewed his doctor, one of his lovers, three people who lived upstate with him. I met and interviewed the federal agent who had arrested him, a former preacher who had left the church after meeting him. All of them said the same thing: Ben had changed their lives. He could perform miracles. They believed he was the Messiah.

Normally I'd laugh at the things these people told me. Had I not met him. Had I not seen what I saw and felt what I felt. I would have laughed. Dismissed them as crazy. But they weren't. None of them were. They were reasonable. They believed. And he wasn't asking them for anything. He didn't want people to worship him, or pray to his God, or to follow the rules of a book, or give him anything. He didn't have a big church. Or a weekly television show. He didn't want publicity. He told them that he loved them. And that they should love each other. And that nothing else mattered. That God was something beyond our understanding. That we should live our lives in a way that made us happy. And not follow rules simply because we're told to follow them. Or worship a God that no one has ever seen, or had any contact with. He was telling them things all of us know. We can be redeemed through love. Do not let imaginary characters dictate how we live our lives. Within the context of religion, these ideas were warped. Manipulated. Fucked. And he showed them that.

I checked on his status every hour or so. Called the prison to see if there was any change. After three days he stopped seizing. He was asleep for twenty-four hours after that. When he'd been stable for a day, the court scheduled his exams. It was a much faster process than normal. I tried to stop it, slow it down, but to no avail. The court and ADA were being pressured by the prison. The warden thought Ben was a danger to both himself and other prisoners.

He also said the prison's hospital facility was unequipped to deal with his epilepsy, the source of his mental illness. Ben's brother supported the action. He told the ADA that he thought Ben was, at the very least, profoundly mentally ill; at the most, a homicidal and suicidal maniac. The situation at the prison was becoming tenuous. Other prisoners were demanding he be released into general pop. Those who saw him at the medical unit all walked out claiming he had changed them. That he could heal people. Make their rage disappear. Make their addictions disappear. Give them peace. What normally might have taken months took days. And I had no defense. Ben would not speak to me about the case, or provide me with any information that would help him. And the witnesses I had interviewed would have worked against him. They would have supported the notion that he could speak to God. That he was the Messiah. That he was somehow going to change, and/or end, the world.

The exams took place at the prison. I was allowed to attend them, but not to participate or interfere in any way. I sat in the back of the room. Ben was shackled to a chair. He refused to answer any questions. He did not acknowledge the psychiatrists in any way. He just sat and stared at them. They asked basic questions. Do you understand why you're here? Do you understand the charges against you? Do you know who your lawyer is? Do you know what state you're in? They got nothing. Between sessions, I told him that if he didn't answer the questions, he would be declared incompetent. He told me that it wouldn't matter what he said. That he did not believe the court had any rights over him. That by answering the questions, he would be acknowledging that it did. That the system was designed to do what it did. That it would kill him as it had killed, or was killing, millions of others. I also brought in a psychiatrist for an examination. I hoped that Ben would come to reason in some way. He would not speak to my psychiatrist either. I kept asking him to see reason, to be reasonable, to act reasonably. He smiled and told me that he, in his defiance, was the only reasonable person in the entire situation. That no one with any reason would submit to the court, or acknowledge the authority of the criminal justice system.

The hearing itself was swift and merciless. The state brought three witnesses: the two psychiatrists and Ben's brother. The psychiatrists both said the same thing. Ben would not speak to them, and would not acknowledge the charges against him. They both stated they believed he was incompetent and unfit to stand trial. His brother spoke about Ben's life. Said there was a long history of addiction, delusions, sexual perversity. He said Ben had believed for most of his life that he was the Messiah. That Ben believed he had powers. That Ben believed he could perform miracles. He said that as a pastor he had been offended by Ben's beliefs. That he had denounced God. And believed in free love and orgies. He said that as a man he felt sorry for him. That he had tried to get Ben help for many years. That he had prayed for Ben and tried to bring him into the arms of God, Christ. Ben had spurned all of their efforts. He thought he was better than God. Beyond God. He thought he was God. An hour after it began, Ben was declared incompetent to stand trial. The judge was a Christian who sat beneath an American flag and swore people into testimony using a Bible. He ordered that Ben be moved to Bellevue, where he would be evaluated and treated. He also ordered that his brother, Jacob, become his guardian and be responsible for decisions related to Ben's treatment.

As Ben was led away, he looked at me and said thank you. Those were the only words he spoke that day. He started seizing in the back of the cruiser as they were transporting him to the hospital. He didn't stop for seven days. Seven days of continuous seizure. When he stopped, he would not speak or acknowledge anyone who worked at the facility. He was put on a unit with other patients. He seemed to calm them, and was seen whispering to them. Fearing some type of issue similar to the one at the prison, hospital staff moved him into segregation. Essentially a rubber room. He was diagnosed as a paranoid schizophrenic with Messianic delusions. He was given massive amounts of psychotropic drugs, but none seemed to have any effect on him. He started seizing again and was given massive amounts of antiseizure medication, but none seemed to have any effect on him. He was kept in segregation and forced to undergo electric shock therapy. It had no effect on him. After three weeks, the physicians at the hospital recommended he be given a temporal lobe resectioning, a relatively common procedure and not particularly dangerous within the scope of brain surgery. They believed that by cutting out part of his brain they would be able to stop the seizures. Again he was strapped down. He was wheeled to a surgical suite. He was given anesthesia. He was given extremely large doses because of his resistance to previous drug treatments. An hour into the surgery, as one of the surgeons was about to begin the resectioning, Ben opened his eyes. His skull had been opened and was literally lying on the table next to his head. His brain was exposed. The surgeon had a scalpel in her hand. The scalpel was just above the surface of his frontal lobe. From her account of the incident, he looked directly at her and he spoke. It is finished.

III MARIAANGELES

Ben used to talk about our souls. Said the idea that we had souls was something silly. Ridiculous. Like something a child would think up. Said people who believed we had these spirits inside of us that would survive after we died was fools. That people was living their lives for something we didn't even have. Something that wasn't even possible. He used to say we had brains. It was all in our brains. And more and more and more, doctors and scientists and people who be living in the real world were coming to understand that everything we is, everything we feel, everything we know and experience, every emotion we got and every thought we got and all the pain we got and all the love we got, it all comes from our brains. There ain't such a thing as a soul. You believe in that shit, you just stupid.

I don't know exactly what happened. Doctors tried to explain it to me but nobody could ever get their story straight. They was all worried, nobody wanting to take the blame, nobody wanting to just admit that what happened is what happened. That's how it is in America today. Everybody blaming everybody else. Even the fucking president do it. Used to be the buck stop here. Now it's always somebody else fault, don't blame me, I'll take your money and fuck you but it ain't 'cause of me. All I know is the end result.

One of them killed Ben. They cut his brain and they couldn't stop it bleeding and when they did it was already fucked. It was fucked beyond fixing. It was fucked beyond anything. Like he said, we ain't alive 'cause we got souls, we alive 'cause we got brains.

When they finished with that surgery, he was gone, but there was enough of his brain left that he kept breathing. It was the most fucked thing I ever saw. This beautiful man, this man who knew shit nobody for thousands of years had known, this man who could change your life and change the fucking world, he was gone, but his body was still working. They laid him down in a bed and he stared at the ceiling. You sat him in a chair and he'd stare straight ahead. You'd turn him on his side and he'd stare at the fucking wall. He didn't move. He couldn't move. He'd blink but nothing else. They gave him all these tests. Testing his reflexes and whether he felt pain or whether he could hear somebody or know what they was saying. All negative. He was a shell. A body that could breathe and be alive but nothing else.

They moved him out of Bellevue. Said they needed more room for more of the crazy motherfuckers that was crazy for real. Sent him to some home in Brooklyn where he could be cared for. Cared for meant making sure his feeding tube was hooked up and his diapers was changed. It wasn't hardly more than that. Sometimes they'd turn the channel on the TV they kept in the room. Sometimes they'd move him a little bit so his bedsores wouldn't get infected. It was him and two other men in that room. One of them was a vegetable like Ben. Had been in a car wreck. Some drunkass had hit him. His wife would come every day and hold his hand and talk to him. She'd read him the Bible like she thought it was gonna do some fucking good. She'd get down on her knees and pray for him. The other man might as well have been a vegetable. He was a gay man who'd got beat for being gay. Nobody ever came to see him. Most of the time he was staring too, but every now and then he'd start groaning, trying to move. It was almost more sad 'cause he had some inkling he was fucked. Some inkling of what he used to be. Some inkling that he was alone and he was gonna be alone for the rest of his fucked-up miserable life. Most days the orderlies would just line the three of them up in front of the TV. They'd shit their pants and piss on themselves. If they was lucky, somebody would turn the channel. In some ways it wasn't much different than how half the people in the fucking world lived. And whether they believed it or not, none of them, not Ben or the other two, or all the rest of the motherfuckers in the world, had a choice.

I came twice a week. I'd moved back to the Bronx. Back to the same apartment. After everybody heard what had happened, we left the farm. Maybe a few people stayed, but most of us went back to whatever we had been doing before we went there. We didn't stop believing in what Ben taught us, or how we lived with him, we just spread back out. Decided to take it back to the real world. That's how it always started.

There was one person. One person who understood. Who could see. Who knew. And that person would share what they had, and it'd just spread 'cause everybody touched by that person would be sharing it. In Ben's case there were enough of us. Enough to help each other and maybe some others. Enough to know what it felt like to feel real love. To see real love. To live with real love. To share real love. Love that wasn't about hating or judging or where you was from or what color you was or where you grew up or who you loved. There was enough of us that had been changed that we could change some others. Change them over before all this shit goes fucking boom and explodes.

Mercedes had plenty of people helping out with her. She was growing up real sweet. She'd always ask if she could come see Ben 'cause she missed him so much. I'd kiss her goodbye and tell her some other time and ride the subway over and come and sit with him and hold his hand. I knew he couldn't feel it, but I did it anyway. And I'd talk to him. Nothing like all that God bullshit the other man's wife would talk about. Just tell him what was going on in my life. I was working at a clothing store. I was doing school at night to get my GED. I was starting Mercedes on letters and numbers so I could get her into a better school. And I was pregnant. I was pregnant with Ben's baby. I knew he wouldn't know, but I'd tell him anyway. I was gonna have his little baby.

It wasn't the first time I'd been pregnant with him. First time was when we was at the farm. I'd known right after we got there and Ben and I talked about what to do and he said it was my choice. I asked about what God would say to him about that and he laughed and said God didn't make choices about what women did with their bodies. Women got that right. Only women got that right. No man, no God, nobody else did. And he said if I didn't want the baby, he would go with me, and hold my hand, and love me, and make sure I was okay when it was over. And we went, and he did what he said he would do, and it was the hardest moment of my life, but sometimes you got to make hard choices. And at that point, being on the road and not having no money and not having no idea about what the future would be doing, I couldn't have that baby. I remember when we was walking in. All these people had signs about God and us being killers and was yelling at us. They had verses from the Bible on their t-shirts. Ben just smiled at them. And that got them real mad, even madder, and he just kept smiling. One of them got real close and called him a murderer and said he was going to burn in Hell. Ben took the man's hand and kissed it, kissed it real soft and long, and it looked like that man was going to die, and his friends was all shocked. Ben let go of his hand and whispered something in his ear and the man smiled and hugged Ben and walked away. I ain't got no idea what he said, just what I saw. Ben loving another man. There ain't nothing wrong with a man loving another man. It's all the same. It's love.

I was keeping this baby, though. I wasn't expecting it to be no Messiah or nothing like that. All I wanted was a healthy little baby. A healthy little child that was part me and part Ben, this man I loved with my whole heart, and this man that loved me, loved everyone he knew. I would tell Ben about how I was feeling, what I was feeling, what I was eating, the names I was thinking about, had some for if it were a boy, and some for if it were a girl. I'd tell him about my dreams, about how maybe we was gonna go back to the farm after I got my GED, about how maybe I hoped I'd fall in love again sometime. I'd tell him about how people was still showing up at the apartment sometimes looking for him and people was still talking about him in the ghetto and the jail. When I got sad, and I always did get sad, looking at that shell where there was once a beautiful man, looking at the vegetable where there was once the man I loved, I'd tell him how much I missed him and loved him and wished he'd come back to me. I'd ask him to perform one of his miracles on himself, to make himself better, to heal himself so he could get up and walk again, and talk again, and smile again, and hold my hand again, and kiss me again, and say my name again, just one more time I wanted to hear him say my name, and I wanted him to love me again, and make me feel perfect and beautiful and peaceful and safe again. I'd ask him, and say do it Ben, please do it for me, but he wouldn't do nothing. And even if he could, I knew he wouldn't. Thing about him that made him what he was and who he was, if he had one more miracle, one more hiding in his back pocket, one more hidden in his cheek, he'd use it on someone else. If he had two, he'd use both on other peoples. If he had three, there'd be three lucky motherfuckers out there. He wouldn't ever do nothing for himself. He'd always give before he take. He was giving until it all got took.

After a couple months, my belly was getting real big. The people at the place knew me enough to let me take Ben outside sometimes. They'd put him in a wheelchair and strap him all up so he wouldn't fall out, not that it would make a difference. I'd bring a blanket to put under him to help with his sores, which would be seeping blood and pus and looking like they hurt real bad, even though I knew he couldn't feel nothing. I'd just push him around the neighborhood. Tell him what I was seeing and smelling and hearing. Make up little stories and shit about the people that'd walk past us. The facility wasn't far from the water, and sometimes I'd go down to the boardwalk along the ocean and I'd sit on a bench and put Ben's chair right next to me and hold his hand and watch the waves come in, one after another. And they kept coming, one after another, just like they'd been doing since billions of years before there was any people on this planet, and just like they'd be doing billions of years after we had killed each other and was gone. It made me feel small, watching those waves, realizing how little a mark we made on this world, and how we was just one little planet in a universe so big we couldn't understand it, and how short we was alive in this life that we got, and how we got to take it and use it the best we can. Not to do anything but love, like I was loving Ben by holding his hand, and he had been loving me by changing my life.

Summer turned to fall turned to winter. I was almost ready to have our baby. Mercedes kept asking about Ben so I decided to bring her along one day. I also had pictures of our baby still inside of me, sonogram machine pictures that I wanted to show Ben and put up on the wall behind his bed. We got to the hospital, and they had him all ready to go. I had asked if we could take him out to the boardwalk, even though it was cold and had snowed a little the night before. He was wearing a winter coat and a cute little hat and some gloves that was worn down but would still keep his hands warm. Mercedes was all excited and a little confused about why Ben looked the same but couldn't move or talk or do anything. I thought about what to tell her, but she wasn't ready for the story, for the whole story, for the story of Ben's life, and who he was and what he did and what he meant and why they killed him, their courts and their orders and their surgeons with their scalpels. Why they killed him, with their bullshit laws and religions. I thought about what to tell her, but she wasn't ready, so I said Ben was just being quiet for a little while and left it at that. We went to the water. The waves were still breaking. There was an inch or so of snow over everything. We were the only ones making tracks. A newspaper blew by us, and I could see all that was in it was bad news. People dying, people killing, governments lying and starting wars, corporations robbing and thieving. Same as the news had always been, same as it would always be. We went to a pier that went out into the ocean, and it was a little windy and a little cold and the waves were louder, breaking right underneath us, just like they had been doing for four or five billion years, and just like they would be for four or five billion more. All those waves, one after another, one after another, just rolling along, rolling into the shore. We got to the end of the pier and stopped. I was going to turn around but my phone rang. It was someone calling about a job I had applied for and they was wanting to schedule an interview. I took the call. I was holding the phone with one hand and Mercedes with the other. I didn't think Ben would be going anywhere. He didn't have no brain left. He couldn't walk or talk or move or think or feel or do anything. I didn't think nothing. I turned around and took the call. It lasted like a minute or so. Wasn't nothing, just bullshit about time and place, shit that we all deal with and think matters but really don't at all. When I turned back around, Ben was gone. His chair was empty and the clothes was sitting on it and he was gone. The cute little hat was right there, and the gloves. He was gone, though. I didn't know what to do, whether I should scream or cry or laugh or what to do. There was no possible way what was happening could be happening. I didn't hear no splash and there weren't no tracks anywhere except mine and Mercedes' and the ones that got made by the chair. And later, after the cops came and they looked at the videotapes made by the security cameras, there wasn't nothing to see. One second Ben was sitting there. The next second he wasn't. And I didn't know whether I should be crying or screaming or laughing or what, but I felt love, I felt the same kind of love I had felt when he was with me, when he was alive, it

was inside me still, and I picked up the hat, and it was still warm from where it had been on his head, and I looked out across the ocean, and I looked out across the sky, and I took my daughter's hand who I love so much, and I took a deep breath of cold winter air from the sea, and the sun was warm on my face, and I smiled and I thought of him, and real quiet-like I said it, and not just to him, but to everyone, to everyone everywhere, 'cause that's what it's really about, what it is really all about.
I love you.
I love you.
I love you.

Thank you Ben Zion Avrohom for your life. Thank you Mariaangeles Hernández, Mercedes Hernández, and Ben Zion Hernández. Thank you Charles Kelly Jr. Thank you Dr. Alexis Donnelly. Thank you Esther Avrohom. Thank you Ruth Avrohom. Thank you Jeremiah Henry. Thank you Rabbi Adam Schiff. Thank you Matthew Harper. Thank you John Dodson. Thank you Luke Gordon. Thank you Mark Egorov. Thank you Judith Cooper. Thank you Peter Wade. Thank you David Krintzman. Thank you Eric Simonoff. Thank you Jenny Meyer. Thank you Courtney Kivowitz. Thank you Ari Emanuel, Christian Muirhead, Alicia Gordon. Thank you David Goldin. Thank you Andisheh Avini. Thank you Richard Prince. Thank you Ed Ruscha. Thank you Richard Phillips. Thank you Dan Colen. Thank you Terry Richardson. Thank you Gregory Crewdson. Thank you Larry Gagosian. Thank you Jessica Almon, Britton Schey, and Aaron Rich. Thank you Roland Philipps. Thank you Olivia de Dieuleveult and Patrice Hoffman, Sabine Schultz, Claudio Lopez de la Madrid, Job Lisman. Thank you Melissa Lazarov, Alison McDonald, Nicole Heck, Sam Orlofsky, Jessica Arisohn, Rose Dergan, Kara Vander Weg, Darlina Goldak, Andres Hecker, Paul Neale, Julie Van Severen, Jennifer Knox White, Sarah Lazar. Thank you Carter Burden III. Thank you Dr. Alexis Halperin. Thank you Mariana Hogan. Thank you Rabbi Adam Mintz, thank you, thank you.